THE RECKONING
OF BOSTON JIM

The *Reckoning* of Boston Jim

a novel

CLAIRE MULLIGAN

BRINDLE
& GLASS

Library and Archives Canada Cataloguing in Publication
Mulligan, Claire, 1964-

The reckoning of Boston Jim / Claire Mulligan.

ISBN 978-1-897142-21-9

I. Title.

PS8626.U443R43 2007   C813'.6   C2006-906709-0

Cover image: British Columbia Archives, B-06646 by A.E. Stanfield, 1899
Author photo: Claudia Molina
Map on page vii from "Wagon Road North."
Used by permission of Heritage House Publishers Co. Ltd.

The author wishes to thank the Canada Council for the Arts for their support.

Canada Council   Conseil des Arts
for the Arts   du Canada

Brindle & Glass is pleased to thank the Canada Council for the Arts
and the Alberta Foundation for the Arts for their
contributions to our publishing program.

Brindle & Glass is committed to protecting the environment and
to the responsible use of natural resources. This book is printed on
100% post-consumer recycled and ancient-forest-friendly paper.
For more information, please visit www.oldgrowthfree.com.

Brindle & Glass Publishing
www.brindleandglass.com

1   2   3   4   5   10   09   08   07

PRINTED AND BOUND IN CANADA

To refuse to give, to fail to invite, just as to refuse to accept, is tantamount to declaring war; it is to reject the bond of alliance and commonality.

—Marcel Mauss, *The Gift*

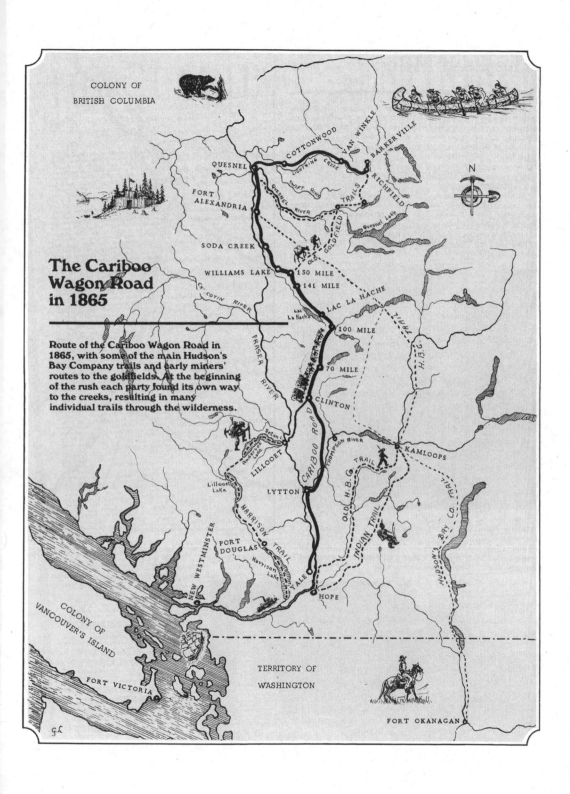

COLONY OF
BRITISH COLUMBIA

N

COTTONWOOD

VAN WINKLE
BARKERVILLE
RICHFIELD

QUESNEL

LIGHTNING CREEK

SWIFT RIVER

QUESNEL RIVER

TRAILS

FORT
ALEXANDRIA

GOLDFIELD

Quesnel Lake

SODA CREEK

150 MILE

OLD

141 MILE

WILLIAMS LAKE

Lac
La Hache

LAC LA HACHE

CH. COTIN RIVER

**The Cariboo
Wagon Road
in 1865**

100 MILE

H.B.C. TRAIL

FRASER RIVER

70 MILE

Route of the Cariboo Wagon Road in
1865, with some of the main Hudson's
Bay Company trails and early miners'
routes to the goldfields. At the beginning
of the rush each party found its own way
to the creeks, resulting in many
individual trails through the wilderness.

CLINTON

Seton Lake

CARIBOO ROAD

Thompson River

KAMLOOPS

LILLOOET

OLD H.B.C. TRAIL

Lillooet
Lake

LYTTON

HARRISON TRAIL

INDIAN TRAIL

PORT
DOUGLAS

HUDSON'S BAY CO. TRAIL

NEW WESTMINSTER

Harrison Lake

YALE

HOPE

COLONY OF
VANCOUVER'S ISLAND

TERRITORY OF

FORT VICTORIA

WASHINGTON

FORT OKANAGAN

GL

ONE

When he offered recompense the Dora woman said: "Not to worry. Think on it as a gift, for your birthday, like."

From the bench outside her cabin he could see the sun near touching the waters of the bay, near touching and yet the air remained warm, and the sky remained the blue of full day. "Have none," he replied.

"None? Ah, well and so, it's just an ordinary gift, then. But if you like, you can bring me something when you're back this way again. Not that it matters."

But it did, of course it did.

Victoria, 1863, and this afternoon in May is nearly done. On Bay Street Bridge a water cart holds up and allows a buggy to pass. The buggy rocks precariously, the driver cursing. There is the smell of offal and rotting fish, of wood smoke and sea brine. There is the caw of gulls and a strip of cloud and a moist, lingering wind.

A man, that man, makes his way through the alleys of the shack town where the Chinamen live, past wafts of joss stick and opium, of brimstone, also, if one is fool enough to believe what others say. His rucksack is laden with furs, and the head of a marten, still attached to its pelt, lolls out and seems at a glance like the head of some grotesque, sleeping child. He wears patched trousers tucked into battered boots and a buckskin coat over a shirt of flannel red. At his belt are a bowie knife and a revolver. His face is best fit for scowling, the nose broad and crooked, the lips a splice in a mat of reddish beard. His hair is a slightly darker shade and is long to his collar. He is not particularly tall and not at all clean and no doubt years younger than he appears. He looks, all in all, like many of the disreputable men about, Americans mostly, who came seeking gold in the Fraser in '58 but who stayed on because there is always more gold in some more distant place. And so what distinguish this man, though few have seen them, are the scars that start just below his collarbone. Though thin-lined and old they form a readable pattern still: JAMES MILROY OF BOSTON. He was perhaps five or six when the People brought him to Fort Connelly. The scars were new then. The Chief Trader, one Hiram Illdare, called him Jim to distinguish him from the two Jameses who were there already. The engagés, however, called him Boston Jim and soon enough he thought of himself that way as well. Having never had a name, it seemed as good as any.

And so this man, this Boston Jim, stops at the plank that crosses the Johnston Street ravine where the shacks list on stilts over the muck and refuse of the creek. Now makes his way down Government Street, past the Colonial Hotel and the Star and Garter and the Hôtel de France. Pianos clank out discordant tunes and a man in a sky-blue waistcoat jigs drunkenly on a stair. He walks past men playing cards on upturned barrels, past sailors and miners and company men. Most can be described by what they lack—an eye, a leg, a finger or two, any number of teeth.

He turns at Fort Street, by the last bastion of the old fort itself. In the square he passes the barracks, the scaffolds, the proprietors of beer wagons calling out their prices, a greybeard preaching to an audience of none. This is where the Indian women sit, selling shellfish and potatoes and camas. He slows as he passes them, studying their faces as he always does and though he recognizes most of them, the one he always seeks is not among them.

On the docks at Wharf Street a steamer is being unloaded amid much shouting and swinging of ropes. On the far side of the harbour a half-rigged ship tacks past the village the whites call the Songhees. Early in '62 hundreds of people of all the tribes had plied their way back and forth, working for the whites and trading with them. Now, because of the pox, the canoes sit idle at the shore and smoke furls from only three of their square houses. He doesn't fear the pox. In August of 1840 a physician came to Fort Connelly on the supply ship and inoculated them all at Illdare's insistence. The physician pierced

Boston's arm with a lancet. "Ground scab," Illdare said. "Better than any, prayer, eh, young Jim?"

The slate roof of the Hudson's Bay Company store gleams dully in a wash of sun. Nearby a brick warehouse is half completed. A workman ceases hammering and saunters across a high beam. Another work-man calls out in a language that Boston has never heard. Both workmen laugh and it seems to Boston they turn toward him as they do so. He speaks English and French, dialects of Kwagu't, Nu-chah-nulth, and Lekwungaynung. Speaks some Kanaka, some Gaelic. Knows smatterings of Russian and Spanish. Speaks, of course, half a dozen variations of Chinook, the trade jargon of the tribes that even the whites have taken on. Still, many in this place are beyond his comprehension. At Fort Connelly the engagé Lavolier had spoken of the tower of Babel, the curse of languages. He held up a canvas marked with the image of a ladder. After the Fall. Before the Deluge. Babel must have been much like this town then, the people from so many countries and tribes, suspicious of each other, and unintelligible to each other, as when God's vengeance was still fresh.

In the trade room are barrels of molasses, sacks of sugar and flour, boxes of iron tools, titled towers of buckets, stacks of rifles, and stacks upon stacks of blankets—four point and six point even, white, indigo, and red. *Wares, Provisions, Dry Goods & Armaments* reads one sign. *Pro pelle cutem* reads the company crest. Boston takes a certain pride in his ability to read. But no, he has no birthday. "Likely at night," was all Illdare had said when Boston, years ago, had asked when he arrived in the world. He only asked because of Lavolier's calendar. In January angels hovered over the bed of a dying child, the snow piled high at the window beyond. In April lambs cavorted while a shepherd slept and a devil leered. In August the Christ gazed mournfully upward, chest splayed open, heart afire. Boston found some comfort in seeing the months separated so, in seeing the days boxed and counted and named. The days should give an account of their existence. It seemed only fair.

"Good day to ye, sir. A fine day. I am Mr. Gifford. Furs to trade? I am at your service."

3

He is a youngish man with an ear half-gone. Though Boston has not seen him before he recognizes the cadence of the man's speech as that of yet another Orkneyman. He drops his furs on the counter, says nothing. They encourage pointless conversation, these company men, thinking it creates some kind of bond, thinking they can use this bond to their advantage.

"Needing flour and coal oil, plug tobacco, shot. Needing needles. Thread, strongest you got."

Mr. Gifford clears his throat. "Ah, but it was a devil of a winter, wasn't it?"

"Won't take less then eight pound for the marten. Two for the beavers. Three for the mink."

"That is a goodly price."

"Thick. You've never seen a marten so thick."

Gifford smiles. "Haven't I?"

"No," Boston says, and in such a way that Gifford drops his gaze. Boston prides himself on his trader's eye. He can remember the exact appearance, size, weight, even odour of an object. He can remember the exact profit he made on trades ten or twenty years ago. He can remember, as well, exact words of conversations, the lineaments of faces, the precise turn of events long gone. He doesn't struggle to recall as others do. If he cares to, all he need do is think of how he stood on this day or that. The rest comes in layers: first the words and the manner in which they were spoken, next the odours, then how the clouds were shaped, the leaves patterned, how the birds called each to the other. The memories of the far past are as clear to him as what is happening now, all except the ones from his earliest years, before he woke at Fort Connelly. Those are in jumbled fragments. A wharf on a night of dense heat. The outlines of furled masts and rigging lines. And then he is nestled among sacks and barrels that rock gently beneath him, recalling a thing earlier even, a thing ever out of his reach. Much later and there is a great cracking as a ship breaks apart. A campfire. A canvas overhead. A man who howls and weeps. The gleam of a long, thin knife.

"Let me cipher. I can give ye, give ye . . ." Gifford stares upward, his face rapt, his fingers moving. In all like a damned priest at his rosary.

Now comes the to-ing and fro-ing, the smiling protestations of Gifford, the blunt remarks of Boston. In the end Gifford agrees to a price only slightly lower than Boston wanted. It is enough to buy all the goods Boston requires with three pounds and twelve shillings left to spare.

Gifford hands Boston the notes and coins and a bill of sale in a legible script that notes when Mr. Boston Jim will come and take his goods.

Boston counts the money, his lips moving silently.

"The pox has been a terror, or so I've been hearing. I'm newly arrived, ye see."

Boston scrutinizes a chipped shilling.

"Well, for ye it would be a blessing, mind. For it left ye with few competitors among the Indians."

At this moment no one else is in the trade shop and it is perfectly quiet but for the buzzing of a fly, the ticking of a clock. Boston looks directly at Gifford. It is something he rarely does; for how many faces need clutter his recollections? He takes in the shadows under Gifford's watery eyes, the protruding teeth, the peculiar width of his skull.

Gifford steps back. Puts a hand to his cheek.

Boston pushes the shilling across the counter.

"I'll, I'll change that for ye, sir. Bad money about these days. My apologies."

Boston pockets the shilling and hoists on his near-empty rucksack. He thrusts the needles and thread in his pocket. "Come back for the other goods. Keep them safe, hear," he says and then leaves without looking at Gifford again. He walks back up Government Street, and then to Cormorant, intent on the London Coffee house where the food is good and plentiful, the liquor well priced and unwatered. He notes a lone pig snorting in an alleyway, notes the general decrease of soap lees, ash, and night soil. Last autumn all manner of goats and pigs and cows wandered freely, feeding on just such refuse that was tossed into the streets. This new cleanliness is not the only difference. Now many of the buildings have been painted in blood reds and ocherous yellows. In the blue of watered ink, the green of precious jade. Now several of the saloons have changed their names and one offers a dining room for ladies. Now a spirits store with a false front and canvas walls stands where a heron had walked through clover and salal. Now there is a gun-smith, a carpet merchant, a photographers' studio, an auctioneer or two.

Boston spits out a stream of tobacco and silently curses. He does not like the way the town grows in size and changes in character each time he comes to trade. It makes him uneasy, as if more time has passed than he has realized—ten or twenty years perhaps, and not just six or seven months.

No, he will not stay a day or two as he planned. He will not bother with a bath, nor a night at a Humbolt Street bawdy house. He'll stay only this night. Come dawn he'll make his way back to his cabin, back past the bay where the Dora woman and the other new settlers are. He'll make his traps ready again. He'll not stop and visit as she asked. He offered recompense and she refused. Surely that settled the matter between them.

And now two women give him pause. Their skirts take up the entire boardwalk and sway like great bells. They are talking closely, their bonnets obscuring their faces. Boston certainly cannot go through the two of them; it would be like breaking through a barricade, the sort of action that merits trouble. And he cannot go around them; even he knows this would not do, for then they would have to flatten themselves against a store window to avoid brushing against him in an unseemly fashion.

The women are very close before they notice him. They stop. Boston stops. The older woman wrinkles her nose. The younger woman gazes down. Boston backs up and takes the stairs to the deep mud below, all the while silently cursing these perplexing encounters, these pitfalls, all the while thinking of the Dora woman.

He had been walking for two days along a ragged green trail. Usually it took only a day for this part of the journey, but the rain came on hard and the path churned with mud and he stumbled several times. It was dusk when he reached Cowichan Bay, as the new settlers call it, and torrenting still, and so he sought shelter in a small cave. The next morning was clear-skied and warm. It was then he noticed the tear in his shirt pocket; it was then he noticed that the smoke pouch was gone. Inside it was one hundred and twenty-six pounds, ten shillings. Never more. Never less. It must never be less. It was the same money he had taken from Illdare's personal cache when he left Fort Connelly years ago. This was not stolen money, not truly, for that amount had been owed to him, that much and more besides. His everyday money was safe in another pocket of his coat, in a plain leather bag. But that money hardly mattered.

The tide was rising over the rocks where he had walked. He stood with fists clenched, recalling each footfall. He turned back and searched the path, the bases of the great trees, their roots splaying out thick as barrels. Searched through the ferns and moss, the places where he had stumbled or slipped. Felt light-headed, as if he might retch. Still he searched.

The tide was out when he returned to the shore. That was when he first saw the Dora woman. She wore a calico apron over a blue dress that was hiked to her mucky knees. The dress was ruffled at the collar and sleeves and it shimmered in the watery sun.

Near the Dora woman was a mid-aged Quamichan woman in a tartan shawl and a Quamichan man, lean and grey-haired, dressed in trousers and a pale shirt and a battered top hat. At the feet of all three were baskets heaped with gooey-ducks. The Dora woman looked up at his approach and as she did her blue bonnet slipped back off a froth of yellow hair. The Quamichans eyed him suspiciously, but the Dora woman waved, as if she had been expecting him all along.

"Have you lost something, sir?"

"No."

"Come now. You've lost something. Could be your very soul with such a look you're having there." She smiled then.

He walked past her, thinking she was mocking.

"Was it a pouch?"

He halted. His chest tightened as if held in a clamp. "Was a pouch, yes."

"Tell me what it looked like. I have to be certain, see, before I show you what I found."

"Was a smoke pouch. With tassels. Blue and red."

"What sort?"

"Silk. Silk tassels. Worn out nearly. The pouch has a Raven on it. In beads." He described the colour of the beads, then hastily drew the image of the Raven in the wet sand.

"Ah, enough now. I believe you." She reached into her apron. "Here it is then."

He grabbed the pouch from her and turned his back and counted the money. It was wet and soiled, but there, all one hundred and twenty-six pounds, ten shillings. He put the smoke bag into a side pocket. Kept his hand upon it. The weight of the coins seemed to firm up the wet sand beneath his boots.

"Old money that is. I haven't seen its like since I was a girl."

"You saw it, then."

"Oh, for certain. I didn't count it, mind. I said, no Dora, it's not yours to be counting." She smiled at him. "Won't you come to the cabin and have some coffee? You look as if you're needing it. Ah, it has been horrid, hasn't it? This morning I said to myself, Dora, go to the shore and help out Mary and Jeremiah, and so I did because after that rain I had to get out of doors like, and my roof leaked and I had to put a bucket, but ah, the noise kept me awake so and . . . oh, don't scowl so Jeremiah, *yaka tillicum*, he's a friend, a friend."

She did not cease speaking as she led the way. Boston and the Quamichans followed silently. It had never happened. Not to him, not to anyone he had heard of. Money belonged to the one who held it. If it is found it is not returned, not voluntarily. It made no sense. Perhaps she was wealthy and was showing her largesse. Service and homage, then, was what she would want in return. But she was not someone of great property. He knew that soon enough. The cabin was like the few others in the area, was no more than twenty feet wide and made of unpeeled logs and had a shingled roof and a few flat stones before the door. A sheet and a petticoat heaved out from a makeshift line. Some of the charred stumps about were still smoking, much of the ground unbroken.

The Dora woman told him to sit on the bench by the outside wall of the cabin. He did so, one hand on his rucksack. Jeremiah milked the lone cow in the lean-to. Mary attended to the few chickens scratching inside a wire pen. From the cabin came clattering and bits of song and in a short time the Dora woman came out and gave him barely raised bread and hard cheese and coffee thick with grains. She apologized, said it was all she had. She asked for his name. He told her and she repeated it several times, as if it were something to bring luck or keep evil at bay. She spoke queerly, leaving out the h's and speaking as if she were half swallowing her words. He'd heard English spoken that way, but never by a woman. She introduced herself as Mrs. Dora Hume. The names of her helpers were not really Mary and Jeremiah, those were just the names a priest gave them. They wouldn't tell her their true Indian names. Wasn't that odd? She left no gap for a reply. She said she'd been astonished at first at how many Indians were about. Terrified as well. She was sure they'd kill her in her sleep. But, no, these Indians were kindly folk and oft-times brought offerings of venison and berries. And wasn't it a great source of comfort being able to hire them? To always have someone about? "And where is it you're living, Mr. Jim?"

He gestured vaguely to the hills beyond the bay.

"Ah, I see," she said, and then began talking, an endless stream of words and stories. Boston had never heard such talking before. She said, first off, that it astounded her how people appeared in this place, no announcement, no rumours of arrival. Might be a whole thriving city just on the other side of that thick, high wall of trees, one only had to enter through the right shaft of rare sunlight, say some magic word, in Chinook she supposed, because that way everyone could understand it. Even she could understand it, for she spoke Chinook quite well, thank you. Her neighbour Mrs. Smitherton said she'd never seen such a quick study. Now the Dora woman was speaking of muddy Methodist boots appearing one day as she was poking at the seedlings in her garden, of how they began preaching of God's love, black-suited knees of salvation. She looked up into a face that was promising a heaven paved with gold and full of angels singing the praises of our Lord. She told the man that all she wanted was a little more sun and that she was High Church and then kindly suggested he not stand so on her new pea shoots. He looked down amazed, hands still in the air, and she laughed because by his expression you'd think he'd just realized he was a hundred miles up, hanging onto strips of clouds.

She spoke next of her life in London, spoke of her family without any introduction, as if he knew them as well as she. Well, he did soon enough, certainly.

Boston finished his coffee, made a brief movement of leaving. He would have to leave soon if he were to hire a canoe to take him down the inlet. And so what held him there? He cannot say, but it was impossible for him to move from the block of sunlight, impossible to move away from her voice that was wrapping about him like twine. He should have been more careful. Odd things lie in wait for weary travellers. He knew that as well as anyone.

"And so I signed up on the *Tynemouth*. Can you believe that, Mr. Jim? Ah, but I didn't want to share the fate of my older sister who hoped for greater things but ended up in Dark House lane, selling fish and oysters. I'd never heard of Victoria, and for certain not the colony of Vancouver Island. Anything outside the boundaries of London were like a foreign land to me. I still can't believe I'm here. I'm often pinching myself I am."

Of this sea voyage she spoke in great detail. Of how when they finally arrived in Esquimalt the men lined the road and she had five marriage proposals within a day. Oh, but they were rough-looking characters and she would not be so rash. She had signed a contract to work for the Avalon Hotel and she intended to honour this contract. But then she met Mr. Hume. He begged for her hand. Such a fine man. How could she refuse him? She had wanted to stay in Victoria, but he knew of free land to be had in the Cowichan. It astounded her and still did. "One hundred and sixty acres. We're like Lords and Ladies of the manor, that's what."

She spoke at length of this husband, Mr. Hume, and said several times how he was to come home any time now. She looked to the forest as she did so, as if expecting him to stride forth. Later she changed her story. "I can tell you the truth. You ain't, I mean, you're not a thief or a cutthroat. You have a good face, you do."

Her husband had, in fact, set off just five days ago to seek gold in the Cariboo. He was sure to find it as he was more clever than most and more handsome, too. Didn't women glance at him in the streets? Didn't it make her both jealous and proud? And he knew something of everything—languages and poetry and history and old tales and he'll write his memoirs as soon as he's old. At that point she dashed inside the cabin and came out with tintype that bore her husband's face in muddy shades.

Her way of remembering was not as his, was not like opening a book and seeing it all there, the same each time. She struggled with names and pondered dates and was often turning back to fill in a word or gesture or detail which had escaped her before. Likely, too, events shifted and reformed for her, as they did for most people and as such could not be taken as truth.

Mary and Jeremiah returned and stood quietly by, only then did she pause and so allow him a chance to leave. "Why, the whole afternoon is gone!" she said and looked about as if it might be retrieved from under a root.

He held up a marten pelt, the second best one he had, a paltry offering for the return of his money, for her hospitality. That was when she said: "Not to worry. Think on it as a gift, for your birthday, like."

"Have none," he replied.

"None? Ah, well and so, it's just an ordinary gift, then. But if you like, you can bring me something when you're back this way again. Not that it matters. Just come again and I'll have some better food for us and you can tell me of yourself, because I chatter on so, indeed I do."

The women have walked on, their rain pattens clattering on the boards. Boston thumps back up the stairs, his boots now covered with mud, now heavy as anvils. He cleans them on the boot scrape and enters a haberdashery. He does this small politeness of scraping his boots, but he does not take off his hat, which is battered and sweat-rimmed at the crown.

The haberdashery is long and narrow and is lit with lanterns though outside it is not yet dark. He shifts uncertainly. He has never entered such a place. Why would he? It is a woman's place. Here are needles of all sizes, hatpins the size of daggers, bone corsets and steel embroidery rings, tins of buttons and tins of beads, stiff bonnets perched on wooden heads, and other, unnameable things, their gleaming and sparkling multiplied in the wall of looking glasses. He has no liking for looking glasses. Cannot imagine why anyone does. But this time he pauses at his own image. "You have a good face," the Dora woman had said. He never thinks of his face, whether it is good or otherwise, but considering it, at this moment, even he can see that for most people it would not be a face to inspire trust, not at all.

"Something for the wife, sir?" The woman is as small as a child and her dress is festooned with scalloping and bright coloured bows. Her ringleted hair, however, is grey, her face furrowed, her voice a harsh rasp.

"Need a gift, for a lady."

"A lady? Had you anything particular in mind? Most gentlemen do."

Boston's mouth is dry. "Ribbons," he says after a pause. Women went in for ribbons. For their hair, he supposes, or to pin on their dresses.

They are amongst the gimping and edgings, are of pink or white satin and unfurl from fat rolls. How many? How long? They would be soiled and tangled by the time he gave them. They would resemble shrivelled worms.

"Your expression tells us we have not divined quite the best thing. Come. Look." The old woman now shows him ivory combs, silver scissors, silver lockets, bracelets dangling with cupids and hearts, crystal bottles of perfume. "We know the best way to a lady's heart, oh, yes, indeed."

Boston has now fully entered foreign territory. He does not like it. So many of the objects are small and smooth, but with sharp, un-expected points, with uncertain purposes.

Perhaps the woman, this Dora Hume, is touched with madness, perhaps loneliness has got to her, out there alone in a cabin, her husband away. It's different for women; they subsist on speech and company. He doesn't long for companionship. If he had a family, a wife, a servant, one of these 'friends,' then every night there would be speaking; every night there would be more words that would stay with him until the grave.

The money was his own. It was her own peculiarity, then, her choice to return what was his. It was not a gift she gave him, no matter what she said about birthdays and such. It did not need recompense to show that he was her equal. She gave him water and food, true, but these things are always given to travellers in need. It was expected of her, of everyone, and was, in fact, some kind of law. Such acts are always reciprocated sooner or later and so cannot be considered generosity at all, but rather a way of equalizing. Don't the few trappers in his parts keep a grudging eye on each other? And only last summer he'd helped those Klallams. He found them near his trapline, an old man and his youngest son. They were exhausted and starving and so he took them to his cabin, gave them food, let them sleep on his benches. They had been living in the Songhees village in Victoria until the Whites burned their huts and forced them to leave at rifle point. It was all so that Tom Dyer, the pox, didn't spread to the Whiteman's town, though it was the Whiteman who set Tom Dyer loose among them, who made it so they rotted while they still lived. The younger Klallam showed him the five slashes on his arm and told him in Chinook, in low furious tones, that the slashes were for each of his dead children and one for his wife. Later the old man raised himself up and spoke in a dialect that Boston barely understood, though it was plain he was laying curses, a litany that went on until darkness fell.

No, he will waste none of his time, none of his money earned from his own toil. It was idiotic to even consider it. He was not in her debt. He owed her nothing. Not even this second, return visit she asked of him.

The old woman holds up a brush made of boar's bristles and inlaid with shells. Boston mutters that he must be going.

"I am sorry, so sorry that we did not find something for your lady," the old woman rasps. "Think on it well, and then return. The exact thing is never easy to find. No indeed."

TWO

Eugene Augustus Hume has never liked parlours and Mrs. Jacobsen's at the Avalon Hotel is no exception. In the half-dark of imminent dawn, the bric-a-brac and furniture seem hunched and huddled and quietly animate, like exhausted refugees seeking shelter from some cataclysm. But it is natural that he stay here. It is his home in a way, given that when he arrived in '61 he had stayed at the Avalon for nearly six months. He lived then in a two-room affair for a cracking good price. Meals were included and Mrs. Jacobsen often served him with her own hands. Eugene merely had to assist with errands and with the odd reluctant bill payer, a task he did with tact and soldierly aplomb, though he did not relish it, hearing echoes of his own not-so-long ago protestations in that of his quarry, recalling his own name chalked on the blackboard behind the counter of the tailor, the butcher. He initially suggested that perhaps Mr. Jacobsen should be the one to act the constable. This suggestion astonished Mrs. Jacobsen. He was a partial invalid, she proclaimed, who rarely dared venture from his room on the southern side. And indeed, Eugene himself has never yet seen him up close, only rounding a corner, disappearing into a doorway, poking about in the pantry, enough to ascertain that Mr. Jacobsen is a small man with the furtive movements of a creature who prefers the dark. He is inept, perhaps, but far too ambulatory to be called an invalid. Perhaps Mrs. Jacobsen was referring—and this thought wanders into Eugene's mind unbidden—to his prowess in his husbandly duties.

Eugene strikes a lucifer and lights a candle. The wick is untrimmed and the flame flares high. Above the sideboard is a great oil of some blank-faced, inbred aristocrats picnicking on a hill. A child has crawled away from the group and is a hand span away from an ominous thicket. None of the picnickers seem to notice the wayward child in the least.

He sniffs at a decanter. Ah, quite so. Sherry. It is a lady's drink, but a good a capper as any to a fine evening. He was the last man standing at the Brown Jug, an establishment that was known to stay open for business as long as there was someone to serve, as long as there was someone, such as Eugene, celebrating before a departure into the wilderness. And yet no matter how many times he raised his arm in a toast there remained that fluttering at the back of his skull, as if moths were rising from sleep.

He contemplates a small statue of a cherub, says: "Steel yourself, Eugene Augustus. You have whiled away enough time. You are off to the goldfields, off to see the elephant, as they say. Now there is an absurd phrase, made by men who have likely never seen one of those ponderous creatures in their lives. But then what is two weeks more, or three? The gold, by all accounts, is still tight in the earth's icy embrace where it has lain for centuries—no, millennia. Consider Mr. . . . Mr. Lell, that was the name, and his book about stones and so forth. His *Geological Ideas*, that was it. Consider the vast stretches of time. How after millions upon millions of years, a mountain is still young! It is a stretch of nothing, like an afternoon for us mortals. And our afternoon is as a lifetime to a gnat. Hah, what think you of that, my little marble friend? Your parts are like to be as ancient as the Coliseum, as the very sea itself, as ancient as . . ."

"Mr. Hume. Is it you, sir? Are you there?"

Eugene starts, mouths a curse as sherry spills on the carpet.

"I heard voices. I was terrified out of my wits. I thought I might faint."

Mrs. Jacobsen stands in the doorway. One hand holds a wrapper closed over her nightdress, the other a candle in its holder. Her hair, a robust red in better light, here streams darkly over her shoulders. And though she is affecting terror, affecting a heaving of her considerable bosom, it is doubtful she has ever fainted in her life. Not that this matters. She was beautiful once and thus can be forgiven much. Indeed Eugene sees her, not as she is now, but as she was thirty or forty years ago, with a regal, formidable beauty, the likeness of an Athena. He does not often boast of it, but he has an astonishing ability to detect the lost lineaments of beauty, much the way an archaeologist detects a once splendid city under rubble.

He covers the spilled sherry with his foot. "My apologies, madam, if I have awoken you. I cannot sleep."

"You cannot sleep? Have you tried Doctor Helmcken's blue pills? Have you tried a purge? An iced bath? It draws the agitation from the limbs. It steadies the mind."

Eugene admits he has not tried any of these remedies but will, of course.

Mrs. Jacobsen is filling his glass and now her own. He notes that she is remarkably powdered and rouged for one awoken in a fright. Notes also (how can he not?) her wrapper shifting open to show the complicated affair of her nightdress, the ravine between her once no doubt splendid breasts. He murmurs his thanks. Mrs. Jacobsen sits on the divan. He is relieved to sit also, for the late hour is bringing with it an unsteadiness of posture. He chooses the nearest armchair. His knees rise uncomfortably high. He will be glad when a taller monarch comes to the throne and the furniture is no longer made in deference to a woman the size of a gnome. His father, God rest him, had chairs from the reign of King George. Card playing chairs, high enough so that a tall man could sit with some dignity. They were the only items of furniture his father brought with them as they moved from this inn to that lodging house. *A man without a chair is nothing*, his father said, in one of his more philosophical moods.

"I, too, am often restless." Mrs. Jacobsen says. "I, too, am often afflicted with wakefulness. Did you know it travels through a family line? Did you know that my Great Aunt Wilhelmina did not sleep for twenty years?"

"I did not know this. But it is fascinating, truly so." Eugene smiles, showing his array of fine teeth. Mrs. Jacobsen's stern countenance transforms before this smile, before the manly presence that is Eugene Augustus Hume. He stands a head taller than most. Is broad shouldered and well featured with a clean-shaven chin and waves of chestnut hair. He wears checkered trousers in shades of brown, a matching frock coat, a fawn-coloured waistcoat, and a cravat of burgundy silk. All of which bring attention to the fine amber of his eyes. His top hat is on a side table as are his gloves. Not for him these coke hats and bared hands. And he has that way of looking about, as if he is always ready to leap to the rescue. Dashing, in a word.

"Mr. Hume. If I may ask. If I may be forthright. Do you feel at home here at the Avalon? Do you feel as if you are suited to its environs?"

"Indeed, madam."

"Then I have an offer. A proposal."

"A proposal?" The moths arise as he takes a good draft of sherry.

"I would like you to stay and have Mr. Vincent's position. Would that be agreeable? Would that take you off this silly notion of the Cariboo?"

"But you have only recently hired him."

"He shakes. He is forever making mistakes in the accounts. He often sleeps throughout the afternoon. And he quails completely at bill collection. I am certain we can find an agreeable arrangement."

"But the steamer leaves. I am booked and . . ."

"And how many make their fortune? How many return, in fact, as paupers? Truly, sir, how many return not at all, but perish of this or that?"

"I have attempted far more difficult journeys, I assure you. Journeys rife with indescribable dangers. It is just . . ."

"Just? Yes? It is just?" Mrs. Jacobsen says, though the name is there, as if scrawled on the air between them.

"That I have certain obligations. The Cowichan, my land, and . . ."

"And? Miss Timmons? Is that what you mean? Have you married her, by the by? Should I offer my belated congratulations? Should I inform all my acquaintances?" Mr. Jacobsen smiles as if this were merely gay repartee.

"No, that is to say, not yet. I am waiting until I have sufficient means to provide a grand breakfast feast after the ceremony. It would be a disgrace to the name of Hume otherwise. Until then we are married in our souls, that is, as they say, in the custom of the country, a union that has a long and honourable tradition here. Even good Governor Douglas and his lovely dusky wife . . ."

"Indeed, but that was long before the arrival of proper ministers. We have ministers aplenty now. We have churches of every stripe. Perhaps you have not tied the knot because you have realized that it would be unwise? Perhaps that is why you cannot sleep?"

Eugene frowns and sadly shakes his head.

Mrs. Jacobsen twists her hair between her fingers. "I am sorry. I apologize. My jests sometimes do not sound as they should. I . . . it is just . . . you see, when you left with Miss Timmons I was shocked. I was astounded. I gave that young woman employment, a fine little room, as many sweet buns as she cared to stuff herself with and wages that were much higher than in London, or any other great city of Europe. What's more, I offered her friendship, albeit the restrained friendship of an employer, of an older, wiser woman, but still. And how did Miss Timmons thank me? She left before her contract was completed. And with a lodger."

She said *lodger* as if she had forgotten that Eugene was this very same man.

Eugene wonders if he, too, should speak plainly. Should ask what a married woman, any woman, is doing in the parlour with a "lodger" at these dark hours, and in her nightdress yet, drinking sherry, mentioning baths.

Eugene, however, is nothing if not a gentleman and so decides on a fond sigh. "Ah, my dear Mrs. Jacobsen, do you think me so lacking in honour?"

"I did not mean . . ."

"I will return. I will marry her. I have given my word. But you have hit upon fragments of the truth, for in England, in that other world, Miss Timmons and I would never have been united over the chasm of class and fortune. But this is a new land. The rules are turned wholly 'round. Possibilities abound."

"I thought so once as well," she says quietly.

Eugene pushes himself up from the chair. "I am booked on the Thursday steamer. I thank you for your gracious offer. If circumstances had been different do not doubt that I would have grasped it without the slightest hesitation."

"Thursday? But is it not already Tuesday? You have your supplies? You are prepared?"

"I am quite prepared."

"Mr. Hume, sir. I spoke rashly just now. Will you allow me to make amends? Will you extend me the pleasure of your company tomorrow evening? I shall have Ah-Sing prepare a roast duck. Your favourite, is it not? We will talk of the latest inventions, of that war in America." she smiles softly. "And other such safe and simple topics."

"I would be honoured," Eugene says and presses her bare hand to his lips, inhales the scent of powdered roses. "Good night, dearest Beatrice. You who have been so kind, so full of gracious understanding. Do not doubt I remain your servant."

The use of her given name renders her speechless excepting a mutter of "Good night, sir, that is, Eugene."

He listens for her steps up the stairs, and then the slow creaking shut of her door. She had once asked him into her room on some private matter then suggested that if he stayed it would not be unacceptable.

"My principles will not allow me to compromise your reputation," he had replied, but with resignation and regret, as if his principles were grim, unyielding relatives.

Morning casts a grey light over the painting of the oblivious picnickers. He will be glad to be quit of its sight. Dora called them a cheerful lot, but then she is likewise blessedly oblivious. Mrs. Jacobsen described them once as "awash in love" and added that they were her Parisian ancestors before the revolution came between their heads and their shoulders. Eugene thinks it far more likely that her ancestors would be depicted as peasants toiling in some mud-soaked field, but when is he one to quibble at inventiveness?

The bottle of sherry on the sideboard has a finger width left. Eugene holds it up. "Let's kill you off then, soldier, before we do anything rash."

THREE

At the London Coffee, House Boston orders beefsteak with potatoes, a glass of whiskey, coffee and pie. The serving woman has
a wattled neck and wears three great rings. In the autumn she wore
only two. Her dress then was also green, but of a darker hue. She does
not recognize him. Would not, he supposes, even if she scrutinized
him. And he makes no sign that he recognizes her. What would be
the purpose in that? He recognizes faces he has known for years and
those merely glimpsed, faces seen in windows and doorways, infants'
squalling faces, and the faces of the dead, staring at the clouds. The
remembered crowd his head to bursting, and cause an ache at times as
if they were hammering at his skull. That is why he rarely looks directly
at people unless he need intimidate. That is why he prefers his own
company, if *prefers* is the right word.

He chews slowly. The food does not taste as fine as it usually does,
the thought of his owing having returned to plague him.

The serving woman takes his plate, asks if Mister is attending
the entertainment at the Victoria Theatre. It is a splendid show. The
famous Miss Annabel Anderson, the astonishing Professor Hinkeman.

"Nothing better than a piece of theatre," the Dora woman had said,
and then described her favourite shows—*The Cripple of Fenchurch
Street, A Chaste Maid of Cheapside*. Her hands moved constantly as
she spoke, now pressing to her chest in imitation of a tragic heroine,
now running over the shape of a corpulent actor. "People were always
saying it was a great shame I never chose the stage. Didn't Mr. Hume
himself remark I was a regular dramatist? Oh, I know what you're
thinking, that it's not a thing for a lady. But I wouldn't be in one of

those penny gaffes where people throw spoilt cabbages if they're not liking what they get. No, I'd be at the Royal. I'm talking of the Royal in London, mind. I been there once. Oh, such a grand place! Such lime lights! I seen Lily Kurl there. I'd be one like her, see. Her sort get the respect of the gentry, they do. Ah, to have hundreds of folk tossing you flowers, all adoring you, all cheering. And tell me what you've seen now. Surely you've seen some entertainment? A magic lantern show? A cosmorama?

"Not in the habit of the theatre," Boston said, caught off guard. What do you get for your shillings, your dollar? Nothing solid, no piece of knowledge that could be put to any use. But now it seems there might be some value. For he could attend an entertainment and later tell the Dora woman what he has seen. That will be her gift. It will cost him nothing but his entrance fee. When he has finished the telling she will smile and clap her hands and he will go on, unburdened of his debt, and all will be as it was before.

The Victoria is nearly full. Red velvet curtains hang heavy on brass hooks. Plaster cherubs and mermaids adorn the lintels and balconies. A man on a ladder trims a coal lamp. The ladder totters and he wails, much to the merriment of the crowd below.

The entertainment is late. The crowd grows restless. The few women present crack open fans. The men lean back, inspect their pocket watches, *hallo* across the crowd. Boston takes a seat in the mid-region. All about him are the crosswinds of gossip. There is Mr. Mifflin Gibbs in the best balcony, he with that fancy grocery and provisioning store. How dare a coloured man place himself so high above them? There is the bone merchant Mr. Wang and there the cobbler Mr. Isaac. There Mr. Applegath, and there Mr. and Mrs. Laforge, putting on airs, the damned rebs.

A scuffle breaks out to shouts of encouragement just as the curtains jerk open, just as the revel master, a red-whiskered man in a top hat, calls out for attention. After an interminable preamble he bawls out the names Master Henderson and Little Miss Olive, demands applause that is heartily given. Miss Olive, ringlets bobbing, leads the sullen Master Henderson, a thick-limbed boy in too-small britches. In the pit the piano man begins a gentle tune. The children sing:

Oh blessings forever on Aileen Astor!
She is as good as she is lovely and twenty times more;
Her sparkling blue eyes and magical smile
'Tis the hardest of heart my love doth beguile

The whiskey-soaked man beside Boston sniffles and wipes his nose with his hand. "Ain't she just like my little Sophie. Oh, my girl." He stands and shouts: "Hear! Hear!" Stumbles against Boston. Boston looks him full in the face, takes in the bulbous nose, the scrofulous skin, the marl-coloured eyes aswim with tears.

The man apologizes profusely, to the ceiling, the floor. Explains as he sidles away from Boston that he must stand closer, that his eyes are weak and always have been.

The revel master again holds up his hands for quiet. "Ladies and gentlemen. You have heard, you may have witnessed, certainly you have awaited with great expectation, the legendary Miss Annabel Anderson of San Francisco, back by popular demand to present her world-famous Spider Dance!"

A young woman strolls out. Her dress is of purples and greens. At her neck is a long white scarf. She gazes about half-smiling as the crowd cheers. Is she pretending to pick flowers? What sort of entertainment is this? She looks at her hands with mild concern, inspects them more closely. Her shriek is enough to shatter glass. The piano pounds frantically as Miss Anderson flails at her bodice and skirt, tears off her scarf, lashes it over her throat and back. Now she is lifting her skirts high and showing red stockings and now jigging in a circle, all to the hoots and calls of the audience. This goes on for a time, and then, for some sort of a finale, she tears her hair from its neat arrangement, her shrieks timed to the piano chords until the piano abruptly halts. She smoothes her hair back from her face, curtsies to the audience, to its thunderous applause. The floor shakes from the stomping. The curtain rushes closed.

Boston is mystified. He'd been expecting real spiders, but here the woman was only feigning. At least the People who lived by Fort Connelly did their best to make it seem real. Perhaps it would be better to tell the Dora woman of their entertainments. Of, say, the girl who was sent to the ghost world. A chisel was thrust through her temple.

Blood flowed from out of the wound, from out of her mouth. Her eyes popped out of bloodied sockets. She was cast into a fire from which ghostly voices came and was not seen again for five days until another ceremony brought her back, healed and whole. Yes, Boston could tell her of this, and also of the wild men who tore flesh from each other to feast upon. And of the great masks that flew about the houses and transformed—now a bear, now an eagle, now the face of a man in torment. It was theatre and trickery, all of it, but was also a way of making deals with the spirit world. As such it had some purpose. Not like this idiocy.

"And now for our main billing of the evening, an Electromagician and Spiritualist of the highest order, on his final world tour before retirement, Ladies and Gentleman of Victoria please welcome the esteemed Professor Eliab Theophilus Hinkeman of New York City!"

The piano plays a dignified strain and the curtains part again. Professor Hinkeman has a shock of silver hair, a neat silver beard. He stands motionless on the stage, one hand grasping his lapel, the other a thick cane. Beside him is a young woman in an unadorned dress of palest grey. He introduces her as Miss Frielan, orphan niece, faithful assistant. Then says: "Ladies, gentlemen. Be warned. The faint of heart should take their leave now, for I am about to show you what lies beneath the skin of the world."

The crowd mutters and shifts. The ladies glance at their escorts, lean closer.

"I require a volunteer for my first exhibit. From him I will pull the very form of his soul. It will not cause pain, nor injury. It will not affect him in any way. My talent is only to make clear what is before us all if we but only look."

A young man clambers onto the stage at the encouragement of his friends. He has scrubby moustaches, a jaunty hat. His friends call out "Leewood, Leewood." He shields his eyes with his hand, mouth agape, looking out into the audience as if he were a sojourner sighting a country of dangerous marvels.

The Professor frowns in concentration, reaches behind Leewood's neck and pulls a rabbit from out of his collar. The rabbit twists in the Professor's grip. The audience hoots and laughs. So it is a comedy of sorts. The Professor puts the rabbit into a bag held by Miss Frielan and studies the bulbous eyes, the reddish hair of the next volunteer.

He claps his hands over the man's ears and yanks out two goldfish. Miss Frielan holds out a bowl of water. The Professor bows. The crowd shouts for more and the Professor obligingly pulls a snake from the pocket of a bespectacled, clerky fellow who scowls and shouts "ridiculous." It is a simple trick, but it may make the Dora woman laugh if he tells her of it. Certainly the men about him are guffawing so hard that some are near to choking.

The Professor now makes a matchsafe vanish and then appear in the pocket of a man at the back of the crowd. He stands playing cards end to end until they reach the proscenium. He speaks constantly to draw attention from the deft movements of his hands, from what shouldn't be seen. Speaks of his soldiering youth, of his escape from the Sultan's prison with aid of a beautiful harem girl, of impossible landscapes of sand, of his apprenticeship in magic in the dens of Goa and Seville, of the loneliness of his life, until Lila, dear Lila, Miss Frielan, his orphan niece. "Stand centre stage, my dear." She is pretty and demure in the light of the coal lamps and candles, someone's cherished daughter, someone's faithful sweetheart. The Professor passes his hands over her eyes and she takes on the aspect of one asleep. He assists her to stretch out on a table, then holds his arms over her. The crowd gasps. She is rising. She is suspended in midair, not limp, but as if she were made of stone. The men point furiously and reassure each other they are witnessing the same thing. The Professor lets her gently down. She rises to loud applause.

"Miss Frielan, ladies and gentlemen, has a sensitive soul. She is clean of sins. It is only for this reason she can float like an angel. But, and this my friends is a truth, she also attracts spirits by her gentleness and purity, the way a warm hearth attracts the living after a day of wind and rain. They pass through her, whispering messages for those who are still among the quick, for those, perhaps, who are here this night."

"A post office, is she?" someone shouts. There is laughter of a nervous sort. Miss Frielan looks sorrowful. The Professor grimly searches the crowd.

"I must ask for total silence for this, our final marvel. I must ask that each and every one of you retain his breath until I shout 'Release.' Only then will the spirits visit us." Professor Hinkeman counts to five and all in the crowd gulp the air, all except for Boston. He sits while 'round him cheeks bulge and eyes grow round. Spirits are of no use to him; it is hard enough to navigate among the living.

Miss Frielan begins to tremble. Her limbs jerk. Her eyes roll upward.

"Release!" the Professor shouts. He feigns a stagger at the force of the exhalation. He raises his cane. "They are here!" The audience gasps in its next breath, and such a gasp it is. The air is of a sudden thinner, colder. There is a shift from jocularity to unease. It is as if a threshold has been crossed. Boston knows the feeling from the winter festivals of the People. He does not like it.

"Oh, Frank, you'll be striking riches," Miss Frielan says, her voice querulous and high. Then in a voice deep and manly: "Thomas, my son, you have my blessing for your journey." And so it goes. She speaks in French, Italian, German, in the accents of England and Ireland and America. She is the voice of lovers, mothers, sons, and friends, all who have concerns and advice, premonitions and warnings for Amos and John, for Jacques and Antonio and Wilfred.

Of all the tricks this is the most simple, and yet the one that draws the most excitement. For here is the suggestion that the future has a discernible path. Not too late? For what? The pronouncements are vague enough to apply to anyone with those names, which are all common enough.

"Ah, Jim, do not forget your obligations. You will regret it mightily if you do." Miss Frielan says this in a flat, unsexed cadence. It is the voice of no one Boston has ever heard. Trickery, damned trickery.

After a time more of this, the Professor taps Miss Frielan on the shoulder. She starts and flutters her hands as if troubled by butterflies. Professor Hinkeman and Miss Frielan bow and curtsy. The crowd claps and cheers. The piano plays a rollicking tune.

Boston walks into a night that is moonless and smells of rain. The theatre crowd jostles past him. In a nearby alley a lantern swings in the dark. Someone is tunelessly whistling.

"I once knew all the words from the *Dovecot Lovelies*," the Dora woman said. "I'm not jesting. I could sing them at the drop of your hat. And I did, too, when we was invited on board the *Grappler*. Surely you've seen the Navy men all got up in their splendid uniforms. Such brass buttons! Such bearing! After I sang, the sailors played the fiddles and accordions and Mr. Hume sang 'The Rat Catcher's Daughter' in his fine baritone. And later we watched a burlesque of *Babes in the Wood*. Oh, but I couldn't stop laughing. The sailors they looked so funny in their bonnets and skirts. And we had ginger beer and apple cakes and we danced until the sun was rising. How I love to dance. How I love music. And here it's so quiet; it's so dull."

Boston halts as if he has come up against an invisible wall. He will only tell her of the theatre? Speech has no substance, no worth that can be calculated or traded. It must be a gift with form and weight and high value, for what she returned to him had high value indeed. Without an appropriate toll, as it were, he can no longer take the route past the bay, and this is the most convenient route by far. He'll have to scramble through uncut bush like some fugitive. And then it is still possible he will encounter the Dora woman here in Victoria some day, perhaps years from now. She said she comes to town whenever she can. Certainly she is the sort who would wave from across the street. How can he say, when questioned, that he was too skint to spend good money on a gift? He might as well slap her face, howl insults.

No, it is not sufficient to tell her stories of the theatre. Perhaps he could work for her, make a fence, chop down a tree or two. But she has Mary and Jeremiah to do such tasks. That Miss Frielan was no one's orphan niece, not with that Adam's apple bobbing in her throat, but she did hit upon the truth—obligations, ever obligations. The Dora woman asked that he bring her something. He nodded and so made a deal, and never has he gone back on a deal. That would upset the precarious balance in the world.

FOUR

Now that the bottle of sherry is truly dead and gone Eugene has no excuse but to make his way down the hall. He pauses at a closed door. It was here he first saw Dora. She was carrying a mountainous load of sheets, was hung up on a doorknob, was tugging and turning and becoming enchantingly entangled.

He unwound her gently, gathered up the sheets from the floor, introduced himself and said "Poor pretty bird, to be caught up so." She was speechless for the first and only time. He apologized for his sudden appearance, though he realized soon enough that it was the remarkable roundness of her eyes that made her appear so startled, so amazed. After that incident he saw her everywhere. It was as if she were multiplied, this Dora Timmons, this hopeless maid of all work. She is touching her finger to her tongue and then to the sad iron, is listening for the iron's slow hiss. She is polishing the limbs of the bronze at the foot of the stairs, filling small pillows with lavender and sage. She is working the pulleys of the chandelier in the entrance. He holds the lamp while she fills each portion with coal oil, then he pulleys it gently back until it is snug against the blackened medallion, in all as if he were a regular manservant.

What is it about her that drives him to distraction? She is not a great beauty. And she can barely manage the rightful exchange of conversation, has to be guided with interruptions that would be appallingly rude with anyone else. For Dora talks unrelentingly, her round eyes barely blinking, one story transforming into the next without a breath to allow a comment, a change of subject, a chance to escape. Indeed, Mrs. Jacobsen was correct when she said once that Dora could pinion people with her chatter as expertly as those naturalists pinion insects on a board.

The best explanation for her appeal, Eugene decides, is that her clothes always seem to be slipping from her, as if nudity is her natural state and her body is always straining toward it. It is her barely laced corsets, the flush to her cheeks, the dramatic panting after exertion, the perpetual half-pinned state of her hair, and that way she comes so close to people and peers into their eyes. She looks, in fact, as if she is forever hurrying from one liaison to the next. She is shocking really, deliciously so.

How is she faring? At this moment he feels near sick with worry. She had wanted so desperately to join him, but his reason prevailed. They would lose the land if both of them were gone. Squatters would take it. And the goldfields, by all accounts, were no place for a woman. And he would never forgive himself if on their journey they were attacked by a pack of bears. "Do not worry, my love, I will write each and every week," he promised. "And you must write to me."

"Ah no, no. You haven't taught me the letters yet. I can't write proper, Eggy, I can't."

"Mrs. Smitherton will help," he said. "Though I beg you, dearest, do not use that moniker in your missives." Do not use it ever, he would have said, but by then she was in his arms, her breath warming his neck, his chest, and so forth.

"I will return, my darling, with fortune in hand. Do not trouble your heart."

Eugene raises an imaginary glass to Mary and Jeremiah who, though Catholic converts, have both been well vouched for. To the Smithertons, who have sworn to look in on Dora each and every day. They are an older, childless couple, both tall and thin and beaming with brotherly love. They are friendly with the Indians to the point of asking them to tea and serving them platters of vegetables from their very hands. They are friendly with the young pastor also, and come on occasion to his services at the butter church. When the pastor sees them there, as gravely polite as two children, his face lights up with the joy of the hunt and he expounds on the divinity of Christ, the vast evidence for it all, for they, being Unitarians, do not believe in such things. The eschewing of all meat but fish, however, seems to be their own peculiar affectation.

"Trust only the Smithertons, and Mary and Jeremiah," he told Dora time and again. It is not that she is a bad judge of character. She does not judge character at all. She sees a halo of good around everyone. He gathers that her father was the same. Certainly she speaks well of Thomas Timmons. Eugene wishes he could speak so well of his father. But no, his father, Sir Alfred Hume, had the rude, bleary stare, the rumpled clothes, the general ill temper of one rousted rudely from sleep. He was from a line of sons who had steadily milked the family fortune, leaving Eugene with nothing to rely upon but his wits and fine bearing. Thank Christ for Aunt Georgina, the forgotten widowed sister to his long dead mother. After visiting her countless times she gave him five hundred dollars as well as the idea that the colonies would be a fine place for a man such as himself. "I suggest that you stay and never return," was her sage advice.

He leans against the door, opening it with his weight. His supplies are heaped in one corner of the small, gabled room, are soon to be packed in his three trunks and good sized rucksack. He has a linen shirt and one of blue serge, a pair of moleskin trousers, and one of wool, socks, collars, an anorak, a blanket coat, a broad-brimmed hat as well as a top hat with hat box, a bed roll, a canvas tent, a compass, a barometer, a leather-bound notebook for the writing of his memoirs, a sketch pad (for he had some talent at sketching as a boy), a rifle, a new revolver, a matchsafe, a knife, a kettle, a fry pan, a folding candlestick, a leather drinking cup, three jars of antimacassar oil, good wax candles, a book jack, a lantern, a portable writing set with desk, a travelling games board, a moustaches comb, a clothes brush, a kerosene lantern, a brass telescope, a stout walking stick, and several books of poetry, as well as other sundries. Most importantly, he has several copies of his letter of introduction should he meet with the scions of the goldfields. The letters, impressively affixed with a large red seal, outline his three years at the college of Oriel, his year as a commissioned lieutenant, his posting in the Crimea. They extol his character, mention that his father was knighted for service to the Queen, and hint that an Earl lurks somewhere in his family tree. Every time he handles them he is glad that he found that out-of-work clerk. The man had such a fine hand and such a way with signatures.

Finally, for his adventures as a gold miner he has brass tweezers for plucking gold, a tin pan, a pickaxe, a magnifying glass, and a magnet, which the provisionist told him he would surely need, though for what purpose Eugene did not ask, not wanting to prove himself a green hand. The tome on alchemy, though not useful exactly, will no doubt provide him with amusing anecdotes with which to regale companions. Food and shot he intends to purchase in Yale.

And thus he is ready, is he not? There is no reason to delay. He has been newly shaved, his boots newly blackened, has had himself photographed at Fardon, Maynard and Dalby in full miner's garb. He has not neglected his soul, either. He went last Sunday to the Iron Church, famously sent over from England, each piece ready to fit with the other as if it were a giant child's toy. A wonder, all agree, down to its iron pews and iron staves. Unfortunate that it made rain sound as gunshots and the rustling of garments like sails cracking on the high seas. Indeed, on the morning Eugene was there he heard not a word of the Reverend's blessing.

He nudges the pile with his boot. The room is not as large as the one he had previously. If it were then he would be able to organize his supplies properly. But no, in this room the roof slopes so sharply he must get on his knees to perform his morning ablutions at the wash basin. But the lesser space was to be expected. He doubted the wisdom of staying at the Avalon at first. Mrs. Jacobsen's fury when she discovered Eugene and Dora embracing in the pantry—perhaps more than embracing—had been positively Shakespearean. Except for the odd retort, however, she has come around. In any case, it is difficult to have a grievance with a woman who adores you. And where else can he stay for such a pittance? After buying his supplies he has one hundred and seventy pounds left to his name. This hundred and seventy pounds seemed a goodly enough sum until he learned, to his astonishment, that it would be just enough to travel to the goldfields and set himself up. He considers again that Mrs. Jacobsen's offer is not in any way possible. Not that it would be the worst of fates to have such employ. There would be some dignity in it. But how the tongues would wag! He is thirty-one. By no means a stripling, but hardly doddering either. And Dora. It is soothing, at times, to listen to her talk. It is like the burble of water over stones. And what a relief to not have to be the fulcrum upon which a gathering balances, as he is often expected to be. But other times her talk becomes tiresome, yes, tiresome. It is as if she has the souls of twenty women and they all must have their say. Often he is certain his future does not contain her, and then she looks at him in just such a way and they tumble into their bed and he hushes her quiet, laughing as he does so, insisting that the Smithertons a good mile off might well come running to save her from marauding Indians. And thus he falls in love with her for the hundredth time, the thousandth.

He draws the lace curtain aside. The dawn sky is the shade of an old bruise, the street a mess of mud and animal droppings. A thud, and a cur comes yelping out of a tin shop. Someone shouts in Russian. He pushes the window up, leans out. No, not Russian, but something like it. Were you in the Crimea? Were you at Sevastopol? He is often asked this when he makes mention of his soldiering. Yes, indeed, he was Lieutenant Hume for nearly a year. Sometimes he also mentions that he had a splendid uniform. He should boast more of his soldiering adventures. Colour them in mightily. In this place it seems de rigueur. He has met a man who sailed with Sir John Franklin, another who escaped from South Sea Cannibals, another who discovered a new species of beetle. Everyone here is a Darwin, a Byron, a Wellington. But, no, he does not boast of that time. For it only brings back the disorienting roar of the cannons, the gun smoke, the reek of spilled bowels and guts, all of which made for the understandable error of running to the left instead of the right. Once separated from his battalion what else was he to do but take cover under the masses of the newly dead? Should he have stood up, shouted and so been shot through the heart? Ah, but no matter how he justifies, no matter how he re-imagines the scene, he has to admit some lack of foresight, courage even. Yet he survived, did he not? He was encouraged to sell his commission shortly afterwards, which he was glad enough to do, a Lieutenant's pay being meagre at best.

The cur disappears into an alley. He will go to sleep when he sees a living soul. Ah, there, a cluster of Indians on the James Bay mud flats. The tide is low. They must be gathering clams or some such. And now two young swags coming from a night on the town, exclaiming about a Miss Frielan. "Imagine hitching yourself to a girl like that!" says the one.

31

"She'd be always floating off, wouldn't she," his friend says.

"True. And what's bloody worse, she'd always know what you were thinking."

Laughter and back clapping. Now a woman hurling ashes into the street. The first Whiteman then, not counting the town crier. There, Mayor Harris, all three hundred pounds of him, making his ponderous way over the James Street Bridge. He is on his way from his butcher shop to the so-called Birdcages, that tasteless conglomeration of architecture that passes for the halls of government. Eugene would even now be striding those boards if not for that damned dinner party, the one he attended in the spring of '61, when first he arrived. Yes, if not for that he might even now be insisting the streets be wholly lit with gas, the spirit prices regulated, the bathhouses inspected. Why had no one forewarned him of the idiosyncrasies of the colony? Come now, Eugene Augustus, why had you not attended to your observations?

Consider. At that fateful dinner the servants wore morning suits when they should have worn black. One looked a half-breed; the other was a Chinaman whose long queue Eugene swore he saw dipping into the soup. The table was so full of epergnes and wilted flowers that Eugene soon enough gave up engaging the people opposite him in conversation, fearing for his neck. Behind him an unshielded fire blazed high in the grate. Governor Douglas sat at the head of the table. He was a burly man with the countenance of a drover. His dinner jacket fit him badly and was bristling with medals and epaulettes, lace and gold chains. His hair stood out on either side of his head like grey handles and at dinner he sawed at his bread with a knife, not once did he break it by hand.

Next to the Governor sat one of his lively, dark-eyed daughters (the Governor's wife was indisposed, always indisposed) and then Arthur Bushby, the young, gladsome clerk of the High Judge. The High Judge, the much admired Matthew Baillie Begbie, was not in attendance, much to Eugene's disappointment. Arranged down the table were the worthies of the town and their wives. The men had weather-battered faces, their wives unfashionable dresses. All ate with a gusto Eugene had not seen since his time in the army. Ah, but when in Rome. Thus he sampled every morsel offered, the clam soup, the roasted salmon, the saddle of mutton, the oysters and pigeon pie, the assorted creams and ices. He sampled as well as the sherry, claret, punch, champagne, port and Madeira. How could he not, given the numerous toasts to the Royal Engineers? They who were building such a splendid road, who have kept the colony from falling into American hands. Fortunate that a rebellion will soon be keeping the Yankees occupied. The guests looked vaguely downward when they spoke of America, as if America were a lesser form of hell. The absent High Judge was toasted also, such a remarkable figure, such a paragon of English justice, not for him the law of the bowie knife and the Yankee colt.

Then Eugene was asked his opinion on how the colony might attend to its future. He cannot recall by whom, but surely he was asked to stand and speak, surely. And so there he was, saying that in all his travels he had never seen a place where so many races commingle. He was inspired by the talk of the Judge and his law-making, as well as by the harangues of a barrister from Bath who he had met on the ship round the Horn. His theories stuck to Eugene, burr-like, almost without Eugene's noticing, as certain facts and theories often seem to. The barrister disembarked at San Francisco and left Eugene with his preposterous ideas. If Eugene ever sees him again he might well thrash him. For there stood Eugene, telling how the progeny of commingling have peculiar tendencies, criminal and otherwise, and that laws must be applied to these progeny accordingly or else colonies such as Vancouver Island would not thrive. He spoke of how a white father and an Indian mother create a Mestizo or Mestiza. An Indian Father and a Negro mother create a Zambo. A Chinese father and a Negro mother create a . . . it slipped his mind that one. But, yes, and a mulatto mother and a white father create a Cuarteron; a white father and a Cuarteron create a Quintero. And a white father and a Quintero? Now what do you surmise?

The Governor said that ciphering was never his strongest suit. The tone of his voice alone should have discouraged Eugene. Some of the guests looked bemused; yes, bemused at a man digging his own grave. The rest examined their silverware.

"White! Ladies and gentleman! That is, it is possible to come full circle."

The room was silent. His glass was unfortunately empty; his throat was dry, the room fuggy and hot. Certainly he should have sat down then. He is as bad as Dora at times, the way he speaks with such reckless disregard.

The Governor hurled down his napkin. Stood. What did he shout? Eugene cannot recall, only that the other guests joined in, only that he was soon being escorted to the door, and then a slap of cold rain, a lash of wind. In short order he learned that many of the guests were retired company men whose wives had Indian blood, some even had Indian blood themselves. And though the Governor's father was a Scottish merchant, his mother was a Mulatta from Barbados. As for the Governor's wife, Amelia, she was the daughter of a Cree princess and a Nor'Wester. And thus it did indeed become complex, particularly now that their daughter Agnes was married to the Judge's English clerk Mr. Arthur Bushby.

Eugene hauls off his boots and stretches out on the narrow bed, consoles himself with the thought that one day the event will sink beneath the surface of memory like the last vestiges of a shipwreck, until all that is left is a word, flung out like a faint call of distress.

FIVE

The shacks of Humbolt Street are a jumble of canvas and weather-beaten wood, of racks festooned with fish, of refuse. A boy chases a wounded gull. A patch of wild rose quivers with songbirds. The mud flats gleam just beyond, and from somewhere comes a funeral lament.

Boston is recognized by many. They invite him to buy clams, baskets, woven platters, blankets and mats, each tribe with its own specialty. Women name their price in shillings, dollars, or whiskey. Men offer for those women who stare out blankly, who have been captured in raids or bought. A few Whitemen also offer for Indian women, or suggest a look inside their 'dance halls.' This is a new trade, unheard of before the Whiteman came, and shared more or less equally by all the Peoples. Boston looks the women over closely, as he always does. He sees no sign of Kloo-yah, however, and so he walks west, past the Australia Hotel high up on its pilings and poles, then over the James Bay Bridge, and so onto Beacon Hill near where the horses race and the rich play their croquet and lacrosse and cheer mightily, as if a war were being won. There he makes a small fire and takes off his overshirt and sets out the needle and thread. He tucks the smoke pouch with its antique money into the torn pocket of his overshirt and sews it over three, four times. Tests its strength, then puts the shirt on again, relieved to know the money, that money, is where it belongs. Only now can he stretch in his bedroll, his head against his rucksack. As always, he waits for sleep to find him. He needs only three or four hours a night. Once it gave him some small satisfaction, this knowledge that he has more hours in his life than most.

The moon rises, is full overhead. The stars fade. "I oftentimes dream of my father," the Dora woman said. "He's calling me, but I can't help him. And you then? Are you ever plagued by nightmares, Mr. Jim?"

He said *no*, not mentioning that he has no dreams, bad or otherwise, and is glad of it, for he would not forget them as others claim to, once the eyes are washed, or breakfast taken, or once the forehead is exposed to the sky. At Fort Connelly, Lavolier scribbled down his dreams, seeing in them instructions from angels, warnings of damnation. The People near the Fort also saw dreams as full of meaning, as messages from the dead, as movements of vagrant souls. Kloo-yah dreamed of a woman with the head of a spider. She dreamed of it for many nights and said that the dream was for him, but how she could not say. She dreamed also of the wounds on his chest. It was as if they were her own, she said. She recognized the wounds as the symbols the Whitemen made and mouthed over, but she did not ask what the symbols spoke, and he did not tell her, fearing the power of the words as much then as he did now.

Curios. Scientific instruments. Musical Apparatus. Ingenious Devices & Novelties. All Fit for the Most Discerning of Customers. Mr. Obed Kines, Proprietor & Expert.

Boston waits nearby until the shop opens for the day. It is new. A raw wood smell overlays that of peppermint and cigar. A flag with stars and stripes hangs overhead, proclaiming Mr. Obed Kines as an American from the Union States. He wears a paisley waistcoat and a tight high collar. He is red-faced and nearly bald and he rests his fists on the glass case as on something he has conquered.

The local curios are on a table by one wall. There is an entire tea set woven of birch bark, arrowheads with symbols in ochre, and argillite carvings made by the Haidas in their island strongholds to the north. Boston has heard that the Whites buy these carvings for their mantels. But she would not have a mantel, only a stove. For her windowsill then. But what would she make of such dark things? There is the beaver, the whale, the eagle. They glare and snarl. There is the carving of a man. His hands are shoved in his breeches, are close in upon his crotch. His features are that of a Whiteman, his expression one of idiocy.

"Pretty things I like," she said. "And novelties. Not that I have such things in my home. No indeed."

He peers into a stereoscope, into a miniature tinted scene of two women on the edge of a cliff. One is standing on the shoulders of the other, her arms held out for balance. The illusion of depth is so strong it seems she might at any moment tumble into the abyss. The Dora woman spoke of stereoscopes, said that Mrs. Jacobsen kept a lovely one in the parlour of the Avalon Hotel.

He straightens. Better to buy something she has not seen before, else she might wave the gift aside as she did the offering of the marten pelt, else he might have to start anew.

The brass ball fits into the palm of his hand. It opens to show a globe. The concave side of its casing shows the constellations, the starry arch of the heavens.

"The saviour of many a mariner," Kines calls. He is attending to another customer, is wrapping a many-handled thing in swathes of brown paper.

Boston closes the brass casing and puts it down. She is not a mariner. It is a novelty, certainly, but a gift should be of some use. Now these.

Kines is at his elbow. "They do not come cheaply, sir."

"That one."

The music box is disguised as a prayer book. Kines demonstrates its repertoire of canticles and hymns. Church is not something the Dora woman mentioned with any enthusiasm. Boston points to an harmonium. Kines turns the crank. Boston knows the tune, Illdare having hummed it once.

"Bach," Kines says, "a damned Kraut, but what of it?"

An assistant enters from a back room. He is a young man with freckled arms and teeth lapping his lower lip. He busies himself with checking through a sheaf of accounts that bear Kines' signature in a large, square hand. Customers come and go. Boston studies another music box, from which a porcelain lady slowly rises. She revolves on a velvet platform to a tinkling tune. Her infinite doubles, reflected in the mirrors behind and below, stretch back to a vanishing point. He has seen such things before; no doubt the Dora woman has as well. It would not be long before she tired of it.

"Are you searching for an item for yourself?" Kines asks.

"No."

"A friend?"

"That one."

"Ah, my most valuable item. It is an automaton. Direct from Europe."

Kines places it on the counter. It is a hand's span wide. The dome arches over trees fashioned of what might be clay. Painted on the inside of the globe is a waterfall and a distant hill with a castle. Inside the globe is a couple in clothes the likes of which Boston has never seen. The woman's hat is a high cone; the man has shoes curled up like fiddle-heads. They wait amid the trees, one opposite the other. Kines turns the key and they twirl about each other to a stately tune that Boston has never heard. A swan glides by, then vanishes behind the waterfall.

"It was wrought by a master Venetian craftsman for Duchess Saphina herself, a woman of gross appetites, as are all aristocrats. The dancing woman is in her likeness, down to her dimpled cheek. The man is Antonio, one of her many lovers, a captain of the guard who was banished when the Duke became suspicious. Lovesick Saphina ordered the automaton made so that each night she could see herself in her lover's embrace, so that each night she could relive the night they first met, when first they danced to the strains of the very music that you hear now."

Boston has never seen the like. It will be enough, more so. It is an ingenious thing. Still . . . he lifts it to see the mechanisms beneath. Such things are plagued with rust, with delicate spokes and cogs that break at a nudge, or work only for the one who displays them.

"What's the cost?"

"Ah, you must understand, given the story behind its creation . . ."

"Some story don't make it worth more."

"I should think it does."

"Ten pounds. Give you that."

Kines smiles broadly. "I do not accept pounds. A monarch's head does not belong on a coin, nor a bill. It belongs on a spike."

"Dollars then."

"One hundred."

"What fool do you take me for?"

Kines frowns and reaches for the automaton. Boston is handing it to him when the assistant, crouching below the counter, grunting over a crate, straightens abruptly and bumps against Kines. There is a fumbling as of three incompetent jugglers, and then a shattering.

SIX

"To gold by the fistful! The cartload! The motherlode!" Eugene calls and raises his glass to the other men clumped about him in the saloon of the paddlewheeler ss *Champion*. They are anchored in a sheltered bend of the Fraser River on an evening that is cool and faintly misty. Whale oil lamps sway overhead amid the pall of tobacco smoke. A night bird flaps against the window.

The men raise their bottles and glasses.

"Here's to chasing, how it say, the Gold Butterfly!"

"*Salud oro. Nada mas pero oro.*"

"*D'or! D'or!*"

"To gold and the bleedin' captain! He says this girl's the fastest, if she ain't we'll use his bones for fuel!"

Laughter. Shouts. A dangerous edge to the whole gathering. But Eugene knows it will not turn, close though it may come. There will not be that sudden shift from joviality, sizing ups, verbal parlays, into accusations, flying fists, knives and pistols. It is his particular gift, this being able to predict the life of a revelry—if one is about to begin, how it will end, if it is possible to create out of sullen looks and tired companions an evening worthy of remembrance and retelling. He would rather, say, have the gift for poetry, be as Shelley, Keats and Byron and live passionately through words alone. He would rather, even, have the gift for mathematics and plumb the secrets of God's universe, like Newton, or like that chap with the telescope. But, ah, one must make do with one's own gifts.

Eugene looks to the two men who must be brothers, both being pale and thin-faced and both wearing near-identical apparel: fustian jackets and corduroy trousers and neat caps on black curls.

"Welsh is it? How do you say gold then, in Welsh?"

"*Aur*," says the one. He is not smiling, nor is he drinking.

Eugene growls in imitation and the men about him laugh. He is speaking of the unnecessary difficulties inherent in the Welsh tongue when an American of some kind interrupts him. "If you say that word 'gold' too much it don't make no whoreson sense. You start thinking maybe that ain't the word. Could be any old fart-ass sound. Who decided it'd be that word, not something else?"

"Gold is our word, is German word," a man says jovially. He is thick-bellied and dressed as if for a Sunday outing, has a great silk handkerchief with which he expertly blows his nose. Even Eugene, fond as he is of good apparel, had the sense to wear his blanket coat, his broad-brimmed hat. His checkered frock coat and trousers, his cravat and waistcoat, his collars and top hat, are all nicely packed, at the ready for a suitable occasion, which this, most assuredly, is not.

"Your word is it?" the American says, half rising from the table. He is a ludicrous specimen. Is a jockey-sized, arm-flailing, revel-wrecker who can barely sit still and have a civilized drink.

"Gentlemen! Friends! It scarcely matters. Words are the one thing shared by all. They are free. Ale, however, is not." Eugene shakes the jug at an Italian who is dozing on the bench, nose buried in his beard. "You are standing treat next, sir. We agreed, a round each to wash down that abysmal feed."

The Italian explains in broken English that he is tired, that he has had enough.

"Enough? Is that what you will say when you are digging for your gold. Enough! Oh, I cannot dig any longer. I cannot pan. I am so weary. And all the while the gold lies beneath your boots. All the while it shimmers just beyond your reach because you have had, what? Enough! Never!"

"That's telling him!"

"*Genug? Nein!*"

"*Bastante? Nunca!*"

"*Assez? Non!*"

The Italian stares at them blearily, shambles now to the bar where among the men is a large quantity of Les Canadiens in scarlet vests, their boots on the rails, their faces veiled in pipe smoke, talking in the way of conspirators.

"What shall we call our mines then?" Eugene asks. "Ah, better. A contest. We shall ask the captain to choose the best. Each man put in a . . . a greenback is it? The winner takes all."

The men debate, up it to two dollars each, then wrestle money from pockets.

The German volunteers to search for the captain. "Stupendous! Marvellous!" he says as he ambles off.

"And you, sir? What of you?" Eugene asks the sad-faced man who has just entered. "Shall we call your mine The-Close-at-Hand?" The man scowls, makes a rude gesture at which Eugene only laughs. Poor bastard. Apparently he had thought he would be let off directly at the mines. Did not realize there was a five hundred mile march before him. "Quite so, but one should be better informed. One should be better prepared," Eugene says this quietly, so as not to be heard, not a difficult feat as words, unless loudly spoken, are being swept up in the general din of the festive.

The German returns with a man whose uncovered head shows a scalp afflicted with a rash. "The Captain not come. But Mr. Fere, he is the purser, he'll make it for a dollar, to take out the winnings."

The others agree and then the ludicrous foul-mouthed American shouts: "The Jessica Bell!"

Eugene stays with his original choice—The Croesus Cache. The Welsh brothers come up with Hawddamor. A Frenchman calls out Marseille. A Spaniard, Santa Maria. The German begs off, saying something about boots. He settles back with a cough and watches the proceedings with a lively interest, as if he had been the one to think of the contest entirely.

The purser stares at them sourly. Eugene knows he has lost already. He decided on The Croesus Cache in the assumption that the captain, teeth-picking aside, would have some education. But how would this grey-faced drone know of an ancient king said to have incalculable wealth? Ah, well, he'll know less of some backwater French city trod on by history and happenstance. And he does not seem a religious man either, given the cursing Eugene heard from him earlier. The Spaniard is out, then. And by the way he stared at the Welsh brothers, Eugene doubts he has time for the delightful, mysterious rhythms of languages not his own.

"The Jessica Bell. I'll be picking that one. Women's what we're need-ing 'round here. Not more men with their heads stuck in the clouds."

"I knew it," Eugene says. "To women. The lovely devils. Congratu-lations Mr. . . . Mr.?"

"Oswald. Ain't Mr. Nothing. Oswald is god-blamed all."

"Ah, then congratulations, Oswald." Eugene raises his glass. The American takes little note of this sportsmanship. Instead he scoops up his winnings, nearly forgetting to give the dollar to the purser who is standing by with one long hand open.

"A song now, friends!" Eugene shouts.

> *Faintly as tolls the ev'ng chimes*
> *Our voices keep tune and our oars keep time*
> *Soon as the woods on shore look dim,*
> *We'll sing at ta da, ta da, Ah, hell*
> *Row, brothers, row, the streams runs fast*
> *The rapids are near, and the daylight's gone, no,*
> > *past, the daylight's past.*

He sings the lyrics more or less on his own, though the others heartily join in the chorus. The German grabs one of the Welsh brothers and leads him in a dance. The Welshman grimly follows his steps. Puffs of soot rise under their boots. Les Canadiens thump their glasses, then join in the dancing. Oswald pulls out a mouth harp and plays, to Eugene's surprise, not badly at all.

There are more songs, more drinks, more dancing. The saloon floor shudders, rocks. Eugene learns a Scottish jig, a Canadian reel. The German is his partner now. The man insists on leading, treads heavily on Eugene's boots, smells of camphor and mint. Eugene begs off and grabs a jug that is being passed about. His glass. Damn. Where? Ah, well. He tilts the jug back, looks full into a lamp that sways as if in gentle disapproval. This night is nearly as splendid as that soiree aboard the ss *Grappler*. As usual, Dora cared little for propriety, nor did she notice the restlessness of her audience as she sang penny-sheet songs loudly and off-key, not minding that her hoops were hiked high to one side as if a great hook were attempting to hoist her into the sky. Ah, but then how they danced! She was not leaving his arms. Not ever. How sure he was! They kissed shamelessly. It was as if their love had woven a chrysalis about them. Her lips tasted of ginger beer, her throat of sea air, her hair of the precious, rare lemons he had given her earlier, holding one in each hand, his thumbs stroking their nubs. She grasped them and laughed and then sliced them full open and squeezed the juice through her hair to make it shine ever more golden. He had never thought of himself as lascivious until then.

"I didn't dare say, but we met before, you and me," she told him that night. He said, yes, in his dreams. She told him, no, in London. He had been with some friends in Newcut market. He had dropped to his knees when he saw her and begged her to come to the colonies with him. Eugene said it was quite likely. He and the fellows often went slumming, begging kisses from comely girls in not-so-comely streets. It was what many students did.

She looked so disappointed that Eugene explained hastily that he was jesting. Of course he remembered her. He used the word *fate*. He used the word *destiny*. Even the phrase *love at first glance*.

He takes another drink, stares at Oswald to erase the thoughts of Dora, to ease the hardness in his crotch.

The night wears on until Eugene is nearly alone in the saloon. He braces himself against the faint shifting of the paddlewheeler, plans how best to navigate the stairs to the bunks below. He has overdone it, will pay dearly tomorrow. But it was worth it, surely, to forge a few friendships on the way to the goldfields. The Italian would make a fine partner. See his hands? Size of shovels. As for the Welshmen, they look as if they were born underground. That makes four, himself included. Perhaps a carpenter or two. No more needed than that. Keep a balance between profit and practicality.

Eugene sings: "Dora! Dora! My adored, my adorable Dora. We'll be rich as Croesus. We'll be Mr. and Mrs. Midas. Oh, give me your golden heart."

"Shut your bloody caterwauling!"

Eugene peers down the stairwell. "What, ho, a fellow Londoner is it? You've been hiding good man. Come up for a song."

"You'll be singing a fucking dirge if you don't bloody well shut it."

There is laughter, and *hear hears*.

Eugene settles for humming. Goes out on the deck, steadies himself and walks, hand on rail. Good that he is not as his father was. Eugene can hold his drink, does not transform from a quiet gentleman into a choleric, violent, incoherent lie-about. When in his cups, Eugene is merely more Eugene-like—more talkative, friendly, more witty, more ready with songs and observations.

The ragged line of mountains is faintly agleam with snow. Eugene points, though there is no one to note, how the moon is cradled in the antlers affixed to the wheelhouse. On the foredeck the Indians, Coloureds, and Chinamen huddle among the cargo. Poor devils. The deck there was hot as pokers this morning what with the boilers beneath going full throttle. He had stood there for two minutes in his socks before jigging and cursing, much to the amusement of the Missouri men who had bet him a dollar that he could not outlast one of their own. He had, however, and has the dollar still in his pocket to prove it.

Chill in the air. Foredeck must be tomb-cool now, what with the boilers shut down for the night. He knows the feeling, hot and cold, hot and cold, never anything in between.

Eugene wakes to a high-pitched whistle. A jarring sends him near tumbling to the floor. Whiffs of whiskey and malodorous socks.

"Scuse it," says his neighbour, jumping from the bunk above, his boots grazing Eugene's head. The man blurs, solidifies. The American. Damn him. Eugene's head pounds and he has a raging thirst. Never again. Not that rotgut. What was in that jug, not tanglewood surely? He has vowed never to drink that insidious local brew. Ah, well, at least he drinks from a glass from time to time, not like these others sprawled about, snoring and gabbling, bottle suckers to the last.

On deck the air is hardly finer, what with the steamer billowing out smoke as it surges ahead. The men jar against him, drum their fists on the rail and call for greater speed. Eugene would rather they call for greater caution, has heard tales of boilers exploding, men and animals sent sky-high, the river stained with blood, choked with flotsam and gore. He sighs. The camaraderie of last night is gone. Each man is now a competitor of the other. Each man may stake the ground the other should have staked. Take his gold. Take his glorious future.

The currents coil through the grey-green river. He tries to find this mesmerizing. Would like to be mesmerized just now. They pass an Indian village on the bank—wood smoke, bark-snarl of dogs, shouts of children running to see them pass. Children everywhere the same, not wanting to miss an event, wanting to be the ones to say: "Did you see?" "You won't believe." Eugene waves to them, dredges up a sense of wonder. A fine day after all, splinters of sun through pale low clouds. A promise of warmth later on. Rounded hills on either side now, pines clinging there. He looks to the bow and sees the suggestion of some great thing gliding by. It is longer than a billiard table, white as bone. Sturgeon? Whale? The vastness of the place astounds him, as if everything is stretched beyond the scale of imagining. Yesterday afternoon they passed through an enormous flat valley hemmed by white-capped mountains. The trees there were so tall it was easy to imagine that, like Jack the giant killer, a man could climb and climb until he reached another world entirely. He saw marshes large as small seas, and bogs aswirl with enough birds to blacken the sun.

In comparison the swathes of new-cleared land were laughable, minute. A few stumps, ten feet across or more, were charred and smouldering. Two men worked a cross saw, and a woman without her crinolines heaved an axe at nothing that he could see, the immensity of it all, he supposed, the futile task ahead. He sent out his sympathy with a wave for he knew the feeling well, had had to fight the impulse to cut and run when he and Dora first arrived in the Cowichan. One hundred and sixty acres, yes, but of trees two hundred, three hundred feet high, of impenetrable bramble, of wolf dens and worse. Impossible to imagine it transformed into the rolling hillsides of England, dotted with sheep and divided neatly with fences. He felt an interloper. And then the neighbours coming to assist, if neighbours are what one could call people who lived miles away, beyond sight. But there they were, twenty of them at the least. Together they hacked at the trees, tore up stumps, sang songs to keep up their strength. The women cooked great pots of salmon stew, brought out bannock, pie, and ale, blessed ale. Enough was cleared so that he and Dora could plant a garden and build a cabin. "Don't worry, dear, we help each other," Mrs. Smitherton said each time Dora proclaimed her gratitude. It was as if Dora did not comprehend that they would be called upon in return. Eugene is wiser in this regard and has already decided that when he returns, flush with gold, he will hire a man to return help with the harvesting rounds, with any roof-raising for new settlers. For after this excursion, he intends to live as a gentleman should. He will congratulate others on their labours. He will pay them generously and they will touch their hats when he and Dora pass in a carriage and four. Perhaps in time he will be known for his charity.

Hills now giving way to cliffs, patches of red earth scoured out of grey stone.

"Ah, this wind, it not good for, what is the word? Constitution, yes?"

Eugene blinks and straightens. The remains of breakfast adorn the man's sand-coloured whiskers. Ah, yes, the German from last night's festivities. In the light of morning his grinning, fleshy face shows evidence of powder, his incongruous dress-clothes evidence of long wear.

"Yes, that is the word," Eugene says with finality and continues his contemplation of the river.

"How is? How you say it? Your courage this morning?"

"Jolly, sir, staying down nicely."

"We not long till there."

"No, I suppose not."

"You are English?"

"I am a Londoner," Eugene says, thoroughly irritated now with the man's persistent cheer, the persistent thumping in his own head that nearly matches that of the paddlewheel.

"You are to be a miner?"

"Yes, only for a time."

"I am boots."

"Mr., rather Herr Boots, yes, of course, we met last night. You are the German. Now if you . . ."

The man laughs uproariously. Wipes his eyes. "Oh, I am sorry. No, my name is not Boots. My name it is Matias Schultheiss. And I am Prussian."

"Ah, quite so, not boots. Not German."

"No, my apologize. This English, it is thick on my tongue. I sell boots. Gumboots. They are needed by miners."

"I have boots, Herr, Herr . . ."

"Schultheiss."

"Herr Schultheiss. Quite so, and here they are, at the end of my feet. Made by a boot fitter in Victoria. I have, I assure you, no need for more."

"Ah, no, I take them to goldfields. No, not I, a pack train. I sell there." With the flourish of a conjurer the Prussian takes a silver case from out of his vest pocket. Opens it to show Eugene a row of stuffed paper cylinders. "You have tried the Turkish smoke?"

Eugene grimaces. "I do not indulge in tobacco, sir, I find it dulls the senses."

"Ah, no, it sharps them. It make the breath!" He beats his own considerable chest. "Think it as good thing from your war in Crimea. They are, so, what is the word, *gelegen*, ah, yes, convenient, a convenient invention. Think, hah, all the stupendous inventions that come next from this American war!"

Eugene shrugs, is barely listening while Herr Schultheiss expounds on some outlandish plan to make Turkish smokes of his own and sell them in neat little boxes. He will have his name embossed on the cover. "Like to the old Kings. I am to have my names and symbols in all places, so that always the people think, aha, I know the name. It is good name."

Eugene finds the idea completely vulgar but at the risk of encouraging further talk says nothing more to this man who is not a gentleman down on his luck at all, but a scheming merchant. At least he can stop Dora's talk with kisses; at least she knows he rarely has the heart for conversation in the mornings, and only a half-heart for it during the day. He is an evening talker. Surely that is obvious. The paddle-wheeler shifts. Reverses. Drifts sideways. Now what is Herr Boots saying? Eugene glances over. The Prussian is pointing straight ahead, his mouth open, letting out a deafening roar.

SEVEN

In Rupert's Land Jedidiah Coom has seen how sled dogs find their hierarchy in the trace. He allows the chain gang to do the same, watches with implacable good cheer from the back of his horse, Kingdom Come, as the prisoners emerge blinking and stiff-legged from their cells at dawn and arrange themselves with growls and shoves at the line of waiting leg irons. Coom nearly always guesses the end sequence of the chain gang correctly.

The leader is Claude Dupasquier, a mixed blood of labyrinthine ancestry. Directly behind him is his younger brother Marcel. They are fierce, green-eyed men with shanks of black hair. Coom treats them with some respect, allows them a larger cell, extra rations, easier tasks, and when they speak in their odd patois—no doubt mocking him, no doubt plotting—he resists the urge to whip them. They once, after all, belonged to the Voltiguers, a regiment that kept the peace in '58 during the Fraser Rush when a canvas town erupted out of the mud 'round the fort and the Americans swarmed like bottle flies. The Dupasquier brothers wore extravagant uniforms then and one of them always walked three paces behind the Governor. Three months for them this time for brawling in a saloon.

Next in line is the coloured man Enoch Handel. He is a tinsmith and former member of the African rifles who is serving a month for throwing night soil into his neighbour's yard. Next is the new man, Boston Jim, a mixed blood as well, by the look and manner of him. Coom has heard this Boston Jim speak only once or twice and though of average height and build he has a way of keeping to himself, not out of fear for the others but out of a kind of disdain. Coom has seen the like. Men who hoard words like they were precious coins, who prefer the middle ranking of the chain gang so that they may watch both ends, so that they may remain unnoticed. They are the most unpredictable, these men who care little for status, and the most vengeful. Did not this Boston Jim smash the property of the curio dealer Mr. Obed Kines, and then the nose of Kines himself when payment was demanded of him? He was fortunate the justice gave him only six weeks, that he did not order him to pay for the replacement value of the curio. But then the justice had no love for Mr. Kines, known for his insults to the monarchy in general and to the Queen in particular.

The Russian Ivan Petrovich is next. By some accounts he deserted a trading ship some thirty years previous. He is stick-thin and grizzled and ties his spectacles 'round his head with a grimy red ribbon, wears a battered top hat, a frayed silk cravat. Not only for such pretensions does Coom despise him. Petrovich is a bootlegger. He sells tanglewood to the Indians though such trade is clearly outlawed. Spirits are a vice that Coom once indulged and has since foresworn, along with tobacco and cards and all women except his blessed wife.

Behind Petrovich is one Tom McBride, a stunted lowland Scot. His voice is high-pitched and nasal. "Been punched once too often in the face?" Coom asked him, jovially enough. This McBride is the very neighbour who accused Enoch Handel of throwing night soil into his yard. Much to his chagrin, he has been given a week for lighting Handel's fence on fire. Much to Handel's satisfaction.

"Perhaps on the chain gang you two will learn some form of co-operation," the justice reportedly said. Though Coom, having noted McBride's constantly aggrieved expression, does not share the justice's optimism.

Toolie is second to last. He looks mournfully at the others with odd eyes in a pale fat face. He purses his moist lips. "Good morning," he says finally, and closes his eyes in exhaustion. Coom works up a Christian pity for him. An idiot, after all, cannot be held to the same standards as others. Still, Coom is determined that his chain gang be well-ordered, presentable, and useful; and thus he has warned Toolie that if he shits in public on his watch, he'll be forced to dine upon it, and if he exposes his privates he'll be heartily flogged.

The boy Farrow is the last. He is an Irish waif for whom Coom had to order small leg irons made. He stumbles often and holds up the work and lately has been given to fits of crying. For months he slithered unnoticed into the finer homes of the citizenry, causing alarm and a belief that a large gang of thieves was at work. The constabulary found him living in a driftwood shelter near the mud flats. He was surrounded by silver plate and small mantel clocks and a profusion of jewellery, most of which was returned to its grateful owners. Coom cannot recall the length of his sentence. Not that it matters. He is the sort who will spend half his life in jail. Bred in the bone, it must be, when one starts thieving so young.

Today, the third of June, these eight are breaking rock. They swing their pickaxes in a sidewise motion so as not to split the skull of the man behind them. "It has happened before," Coom warns, and chuckles at the remembrance. Later they use the rock to fill in the potholes that have appeared after the days of hard rain. Some of these potholes are posted with the warning *bottom not found* and are a mystery to learned men, though children say they are the wellsprings of the underworld, and play a game of leaping across, Indian and white children both.

Sunset and the hour arrives for Coom to escort them back to Bastion Square. "A little singing, boys, to lift the spirits of these good townspeople who have to see the sorry lot of you. Come on, boys, *Abide with me, for it is toward evening and the day is far spent. . . .*"

His charges, except for the Dupasquier brothers, except for Boston, join in half-heartedly, not wanting the whip on their backs.

"God keep you well," Coom calls as the gates of Bastion Square close behind them.

"And goddamn you to hell," the Dupasquier brothers say, once Coom is out of earshot.

The cell of the Dupasquier brothers has rush mats and high barred windows and a table with chairs. Boston's cell is no more than four paces long and eight wide. It is dank. Rats rustle in the reeking straw. At least he does not have to share his cell, as Farrow and Toolie do. If he were forced to share with the likes of McBride or Petrovich he might well have to thrash them and so extend his visit. Even now Petrovich is lamenting for good whiskey and McBride is berating Enoch Handel, the black bastard prick, and questioning over and over what kind of justice would give him, a Whiteman, an equal sentence. Finally one of the Dupasquiers tells McBride to stop his whining or he'll cut his throat. At this Handel laughs, enraging McBride so greatly that he batters at the walls of his cell.

The jailer snuffs out the corridor lamps. Boston paces, his legs light after the leg irons. Smashed Kines' tawdry automaton did he? Thrashed Kines with no provocation? It was the clerk's fault for rising so abruptly, and yet the clerk was the one who swore alongside Kines that Boston hurled the automaton to the floor. It was Kines who made to punch him; Boston only served it back to him. That, too, Kines and his clerk denied. Boston will seek his retribution when he is set loose. It will be the type of reckoning he knows, but this with the Dora woman, it chafes him constantly.

He settles at last in the straw. Sifts through her stories, her life, every word returning as clearly as the day it was spoken. A clue is within the stories as to what he should do; he is certain of it.

"Come in, good lady. Come in," her father says to a woman. Assures her they can negotiate any price. The drapery is on a twist of a street not far from Newcut Market. It is small, but ah, what pride the Timmonses all take in it. They have cambric, baize, and muslin, printed cottons, worsted damask, French marino, linen ticking and bleached duck. They have cerements and swaddling, shawls and fans. Her father was a costermonger of renown before he married and well he knows the art of the sale. He stuffs handbills in letter boxes, announcing a sale on "infinitesimally damaged goods." Proclaims that new stock is fast arriving, as for the old, "for you, ma'am, I'll make it such a price that you'll be wondering how it is I feed my five children." He winks when he speaks like this so that his patrons might know it is only a game of which they are part.

Her father is now laughing at a customer's jest. Now full of drink. Now spending lavishly, mutton and ale for all. Now cheerfully boasting that he can thrash any man. Wasn't he the best boxer in Newcut? Look here, he's stronger than a man half his age. Anyone wanting a gentle thrashing step his way.

He rubs his hands together as he often does, even on warm days. Dora watches intently, a mess of straw-blond curls falling over her cheek. Surely one day something will burst forth from his palms: fire, a bird, a sweetmeat, a coin. It is that aura of generosity he has. "You're cursed with it," Dora's mother says and looks at him with adoration, nothing less. Dora's father spins Ethel in a tight embrace and continues to buy useless carnations from the flower sellers, continues tossing coins into the tin of old Hannah. He strolls through the market in the early evening. The street children bob toward him. They are the drownlings of the London streets and he, her father, is a great raft of a man.

Her mother says: "You give too much. We must think of the future, darling. The girls must have dowries, the boys apprenticeships." Her father drops to his knees and begs forgiveness, spreading his arms wide, as if to encompass the world. Dora's mother laughs girlishly. She is blue-eyed and black-haired. Her hands are white and tapering and astonishing in their elegance. In contrast, Dora's father is a lion of a man—golden-haired, strong and tall. Their love is legendary. The beautiful Ethel could have had her choice of any respectable shop-keeper and instead chose Thomas Timmons, a costermonger with barely a farthing to his name. Ah, but soon they will have a shop on Regent Street. It is Thomas's constant promise. No longer will Ethel's family scorn her choice of husband. The Timmonses will have extravagant displays behind plate glass windows and five men clerks standing ready behind counters long as roads. They will have lace of such fine work-manship that a magnifying glass will be needed to show details hidden from less worthy eyes. No longer these coarse draperies. They will have lawn, glazed worsted, harateen, velvets, silks, and damasks. Dora can see it all so clearly. And are not they being prepared for this step upward? Dora, though she is fourteen now, is not yet to be married. Not for her the black-toothed, spindly boys who come to pay their respects. In their two room flat above the shop, Dora's mother is teaching Dora and her brothers and sisters to speak so they do not sound like gutter spawn. She is teaching them what she knows of reading and writing. Not for her children the ragged schools. She insists her daughters put aside knitting and devote their precious spare hours to needlework. Dora is not the most skilled at this art. Look at this sampler, at the letters slanting downward, tufted with broken thread. And look at this embroidered round of a girl on a swing. The girl's hands are marked with wayward stitches like so many wounds. No, what Dora loves is the clink of coins, the cutting and packaging, the exchange of news, the cajoling of a difficult client. She wishes to work in this "Ah, but soon shop," and tells her father so.

"Who has ever heard of a lass waiting on customers in the finer stores?" her father asks and pinches her cheeks. "Promise me you'll marry some good man and become the angel of your house, and your old father will come visiting on a Sunday."

Dora grabs his hand and promises. Promises that she would give up the very world for him, her darling father. He need only ask.

Morning and from atop Kingdom Come Coom shouts: "March on, boys! Faster now, you are off to do God's work!" They shuffle through the streets in their leg irons, each of them carrying a shovel. A wind blows in fits and blasts, sends hats tumbling as if a hand has thwacked them aside, whistles through the slipshod construction of the town. McBride nudges Petrovich and tells him eagerly that this wind can flip crinolines inside out like so many cheap umbrellas. Petrovich ignores him, curses in Russian and English and stumbles against Handel. Petrovich's hands are shaking. Sweat drips from his chin though it is hardly hot. He has begged each of them to procure him a drink, has promised to pay handsomely for it. "I have money. I have it. Yes?"

To Quadra Street, to the Church of St. John the Divine. Coom stays so close behind them that Kingdom Come's hot breath ruffles Farrow's hair. The convicts are to dig the graves for twenty-odd Indians from this tribe and that. They were Anglican converts who died of some fever. "Sort of sickness that would make a Whiteman merely sniffle," Coom says and then wonders aloud how the Indians have thrived for so long. He halts Kingdom Come outside the church. The horse paws the ground, snorts. "Easy there," Coom says soothingly.

A Reverend appears in the churchyard, points at some unused ground a distance from the regular gravestones, then hurries back into the church, the wind gripping his black coat and seeming to pull him along.

The rocky ground is dense with brambles and rubbish. A tree stump splays out long, gnarled roots. The corpse of a dog lies bloated, its legs stiffly skyward. The convicts clear patches of ground and strain at the shovels. Each man is chained so close to the other that their grunts and odours intermingle and they are like some immense multi-legged insect burrowing vainly into the earth.

By the afternoon the graves are half dug and the men allowed some rest. They huddle under the trees as a wind-driven rain turns the earth to mud. Petrovich is now cursing constantly under his breath. Froth speckles his lips. The boy Farrow is sobbing. Toolie shows his hands to Boston. They are blistered and bloodied. He licks his palms and whimpers.

"Back to it, boys!" Coom shouts. He jerks the end of the chain. Turns his back to attend his horse. A clod of dirt clips him in the ear. He doesn't roar, nor shout. Not Coom. He turns calmly. Studies them with an amused air. He draws his revolver, pulls the hammer back.

"I am a patient man. It is one of God's gifts to me. And thus I will walk out of earshot. Five minutes you will have, and then the miscreant must be given up. If not, all suffer twenty lashes. Understood?"

He mounts Kingdom Come and turns his back again.

"Damn you, Petrovich," Claude Dupasquier hisses. "You only got a week more."

His brother kicks at Petrovich. Handel chuckles.

Petrovich stares miserably at them, whispers: "You wouldn't give me up? One fucking drink is all I need. His voice, Coom's, it burns here in my head. He is the devil's whore, yes? The devil himself for all he talks of God. I was not trying to hit him. I am surprised as all of you, yes? Please, I beg you." Petrovich is trembling as he drops to his knees. Claude grips his collar. Is ready to haul him up and shove him forward when Boston says: "Take the blame for you, Petrovich."

The others stare at him.

"Take it for me? Yes? You are not jesting?"

"Cost fifty dollars."

"Fifty? I have, have only eight. Eight. I can give you eight, yes?"

"Three minutes, boys!" Coom shouts.

"Make it sixty," Boston says. Sixty would be enough money to buy a fine gift for the Dora woman; he need spend no more of his own.

"I have eight only, no wait I remember, I have fifteen, yes? I give you fifteen today and the rest I give you when you are free. You come to me at the shacks on the inner harbour. Ask for me. I give you the rest. On my honour. My word, yes?" He extends a shaking hand.

Boston takes it briefly. "Give it now, then. Forty-five later."

Petrovich fumbles in a coat pocket, gives over the soiled bills.

"Time's finished," Coom roars, striding toward them.

"Did it," Boston says. "Threw the dirt at you."

"You? By God's grace, I wouldn't have thought you such a fool. Hah, but I am not particular, neither is the whip."

Although a physician has dosed him with laudanum and dressed his back with salve and clean linen, the pain is still fierce, albeit preferable to the company of the chain gang.

He lies on his side on the stone floor. This cell is not much larger than a coffin. Light comes through a crack in the ceiling in the early mornings. Utter darkness otherwise. Not that he fears the darkness, feels absorbed by it rather, feels he might walk straight through it and so to freedom. The Dora woman is the one who fears the darkness, said she had never seen anything like the Cowichan night, rolling in with no street lamps to stop it. She described then the lanterns from the boats on the Thames, how at night they bobbed and wove, like fallen stars struggling to shore. And if you walked along Park Lane when the season was in progress you'd see the quality pouring into houses so ablaze with torches and great chandeliers that the walls seemed afire.

"Don't be worrying about the darkness," he should have told her. "Day's just as fearsome." It was as simple then to wander from the human realm into another, quite similar, realm where the bear people walked and the salmon people swam and where the skookums had their lairs. The borders were hazy, unmarked. You could step into it the way you stepped into moss that seemed to cover a rock or fallen tree only to find your foot sinking slowly into a green mouth. You could, as he did, see something small and winged and human-faced, though hideous in aspect, flitting through dusk shadows. And you could hear, at times, a vast moaning that was not the wind, no indeed.

He shuts his eyes. Shifts to ease his back. It is a Friday evening when the miseries begin. Dora's father is at large in his old haunt of Newcut Market, is boasting that his wife is the most splendid female about, better than any other wife. "Better than yours, sir," he calls to a passing rubbish carter. Soon enough the crowd forms a ring around her father

55

and the rubbish carter. Dora squeezes between the shifting legs, hauling her younger brother with her. The rubbish carter is immense, a fortress unto himself.

Hard to say how it happens. They are boxing and circling each other, her father not cheerful now, the rubbish carter snarling and lashing out with a great fist. Her father falls onto the cobbles, does not break his fall, does not move after falling. He's not dead, but never the same. Now he lives only in the instant, cannot recall if he has just eaten or shat, cannot recall his children's names, nor his wife's. He sits on a stool in the shop and says nothing to the patrons, says nothing at all for hours, his mouth jarring open at a fly trekking over his knuckles. Occasionally tears course down his cheeks. Occasionally he speaks clearly for a few moments, calls for his children by name and then, as if a door has been shut, the glassy stare returns. It breaks Dora's heart to know her father is imprisoned in his own skin. She would like to save him, but how? She cannot imagine how.

Her mother is afflicted with melancholy, can barely manage an exchange of pleasantries with the patrons. Not that these patrons are seen much of late, the sight of the once bold Mr. Timmons being more than they can bear. And there is competition. A new drapery has been set up two doors away. The proprietor has self-generating lamps and wears a fantastic yellow coat embroidered with tulips and peacocks. He has such quantity of stock it seems his doors might burst open and spill rivers of fabric into the street:

Their luck dribbles away. Her mother croons to her few coins and ignores her children who are given little to eat except potatoes and black-spotted bread. Ah, but she is not cruel. She longs for her husband, combs his hair and sings mournful songs to him. "Come now, Tom," she says. "Come on now." It is as if she believes he is perpetuating a complicated joke. Often she sobs in misery, swears she can hear the creaking of the workhouse door.

Dora's older sister marries into the oyster sellers and pries open shells with her husband on Dark House Lane where the fish are piled in great, slippery walls. Dora crouches near her sister's table like a dog. When her husband is not looking her sister slips her an oyster. She abhors the oyster's soft fleshiness, gulps it whole and feels like someone forced to cannibalism.

Her youngest brother dies. Dora carried him on her back when he was an infant. Fed him his first gruel. She cannot bear that he has died. She grows furious at her mother, at the cold room, the meagre food. Her two other brothers run off one day and take her mother's coins with them.

Worse and worse. The landlord pounds at the door of their flat. Now Dora and her parents are forced to live in the shop. Dora wraps herself in lengths of woollens. She can tell one drapery from the other even in the dark, by their texture, their scent. This one smells like dried grass. That one feels like sand, finely woven. They give comfort to Dora, but not to her mother. "Don't be crying so, mama," Dora says as cheerfully as she can. "I'll be taking care of us. We'll have that shop on Regent Street yet. How grand it shall be."

Fire was what the Dora woman spoke of next. She shook her head as she did so, as if to deny what she was saying. Her father must have upset a candle. Difficult to say. Dora remembers only being on her knees and coughing up black phlegm amid the spellbound crowd, that and the billows of black smoke and then the firemen with their great-coats and useless pumps, their apologetic assurances that it was too late to save the two still within.

After his week in solitary, Boston is returned to his usual cell. Boston says nothing when the others greet him. He eats his bread and cornmeal gruel and then follows the other prisoners into the high-gated yard. It is Sunday and they have a half day of rest in which to contemplate their sins. The others mill about. Not Boston. He does not mill. Has never done so. He stands near the gate and keeps an eye on the other prisoners, on the street. A group of Indian and mixed blood children gape at him through the bars. The girls are in clean white pinafores, the boys in short pants. A nun hurries them on, her face afloat in the black expanse of her habit.

"Round of cards, yes? Poker?" Petrovich pulls a miniature pack from his sleeve, slyly winks. "The jailor, he'll not see."

"Cards," Boston says and spits in the dirt. He dislikes such games entirely, the closeness of the others, the gloating when the winning is done. He keeps track easily enough of the cards and the likelihood of which will appear. Even so he has lost often enough to know that it is not worth his time. Once it was to a Whiteman with a flat-topped hat and a cane, once to an old Salish woman with a silver tooth, once to a fat Chinaman who spoke English as if he were born to it. They cheated, of course, but he had known they would when he sat down. It was part of the contract and could not be complained about. Still, he had thought he could best them.

"You have fifteen. Play me at hand with that," Petrovich says. "And you have credit. I have not forgotten. Thirty-five dollars. Yes?

Boston spits near Petrovich's boots. "Forty-five more. We agreed on sixty in all."

"Yes, ah, yes, sixty. I forgot. Forty-five more. I am good for it, yes. I am out tomorrow. You come to find me."

"I'll find you, now fuck yourself off."

Petrovich chuckles, as if Boston is joking, then sidles off at the beckoning of Tom McBride.

EIGHT

June 6, 1863

B eloved Dora,
Do not fear, my dearest heart, for I have arrived safely in Yale this
day after a most exhilarating journey from Hope in which God was
being called upon with all manner of tongues by the motley &
malodorous guests & crews of the ss Champion, *as our trusty captain led*
an intricate dance through a cauldron of roiling water while the cliffs
frowned down upon us. Never have I felt the like of such currents which
threatened to dash us against the cliffs or else send us spinning into the
whirlpools alike to those which are said to herald the Kraken rising from
the ocean's depths! The paddlewheel beat backwards and still we hurtled
forward while the spray baptized all aboard whether heathen, Christian
or Jew & the bell gave clamorous directions to the crew who ran about in
a dither until at last the rough dock of Yale & the spire of its new church
could be seen by all & so we praised God once more & then let out a
lusty cheer & now we can go no further for beyond Yale the Fraser is truly
impassable for here lieth the Devil's Canyon, or Hell's Gate as it is so
colourfully called. It is here in Yale that I am provisioning as well as
tying knots of friendship with several companions with whom I scraped
up on an acquaintance on the Champion & who, I am certain, will be
willing investors in my mining venture. Astonishing how quickly
adventures bind people together! Astonishing how quickly friends are
made here in this country where no one has any history with another!
I have encountered a representative of nearly every country & enclave in
Europe & a great many Canadians & Americans, though the Americans
are said to be hardly as prevalent as in previous years, due to the War of
the Rebellion there. The Celestials seem to be spontaneously generating

*from the soil & are said to pull gold from claims that the most desperate
of Whitemen has abandoned for better & as for the red Indians they are
plentiful & are responsible morning & evening for a bucket brigade that
brings water to these buildings that are as crude & unembellished as a
child's toy blocks & still smell of the forest from which they were hacked.
Of these Indians often a noble-looking specimen can be espied & as there
are so very few White Women their women provide a parody of Christian
marriage to lonely men who have chosen to dwell out their days in this
wilderness. I believe that it would not be . . .*

Parody of marriage? "Bloody hell," Eugene mutters.

He draws a line through the sentence. The ink blotches over a
good quarter of the page. He curses again. Loudly. A page is worth at
least the price of a brandy. Yet Dora is worth it. Certainly. He imagines
her waiting each week for the post, disappointed when nothing from
him arrives at the dock in Maple Bay. Difficult though it is for him, it
is doubtless more difficult for her. But then isn't it always for women?
Condemned to wait, darling Penelopes, the lot of them.

He sets the paper aside for fire starter, straightens out his writing
set. It is no simple matter to think in this pressed-in room, its wallpaper
blotched and peeling and embellished with the smashed remains of
insects. It is no simple matter to write on this listing table amid the
smell of the last tenant's boots. Why had he troubled to rent a room at
all? To have some privacy? Hah! Given the volume of noise from the
saloon below he might as well be stretched out under a bench with all
his adventuring brethren.

On with it, Eugene Augustus. He dips the pen in the inkwell, waits
for the ink to hold to the nib. This time he begins with the trip from
New Westminster and how the captain—no doubt noting the strength
of Eugene's voice—bid him ring the bell for departure.

*For the span of over three hours I rang & called out: "Yale! Yale! All gold
seekers on board. Last call. Last call!" You would have thought me a
regular costermonger. For this service the captain paid me two dollars &
though this may seem a princely sum for such a minor task here it will
barely buy a loaf of bread. But that was not all, my dearest heart, for we
paying passengers were expected to lend a hand with loading wood &*

cargo & when we became stranded on a sand bar we were called upon to leap out & pull the sternwheeler along with a tow line—at which you can imagine the disgruntled mutterings, that is until I leapt out onto the sandy shore & made a fine example that the others soon followed—even though we were hardly needed for the great wheel walked her charge over the sand & it was the strangest sight, as if a fish had suddenly pranced up on shore!

He pauses. Yes, he can see the stranding scene as clearly as if it actually happened to him and was not merely something of which he had heard. Inspired, he adds in an Irishman who was nearly swept overboard as they charged through the riffles. Fortunate that Eugene grabbed him by his belt.

He signs *Your beloved Eugene* with a flourish, blows the ink dry, wishes the pale, smooth page were her skin, wishes he could have written endearments, ribald jokes, of the way his soldier stands at attention for her each morning whether he wills it or no. But Dora depends upon Mrs. Smitherton to read his letters aloud, she being no reader. She sees his looping, ornate hand, his tremendous Fs, his Hs (that a tutor once said indicated greatness) as a script as mysterious and intricate as that of the Persians, the Chinese. As for writing, so far Eugene has only been able to teach her how to write her name and his. The first time she legibly wrote the words Mr. and Mrs. Eugene Hume (for he has assured her they are as good as married) she stared at them as if they were a talisman, as if she thought, as the Indians were said to, that writing had some magical properties (for why else would the Whitemen depend upon it so?).

She practiced writing *Mrs. Eugene Augustus Hume* until Eugene said it looked as casually done as the signature of a barrister, and then he tucked the paper into her bodice. She was not shocked; nothing of that sort shocked her. For days after, whenever she presented the paper to him it was a signal for trundling off to their bed, and this often as not in the full light of day. They would wallow in each other for hours while the chickens clucked hungrily outside and the fence holes remained undug, the garden untended.

"At ease, soldier," Eugene now commands, to no avail whatsoever, and so resorts to imagining Mrs. Smitherton. She is adjusting her spectacles. She is pronouncing each word of his missive as if it were an item in a quotidian list. No, she would not do justice to his endearments and ribald jokes, and neither would her husband, though they are kindly, irreproachably honest people to whom he is now firmly in debt. And at least he can trust them not to speak of him disapprovingly. He must find something with which to thank them for taking care of Dora. A nugget would do nicely. He will put one aside.

He makes an oath now to the inkwell that one day he will teach Dora to properly read and write. He will teach her to speak with the cadences of his class, to dress with a simple elegance. He can clearly see himself, sometime in the middle future, leaning over her as she sits at a fine desk. Before them a window hung with velvet drapes holds a view of Victoria's Oak Bay in which sails glint and steamers puff out fat clouds. Governor Douglas and his wife will be calling soon, but for now they have time. He is teaching her to write the names of their children: Euphenia, Thaddeus, Leander, Persis, Octavia, Jules. A musical roll call and all are hale and hearty and tumbling about in the rooms nearby.

From the saloon below someone scrapes at a fiddle. A quarrel begins, then fades as the men are sent to grapple in the murk of the street. Eugene has earned his evening now. He takes the narrow, treacherous steps to the saloon. From five paces calls to the barkeep: "Mr. Culky! A glass of HB, no, of your finest cognac."

"Try your luck at the Frog's place, then. All we got is Old Tom and grog. We don't put on the frills here."

"The question was not meant as a criticism of your establishment, sir. I merely assumed . . . ah, a glass of your finest Old Tom then."

Culky's expression does not change as he pours. His face seems, indeed, to have long ago frozen into a wince.

Now, Eugene Augustus, how will this evening progress? Concentrate, man. He surveys the room. Sees seated men and standing men and milling-about men, sees stumbling men and fiddle-playing men and billiard-playing men there in another small room. Sees men of all nations united by a thirst for gold. A masculine landscape inhabited by not even one example of the fairer sex. Ah, what Eugene would give for a whiff of rosewater, a sea swirl of skirt.

He drinks and the whiskey is a pale burn in his throat. Difficult to predict this evening, difficult indeed.

At the faro table the dealer sweeps up cards from the green felt. The case keeper, a Chinaman, records the cards on an abacus. A simple game, the odds against the house. One merely has to bet which card will now turn up and in which order. All it takes is a good head for numbers and an honest table for one to eventually win. Unfortunate that Eugene has never had a good head for numbers. It is why he avoids the cards and the dice and the wheel, bets only on those outcomes over which he has some control. Now Dora, she could have been a regular sharper, for though she can barely read and write she can add, subtract, divide, even juggle large sums. "I see them falling into place," she said with an irresistible shrug that engaged her entire form. "I see them like it were raining numbers."

The faro dealer gestures to an empty space at the table. Eugene smiles and shakes his head, calls over to Mr. Culky for another shot. "And two for the gentlemen at the end of the bar." He points to the Welsh brothers who are holding onto the bar railing as if assailed by a whirlwind. They stare dubiously as he approaches. When he met them on board the ss *Champion* he had not realized their English was so poor. Finds he must rely on broad gestures and loud, clearly spoken words. After they are finally made to understand they shake their heads. They are meeting their brethren in Camerontown, Eugene gathers. A mine is started there already. They have no need for partners. Eugene sighs. Looks about again. The Italian is not in sight, neither are the Missouri men. Les Canadiens are at the faro table now. They are cursing in their peculiar French. Their backs form a barricade. At the chuck-a-luck table an Indian man in a cocked hat tosses dice with a practiced hand. The light is fading and for a time the raucous crowd is half-figured and ghostly. Now an Indian boy lights tallow candles that are speared upright in wax-heaped bottles and give off trails of black smoke. They smell more foul than most tallow candles—of burning sheep fat, of carcass. Nothing like an odour to stir the pot of memory—a battlefield in the gloaming and all about corpses of horses and men are afire like a scene from some medieval poet's hell. Eugene mouths a curse. He is excellent at forgetting many things, why not that scene? He gestures to Culky who fills his glass without a word. Eugene straightens. The evening is not yet over. There is still hope, still reason to stay.

The door cracks open. Oswald. Behind him is Herr Boots. He is grinning foolishly, is in need, obviously, of some kind of protection from this Oswald, who is waving his arms as if he has just walked into a line of drying petticoats, who won last night's bet by a hair.

"They're horse-shitting, them that says it's sitting around. It ain't like the Fraser, wheres any harebrained fucknit can get at it with a pan. It ain't like California in '49 neither. It's more hidden than a nun's twat. You gotta read the land, see. Gotta dig through rock to get the mother-lode. Need more than sluices and such shit. Need shafts and a pump to keep the water out. Gotta have money for all that. Gotta have a company. Boys on their own are turning up dead and bear-chewed in the hills. Ain't no place for a man alone, less you're a god-blamed Indian. Don't be listening to them fucknits that tell you otherwise. Listen to me. . . . Yeah, can we do something for you?"

"Ah, Mr. Hume," Herr Boots says. "I happy to see you again. *Sitzen.* Here. Mr. Oswald he is speaking of mining. He knows much of it. He make big strike in Sierra Nevadas."

Eugene smiles. "Truly? Then why the deuce are you here?"

Oswald stares grimly at his hands. Eugene sits.

"He here because he have bad partners. Bad men," Herr Boots says.

"I trusted the wrong ones, see, sons-of-whores and mongrel bitches. I got too goddamned good a nature. Not this time."

"Mr. Oswald is expert at mining. He look for investors."

"But what of your boots? Herr . . . what of your venture?"

"Oh, I sell boots and then have money. Maybe I look to buy in a mine. I not sure."

"Call the mine The Jessica Bell, after my fiancée. Won that whore-son bet, didn't it? There's a sign for you."

"Herr . . . ah, Schulmiss."

"Schultheiss," the Prussian says, chuckling, always chuckling, as if life were some great joke.

"Quite so, Herr Schultheiss. May I speak with you in private?"

"Say your mind, Pume, don't be sneaking around like a mongrel with its head up its arse," Oswald says, grinning.

"Hume, the name is Hume, I say, and no. It is just . . ."

It is just that the Prussian is a fool to trust this swine-tongued Oswald. Oswald is a diminutive powder keg, a not-so-eloquent liar. Good natured? Eugene would have laughed if it had been appropriate. Mongrel? Eugene would have called him out for a duel if Oswald had not been jesting.

"Just that I, too, will be starting a mine and . . ."

"Yeah, and how you gonna choose the fuck what spot? I knew a gentleman-sir like you who thought if he horked snot on the ground it'd come up gold."

"I shall study the lay of the land," Eugene says with dignity. "I am not a green hand."

"You ain't? What's a stringer then? What's the fuck difference 'tween a sluice and a cradle?"

"I am not interested in proving myself to you."

Oswald laughs, shows a mouth of chipped, tobacco stained teeth. "Can't take some jibing, can you? Well, if you don't know bum squat about mining, maybe you got some capital. Maybe you wanna invest in The Jessica Bell. I might consider it. Christ's clinkers, but I might."

"Your confidence is remarkable, Mr. Oswald. And now, if you will excuse me, gentlemen."

"I ain't no gentleman looking for a lickfinger. Bumtags are more use 'round here than gentlemen. Most of you got less money than a fucknit shoeshine. Here's my advice to you, Pume, or Hume, or whatever it is. Don't be putting on god-blamed airs. Don't be thinking gold'll be jumping out at you just cus you got some dandy-ass name for your mine. I'll tell you this. It's us that run the show here."

Oswald sits back and grins. Schultheiss mops his brow and smiles apologetically. The moths rise at the back of Eugene's neck. He is tempted, nay, determined, to return to his room for his revolver and take out this dwarfish fiend with one shot. Easy Eugene Augustus. Consider how that would set the evening on a course entirely different from the course which you had planned. And was the insult so great? Perhaps in the staid environment of the Old World it might have been. But here the old rules no longer apply. And look. The men about Oswald are not taking it so seriously; rather they are chuckling and snorting.

Let the Prussian be taken in with this piglet-brained Yank, then.

In any case, what profits can he expect from such a quotidian item as boots? Some novelty might bring him fortune, but *boots*?

Eugene makes his way outside. The air smells of pine and wood smoke. The night is cloud-dark, edged with winter. Men jostle past him on their way from one saloon and grog shop to the next. There is the California House, the American flag lifting feebly in the breeze. There is the dirt street and then the sandy bank sloping sharply to the river. What happens at high water? Perhaps the denizens huddle in that diminutive church higher up. Perhaps, indeed, another line of buildings once faced these. It almost appears so. Perhaps the opposing street was seized by the thick muscle of the river and smashed to pieces, leaving only the steep sandy bank. He straightens his shoulders, his hat. Another man, without his confidence, might well be discouraged by that troglodyte, Oswald.

"Over here! Find the lady! Find the lady!" The man calling this is setting up three cards on a crate. Now holds up a candle lantern. "Easy to do. Anyone can win. Come look. Just look. You there, and you."

Men pause. Glance. One steps to the challenge. He loses the first attempt, then the second. On the third he wins three dollars. The tosser hands the money over grudgingly. "Good eye, sir, good eye. How about another round while your luck holds?"

The winner shakes his head, stuffs money in his pockets.

A man steps up. He has an impressive dark beard that falls near to his belly. He sways slightly. "My father won a quid at Find the Lady once. At a fair it was."

"Play a round for free. For your father's sake, then."

Eugene watches from just out of the circle of lamplight. The man at play is young, he notices, and the beard only a young man's attempt at a fierce countenance. He also notices a man leaning against a nearby stable wall, and then another man by the river, squatting near a tree.

The tosser shifts the cards one over the other. He is hatless, his features there for all to see—the greying hair reduced to a monk-like fringe, the sloping chin that gives him the appearance of weakness, of indecision. As for his accent. Some hint of the emerald isle in his ancestry. The colony of Nova Scotia? New Found Land? No matter, such dealers are a race apart whatever colony or country they have scrabbled from.

The young man loses the first game, plays another for free and wins. Now is the time. Yes. The tosser suggests a small wager. A mere quarter dollar. Shillings acceptable as well. The young man is fumbling in his pocket. Is humming a cheerful tune when Eugene steps up. My God, he may know little of mining, but he has spent enough time slumming to know of sharpers and their tricks.

"I would not recommend it, young sir. You will not find the lady. You will never find the lady."

"Mind your own affairs there," the tosser says.

"You have already been duped. The player before was an accomplice, a shill as it were. Another two are on the lookout should an authority come about and question the dealings."

The tosser stares at Eugene. "You calling me a cheat?"

"My father won a quid at Find the Lady once," the young man says. "At the fair it was. He bought us taffy and caramels. It was right jolly."

"Indeed? Well, I assure you, young sir, you are more likely to find the Lady of the Lake than the lady of the cards. They have many tricks, these men."

The young man looks to him wide-eyed. He is stroking his ridiculous beard as if it were a cherished pet. Has Eugene met him before? Perhaps, though likely it is merely that particular gullibility of youth that is familiar.

"Here, it's only a bloody quarter," the tosser says.

"And then a half dollar and then a whole. And then the man's entire purse, and if he is unwilling to part with it, strong encouragement to give it up, eh?"

The tosser stands. The squatter on the bank stands. The figure by the stable shifts so that he is no longer leaning. Squares of light fall into the street as doors open and shut. Spinet and fiddle. Shouts and catcalls.

The man from the bank approaches, bringing with him a smell of onions and ale. He has the bulk of a wrestler and is likely armed. Eugene is tempted to let the young fool learn his lesson, be pummelled to bloody bits. Courage, Eugene Augustus, do not cut and run, not from this engagement.

"I advise we walk on," Eugene whispers. The young man stumbles to one side. Eugene rights him.

"Where's my lady, eh? My father found her. A quid he won. It was right capital."

The bank man stands behind the tosser, sucks his breath through his teeth. Why should Eugene risk his neck for a stranger? He takes one step back. Two. Half turns. His heart pounds. The man from the stable blocks his escape. He is the tallest man that Eugene has yet seen in the colonies. His shoulders are as wide as a door. His hat, a wide-awake, shadows one eye. Indeed, he is well-dressed for a muscle man, has a frock coat and high boots that gleam even in this derisory light.

"I should warn you," Eugene says. "I am an Englishman, and a soldier of the Crimean, and . . ."

"And full of the Dutch courage, I'd say." The voice is the sort that could command the trees to bloom, waters to part. It seems to have an echo of its own. The bank man backs off. The tosser stuffs his pockets with cards. Tips over the lantern in his rush.

"Arthur. This is unlike you entirely. As for you, sir." The man comes closer, looms over Eugene. Few men can loom over Eugene. It is not something he likes. "My thanks for trying to save the pockets of my clerk. And now Mr. Kinnear and Mr. Jevowski, is it? Either cease your nocturnal swindling or be gone from this town."

"'Course, your honour, 'course," says the tosser, Mr. Kinnear. "Just a game. Not a swindle. Not this one. Didn't know he was your clerk. Didn't know. 'Course. Good evening to you. Good evening."

A full moon is rising over the hills and flushing its light down the street. Arthur is singing "Beautiful Dreamer." The tall man is inviting Eugene for a coffee at Captain Powers's Hotel and introducing himself as Matthew Baillie Begbie, High Court Judge. Kinnear and Jevowski are nowhere in sight.

They sit in upholstered chairs in Captain Powers's front room, their legs sprawled out toward the fire. The chandelier lamps are lit. The Judge's hat sits on a wrought iron table. His hair is black, thick and richly oiled. His eyes are a remarkable blue. He wears a Van Dyke beard, moustaches waxed to tasteful points.

The noise from the saloons is muffled by distance. Arthur has gone off to bed. Eugene knows where he saw him now—at Governor Douglas's table nearly two years ago, on the occasion when Eugene was ushered so ignobly out the door. Arthur's face was less enveloped with hair then, which is why Eugene failed to recognize him. Wasn't young Arthur married to one of the Governor's daughters? Yes. To one of the *les belles sauvages*, as Eugene has heard them called. Ah, at least this evening is turning out splendidly, just as Eugene felt it would. They are smoking cigars, the Judge's own, and sipping coffee from China cups. They have exchanged pleasantries on the weather (promising) on Captain Powers's coffee (excellent) and on the war raging in America (tiresome).

The Judge blows a white ring that blooms against the window pane. Eugene attempts the same, coughs. He has never acquired a taste for tobacco. Still, he could hardly turn down the offering of a cigar from such a man; it would be alike to turning down the offering of his hand; it would be disrespectful of their common bond. For they are both Englishmen, they both prefer their coffee black. Most importantly they both attended Cambridge, though when the Judge, delighted, presses Eugene for dates and reminisces about this doctor or that, Eugene regrets that he had brought the subject forward. No point in explaining to the Judge that he would have completed his three years, certainly, but there had been the problem of the money, the problem of being unfairly sent down. The bulldogs, those greasy wardens, took a special delight in tracking him when he and his companions were out enjoying an evening. They hardly cared that one could not merely snap one's fingers and so be transported across the environs.

Eugene decides it is as good a time to piss as any. "If you will excuse me. I must step outside. The coffee. I am not accustomed to such excess of liquid this time at night."

He pisses against a wall and as he does a dog slinks past, staring at Eugene over its shoulder, as if there were a price on its mangy head. Eugene belts his trousers and now notices that the clouds are in retreat and the moon is looking low enough to roll down the street. It is full round and the patterns upon it are as delicate as lace work, astonishingly clear. To Eugene's delight a line of poetry ambles into his recollections. He had read it in some English periodical, and then again on the wall of a necessary here in the colonies.

Eugene returns and takes up his cigar. "Ah, Bright wandering coquette of the sky, whom alone can change but always be adored."

"My pardon?"

"It is a fragment from that incomparable poet, Percy Shelley. It has only just been discovered and published."

"Ah, but was it not: Bright wanderer, fair coquette of Heaven?" the Judge asks.

"Possibly."

"And then: To whom alone it has been given to change and be adored forever. I could be in error."

"No, those are the correct lines, now that I think on it. Quite so."

"I am glad to meet a man who prefers poetry to gambling."

"Indeed, sir, I swore an oath to my dying mother that I would touch not the cards, nor the dice, nor approach a gaming table. I will honour that oath."

"*Ad praesens ova cras pullis sent meliora.*"

Something about chickens and eggs, which comes first. No, that it is better to have an egg than a chicken. "Quite so," Eugene says.

"But what of searching for gold? Is not that a gamble?"

"In a manner, yes, but the differences bear analysis. For it is due to one's own exertions that gold is found, it does not merely rely on the turn of a card or a dealer's honesty."

"That is true," the Judge admits with a small smile. He adds more coffee to Eugene's cup and then his own. "And you served in the Crimean?"

"Yes."

"A noble cause."

"Yes."

"Who can forget that brave charge by the light brigade?"

"Not I."

"Although it was said to be not wholly necessary. But then, *errare humanum.*"

The whole war was unnecessary, Eugene thinks. The whole war was full of human error. It was foolishness that masqueraded as courage and best not spoken of. "Quite so," he says.

The Judge presses with more questions. Has he met the Governor? Has he not letters of introduction? A man of his standing and experience must. "I would be pleased to see them."

"I thank you. It would be an honour, your honour. It is just that I have left them with my wife."

"Ah, perhaps at another time. When we are both in Victoria."

"Yes," Eugene says.

"It is astonishing how many are forged, and so poorly at that."

"Astonishing," Eugene says.

"Indeed," says the Judge and thankfully now speaks of French poetry, the moral role of princes and kings, the theories of Mr. Darwin. "You must have attended a great many interesting lectures while in London."

"Certainly," Eugene says. London lectures. They always started out well. Soon enough, however, the endless extrapolations, explanations and examples sent his thoughts drifting over the student watering holes like a lost soul.

The Judge is now speaking of the rights of the populace, states strongly (as Eugene was finding he states all things) that British law be equally applied to all, whether the man be red, black, white or yellow. "The law is colour-blind," he says.

"Quite so. That is why she is blindfolded. Personally I have always found the image appealing."

"It makes no difference if she is blindfolded, metaphorically or not. She does not differentiate the yellow from the brown or black."

Eugene agrees, for he would like this to be a most agreeable evening. In any case, the Judge's theories make a great deal more sense than those of that damned barrister from Bath whom he met on the passage over. The Judges theories are simpler, easy to recall. His stomach tightens. What if the Judge has heard of his evening at the Governor's? His disgrace? No other word will suffice. Thank Christ that this Arthur Bushby did not recognize him, though did he not wink before he stumbled off? Surely not.

Eugene hastily offers up Dora, how she is alike to the ruddy-skinned, strong limbed women painted by that Flemish chap.

"Rubens?"

"Exactly so."

"Good that you are happily married, Mr. Hume."

Eugene admits wholeheartedly that he is. They continue with the topic of women, the absurdity of crinolines, the darling manner with which women peel an orange, their unfortunate lack of rationality. "Yet this is the thing," Eugene says. "A man must make his fortune first.

He must settle in the world before he binds himself. For women it is different. They are older creatures than us. Yes, I think this is so. They are as wise at eighteen as we are at thirty. They have no need to go off travelling the continent, no need to be studying geometry or philosophy. They are prepared from the cradle to get on with the business of life. Dora, that is, Mrs. Hume, is never plagued with doubts, never sleeps poorly. She chatters cheerfully from morning till night. Sometimes I wonder whether she knows if it is I standing there or merely a wooden post. Sometimes I wonder if I sent another man in my place if she would even notice."

"She would, I do not doubt. Women notice much more than we credit them."

"Indeed. Are you planning marriage? If I may be so bold as to ask."

"Not as yet. I have much work to do before I can contemplate such a state." At this the Judge looks at the mantel clock. "I must to bed now. I continue my circuit come morning."

"If you are needing companionship . . ."

The Judge is not. The Judge will be halting at near every roadhouse and ensemble of men, trying cases both petty and severe. He and his small party will be on forest trails, breaking through snow.

"Snow?"

"There is snow in the high country. Have you not heard?"

"Yes, but it is now June."

The Judge smiles. "You will find the weather here quite inconstant. Take it up as a challenge."

He stands and offers his hand. Eugene likewise stands. The coffee has worked its magic; he is steady.

"Good night then, Matthew," Eugene says, for somewhere during the evening they exchanged their first names. Somewhere in the evening that kind of a bond was forged. "I trust we shall meet again."

The Judge smiles sagely, warmly. "We shall indeed, sir. There is only one destination after all."

NINE

"Have you ever been to London, Mr. Jim?"
He said no, thought again how she asked the oddest questions.
London? Why not Africa? Why not the sun?

1862. The new Westminster Bridge is opened with great ceremony. At the zoological gardens in Regent's Park an infant giraffe stumbles upward to the urgings of the crowd. And in South Kensington preparations for the International Exhibition have begun. It will be as great as the Great Exhibition of '51 and all London talks of it. Even Dora talks of it, though she doubts she will see much of it. In a cramped, windowless room off Bond Street Dora and a dozen-odd other women are far too occupied with sewing gowns for the quality. Her skills are not fine enough for the tailoring, not even for the making of ruffles and bows, the edge-workings of lace. Her fingers are not the lily stems of Marie, barely twelve, nor the deft blur of Miss Grower who at thirty looks to be fifty. No, Dora's clumsy fingers are fit only for the sewing on of buttons and large beads. Even then the sweater, Mr. Haberdale, frowns at her work. He is pot-bellied and scoured with wrinkles and is everywhere at once. At the end of the day he tells the women to open their mouths so that he may inspect for buttons hidden beneath their tongues. Women, young and old, have been known to steal in this manner. He explains this to Dora and inspects so closely, for so long that Dora would love to spit a button into his rheumy eye.

In this month of April they are frantic with work. The Season is near to hand. The working hours stretch from twelve a day to fourteen, and then to seventeen. Mr. Haberdale orders restoratives of nutmeg and gin. He orders, as well, a clock that strikes each hour and releases a mechanical bird that belabours them with its cries.

"But do you know. I half-enjoyed it at first for all that."

Boston nodded. Thought of the growing lateness of the hour. But he did not leave. It did not seem right to leave.

This is the closest she has yet come to the quality. She imagines that after all this frantic preparation she herself will be attending the balls, the teas, will be riding in Hyde Park, or calling on an acquaintance in the afternoon. It is as if she herself is preparing for the market of marriage. And she loves, indeed, the wondrous gowns heaping the table, the lush colours—apple greens, coral pinks, the purplish-reds of magenta and solferino, named so for battles of the Crimean and not out of fashion yet. And though her fingers may not be deft they have an astonishing knack for assessing say, whether a silk is from China or France, whether a lace is from Nottingham or Holland. She has won admiration for this, has won admiration also for keeping spirits up by telling stories and jokey tales, or did, until Mr. Haberdale commanded silence with the tone of a Reverend high in his pulpit.

At night she dreams of buttons—buttons of shell, buttons of bone, of ivory and silver, enamelled buttons painted with fabulous scenes. She dreams of lines of buttons that stretch to the sky or roll into cracks of the floorboards and then of Mr. Haberdale begging that they be gently prised out. She dreams as well of beads, a lustrous snow of them, delightful until the beads become the size of fists and begin to stun birds, shatter windows, until they find their way into her mouth and she chokes and wakes to a cold room, a pounding heart.

"Though sure I made the best of it. Do you know what I'm meaning?"

Boston muttered he supposed he did.

She is in bespoke tailoring, after all; she is not a slopper in the East End slaving at those treadle machines, making identical drab gowns for whomever chooses to buy them. She earns twenty pounds per year and is reasonably fed and has lodgings with the other seamstresses in a room down the stairs from the workroom. She shares a bed with only two others—Mrs. Tavenshaw of the gypsy-dark skin and the mumbling Miss Plamouth. And she has an admirer, doesn't she? Mr. Haberdale's son, no less. The elder Mr. Haberdale disapproves, but the younger Mr. Haberdale has an income of his own from investments of one sort or another and will not be deterred. Marriage into the family of the Haberdales! A moderate wealth. Puddings. Sweetmeats. Roasted pheasant. A wood fire in each room. A great step up indeed. And yet the other seamstresses are not as jealous as Dora wishes they could be. Nor is Dora as grateful as she wishes she could be. And why ever not? Well and so, because the young Mr. Haberdale is ugly as sin. No other, gentler expression will suffice. He has a sprouting of orange hair, eyes the shade of agates, and a mouth crowded with yellow teeth. He is a young man by the calculation of his two and twenty years but seems to Dora some creature born underground centuries ago and raised on sour mash. He does not engage in small talk but speaks in passionate spurts of politics and policies, and then lapses into ominous silences that Dora has to fill with words, as if she were a convict bargaining for her life. And why can he never look upon her face? Why fix his gaze on her throat? Still, she accepts his invitations once their hours decrease back to twelve, once Sundays are again a half-day free.

Inexplicably, their first outing finds them at the tanning factory where the men labour at noxious vats. The pure finders come in with their reeking buckets and carts. One lad boasts he has the pure not only of Lord so-and-so's mastiffs, but also that of the Lord himself, thus his offering is certain to tan a hide to the finest quality. The foreman cuffs him. Dora protests to Mr. Haberdale. She can barely breathe; her dress will become soiled. And what does Mr. Haberdale do? He takes her to a match factory and points out a woman, her jaw glowing palely green with the fossy. He takes her to watch the destitute men breaking granite for their bread. He takes her to the slave market at Bethnal Green though he has no intention of acquiring a servant. He points out the chimney sweeps, the crossing sweeps, a young girl holding out an orange as if she were holding out the world. Points out these things as if Dora has never seen them, nor known of them. In the vast market of Newcut he buys nothing and asks that she does not, that she merely observe. And so she observes a Punch and Judy show. Punch beats Judy with a stick and casts their baby into the oven. Judy leaps about in puppet fury. Dora laughs. Mr. Haberdale does not. Indeed, he frowns so hard it seems the points of his mouth might peg him to the ground.

"My father often took me to see these shows," Dora says, "it's why I like them so," and then tells him about her father's demise, his miserable half-life and then the fire that truly killed him along with her mother and all that they had worked for. Tears spill from her eyes as she tells him this. And his reply? He asks her opinions of the proletariat.

"The what?"

"The workers! That is, the labourers! The toilers!" he says, gesturing all about him.

"A fine lot for the most part," Dora replies, bewildered.

Mr. Haberdale sighs, but then he is ever sighing like some benighted swain.

Dora supposes all this odd behaviour is in preparation for a mysterious business venture. Perhaps Mr. Haberdale is hoping to challenge his father. Certainly he has asked her to not mention, should his father ask, that they have been visiting low neighbourhoods and wretched factories. In the end, Dora hardly cares about Mr. Haberdale's purposes. She has only so much free time. She does not wish to waste it watching the labours of others, feeling their misery seep into her as if her skin were a sieve. "The Seven Dials is where I want to go," she says. "You may come or not." Mr. Haberdale trails her reluctantly, momentarily cowed. From one Mr. Cohen, an old acquaintance, Dora bargains for a matching bodice and skirt. The fabric is a damask with green and yellow stripes. The trimmings are of lace and crimped silk. She buys, as well, her first true hoops. She spends near the whole of her scanty savings, but the style is of only a decade past; the tears and stains are moderate and easy enough to mend and scrub. She is most pleased with her purchase, even though Mr. Haberdale asks how it is she can wear cast-off garments, that is, how she can become a rich woman's shadow, a tatterdemalion in fact. She barely attends him, insists now that they eat and drink and be among talking and laughter.

Mr. Haberdale acquiesces readily enough and takes her to an old-fashioned coffee shop with high-backed pews and tables pocked with burns and scattered with periodicals. Through the charry air Dora sees only one other woman and this a woman of dubious morals and so she smiles only from politeness when Mr. Haberdale introduces her to a group of youngish men in decent coats, all who greet him companionably enough. It seems the younger Mr. Haberdale is known here.

Possibly even liked. She cannot recall the conversation, cannot recall their faces, only that the coffee dished from the vat was bitter and hardly warmed and the word *proletariat* rose up again and again. And then Mr. Haberdale stands and asks her to stand. She, apparently, is to be an emblem. She is of the exploited. "Look upon her hands," he says. Dora lifts them up hesitantly and the men gasp as if she were holding up bloodied stumps. Mr. Haberdale clears his throat. Never has she heard him speak for so long and so passionately and with so little faltering. "This woman slaves in obscurity in poisonous rooms while below roll the carriages of the bloated rich and all about the shops are bursting with goods made of blood and ceaseless toil. In a year, that is, six months, her beauty will be gone. She will be hunched, her hands like claws. She will be consumptive! Blinded! She will descend to the slop trade and then, if still unmarried, she will supplement her wages with the wages of the street, will become, yes, a dollymop, and descend at last fully, that is, into that most degraded of trades."

Dora protests. She will never become . . . how dare he suggest. . . . Her cheeks burn. She is of a sudden aware of the tawdry brightness of her gown here in the coal stained coffee-house. She dashes out. Mr. Haberdale catches her in the street. He shouts to be heard above the street callers and the clatter of wheels. "I am sorry, my dearest, that is, I apologize. I beg. Please. Do you not see? The workers, the labourers I mean, those in the street, that is, the people, yes the people, they must be told of, that is, they must be made aware of their own misery. Only then can the revolution begin." That was all he was attempting. He did not wish to humiliate her. Soon such a word as humiliation will be forgotten in any case. His voice catches. Tears are glistening in his eyes, much to her astonishment.

"Made aware of their misery, that's what he said, Mr. Jim. How can a person not be aware of their own misery? That was the most absurd thing I'd ever heard. It is alike to not being aware you had a broken limb."

Boston muttered some agreement and noted that a spider had woven half a web by this time, there in the join of her cabin door.

To atone, to explain, Mr. Haberdale takes her to the library of the British museum and after some searching, finds a man at a table, scratching at a notebook, a barricade of books about him. He is dark of hair, well-featured and weary-eyed, his accent hushed and heavy. Dora is introduced and then Mr. Haberdale and the man whisper and nod as if the keepers of some great knowledge. The man is an exile of some sort. "He has written a great Manifesto," Mr. Haberdale later tells her in the green shade of Hyde Park. "It will revolutionize the world, that is, I mean to say, we shall all be equal. The workers will have control of the profits of their labour and then all of mankind will eat and drink their fill and have clothing enough and then, only then, will they practice the high arts, music, that is, and poetry."

Dora had never heard such nonsense and tells him so. Why should the quality want to be equal to the lower orders? Why indeed should Mr. Haberdale? And what of the organ grinders, are not they making music and on a scrap of bread a day? What of the tract sellers? "There's your music, sir, there's your poetry."

"You do not understand, no, not at all. I will teach you, that is, instruct you, and you will become a champion, indeed, a paragon, a gleaming light for the cause." He kisses her cheek then and it is like being rubbed with a mollusc. She tells him she will no longer see him. She will no longer step out with him of an evening nor a Sunday, un- less . . . unless perhaps it is to the Cremorne Gardens? Mr. Haberdale calls it a gross leviathan built on the backs of the poor or some such thing and yet in the end he acquiesces, daring as he does so to look at her face, her eyes.

"Ah, but it were grand, Mr. Jim. You have never seen the like here. Imagine you are in a dozen countries at once. Imagine China temples and Swiss houses and snake charmers and a great maypole and dancing, 'course, and fireworks, oh, like a fiery garden in the sky."

They are watching an operetta when a voice at Dora's elbow says, "Ah, it is this I missed some." Another voice agrees wholeheartedly.

Both are dark-eyed, plump and bustling, both have a wealth of black glossy curls. They are identical, in fact, excepting the fine scar on the cheek of one, the plumper figure of the other. Their dresses are splendidly ornate, multi-coloured affairs with skirts round as tabletops. Dora falls into conversation with them while Mr. Haberdale frowns, once again.

"A seamstress for the quality! Ah, where we live seamstresses are rare indeed."

"Rare as coal fires and starlings."

"Yes, sister. Oh, the things I do not miss. Oh!"

"I must ask, and begging your pardon . . ."

"From the Antipodes!"

"Oh, the other end of the world!"

"We are from Australia! Australia!" they say in unison.

"How delightful!" Dora says, and claps her hands. Mr. Haberdale takes Dora's elbow. But Dora cannot be spun like a top. She firmly plants her feet. "And what is it like there? You must tell me."

"The birds make you think of a painter gone mad."

"Gone quite mad. And there is an animal that hops instead of runs, truly."

"Hops, yes. Oh, it makes me laugh each time I see them. And there are men so black they seem made of night."

"Oh, and so many marvels, endless marvels."

"But no fine seamstresses, very few!"

"Oh, and such a scarcity of good lace."

Dora can hardly tell which is speaking. She fears that if she continues to look from one to the other her neck might snap. Their sentences stack upon one another and build, eventually, their story—twin orphan girls sent off to the Antipodes by the parish priest. In their possession are letters of betrothals to two stalwart brothers, not twins, but close enough in age and temperament and happy to live close to each other for all their days. The Placterton Brothers are brewers with a thriving business. Famous in Melbourne, truly. They are not convicts, nor bolters, nor descended of either, the sisters make this clear, turning sombre ever so briefly.

"There's some here who look down on us."

"Oh, but we hardly care, hah."

"Not a whit, no. Let them rot here in soggy old England."

"Are you married then?"

"Yes, are you?"

"No," says Dora, not looking at Mr. Haberdale who is grimacing and fidgeting.

The plumper sister's gaze passes over him, expresses sympathy. "We have heard that Miss Burdett-Coutts is once again planning to send good women off to the colonies."

"Oh, yes, sister. It is one of her great causes. To the Americas this time!"

"No, it is the Canadas."

"Yes, sister, you are right. That was the island. Fabulous riches there. The streams are full of gold. The men are all handsome and rich as can be imagined and not a woman amongst them."

"Oh, they are lamenting for wives! They care not a whit for position or dowries. Not like here in soggy old England."

"The female immigration society, dear. They arrange everything. It is all very safe."

"All very honourable."

"It is time we left, Miss Timmons," Mr. Haberdale says.

"My goodness! I do believe I've heard of this Miss Burdett-Coutts," Dora says to the sisters.

"Of course, you have," Mr. Haberdale says. "She is that worst of the bourgeois, that is, of the philanthropists. She gives money away as if it belonged wholly to her in the first place, that is, I mean, as if she should be applauded for it. It should be taken. Yes. Taken! All of it, not given out in dribs and drabs . . ."

"But your friend, that Mr. Marx and his family. Don't they live in one of her charity buildings?"

"We must go now," he says as if he has not heard this question at all.

"Yes," Dora echoes, "we must indeed."

The outings continue, but no longer to factories or to the meetings of radicals in cramped coffee rooms. Mr. Haberdale the Younger now seems determined to please her. They view the enormous panoramas at Burfords in Cranbourn Street, the waxworks of Madame Tussuad. They attend the Oxford Music Hall where Dora catches Mr. Haberdale tapping his toe. "Only out of impatience," he insists, and gives his usual frown. On a common green they clamber into the coach of a whirligig and are soon being heaved into the sky. From this vantage Dora sees, for the first time, her city in all its vastness and muted chaos and wonders if it is indeed a monstrous place, a devourer of the innocent, as Mr. Haberdale insists. How she desires to continue rising higher and higher, to leave the city entirely.

Ah, but then a month or two passes and she has nearly forgotten this desire, nearly forgotten the Antipodean women. Indeed, she has nearly resigned herself to Mr. Haberdale, though he has not proposed marriage, though he has said marriage is a custom that will soon be abolished. And yet, and yet, something rankles. It is as if she is inhabiting a life for which she is not meant. She has felt so ever since the fire took her beloved parents and their beloved store.

Then one evening her life finds its true course. She is walking alone near Newcut Market, seeking medicine for Miss Grower who has fallen sick. A yellow fog shrouds the buildings and street carts; it turns the street lamps a sulphurous yellow; seems to muffle the sounds of hooves and wheels and the calling out of wares. People appear out of this fog, stream past her, then disappear, like apparitions at a magic lantern show, all but a group of students, reeling with laugher and drink. They halt before her and their leader (he must be their leader for he is the most handsome) drops to his knees. "I am leaving soon for the colonies," he cries. "For the goldfields of the British Columbias. I will pluck gold from the ground and so adorn your golden hair. Ah, my beauty, come with me. I adore you. I love you with all my heart. At least give me a kiss before I journey to my fate, to death perhaps!" The young man's face. Oh, how it beseeches! How full of longing it is! She kisses his cheek. He leaps up and tries to pull her along. His friends haul him back. They are laughing as if they own the world and then the fog takes them.

"It were Mr. Hume, you see. I knew it as soon as I saw him at the Avalon Hotel. I didn't dare tell him straight away. I waited till that evening we danced aboard the *Grappler*. I told him that he'd been thinner then and that his hair were lighter, but that it were him for certain. And he said that for certain it must have been. It were a sign, you see, back in that London street. I knew it straight away. And so straight away I sought out the wife of that Mr. Marx to see if she could help with the wheres and hows of finding the Miss Burdett-Coutts and her societies. Mrs. Marx was glad to help me, and I'm thinking it were because she didn't like Mr. Haberdale. Those Marxes were terrible poor, see, and never once had he helped them, thinking, I suppose, that books are alike to food and ideas can pay the rent. As for Miss Burdett-Coutts I met her in person I did, and she were lovely and grave and not at all like Mr. Haberdale said, not a philanthropist at all. And she was happy to send me on a ship to this island. Said such a lively person as myself would be useful there. And true enough in no time at all I felt that this was my place and home and that London was long ago. And it's strange, Mr. Jim, isn't it? How you can live all your life in one place and still feel as if you're not belonging."

TEN

A train trundles through green countryside. Heat waves ripple over farms and church spires. The woman Eugene sees is Dora, but not Dora. She is alone in her seat though the carriage is packed with men. They are hidden behind their periodicals. Dozing over their canes. They are oblivious to the woman, but for him, but for him. Her head leans against the window; her hat brim is crushed against it. Her eyes are closed as if she is sleeping—dreaming of him, perhaps, as he is of her. Leisurely she twists the pearl buttons of her bodice and they ping to the floor. Overskirt, petticoats, chemise. They are falling from her, are lifting themselves out the window to fly alongside the starlings, blindfold the amazed cows. She rolls her stockings down her thighs, eyes still closed, as if under a mesmerist's spell. Next her corset pings open, is a silver carapace at her feet. Now she is naked but for her hat. And this, too, she unpins, the feather of cobalt blue brushing her cheek as she does so. Now lets fall her hair. It is wheat-coloured, shot with copper. Ah, she is dimpled. Luminous-skinned. Her hands caress her throat, her breasts, the round of her stomach, her sanctuary. The men are no longer oblivious. The breathless gold of the moment is gone. They are shouting in a tangle of tongues. Pointing. Cheering. Jeering. Mules lope down the aisle. Oxen smash the windows with their horns. A whistle blasts. The train shatters into black shards.

"Quite so. Shit," Eugene says blearily and watches a square of morning light fold over the rafters. He hopes to fall back into his dream, but it is impossible, what with the mossy film on his tongue, the thudding in his skull, the cymbal crash of plates, what with the birds carrying on like mad heralds, the general din of hundreds of men on the move.

He rises stiffly from the bed. Culky? Is that the proprietor? Why not Procrustes, the nefarious innkeeper who stretched or chopped unwary travellers to make good his boast that his bed would fit any man? For that is how Eugene feels this morning, as if someone has been hacking away at his limbs.

The water in the washing jug is brown and afloat with flies. Already he has a thick stubble on his chin. He will grow a beard. And why not? If he is to be a miner, an adventurer, then it is best to look the part. Next he slicks down his hair with Macassar oil, scrubs his teeth with tooth powder, and adjusts his clothes, having forgotten to discard them last night. A wine stain adorns his topcoat lapel like a tattered rose. How did it get there? He is no dribbler. The Judge will have the wrong idea entirely. The Judge? Bloody hell.

The front room of Captain Powers's establishment is empty but for a tabby cat arranged artfully on a chair. The fire is a pile of ash. Eugene catches his breath. Curses.

"The Judge and his party left at first light," Powers says, as if this should be obvious.

"Ah, quite so, did he leave a message for Mr. Eugene Hume? We arranged to meet."

"To meet? Here? This morning?"

"This morning. Yes. I believe it was this morning. However . . ." Eugene presses his brow. Damn Culky and his rotgut whiskey.

"Perhaps you would care for some breakfast, sir, to sop up your evening."

Eugene cradles a mug of gritty coffee, eats bacon, flapjacks and eggs in the near-empty saloon. Steps outside. Pale sky ringed with clouds. A ruffle of wind. Two men pass by him with a trundle barrow that haws from side to side. Culky's Indian boy stands in the midst of the road and stares after them like the one child left by the piper.

No matter that he missed the Judge. In the goldfields, that is where they promised they would meet, he is nearly certain. He checks his pocket watch. Near to noon. Let the others run off like hares. He will catch them up soon enough.

The stove hisses pleasantly, puffs out green-smelling smoke. Two men—Yale-ites, Eugene assumes, for they are in no hurry to depart—

sit about it with their boots on the rails, hats low on their heads, their cheeks abulge with chewing tobacco.

The man busy at the counter looks gravely at Eugene from over the rim of his spectacles. He bids Eugene good morning and felicitations and introduces himself as Isaac Oppenheimer, provider of all supplies. Soon enough Eugene has bought a sack of dried beans, dried apples, lard, a filch of bacon, coffee, and four jars of medicinal brandy. "Best that you purchase as much as possible now, good sir," Oppenheimer says, and speaks of the prices further up the road in a tone of awe and fear that is best reserved for minor demons. "And how is your shot? Because you shall need much shot. To shoot your dinner and the waking bears. They are most fierce at this time."

"As would I be, Mr. Oppenheimer, if I were rousted from a winter's sleep with no victuals and no woman bear to warm me." Eugene says. He glances at the Yale-ites. They give no sign of having heard this witticism. The one is scratching his armpit. The other spits a brown steam into the spittoon.

"You shall also need mosquito netting. Mosquitoes on further miles are worse than the plague of locusts that the Lord sent against the blasphemous Pharaohs."

Eugene nods in appreciation of this colourful embellishment, decides he is enjoying all around this purchasing from Mr. Oppenheimer, he with his impeccable, ornate English that was most likely learned entirely from antique books. "Three boxes of shot then, and two lengths of your mosquito netting."

"And this? I shall assure you, it is the finest."

Eugene declines the plug tobacco, though he cannot help but smile. Chewing the finest plug tobacco is like chewing the finest dried leather boot. He debates telling Mr. Oppenheimer this, and then decides, no, it would damage their game. For Dora is correct; it is a game, the machinations of a deal. Not that there is room for bargaining here. A large-lettered sign over the counter warns against it.

Mr. Oppenheimer rests his elbow on the counter, lowers his voice so that Eugene must lean toward him, so that the others cannot hear. "You seem a gentleman who shall appreciate this." He pulls a rolled parchment from a leather casing.

"Ah, and what is this? My fortune?"

"Of a manner, sir. It is a map."

"A map?"

"It is the latest map of the wagon road. Drawn by a surveyor of the noble Royal Engineers, one of the very men who did forge a path through the great canyon."

"Is it so easy to become lost? Do I not merely trudge along?"

Mr. Oppenheimer *tsk tsks* as if Eugene asked if he should merely fly. He unrolls the parchment with reverence. "They say of this road that it is the eighth engineering wonder of the world."

Eugene peers closer. "Do they indeed?"

The map is beautifully drawn, the coastlines detailed as lacework, the place names in a precise hand. There is the great rough oblong of the colony of Vancouver Island. There, the colony of British Columbia through which the Fraser River meanders—spliced in places like torn fabric just above the 49th parallel, past New Westminster, past Fort Hope and Yale and then upward into the heart of the colony. As for the wagon road, it begins at Yale and follows the Fraser until, at Lytton, it joins a River called the Thompson. The road now follows this river until 47 Mile House, now heads on riverless past 70 Mile House, 100 Mile House, 150 Mile House and so on. Such dull names wherever they are marked from. Ah, but what poetry can be expected from engineers? The road ends near Soda Creek. Near where it joins again with the Fraser.

"From there you shall take another steamer, until here." Oppenheimer points to Quesnel. From Quesnel a fine line turns at ninety degrees into the stream-veined palm of the goldfields. "No more road. The way is hard here. A hundred miles yet on forest paths."

"Look here, your map is wrong. How can this possibly be called 47 Mile House? It is a quarter way along a near 500 mile route. That means that is wrong by . . . by a great deal."

"These are the mileages calculated from the Lake of Harrison route, from this outpost." Oppenheimer points to Lilloet. "It is not popular now. There is too much portaging, and too many high mountains."

"Ah, quite so. The confusion should be sorted out. Do you not agree?"

Oppenheimer does indeed.

"Well, what else? Lady Franklin's rock? How charming. Did you meet the grand lady when she visited the colony?"

"I did, yes, I did. She is like a queen. She tells me: 'Mr. Oppenheimer, I shall remember always your help and good store.'"

What is an adventure without a map? Even looking at it is somehow comforting. The distance from Yale to Barkerville seems short enough when it is laid out here before him on Mr. Oppenheimer's counter. The "forest paths" from Quesnel to the goldfields suggest a country stroll. Never mind the gaps where the road is not yet finished and the blank spaces that might be gigantic whirlpools or crevasses or barbarian kingdoms or whatever else the imagination cares to colour in. This only adds to its appeal. And he is one for maps. He recalls that now.

Eugene points to the goldfields: Lightning Creek, Williams Creek, Van Winkle. The string of towns: Camerontown, Barkerville, Richfield.

"Can you mark, my good man, where the treasure lies?"

Mr. Oppenheimer smiles. "If I knew such a thing I should be a rich, rich man."

"Hah, quite so, and now that I am quite supplied, I need a conveyance. A good horse would suffice."

Mr. Oppenheimer straightens his spectacles. One of the Yale-ites laughs, says: "Won't find a horse, good or otherwise. You'd best go see the blacksmith. He's got a molly, I hear."

The blacksmith brings her out blinking and bewildered into the sun, like someone long imprisoned. She is fat-bellied, the grey of a felt hat. The blacksmith pats her withers with his speckled hand, tells Eugene that she is a pack mule, owned previously by Cataline himself and didn't he care for her as if she were his own sister? She could get to the goldfields with her eyes closed and is alike to a mule the blacksmith had back in Toronto—affectionate, dependable, sweet-natured. He would keep her himself except that he does not have the space, nor the feed.

Eugene pretends a practiced eye. What does he know of mules? They are hybrid creatures, like griffins and chimeras. They cannot breed, poor sods.

"Is she sturdy?"

The blacksmith says she is indeed, leans his considerable bulk against her. The mule flicks her ears in seeming disdain and does not move.

"Quite so, and her hooves. Are they strong?"

"Strong and newly shod," the blacksmith says, lifting one of the mule's hooves to show him.

Eugene glances down. "And her name? Am I to merely call her Miss Mule?"

"Miss Mule. Hah! Call her that if you want. Her name, though, is Zuri. I think it means good in Cataline's lingo."

The blacksmith asks for forty dollars and when Eugene theatrically waffles he throws in an oiled canvas and an *aparejo*, which looks to Eugene to be nothing more than a leather sack stuffed with straw.

"Bring your supplies, I'll rig her for you. It's an easy business."

But it is not an easy business. Eugene has to make three trips back to Culky's, has to enlist the help of Culky's boy to carry the three trunks and several sacks. The blacksmith stares aghast at Eugene's pile of supplies. No amount of cajoling will convince the blacksmith that it is not too much for both man and mule to carry. Reluctantly Eugene returns to Oppenheimer's. Sells him the so-called unnecessary articles—the folding table, the games board, the tome on alchemy that he has not yet read, the top hat and box, even the third trunk itself.

"And what of the tent?" Oppenheimer asks.

"Won't I be needing it?'

"I would advise to sleep in the air if the weather is fine, to stay at the roadhouses when it is not. Such is best." Oppenheimer says, though for all his concern the price he sticks by is far below what Eugene asked.

Only now will the blacksmith show Eugene how to saddle the mule with the *aparejo* and then how to lash on the trunks and how to secure it all with a diamond hitch. The mule makes no protest except for a slight sinking, as if she were standing on soggy ground.

"Best carry your rucksack if you're able. Enough weight on her as it is. Hobble her at night. Let her forage for grass. Treat her well." The blacksmith glances at the sun. "The Spuzzum Ferry is eleven miles or so on. Roadhouse there's run by Duteau and his half-breed wife. She makes a fine stew. Likely you could make it if you left now."

"Spuzzum?"

"It's Indian for something. Don't recall for what. You'll find there's a lot of that around here."

What had he expected? Towering sentinels rigged up in gold miner's garb? A wayward, black-shawled fate? No, but he had expected some sense of a beginning. He looks back as he rounds a bend, can no longer see the high outline of that tire shrinking contraption outside of Yale, can no longer see any vestige of civilization at all. Thinks of Lot's wife. He is not one to criticize God's decisions. Yet it does seem rather harsh to have turned her into a pillar of salt for simply looking back. It is such a simple, human desire, and harmless withal.

But come now, Eugene Augustus, is not the canyon stupendous? In all your travels through Italy, France, even in your unwanted travels through the lands of the Ottoman Turks, have you ever seen a more ingenious road? Eugene has to agree with himself. He has not. The road, wide enough for a team of oxen, has been hacked and blasted from the cliffs. The bulwarking of rocks and logs is at times fifty feet high. No barrier guards against a wrong step. Not that Eugene trembles from heights. Once swung from a belfry on a dare. But this is different. The swirl of the river works a hypnotist's spell. And this is no Roman road that has proven its strength over centuries. This is so newly built that the cribbing logs are still paler where the bark has been ripped back. And how secure is that cribbing? If the road workers misplaced one log it could mean his death. The entire buttress could crack out from under him. Though it need not be so dramatic; a mere slip would do.

He steers Zuri closer to the canyon walls, tries to eradicate the image of himself pinwheeling into the gorge, his wail heard by naught but the birds and by this mule who would no doubt plod on without him, undaunted, uncaring. His body would be smashed beyond recognition. It would not be found for days, weeks, months, perhaps at all, and who would care in any case about one more lost miner?

He must write a note, yes. He will keep it in his coat pocket. It will explain who he is should his ravaged body be found. It will declare his love for Dora, instruct that all his worldly goods be left to her. He catalogues these worldly goods and comes up with a short list indeed. Ah, but at least his love is endless.

He stops and heaves off his rucksack. It has grown heavier in the preceding hours, has left a great blotch of sweat on his back, a cutting ache in his shoulders. He spreads the map on Zuri's haunches. They are the only souls in sight. If not for the fly-thick turds of oxen and other mules he might wonder if they are the only souls for a thousand miles. The canyon has that sort of eeriness. Has a green liquidity cut with columns of light, an ominous quiet but for the river roiling below. Pines and spruce cling to the dry cliffs, and the shadows of vast clouds stretch over the earth like those of monsters awakening. Where is this bloody Lady Franklin's rock? Her rock should be monumental. Something worthy of her epic search for her husband lost somewhere in the arctic ice. Would Dora search for Eugene with such determination if he should vanish? Or would she wait and wait for a return that never came, become a shadow from lamenting for him? Or would she curse his name, believing he had abandoned her? He doesn't know. He should know. Why hadn't they discussed such things?

He pulls on Zuri's bridle. "Come, damn you, the day has out-run us."

The road dips down and the river breathes out mist. Eugene recognizes fir, balsam, hemlock, maples: comforting trees that might speckle an English countryside. A bird screeches. From ahead comes the sound of rocks dislodging and splashing into the river. Bears? Lions? He hauls out his rifle. Are they being watched? Are Indians clinging to the cliff as stubbornly as the pines? And this mule. Is it possible she is slowing? Smacking her makes no difference. It is like smacking a stone.

"Move! Giddyup! Christ!" His shouts echo back to him. Zuri's ears do not even flicker. It is alike to the dreams where he must run but cannot, as if his legs were mired in molasses. Think of other things. What did Oppenheimer say? That this road is an engineering wonder. The eighth in all the world. But then anything built larger than a grist mill is called the eighth bloody engineering wonder of the world. Which begs the question. What are the other seven? The pyramids of Giza. Cheeps, no Cheops, the largest one. No, that is an ancient wonder. But engineering went into it. They must be the same. And the Colossus of Rhodes, so huge it bestrode the harbour. A lighthouse of some description. A temple. A tomb. And the hanging gardens, yes, of Babylon.

"How many men can name so bloody many? Tell me that, damnit."

Zuri answers with a great mournful blast, as if she has suddenly recalled some great tragedy. It startles a flock of small birds roosting in a copse of trees nearby. It certainly startles Eugene.

She haws again, ends it with a gasping sob.

"Quite so, are you finished? Zuri. It does not suit. Something tragic is what is needed here. Semele? Dido? Medea. Hah, what of Ariadne? Leading her Theseus through the maze. For I will be abandoning you as soon as possible, mark my words. And then you'll have something to mourn."

She flicks her ears. Eugene pushes her from behind to no avail. He hauls on her bridle. She shows her teeth, plods ever slower. Her nose. It shows white where the bridle has rubbed, where the ash once was. At least Eugene thinks it is ash. Not that it matters. What matters is that Eugene has been duped. He has bought an ancient mule, a mule ready for the knacker's yard. For dog meat. Why was he not suspicious? A mere forty dollars for such a prize of a mule? And an *aparejo* and oiled canvas? And hadn't that damned Canadian been over-eager to help him load her? As if to get Eugene on his way before he changed his mind. He could turn back. He has been on the road only four hours or so. He could demand the return of his money. But then he will still have the problem of how to haul his supplies. This decrepit mule was apparently the only one to be had in Yale. "You're lucky to get her," the blacksmith said. No matter, he will return her forthwith to the blacksmith and then reduce his supplies to the barest minimum. He has seen others equipped with one rucksack alone. Come now, Eugene Augustus, who ever returns money once a deal has been made? The blacksmith will merely say the mule had been nosing in the cold forge fire. No fault of his if Eugene could not tell an old mule from a young one. Green hand. Greenhorn. Useless son of the minor gentry.

"Christ's blood and damnation!" he shouts. "Son of a whore!" He curses the blacksmith and all his Canadian brethren—a drab people who will be forgotten by England, wrapped whole in the Yankee flag, and then popped down history's sewer. He curses all mules. A eunuch species, ignoble and traitorous. In no great tales do they figure, none that he can recall.

The echo of his shouts fades. He opens a jar of brandy and takes a steadying drink. Feels the warmth of it down to his boots. A flush of the old courage. Unrolls his map again. "You'll be lucky to make it to Spuzzum," the blacksmith said, no doubt chuckling inside. Yes, Ariadne is slow. She is old. She is most likely stone deaf. But she is moving forward. They are moving forward. The day is still fine. Steady on each and every day. You will make it to the goldfields. Only keep your wits, man.

He takes a great breath. "Come then, my girl. Let us get through this labyrinth." And so they continue, Eugene imagining them merely as two old friends, walking in the park, each pondering alone life's great mysteries.

Two or more hours pass. The light is fading in the canyon and still no sign of this Spuzzum Ferry and roadhouse. Again he checks his pocket watch. At a mile per half-hour or so he should be nearly there. He takes another swallow of brandy. Holds a measure of it in his palm for Ariadne. She licks it with greater enthusiasm than she has shown for anything else all day.

The road winds ever closer to the riverbed. The sky is a cobalt blue. Not a cloud. Hardly a wind. "We could camp, Ariadne. It is possible," he says with little conviction.

Ariadne nuzzles the brush by the road. Ridiculous, this chatting to a deaf mule. Next he'll be chatting to his pickaxe. His tin pan.

He tethers Ariadne and scrambles down toward the broad bank of the river. Drinks deeply from a pooled space and fills his water flask, notices, a short distance on, the smashed remains of a rocker caught in the river rocks, and a glinting in the trees just beyond. He wanders over. Ah, a forest glade. . . . Good Christ. That sweetish odour. He knows it. The road is hidden from view. Ariadne is hidden from view. There is the rush of the river, the rushing in his ears. A ferocious carved bear sits atop some nightmare creature. Poles with torn banners of calico and trade cloth. Spindly scaffolding hung with axes, pipes, bows, arrows, kettles, a wheeled toy. Atop the scaffolding are canoes. In them are bodies swathed and propped upright. One skull is near clean of flesh. Another is half-decayed. A third is intact but for its eyes, which are being picked out by the birds.

"Quite bloody so." He backs away, revolver in hand. Hears footfalls.
"Who's there! Goddamnit! Who's there? I'll fire. I'm well-armed!"
There, along the riverbank, passing not fifteen feet before him.

Indians. Thirty at least, including the children. They wear deer hide, blanket cloaks, trade bangles, beaded necklaces, calico. One man wears a scarlet tunic with epaulettes, another a linen duster. A woman wears a fanciful bonnet, its lace torn to shreds. They have rifles and long knives and carry boxes of goods from tramping lines across their foreheads. They pay him no mind, as if he does not exist. The breeze carries their odour of old leaves, earth, uncured hide. All except the very young are terribly scarred from the pox. Some have one eye that is milk-white, gelid. One woman is wholly blind. She walks with her hand on the shoulder of the boy before her. Eugene could call out *Klahohya* or *Tillicum*. At least one of them must know Chinook. He will tell them he is just a sojourner. Then what? No, they are not interested in conversation. They are not even speaking to each other. Eugene's mouth is dry. If they are hostile, he is doomed. Dammit all. This road is not a place for a man alone.

The man bringing up the rear is slightly built, stoop-shouldered. He wears spectacles, a trade blanket coat, the white of it now grey with dust, the edge stripes of red and green encrusted with dirt. His left eye is a hole, rawly healed. His right eye passes over Eugene, but he gives no indication that he has seen him. And it is not a trick of the thinning light. His matted hair is blonde, his skin dark from the sun alone. Eugene does not call out. Could not even if he wanted to. The people disappear 'round the bend. At that instant a boom reverberates through the canyon. Ariadne haws. Eugene drops his revolver and it clatters on the stones.

"And so you see Hank?"

"Is that his name? Then, yes, I saw him just several miles back. I saw an Indian graveyard as well." Eugene says this to Gerald Duteau, the caretaker of the Spuzzum roadhouse. Duteau glances to his wife who is busy at the stove. She ladles out a plate of stew and hands it to Eugene, instructs him to eat.

"My thanks, madam. I have never smelled anything so fine," Eugene says. He is not exaggerating. He has never been so ravenous. Still, he must concentrate on each bite so that he is not tempted to push the stew aside, so that he does not think of the half-decayed skulls, that sweet and sickening odour.

93

The roadhouse is a one room affair of whipsawn logs caulked with manure and straw. A greased cloth serves as a window, beaten earth for the floor. A fire cracks at the far end and throws shadows over the men already in their blanket rolls. The other men make room for Eugene at the sawbuck table. They are twelve or so all together, Oswald among them. He is picking his teeth with his knife. His boots sit beside him and his heels are bound with bloodied cloth.

"Fucking blasting," he mutters. "Fucking boots."

"It is not always meet to be in a great hurry," Eugene says. "You are familiar with the tale of the tortoise and the hare?"

"No I god-blamed ain't," Oswald says and spits into the fire.

"Ah, quite so, in any case . . ."

Duteau hands Eugene a glass of grog. "On house," he says, and then, after a pause: "And he look at you?"

"Who? Ah, the strange Whiteman. He stared straight at me, sir, but said nothing though I called to him. I said I was a friend in various tongues, but it was as if I had disappeared. Should he be rescued? Brought back to the fold of civilization."

"Christ's balls! He don't need fuck-what rescuing. He's gone Indian," Oswald says.

Duteau agrees that the man has. "He is from New York, this Hank. He came up in '58, with maybe eight more, all green hands. Maybe he was clerk or scholar. I don't know. But his friends, they leave him behind. That in '59. It different then. Not like now. Now it easy. Then we have no roads, no roadhouses, no good cooking like this. And in '58, it worse. Some Whitemen rape the Indian women and the Indians they chop off heads and send the bodies back down river, until us men, we march up river with guns and we make a peace. And in '59 we make own trails. In spring we go along the canyon walls like lizards because the water it toss a canoe like a leaf. The Indians they make boards narrow like hands and hang them along the cliff with the ropes of deer hide. So it is, what? A ledge, yes? But one time it break and a Mexican he fall long time, and the water swallow him and we never see him more. But of this Hank and his friends, they stay too late and winter coming. And this Hank he is sick and his friends they think he die so they leave him with a gun and water and food and go back with the not much gold they have. If they carry him they all die, maybe that what they tell him. After days the Indians come and these Indians pity this Hank and take him to their place. And this Hank he hate his friends for leaving him and he loves Indians now and he marry to one of their women and dress like an Indian and worships the spirits like an Indian."

"And what of his eye? And their eyes?" Eugene asks.

"That winter the pox it come and kill off half the tribe and Hank he take care of them, and some live, but near all have only one eye now and some are blind and most are scarful and ugly. And they put the muck-a-mucks high up with their goods and that is what you see, their graveyard with the old dead and the new. And they say it Hank's fault and that he make a spell because only he not getting sick. I suppose he have pox before or he lanced. And so they going to kill him or send him away—I hear two stories there–but he swears he an Indian and that he not speak English again and he not look at Whitemen again and he take a hot stick from the fire and he cut out his one eye, and now he think that he like to them and one to them."

"He is mad, poor man," Eugene says, and the other men voice agreement.

Duteau shrugs, says: "Now this tribe, none look at a Whiteman now. They say we ghosts, evil spirits, and if they not look at us we go away."

"A tribe of one-eyed men," Eugene says. "Better than Ulysses and the Cyclops."

"I never heard of him and a, whaddya-call-it, Cyclops," Oswald says.

"A Cyclops is a one-eyed giant. His name was . . . was. . . . Ah, it has slipped my mind."

"Whaddya blathering about, one-eyed fucknit giants."

"Ulysses."

"Grant's killing them whore-son rebs. He ain't fighting no one-eyed monsters."

"Hah, quite so. I see we are speaking at opposite ends. I am speaking of an ancient hero written of thousands of years ago. The hero was gone from his beloved wife for twenty years or some such and had many adventures in his returning. You, if I am correct, are speaking of the inestimable Ulysses S. Grant, hero of many battles against your Southern adversaries."

"There ain't no one-eyed monsters in America, see."

"Most likely not."

95

"If there were they'd be in for a holy fucking thrashing." Oswald says this as if daring Eugene to argue with him. Eugene chooses not to. Instead he calls for a toast. "For our first true day on this wondrous wagon road. What do you say, gentlemen? I am standing treat. Mr. Duteau, a glass of your finest grog for each of us here, and one for yourself and your lovely wife as well."

They toast the road, and then an end to the blasting which is holding up their passage, and then to poor Hank. The conversation saws back and forth across the table. The men sleeping are oblivious. Twice Eugene catches Duteau and his wife glancing at him and then each other. It makes him uneasy. He is not so far gone yet. Not compared to some of these others who look and smell as if they haven't bathed in months, who have the look of men born under hard circumstances, their fists forever curled.

Mr. Duteau makes his bed atop the bar to insure that no one has a midnight thirst. Mrs. Duteau hands Eugene another blanket though he has not asked for one. She smiles and pats his arm.

He tries to sleep amid the snoring, his head on his rucksack, his supplies near at hand. What do the Indians expect their dead will receive after all the preparations? A great blue river? Woods of endless game? What, for that matter, is the reward for the Queen's Prince Albert, stuffed with spices in his marble mausoleum? What is the reward for Eugene's dead parents and his three siblings, dead at infancy or in childhood, buried in the family crypt? What will be his? Furniture made of puffy white clouds? God's rays? Winged cherubs? Would that he could believe it.

ELEVEN

Another night in the Bastion Square jail and the men are snoring, the boy is crying in his sleep, and the idiot no longer seems a harmless presence, rather like a creature sucking marrow from fresh bones. How can the bastards sleep so easily? It is as if sleep were one of those small inconsequential actions, like pulling on your boots.

"How'd I dare do it?" the Dora woman stared at Boston, as if he were to have some idea, some reply. The sun was behind her now. At least three hours had passed since she had given him back his pouch with the money. She took her bonnet off. Filaments of hair wavered 'round her head, caught in some imperceptible breeze.

"I'd seen the dead ones, nudging up against the wharves. You get just a glimpse of a shoulder like, or a hand, or a bit of skirt. The water ain't where people are belonging. Cobblestones is where we belong. So how'd I dare get on that ship? I hardly believed this island were real. So, how'd I dare? Where'd I find the courage?" She waited, round-eyed, for a reply. Boston said he did not know and felt that brief lurching, as he always did when ships were mentioned, the watery deep. That was when he should have left. But he could not, not with her voice wrapping 'round him like twine.

Why, the thought of that fine man on his knees, telling her to join him in the British Columbias, that was where she found the courage. His beseeching gaze drew her on like a horse in harness.

Mr. Haberdale the Younger tried mightily to deter her from the voyage. She would be worked to death in the vilest of conditions. She would be sold into a brothel. She would die of ship fever.

"You must, that is, you truly must not go. I care for you, I mean,

I adore you, that is to say I love you, truly." He gripped her hands. His face contorted, became uglier yet. And then, actual tears. It was a most unfortunate sight. He asked her to marry him. Yes, he would descend to it to please her. He loved her that much.

"But it were too late. I was already decided. I told him he would soon enough find himself a nice radical lady who wore bloomers and spectacles and was pleased to spend her time in low coffee houses. Ah, I was cruel, and I felt bad enough right after. But it were like he saw someone else and not me at all."

A fine spring day. Sixty-two women and girls walk two abreast through the parish of Wapping, past the leers and hat doffing of the sailors and watermen and sack sellers, past the mute glance of a mud lark or two, their kettles sprouting bits of wood and iron. They walk past shops that sell telescopes and compasses and coppery instruments meant for measuring stars and wind and the angles of waves. She told Boston this as if he had no familiarity with sextants, chronometers, and quadrants, though he had traded such devices before. Four years ago he found a ship's compass half-buried in the sand of a lengthy shore. Near the compass was a mast speared upright and nearby that, a drowned man. Boston traded the compass for a month's worth of bacon and lard. He was thinking of telling her all this, but she was still speaking of the shops, the endless shops. Of slop sellers with their dreadnoughts and pilot coats, of shops reeking of tar and festooned with ropes. Some shops had true windows that showed a ghostly version of herself inside. How easy, then, to imagine herself with a neat cap and folded hands and saying "Yes, assuredly, sir, whatever you wish. Please, may I direct your eyes."

Mrs. Farthingham, shepherding them from the rear, tells Dora to fall into line. She is a Hussar's widow, is hefty-shouldered and kindly-eyed and possessed of a voice that can carry cross oceans. Dora easily forgives her abruptness. Has a harder time being charitable to Mr. Scott, the head chaperone. He is a sour-faced, untidy man with a wayward eye that forces him to look askance. It is unnerving, as if he is perpetually suspicious, as if he is about to accuse them of following him and plotting misdeeds.

"And then we were on the docks. Oh, Mr. Jim, the people watch the comings and goings at the harbour in Victoria like it were their sole entertainment, but the London Docks, it's where the whole world is coming and going. I saw blacky men and Chinamen. I saw a bird green as lime squawking on a man's shoulder. And then a whole gang of giant men with hair pale as a fairy babe's. They were wearing great blue coats and smoking pipes bigger than their fists."

Such clanking and groaning and shouting. Barrels stacked as high as a house. Vast warehouse doors with bolts thick as a man's leg. Odours of spices and coffee so strong one could live on the smell alone. Odours of rum so strong it seems there are underground rivers of it. And the vessels! Crowded all against each other as far as she can see. Masts high as Cathedral spires. Sails cloaking the sky and copper glinting and cargo swinging and gay flags cracking in the breeze.

They huddle near the dock gates while Mr. Scott exchanges gestures with a warden. The man holds out his hands to show his helplessness. Mr. Scott returns. Announces: "You cannot board until nightfall. The superstitious malarkey of sailors holds that spinsters are bad luck on board a ship. Thus it is best you not be seen parading about and causing trouble." Mr. Scott looks at them, askance as usual, as if pondering whether the sailors might be not far wrong.

They are directed to the benches outside a warehouse that is pungent with the smell of hides. The men waiting there for a chance at labour stand reluctantly so they might sit.

"I've never been to London before. I'm from a farm in Wiltshire," one Miss Joanna says. She has a large nose, a too-broad brow. She begins a jerky sobbing. Poor thing, Dora thinks, to be so homely and so alone. To comfort Miss Joanna, Dora tells of her own past, her family's lovely drapery shop, her days as a seamstress, now forever behind her. She speaks of the unsuitable Mr. Haberdale, of the suitable young man there on his knees in the brumous street, the absolute certainty that happiness awaits her, and awaits Miss Joanna as well. Dora's words are a success. Miss Joanna's sobs trail off. She begins looking about with great interest, then finds the courage to wander off and study a pile of tusks, and all before Dora can speak of the Antipodean twins. Dora turns instead to Mrs. Farthingham, but she is scanning the harbour with such a determined cast to her features it seems she might be seeing beyond the clamorous, seething wharf and so into their future.

They wait until singing from the public houses overtakes the shouts of the day labourers. In the dimming the vessels have become behemoths nudging against each other and muttering conspiracies. Dora's courage seeps away. "Look at our cargo of helpless women," the ships groan and creak. "What fools they are. What fools."

A cloud-striped moon is high overheard. Now they are allowed to approach the *Tynemouth*. The silhouettes of sailors shift and point. Keep a distance. Two lanterns shed a muzzy light over the plank.

"March across as if you are on a large plain, my dears," Mrs. Farthingham says.

"Don't dawdle. Don't look down," Mr. Scott adds.

Some of the women whimper. Not so Dora. She follows Mrs. Farthingham's example, holds her skirts high and plants one foot firmly before the other until she is on the deck. Helps coax the others across, watches the heaving aside of the plank, has barely time for a second thought before they are herded down the narrow hatch. At the suggestion of the Immigrant Ladies' Society Dora has left her hoops behind. She feels insubstantial with only layers of petticoats, and thoroughly unfashionable, but she is thankful for her decision now, watching as a mortified woman is squeezed through the hatch like dough being squeezed into a mould.

In the hold, ship's lanterns sway over bunks that are shielded from each other by grey canvas curtains. At the far end is a long, ridged table, and then their trunks. It will be a five to six month journey the secretary to Miss Burdett-Coutts warned her. Five to six months. Five to six months. It is a desperate refrain that Dora tries hard to keep at bay.

"All accounted for, Mrs. Farthingham?"

"Yes, sir."

"We have assigned bunks so as you do not quarrel. We will not abide quarrelling. You will have two meals a day and a draft of lime every other. You are to keep yourself clean and off the drink. You are not to fraternize with the other passengers. You are not to fraternize with the crew. You will be allowed out on deck in chaperoned groups of fifteen each. Each Sunday you will attend a service given by Reverend Holt. You are expected to be models to your sex. You are . . . now, what is that? Crying? Do I hear weeping?"

The weeping drops to a whimper. Dora cranes her neck and spies the four Grinstead orphans huddling behind the skirts of the older girls. One of the orphans is pressing her fist against her mouth. Her eyes are dark and large, an endless well for the tears pouring forth. The other three orphans hush her furiously. None of them seem more than twelve. All of them are miserable and thin, but none more so than this sobbing girl.

Poor child, Dora thinks. She nods at the girl and puts her finger to her lips, then suddenly wails out "Oh, me, ah!" and buries her face in her hands. The other women stand back as if fearing contagion.

"You're the weeper, then. Now what in God's name are you going on about. . . . What? I cannot understand you. What nonsense is this, woman?"

"Oh, me poor aunt, sir. Oh, I miss her so. Oh, she'll be so lonely."

Mrs. Farthingham pats Dora's shoulder. "There now, have some courage."

"You are not being held here against your will." Mr. Scott says. "You may leave and return to your aunt. The anchor is not to be hoisted for some hours yet."

"Ah, no, see, me auntie she's pa, pa, passed on. She's with the angels. Oh, gracious!"

"Then how can she be lonely?" Mr. Scott demands.

"Oh, ah, because she'll have no one to put flowers on her grave, gravestone, see."

Dora's hands are wet with real tears. It seems she might be able to convince herself that she truly does miss this phantom aunt. It seems she might be able to convince herself of just about anything.

Mr. Scott throws up his hands and continues his instructions. Dora looks over once more. The Grinstead orphan is staring at her with mouth agape. She is not crying; indeed, she is now nearly smiling.

"What's your name, love?" Dora whispers.

"Isabel Lund."

Dora takes to seafaring as if she'd been born to it. She does not retch and keep to her bunk as so many of the other women do. She can barely wait to be on deck each morning. Ah, the wind! It smells like something pickled and delicious. It smells enormous, if that were possible.

And what sights! Flying fish and spouting whales and birds with wings wide as sheets and all under a sky constantly shifting in shape and size and character as if part of some vast cosmorama.

"Are you not afraid?" the other women ask.

"Not a mite," she says. How can such a great vessel crack apart? And Captain Gringshaw—thick-armed and mutton-chopped, ablaze with brass buttons—isn't he the very picture of a captain? And look at the sailors swarming in the rigging, alike in comfort there as the gulls. When the ship plunges into troughs of waves she thinks of a swing in Hyde Park. What a delicious, shivery fear! That brief closeness to the sky. That swooping back to earth.

"You must have sea water in your veins," Mrs. Farthingham says with admiration.

A month out, the ship is afflicted with calm. The sails hang limp and the sun stretches hot on the deck. The sailors mend the ropes and slather metal rails with white lead and tallow. They keep their distance still, but the voyage has been blessed with enough good omens to balance out the women's presence. Porpoises have hurled themselves before the prow. An albatross followed them for a week. And so the sailors now wave to Dora and the other women when Mrs. Farthingham's watchful eye or Mr. Scott's walleyed one is momentarily elsewhere. The male passengers are becoming friendlier as well. They raise their hats and call out *good day*. For them, however, it isn't a fear of bad luck that makes them keep their distance, but a fear of their wives. Ah, well and so, Dora can understand the wives' thinking. For what sort of women would send themselves off to a foreign place to be taken up by miners and ne'er-do-wells or any man with a roll of banknotes? The several who hope to be governesses are acceptable enough, modest in their habits, books often in hand. But what to make of the Misses Finch, Hutchins, and Law? They saunter out on their chaperoned promenades in low-cut dresses and wink at honourable husbands, at not-so-honourable seamen. They make, in fact, no great pains to conceal their former, unmentionable profession. Just as unseemly is the Widow Dall. Two score and six and she has buried three husbands already. "I'll be onto number four, soon as I set foot," she says. "I'll outlive a hundred men." On several occasions she has been reeling drunk. When Mr. Scott or Mrs. Farthingham demand to know the source of her inebriation, she insists she is as sober as a judge she once knew, then laughs uproariously.

As for Isabel, she, too, has taken to the sea. Her cheeks are flushed with colour. Her dark hair has gained a thickness and sheen. In all she is possessed now of a curious, elfin beauty that others remark upon and that Dora is becoming quite proud of, as if she had a part in working such change. At dinner they sit side by side and giggle over the sliding plates, Isabel in awe, as usual, over the abundance of bully beef and hard tack. At night they share the same bunk, often whispering until hushed. Dora tells Isabel of her family's sad fate. Isabel tells Dora of the orphanage. Cold and grey. Grey and cold. She doesn't recall her parents. Her life is a slate, waiting to be chalked upon.

One night Isabel whispers: "Would you like a daughter, Miss Timmons?"

"What is that? Ah, well and so. Many daughters, hundreds and thousands of them."

"Let me be your daughter. Oh, do."

"Surely so, you are like a daughter, or a sister. When we are settled in the colony we will see each other often. We will go for ices. We will go shopping on a Saturday."

"You will not let them marry me off to an ugly old man."

"Issy, love, they're Christians. They'd not marry you off so young. They'll arrange a situation for you. Hasn't Mrs. Farthingham said so? You are to stay with a kind family in a fine house. Aren't the other orphans excited? You should be as well. In time you can choose whoever you like, from a hundred suitors, all handsome young men to be sure."

"I don't want to go into a situation. I want to stay with you. I'll work hard. I'll be a great help to you."

"Hush, now," Dora says, though she should have said: "Oh, for certain. We'll all live together and be like a family." But she will have trouble enough shifting for herself in this new colony, never mind taking care of another. Later, once the lamps are out, she hears Isabel softly crying. Her back is turned. It is a memory Dora will have to bear.

They sail through past the Bay of Biscay, the Canary Islands, Cape Verde, the weather holding fine. "Mark my words all. If this continues we'll arrive a month ahead," Captain Gringshaw announces. He inspects their quarters and asks how they are faring, nodding at their requests for more air, for better food. He gives seashells to the Grinstead orphans. Isabel's is particularly beautiful, is round and flat and bears the image of a many-pointed star. She accepts it with reverence, shows Dora how it fits perfectly in the palm of her hand.

The Captain is gallant to Mrs. Farthingham, but growing cool to Mr. Scott, takes him aside one day and can be seen shaking his head and pointing at an imaginary list. Soon after, Mr. Scott no longer draws the lock on the hold at night. But it is not just Mr. Scott's suspicious nature that likely irks the captain. Mr. Scott is growing more disreputable by the day. Untidy is no longer the word for him: slovenly, perhaps. Stains have blossomed on his trousers. His hair is uncombed, his hands grimy. And his eye. Is it possible it is more wayward than ever? "I'll be finding it in me soup next," the Widow Dall says, glaring after Mr. Scott as he makes one of his many daily rounds.

Boredom begins to afflict them all. Mrs. Farthingham orders a battle plan. The women are to help with the mending of the sailor's clothes. Short plays are to be put on; the governesses are to give readings. They read through *Mansfield Park*, *David Copperfield*, and *Vanity Fair*. Dora cannot bear to miss a chapter, likes Thackeray's Becky Sharp best of all.

"Don't be ridiculous. She is most unpleasant. Indeed, she is the villainess of the story," says Miss Katherine Paul, one of the governesses.

"But I like the part where she's leaving school. She's so brave. She's like us going off to who knows where. Trying out her fortune."

"The unpleasant part comes later, I assure you."

Unpleasant is a favourite word of Miss Paul's. She is a plain woman with thin hair and a constant sniffle. Mrs. Farthingham has put her in charge of improving the reading and writing skills of the women.

"Learning can be unpleasant," she tells Dora. And then later: "I have never had a more unpleasant task than teaching you to read."

"Ah, my mother tried as well. But the words, they crowd together when I'm looking at them. They switch places even. It's like they're playing tricks on me."

"You are being ridiculous again. You must simply apply yourself."

"Here, let Isabel read. She's doing so well, she is. She'll be a scholar soon enough."

The governesses work so hard that Dora feels that she, too, must do her part to alleviate the tedium. She tells the other women about the drapery, about Mr. Haberdale the Younger and his peculiar wooing. She tells them stories of her own devising and stories she has heard through others. The women listen and nod. "Thank goodness this is a long voyage. Or you might never get through all your stories," says Miss Joanna dryly. Dora agrees. She is full of stories, full of a numb kind of hope.

"Have you ever been feeling that, Mr. Jim? As if the future were a fine carriage waiting for you. All you need to be doing is step into it."

Boston said that he'd never been in a carriage, fine or otherwise, not adding that he'd also never dwelled on the future, that the past filled his mind enough.

"Ah, well and so," the Dora woman said and slapped at a gnat that was troubling her neck.

The jail is quiet now. The boy Farrow is no longer crying. The Dupasquiers are no longer laughing over cards. Even the snoring has subsided. No, he has never dwelled on the future, never thought past the next trapping season. But now he has no choice, what with his obligation to the Dora woman. Why would anyone dwell on the future? The future—unlike the past, unlike the present—is mutable and can expand to an infinity of choices. It is as vast as an ocean, and as deep, and is inhabited by every unknown thing.

TWELVE

By late morning of the second day rain curtains the canyon. Within the hour Eugene's boots are as live things. They squelch and burp; they chafe his toes; they slip out from under him, as if playing tricks. The rain fills the brim of his hat then sloshes off in small waterfalls. The anorak, bought in Victoria, guaranteed to keep Noah dry, is soaked through. The road, now no more than an extravagant ledge, churns with mud. The canyon here is perhaps a mere hundred feet across, has a sparser growth of nettled trees, is a tableau of wet browns and muted greens. Below are pillars of rocks inset like a haphazard staircase for some great, multi-legged beast. The dun river roils with spring melt. Foam hoists a splintered tree, hauls it down. The roar is a constant that would drive a man mad if he dwelled here. This must be the Upper Canyon, the Great Canyon, the Hell's Gate Canyon. This was where canoes, rafts, steamers, were smashed by the river's tumult before the building of the road ended the hauling of cargo by water. This was where the Indians ambushed miners and sent their decapitated bodies downriver. Back in '58, Duteau said. Not now. Now the Indians are appeased or else dead from the pox. Now they are apparently cowed into submission like Hank's tribe.

He puts Ariadne between himself and the river, glances above at regular intervals. Sings and whistles and hums. Is comforted when a group of men come up from behind him. He would like to fall in with them, but they are moving fast, with heads down, give only silent, hunch-shouldered greetings. Americans? British? Far-flung inhabitants of the Empire? Who can tell? In the blur of the deluge their rucksacks give them the appearance of lurching hunchbacks.

"I'd welcome a bloody cave at this moment, Aire, never mind a roadhouse." There was one not far back. A beastly looking place, but it would have sufficed. According to his map, Boston Bar is the next place that offers rest and repast. He repeats the words: Boston Bar, Boston Bar, trying to think of a suitable rhyme to put to song and comes up with nothing except *far*. The Duteaus might have informed him when it was best to depart. Otherwise he would not have moved to the spot nearest the fire as the others left at first light. He would not have indulged in more coffee and watched Oswald move with the heedlessness of a child's crank toy, nor watched the competent, comely Mrs. Duteau kneading bread. And when he was prepared to depart, Ariadne proved her muley nature and had to be hauled by both Eugene and Mr. Duteau onto that "ferry"—truly no more than a precarious raft—and even then she hawed as if she were being led to slaughter.

Eugene catalogues her sins—deaf, doddering, imbecilic, pug-ugly— voice raised above the tumult and the rain, rounds a sharp corner and nearly bellies up against a gang of Chinamen. They wear long tunics over trousers and conical hats veiled with rain. The blows of their pickaxes reverberate through the canyon. Just past them is a pile of rubble, evidence of yesterday's blasting. Several more Chinamen heave rocks into the river. One slips and shouts. His companion hauls him to safety. The one Chinaman in English garb directs Eugene and Ariadne over the rubble, past the other workers who are perhaps thirty strong. Mostly Chinamen, but also a few Indians, a few Whitemen. One of these Whitemen stands under the shelter of a rock. He is shaking his head in exasperation and holds what looks to be a yardstick. His scarlet tunic is soaked with rain. His pillbox hat has slipped to the back of his head and his high boots are slick with mud. A Royal Engineer! The Pride of England. Eugene might well have spotted a bird of paradise. He is that delighted, that amazed.

"Hallo, sir. Hallo! A fine job you are doing here. Fine, indeed."

"Keep to the inward side. The rain, man!"

"I thank you for your concern. By the by, could you tell me how far is it to Boston Bar?"

"What's that?"

"Boston Bar, the furlongs, the miles? Surely you would know?"

"Not there! Damnit, there!" He points past Eugene. Eugene turns. A Chinaman stops working and gazes sadly at his pickaxe as if it alone had offended the engineer.

"Good sir," Eugene calls "If the whole cliff must be cut asunder why should not the man start there?"

"Why not? Why not? Get on with ye."

"Hah, is it a Yorkshire accent I detect? I have friends from those environs."

The engineer does not seem to hear him.

Eugene is taking a breath to give his next shout force when a silver light illuminates the scene—the Chinamen assaulting the grey cliffs like gnats assaulting an elephant, the engineer wildly gesturing. Then comes a great crack and then a rumbling as if the earth were about to split in two.

Eugene crouches against the canyon wall. Hauls Ariadne close. Dynamite? Cannons? Damn the Yorky. There is that lightness in Eugene's skull, that hateful moth-like fluttering.

The rumble recedes.

"You might have informed me that you were about to blast! Indeed, sir, you might have."

"It's a storm, man, a storm! Not bloody blasting! Ye can't blast in a storm. Now get on with ye. Stay in the open, away from high points, trees and cliffs like. The lightning feeds on them."

"Ah, quite so, quite so." Eugene catches his breath. His palms ache from gripping Ariadne's bridle; his jaw aches from clenching. He would like to apologize for his brief loss of rationality, but the engineer has disappeared, the workers are hurrying off and he and his mule are alone in the storm like characters in a gothic tale.

Strange lightning. Eugene has never seen the like. It cuts the sky in parallel strokes. An agitating wind. A thrashing rain. He finds a low rocky overhang and manoeuvres Ariadne across the opening so she forms a sort of barrier, crouches behind her and is now grateful that she is deaf. The thunder does not trouble her in the least. Eugene, however, is startled by the massive booms each and every time.

The storm passes surprisingly quickly, leaves a trail of clouds, bushes laden with gem drops of water, and a column of ominous smoke in the distant hills. Eugene leaves the safety of the overhang and stretches his fingers into the burgeoning sun. He is bone cold and wet through. It is not the greatest discomfort he has experienced. The Crimea was worse, certainly, though all that seems to have occurred to a different man entirely. One of hardier mettle.

Boston Bar is a collection of perhaps ten buildings strung dangerously close to the river. A horse stares at him as he passes, a sow feeds on a trough of fish.

"What a blessing to come upon your establishment," he tells Mr. Moore, the owner of the International Hotel. "I was bloody well stormed upon."

"Weather has it in for ya, does it?"

"It does seem so, yes."

Mr. Moore bawls out for one Orvid to stable the fine gentleman's mule, then shows Eugene to a back room that is crammed with bunks. An open fire burns mightily at one end. Men are resting in their beds, others play cards on barrels. Socks and shirts and trousers festoon the bunk beams and ledges. The room smells of wet dirty boots, wet dirty men, wet dirty wool. It is hot as a baker's oven. Eugene looks about, sees no familiar faces. He might even welcome the sight of Oswald at this moment. Perhaps he need only engage the man in his own parlance. *Ain't*, Eugene silently practices. *You bet, Hey there, Damn blamed fucknit.* They might even become something like friends. Everyone likes Eugene Augustus Hume and it rankles that this Oswald seems to view him as a well-dressed cockroach.

Eugene strips to his sodden underclothes and turns himself this way and that before the fire like a choice roast of pork. Remembers Dora sitting by the fire, her skirt hemmed with wet. The hem began to steam as if a fire were beneath her skirts. He told her this and she said there was indeed and he was welcome to try to put it out.

Eugene faces the fire and shuffles closer. He clasps his hands before him, feels as he did when he was thirteen or fourteen and his organ had a will of its own. Thinks of his sister's governess and how she once leaned very close and rapped his knuckles with a ruler, not hard, almost lovingly. She had dark wells for eyes, a rosebud mouth. What hidden reservoirs of power they have, these women, these 'weaker' vessels. It was at that moment he realized this. His sister died of a fever not long after this. The governess he never saw again.

Halfway dry he sits heavily on his bunk. The straw mattress rustles under him, has that pungent odour of squashed bedbugs. He unfurls the map from its leather casing. Curses under his breath. The parchment is soft with wet. The rivers have become bleeding, spidery lines, the lakes pale seas, the place names blurred and unreadable. He hurls the map to the floor and a man striding by leaves his boot print on the island of Vancouver. Eugene holds his head in his hands. Picks up the map, stares at the gibbered lettering. Is this how Dora sees lettering? As if it makes sense and yet does not? Eugene can understand that. It is how now he feels about most things.

He makes better time the next day. The sun shifts through a pewter sky. The rain holds off. The road is grittier, sandier. Stands of poplar. Pines hunkered down like old men resting. Red-throated birds sweep low to the river that is broader now and tamer. A few miners work the bars, Indians and Chinamen mostly, silent at their rockers. The mountains are wedge-shaped, clay-coloured, sparsely wooded. The place now barely warrants the name of canyon. If not for the grouse he would say it were peaceful. Twice now they have exploded out of the brush and sent his heart pounding. Even Ariadne betrayed a nervous flick of her ears. Fortunate that she is nearly deaf after all and thus not given to tearing over hill and dale over a bit of bird, a bit of thunder.

By noon Eugene has stripped off his jacket. He tries singing a London drinking song but the full verses elude him. He is being made anew, that is it. The old songs no longer signify. He needs a song of the wagon road. *My feet are weary. My eyes are bleary. My darling dear is far from here. And it is four hundred miles to the goldfields, and. . . .* What rhymes with fields? It will come to him, surely. For now his mind is rubbed clean.

Past noon and he comes to a rough fence and a field of burnt stumps and then a stable and a barn and a peak roofed house. *Boothroyds Welcome Sogerners*, the sign says. A freight wagon waits there, the oxen lowing and dropping great turds. The wagon is nearly as high as a two-story building and is precariously narrow for its height. Astonishing that such wagons do not topple over in a breeze. He watches the swamper hammer at a man-high wheel. It is not a job Eugene would relish. Better to make a fortune at one fell swoop than spend years carting goods to and fro.

He drinks ale with a chaser of goat's milk and orders flapjacks and steak from a daughter of the place who makes no apology when he questions the prices. Indeed, she sullenly assures him that the prices will shoot upward with each yard he walks.

"Then I best have another ale, my lovely girl, and a brandy, yes, and a coffee." She stares at him and he pities her of a sudden, though he is not certain why. For the unfortunate brows perhaps, for the constant presence of loutish men, for some grim secret hinted at by the twisting of her hands.

He eats quickly, drinks quickly, compliments the cook, and then the girl herself, pressing a quarter dollar into her hand.

"What's this?"

"A tip."

"A tip? You ain't never coming back, so what does it matter?"

"I may come back, miss, I may."

"I won't remember you if you do," she warns, though she watches until he and Ariadne are gone from sight.

The sun glows unfettered. Eugene is pleasantly flush with food and drink. His rucksack seems lighter this day, hardly a burden. The landscape is dry, true enough, but has a simple, stark beauty he had not noticed before. And the birdsong, the air fairly trembles with it. He stands aside to let the freight wagon from Boothroyd's pass him. The bull puncher walks alongside the oxen, his goad stick over his shoulder. High above, the skinner sits against a backdrop of canvassing, his whip at a rest. He calls out something unintelligible over the rumbling of the wheels and lowing of the oxen. Eugene watches the wagon disappear from sight, then tethers Ariadne to a tree and walks into the low bush and pisses for a long while. He is walking back when a grouse erupts from the thickets. Eugene yelps and falls flat on his back. Clouds the shape of flat-bottomed scows sail across the sky. "Here lies Eugene Augustus Hume. Done in by a bird," he says and laughs for a time. That dear girl at Boothroyd's, she did serve the brandy with a generous hand, bless her. He stretches into the warmth of the sun, the sandy earth, closes his eyes for a moment, for two. Opens them to a lowering light. Jerks up to his feet. "Who's there!" He points his revolver here, there. Sees a badger, gamely digging a hole.

The darkness has gathered before he arrives at Salter's Roadhouse there at the base of Jackass Mountain. The oxen regard him, their breath billowing. About him are the silhouettes of outbuildings. The freight wagon that passed him earlier is nearby, its canvas lifting in the gusting wind.

He leads Ariadne to the stable. Unburdens and fodders her himself as there is no assistance to be had. At least he is gaining some practice at this stable-hand business. To some he might even look as if he knows what he is doing.

He dines on beefsteak and potatoes. He is ravenous once more. The conversation drifts about him, as do pipe smoke and cigar smoke and smoke from the hissing stove.

"It's a blessed thing, this road," says a Scot, one Red Olsen. "Once the bridges are done and all the rest, the prices will be coming down, mark my words."

"But there'll be more and more damned greenhorns. Every inch of the creek will be staked by July," says the one called Spitting Bob.

"This why, I think, it call gold rush," says the Dane, and the others nod as if he has spoken words of great wisdom.

Red Olsen. Spitting Bob. The Dane. Lancashire Morton. Thunderman the bull puncher. They are the names of characters in a penny gaffe. Or the names of men who are preparing to pass into legend. They talk of the war in America, the election of Douglas as Governor of both the colonies, his decision to disband the engineers. They debate which roadhouse is the most infested, and who bakes a finer pie: Mrs. Hautier at Lytton's Globe Hotel or old Mr. Ying at Clinton's Colonial. It seems it might have to be settled with pistols, but Salter soothes it over with the skill of an experienced diplomat.

They are now talking of mining, endlessly it seems. Blue streaks. Pay dirt. The special place in hell reserved for claim jumpers and spikers. They talk of the road. Of Jackass Mountain and which is the steepest grade of it. Didn't Cataline himself lose two mules on his last trip?

"I was pondering why it was called so," Eugene says. He has a mulled claret in hand now, feels his mood lifting, his tongue loosening.

Thunderman thumps his tin cup on the table. "It ain't called Jackass Mountain because it's a mule killer. It's called that because one of them highfalutin engineers tried to name it after himself. Was to be Huchins Hill or some such horse shit. So Salter here, and the rest about, said don't worry, sir, we'll make sure it's named after you. And when he left, Salter said from now on we're gonna call it Jackass Mountain."

The room erupts in laughter. The men applaud Salter who is hunched there by the fire, smiling modestly.

"Now the Judge," Thunderman says. "He deserves a mountain named for him, or a lake, but no, not those strutting popinjays."

"The Judge? He was here?" Eugene asks.

"Shore," Salter says. "Not but yesterday. We went hunting, him and me. By God that man can shoot the eye out of fool hen at fifty paces."

"Yes, Matthew is a fabulous woodsman," Eugene says.

"Matthew?" Salter says.

"Yes, the Judge. Matthew Baillie Begbie. I have dined with him many times. We both attended Cambridge, you see, and have much in common, our backgrounds, our ideals. I will be staying with him when I reach the goldfields."

This invites suspicious glances from a few, stories from the rest. Eugene listens closely. The Judge is apt to hold court in a tent with a stump for a desk, or even from horseback in wig and robes. The Judge swore in a Chinese miner by cutting off the head of a chicken. He translated Latin into Chinook for the benefit of an Indian. The Judge near alone keeps the law on the road and in the goldfields and has seen to the hanging of a good many miscreants. Don't the bravest men quail before him? Don't even faithful wives follow him with their eyes?

The conversation turns to the road itself. It is as if the wagon road is a country of its own—a long, thin country that is raw and new and ever-changing, certainly, yet at the same time complete with its own customs, costumes, legends, laws, and expressions, all of which are passed on to newcomers at these roadhouse gatherings the way such things are usually passed on at a mother's knee. And Eugene is part of it now. He finishes his claret. "I will tell you a story of the road."

The voices do not abate. The Dane is speaking of mule trains. Spitting Bob of remedies for scurvy. A good number are discussing the charms of Indian women.

"It is about a man named Injun Hank. It is about Indian graveyards, betrayal and sacrifice."

The gathering grows quieter; a log falls in the fireplace.

"You didn't see him, did ya?" Thunderman asks, for once his voice held low.

"I did assuredly. Why?" Eugene asks with a smile, then wishes he had kept silent. This curiosity. This restless seeking mind of his. It is a flaw, a fatal one perhaps. Of course if the wagon road can be seen as a country then it follows it will have its own ghosts and superstitions as well.

"Everyone who has seen that man has had naught but bad luck," Red Olsen says.

"Ain't even clear if he's alive," adds in the skinner of the freight wagon. He has been quiet until now. "Some say he's a ghost himself. That's why he can't see us. I warned you 'bout him, I did. I told you to keep your eyes on the road."

"I didn't hear you, sir. In any case, the warning would have come too late."

Too late indeed. An Irishman who saw Injun Hank near Rombrot's fell into a ravine not two days after. Before the road was built three Greeks saw just the shadow of him. They lost their way in the woods the next day. They survived the ordeal but the one could not cease shaking, the second hanged himself, and the third died of a mysterious sickness in Richfield that autumn. And then there was the Chinaman. Injun Hank stared at him as he was drinking from the river. A week later the Chinaman complained of stomach cramps and died spewing out black bile.

Eugene asks Salter for more mulled claret. Duteau might have told him of this superstition instead of merely exchanging nervous glances with his wife. As for Mrs. Duteau, she was not being solicitous because of his manners and bearing. She pitied him. Thought him a dead man walking.

The talk shifts back to mining. He borrows a candle lantern and steps outside. Ariadne is sleeping upright in the stable with three other mules. Their sighs are like those of souls in purgatory. He leans against a post. A horse stamps and neighs. Manure and earth. The smell of his own sweat. He looks at the black wind of the road beyond which who knows what lies. Imagines resting his head on Dora's breast. She strokes his brow. "There, there, my love."

"It's all stories, man."

"What! Ah, Mr. Salter."

Salter checks on the feed, then slaps Eugene on the back. "Men here drop dead regular as horses drop shit. All kinds of dying possible. One thing you can't depend on is old age. That thing with Injun Hank, it's a whaddayacallit, a coincidence. Been plenty men who saw him and didn't die. I know a few. But who wants to know about them, eh?"

"No one. No one at all. I quite agree. Exactly so."

They walk back to the roadhouse in companionable silence. At the door Salter says: "The trouble is, 'course, if he saw you. Looked at you."

Eugene attempts a laugh. "Ah, quite so. Are we speaking as old wives do, of evil eyes and such?"

"Evil eye in this case. He's only got the one."

"Quite so. Ah, he did look at me, yes. His eye, that is, was fixed upon me, though he did not seem to see. Sir, Mr. Salter, he is merely an unfortunate soul left to wander the earth with heathens. You do not truly believe . . ."

"No, of course not. Hume, was it? I'm to bed now. I advise you get some shut-eye, too."

"My thanks, but I may enjoy the stars for a time. They are remarkable."

Salter looks upward, puzzled, then ducks through the doorway.

Eugene tilts his head back. There is Orion the hunter, slain by the huntress Diana. There is Cassiopeia who boasted too much of her daughter's beauty. And there the Seven Sisters. What is their story? He can't recall and does not wish to. The starry heavens are full enough of the outcast and the damned.

THIRTEEN

At the crossing of the equator Captain Gringshaw invites the entire party of women up on deck. They are in time to see Neptune clambering over the side. He is dripping seaweed and holding a trident and is surrounded by all his seaman helpers.

Boston scratched his ear. "A God, was it," he said because he had said nothing for a long time now.

Dora laughed. "Oh, no, don't worry, it weren't the real Neptune but a petty officer all got up. And the tribute, you know what that was? No? Beards! The soap smelled something horrible and had tar in it. They grabbed a young man first. Afterwards his face was all covered with bloody nicks, ah, but he was a fine sport and said he never had a better shave. Next they got a hold of some gentleman who had a coppery beard right to his belt. He was livid and kicked and yelled and said what a disgrace it was. Neptune showed no mercy at all. But that's fitting for a Sea God, aren't you thinking? And so off came the beard, and don't you know it but the gentleman actually wept."

Mr. Scott is also held down and shaved. This does nothing for his mood, which has been growing more foul by the day. No, they would not be allowed up for that evening's festivities. Later they hear the thump of dancing feet, an accordion, a fiddle, the hoots and laughter of the passengers and crew.

Miss Hutchins: "We should be let up. We ain't livestock."

Miss Paul: "It would not be unpleasant."

Miss Joanna: "We need good clean air."

The Widow Dall: "Air? We need men is all. Ain't that why we're here?"

Mrs. Farthingham sets off to ask Mr. Scott for his permission.

She returns after an interminable wait. "He relented, my dears, after a long assault. But he says he will not attend. He says, indeed, that he is no longer the champion of your virtue. I, however, have every confidence that you can champion your own."

The women clap their hands. Some even *hurrah*. Now Dora envies those who have brought their hoops and left them hanging like great birdcages at the end of the hold. Such a delight it would be to have them bump and sway as she danced. No matter, Dora is determined to enjoy herself. Never has she seen such a radiant moon. Never has she heard such a hearty cheer as when they come out of the hold, as gracefully as the ladder allows. Mrs. Farthingham is soon enough dancing with Captain Gringshaw and takes little notice of what is happening to her charges who are as fuel to a fire. The Misses Finch, Hutchins and Law dance without ceasing with the sailors and gentleman passengers alike. The Widow Dall holds court with three gnarled sailors. A bottle glints in the moonlight. Well and so, Dora is not one to point fingers. The Widow Dall seems happy enough in the part that has been allotted her.

Dora dances until her feet ache. She dances with the first mate, the cabin boy, the midshipman, and then with the young man who was so sporting when shaved by Neptune. And she dances with Isabel, dearest Isabel.

"How can I tell you what came next?" Dora said to Boston. "Oh, it is terrible, terrible sad."

How to tell? Let the words pour out of their own accord. It seemed to have worked until now. Boston studied the crescents of dried mud 'round his boots. Dora sniffled. He had nearly risen when she said: "The Horn. That's what they call it. The cauldron of the earth. Oh, I had never imagined such skies. The clouds were all purples and browns and sickly yellows, and the winds were moaning, and the sea heaving. It was like the very world were bruised and raging with fever."

Boston sat back down. He was mildly curious as to what happened next. There would be a death, he presumed, or several. And then he would leave. The sun was still above the trees. There was still time before dark.

Had he heard of the Falklands? Yes? Rocky scatterings in a slate-grey sea. Blacky men paddling low, thin boats. A stubby-winged bird that flies through water but cannot through air.

They are allowed off ship for the first time in months. They gawk at the wares in the streets of Stanley. At the Governor's mansion they feast on mutton, oysters, trifle, tripe. Afterwards Isabel holds her stomach and groans. She proclaims that she has never been so happy.

"Ah, now, there will be much more of this happiness business," Dora assures her. "Now sleep, dearest Issy."

It is while at anchor in the Falklands that a gold watch disappears from the cabin of Mr. and Mrs. Parfield, passengers en route to San Francisco. Mr. Scott orders Mrs. Farthingham to search through their charges' belongings.

"My girls are not thieves," Mrs. Farthingham says. Mr. Scott glares at her askance. He raves. She holds her ground until the victory is hers.

"You may bear responsibility for bringing pickpockets and thieves to the colonies, then, Mrs. Farthingham. I shan't and that's that."

They leave the Falklands on a calm day, under a sky the colour of champagne. Dora knows champagne now, having drunk it for the first time the night before. That Sunday they gather on the foredeck to hear the sermon of the good Reverend Holt. He speaks of God's love while clouds amass overhead and a wind tears at his beard.

Now the sailors are lashing things down and clambering in the rigging. The first mate bellows orders through a speaking trumpet. The cabin boy crosses himself.

"Passengers to your cabins!" orders Captain Gringshaw. "You women to your hold!"

They descend into wobbling pools of lantern light. Mrs. Farthingham's fearless voice tells them to have faith in the worthy Captain, in the good Lord. She has lived through storms and battles. This is nothing. "Come now, we must prepare." They secure everything that might shift, then lash themselves to their bunks with sheets. Now Mrs. Farthingham extinguishes the lanterns, citing a danger of fire. She does this quickly, but not before Dora sees her white face, her trembling hands.

Tempestuous. Basterous. Dora understands these words now. A trunk jars loose and hurtles against the walls, exploding out petticoats and underthings. Above is a hideous screaming. "Just the rigging in the wind, just the rigging in the wind," calls out Mrs. Farthingham. The women weep and pray. There is the abrupt stench of vomit. Rats scuttling down the passageway are tossed high. It is no longer like a swing.

There is no certainty of being pulled down each time, no glint of sky and glory. The rolls are so great that the ship stands near on end. It shudders and lurches. Dora longs for some light to hold back the darkness. What is it like below the seas? She cannot imagine the depths. How very cold it must be. How cold she is now. "You must have sea water in your veins," Mrs. Farthingham said. It made Dora proud, now the thought only terrifies her, as if the sea were coming to claim her for its own.

Isabel clutches at Dora. Dora checks the knotted sheets. "Hush, dearest. Think of your fine house. Think of apples, of mutton and meat pies." She tries to say more but her throat is too dry. If she survives she will never leave land again.

For two days' entirety they are heaved and tossed. Finally an hour of calm, a harbinger that they have passed through the worst. "Praise God," someone says. Is it her? She is not certain. She is only certain that something is wrong. Her hands are sticky, as if covered with blood. Her eyes flicker with pain. The swing lifts her high. She kicks at the clouds. They break apart and scatter.

Three of the women take sick, five of the regular passengers, two of the crewmen. The ship's doctor orders calomel and bleeding to flush out the fever. The air of the Falklands is blamed, the food at the Governor's table, the storm itself for bringing malignant air from heathen lands. Dora's throat is made of wool and straw. The cloths on her forehead are heavy as bricks. Mrs. Farthingham murmurs encouraging words. Isabel caresses her cheek. Her face is pale and shimmery, as if submerged in water. "Take this, Miss Dora. Take this. It's for you. It's my best thing."

The object is smooth, round, has a coolness. Mr. Parfield's watch!

"No!" Dora shrieks. "No, I don't want it! I'll be blamed! I'll be blamed! Go away. I don't want you here!" Isabel is crying from far off. Dora remembers little after that. Did she call poor Isabel a thief? She might well have. When the hold finally settles into solid form, Isabel Lund is nowhere to be seen.

Mrs. Farthingham's strong voice wavers as she tells her: Isabel caught the fever not long after Dora did. She died the previous day. The Misses Finch, Hutchins and Law glare at Mr. Scott as if he were to blame. Miss Joanna is again lamenting for the green fields of Wiltshire. Miss Paul says she had never known such a fine pupil as Isabel, nor one as pleasant. The other Grinstead orphans sob and cling together, terrified that they might be next. Dora weeps and weeps. She says nothing about Mr. Parfield's gold pocket watch, though fears it will soon be discovered among poor Isabel's things. Perhaps Dora should not have refused it. She could have taken it and then returned it quietly to Mr. Parfield. She could have said she found it. Ah, she would not have been believed. She would have been keelhauled, her prospects ruined, the clear path to happiness blocked.

Most of the passengers attend the funeral, as do most of the crew, and all the women, and a vast quantity of birds that bob behind the ship like a procession of hired mourners. A light—silvery and lambent—falls upon the ship just as the Reverend Holt consigns the body to the waves in a wrapping of sail. All agree: never have they seen such a peculiar, beautiful light.

"We arrived that September," Dora said, her voice halting. "How I longed for Isabel. I missed her so greatly and felt so badly. I hardly cared to hear the cheers when Esquimalt was finally sighted."

The dock is stuffed with men in their sartorial best. Some row alongside the *Tynemouth* and attempt to clamber on board like love-lorn pirates. Unfortunate that the Widow Dall, who has been saying a long goodbye to her three gnarled admirers, has to be carried off reeking of gin. Dora's turn and she steps onto the dock in her damask dress of green and yellow stripes. Hands reach out. There is the odour of peppermint and sweat and the distinct smell of land—earth after rain, horse droppings, the scent of flowers held tight in the fists of the hopeful. She tries to ignore the faint buzzing in her ears, the failing of heart. How Isabel would have loved to see this. Dora looks through the crowd. A dozen pairs of eyes catch hers. Hat are swooped off, great smiles given. She cannot help but smile in return. It is like she is royalty arriving. When will she, the daughter of a costermonger, when will she ever again be so cheered and heralded? The order of things is easily scrambled in this place. That much is already clear.

They stay that night in the Marine Barracks. In charge is a young naval officer with a chin beard and a high broad forehead. She is reminiscing about the voyage with Miss Joanna when he calls for attention, standing before them as ramrod straight as if he were clasped between two boards. "Welcome to Victoria, ladies. I am Mr. Edmund Verney, the head of the female immigration committee. Please, I must begin with a warning: this is not London. You will find that masculine manners here need some refinement. I must beg you not to wander from these quarters. This is for your own safety. Some of your number have already gone into their situations and within a few days you will all be placed. Now, you will be pleased, or rather I am pleased to inform you that a Regatta will be held in your honour on the morrow. There will be boat races and prizes, refreshments and victuals."

"What about our rich husbands, then eh?" shouts the Widow Dall.

Mr. Verney turns a pinkish hue. "Please, ladies. I hope you have not been led too far astray in your hopes. There are more poor men here than rich. More vulgar than refined."

"What about you?" Miss Finch calls out. "You're a handsome one. You needing a wife, then?"

The women laugh and crowd in closer to Mr. Verney. Mr. Verney steps back. He might be a cat in water, so completely is he out of his element. "Let's give a hand clap for Mr. Verney," she calls. "And three cheers for the committee and all their work!" The women obligingly clap and cheer. Mr. Verney bows and then hurries out the door, knocking his head on the transom as he does so, to the great merriment of the Misses Finch, Hutchins and Law.

Dora is about to take her rest when Mrs. Farthingham approaches her. "I retrieved these from Mr. Scott as you asked, dear. It wasn't easy. He kept saying as how the girls were his charges and his responsibility. Do you know, I believe he feels a little badly. Ah, well, I enlisted the Captain in the campaign and was at last successful."

She hands Dora the bundle of Isabel's things. Inside is a night shift, a comb, and a round flat shell, cool and polished, with a star pattern upon it. It is the very shell that Captain Gringshaw gave Isabel and that she treasured. Dora remembers that now. She stares at the shell. Hefts it. Yes. It is the size and shape of a watch. It is a mistake that anyone in a fever could make. It is a mistake she will never forget.

FOURTEEN

June 12, 1863

D*earest Dora,*
If by chance a century or two hence travellers on this road should
stop at the thriving village known as The Forks over which the flag of
the French presides & if they should seek respite from the frowning
sun at the meeting of the impassioned noble Fraser & the calm
beauteous Thompson & if they were to sit amid the smiling grass, under
the embracing branches of a great, gnarled pine & if these denizens of
the future (let us make them lovers) should glance upward they will
see, carved into the trunk of the aforementioned tree, the names of Dora
& Eugene, the E of which is hooked artfully through the D, & beneath
the date, the year of our Lord June 12, 1863, & they will then gaze
again upon the Fraser River, so brown & muscular & then upon the
phantasmagorical blue of the Thompson & see how it is like a vast
shimmering ribbon in this tableau of hot sands & wind-swept ochre &
they will see in this meeting & mingling a uniting of the power of their
own love, which is inspired by ours, lovers of a century past, & thus carry
onwards, ennobled!

"Not finished?"

"A moment more, I beg you, monsieur."

"Perhaps more ink?"

Mr. Barnard holds out a small glass pot. He is a handsome well-attired Québécois with a neat beard. Nearby a sorrel horse noses the sparse grass, its hide agleam with sweat.

"Ah, quite so, my thanks. It is no simple task to write upon a rock."

"Perhaps you need assistance in composing? I have good skill and charge a small fee only."

"I believe I can manage. Merci, and such."

Barnard gauges the sun against his pocket watch. Nods, pleased, as if he and the heavenly bodies have some mutually profitable contract.

Eugene rereads his paragraph. Yes, he can see the tree as clearly as if he had indeed spent the afternoon inscribing it like a ham-fisted monument carver.

Dearest Dora! Remember our tree! Remember that your love is
a beacon that holds me safe until my return!
  Your dearest, most loving, Eggy.

Barnard folds the letter expertly and slides it into a gummed envelope and then into a bulging saddlebag at his feet.

"That is a quarter dollar for the paper, another quarter dollar for the envelope. Two dollars for the delivering of it. The ink is gratis, sir. And so, altogether it is $2.25."

"What? For a missive? I could purchase a meal, a brandy, a crock, no several crocks of grog for such a price."

"Ah, but is price of the Cariboo. And I, sir, I am the Cariboo's only postman."

Eugene counts out the coins. He should have shrugged in incomprehension when Barnard rode toward him and called out for letters in four languages. Astonishing how quickly money can be spent on the road. He has sworn to be more frugal, but it is not easy. A man must have food and refreshment. A man must have a place to sleep. True, he need not have spent the entire Lord's Day eating and drinking at the Globe Hotel at The Forks, but the food of the sad-eyed Madame Hautier was famous and justly so; he could hardly pass it by. He congratulates himself for not writing of it to Dora. For she might see in his rapturous description of Madame Hautier's cooking a sly attack on her own, which, in truth, was abysmal. Her butter is nothing but runny gobs, her flapjacks hard as flagstones.

Barnard mounts his horse with a parade ground flourish. "Trust in the BX!" he calls out and leaves Eugene in a shroud of dust.

The dust subsides. Eugene mops his brow. Ariadne nibbles fastidiously at a sagebrush. It is mid-morning and already it is a glaring, un-English hot that is melting his patience, his good humour. There are sparse glades of pines, clumps of cactus, and tumbleweeds made animate in the crosswind. There is the blue of the Thompson below, an uncertain breed of carrion bird above, and all about, bare and dun-coloured hills that look to have been newly poured from the sky and left to bake and crack open in the sun.

Eugene feels himself recede. He is at the vanishing point, not the centre. Nothing is the centre here. He hauls at Ariadne's bridle, suppresses an urge to pound her. Since leaving Yale, they have been passed by all manner of travellers—innumerable miners with barrows and rucksacks and mules, the precarious ox wagons, a mule train, a battered horse-drawn carriage, stuffed to its roof with cargo and men, even a one-legged, scurvy-mouthed man who hobbled past Eugene on his wooden leg and spouted prophecy and doom. Most astonishing, however, were the two women of late yesterday afternoon. One had skin black as ebony and wore a broad straw hat aflutter with ribbons. The other had rouged cheeks and plaits of ashen blond. They were riding astride sturdy horses, a sole male escort. Their skirts, free of crinolines, rampant with colour, flared out as their horses trotted by him. Such a delightful contrast in the dull landscape, alike to a stained glass window in a stone church where a parson is droning on.

"Come to see us in the gold towns!" they called.

Eugene raised his hat. "I may indeed," he called, but his voice was caught by a gust of wind and he was left jawing in their wake.

Ariadne stops, twitches her ears. Clang of a bell mare. The clanging increases and now comes the mule train, the largest Eugene has yet seen. The mules carry boxes marked "Dynamite," "Champagne." They carry sacks of flour, sugar, salt, a stove, a door, even a plate glass window held steady by a Chinaman. There are three well-armed Indians and a second Chinaman, an older man, walking alongside a sixth man who is the famous packer, Cataline the Basque: of this Eugene is certain. He has long moustaches and long black hair, wears a clean collarless shirt, a thick belt and high black boots. He greets Eugene in a mixture of bad French and worse English. Ariadne nuzzles his chest. He strokes her neck. "Zuri," he says with an expression that is both surprised and pleased. It is, Eugene thinks, as if he has come across a beloved elder relative who should have died years before.

"Am I to understand that you owned her once, sir? If so, perhaps you could enlighten me as to her age."

"Zuri. Ah." Cataline says and runs his hands over her knees, lifts her hooves, shakes his head in wonderment, now points up the road and mimes a vast load.

"She is managing fine. I am carrying no more than others are. Indeed I had to sell much of my supplies in Yale. I received nearly nothing for them."

Cataline looks at Eugene as if he doubts his intelligence, then adjusts Ariadne's straps, strokes her muzzle, walks on with his tireless walk. The mules crowd past Eugene. Several nuzzle Ariadne. She haws mournfully as the last dust from their hooves disappears into the funnel of the road.

For the next three hours he does not see a living soul except a red fox and some creatures that might have been a species of giant rat. His shirt is stained with sweat and his feet ache hotly in his boots. He looks down from the height of a great bluff to the swale below. Sees the frothy blue of the Thompson, a semblance of green along its banks. Before him is a crude gateway formed by two great rocks on either side of the road.

"Should we take a rest when we reach the bottom, eh, Arie? The current looks mild. We could swim, paddle about like ducks and such."

Ariadne haws madly, rears up. The *aparejo* slides to her withers. Pans clank. A bottle smashes to the ground. Eugene grabs her bridle rope. It tears through his hands. The stench strikes him like a fist.

"What the bloody damnation!"

Nothing will surprise him now. Nothing. If Christ and his attendant angels walked by in miner's boots he would merely bid them good day. And if the sky rained peaches and cream, why, he'd merely help himself to a bowl full.

They barricade the road, as if doing so were part of their normal inclination. Their mud-shaded fur is sloughing off and dangles from their knobbly knees, their serpentine necks, their double humps. Bears he could understand, wolves, pumas, but camels? Why not elephants? Why not unicorns?

"Well now, beasties. This is desert-like country, true, but if I am not mistaken you are out of your geography. Have you escaped from your turbaned masters? Escaped a zoo?"

They swing their heads and stare at him like vicious dowagers. He had not realized camels were so large. Bigger than a horse, than an ox. They are, indeed, about the size that Cataline was attempting to express. Damn him. He could have given better warning.

The nearest one spits and a yellow-green blob splatters on Eugene's shirt.

Eugene steps backward. The camel advances. Eugene hauls again on Ariadne's bridle. Her eyes are wide as billiard balls and she is rooted to the spot. Two other camels appear behind him. To his right is a precipitous incline. To his left a steep bank. What is it about camels? Or are they dromedaries? Years without water. Ships of the desert. Something biblical, something about knitting needles and a rich man. Why didn't he write it down? Because he is not a naturalist. He is an adventurer, damnit, but camels were never in the plan.

The largest one lunges and snaps its yellow teeth a few feet from Eugene's chest. Eugene yells and staggers back. Ariadne now bolts up the bank, showing a dexterity at which Eugene will later marvel. He, too, clambers up the bank, loses his footing in the shale, slides back. Hauls out his revolver.

Eugene's appreciation for comedy stops short at the manner of his own demise. A taste of vomit is in his mouth, a flighty beating in his chest. Should he charge through them? Shoot the leader and hope they scatter? Yet that may provoke them to charge en masse. Better he walk through them iron-eyed. They might be like dogs, who won't chase the fearless. Great God! Is he afraid of camels? He who has braved the road alone for these twelve days? Who braved a sea voyage? The wilderness of the Cowichan? Who has fought in the Crimea, for Christ's sake!

He raises his arms. "Get thee gone, you wretched beasts!" It seems the right thing to say, seems they might even vanish in a puff. They do nothing of the sort. Their stench envelops him like a vile blanket. He is surrounded. He is aiming his revolver. He shuts his eyes, and as he does the shot resounds. The six camels are trundling off. The seventh, the largest, the most dastardly, lies thrashing in the road, a bullet in its neck, the blood forming a great pool. The revolver is hot and smoking in his hand. He is quaking. He has not shot a gun since the Crimean. He has not killed anything since then. Would that he had companions. Someone to joke away the incident. It is difficult to be brave alone. "Bugger it. Fuck it." He walks closer to the beast, reloads with shaking hands. Eugene wishes the sound the beast is making could be called inhuman. But as he knows well enough, there is no end to the tortured sounds that humans can make.

He shoots the second bullet between its eyes, looks away up the road, to the two great rocks that seem now like the sides of a giant vice, looks to the birds that are already settling in the nearby pines, eyeing the carcass.

The nearest roadhouse is owned by a Mr. and Mrs. Barrymore of Devon. They tell him, with little enthusiasm, that he is their first and likely only customer of the day. No wonder, Eugene thinks, what with only a small sign that points down a lengthy, rough path and no sign of life at the spartan building in the shadow of a barren hill. Only after several bangs did the door creak open to show Mrs. Barrymore, lantern-jawed, sun-browned, a blackish dress sagging on her frame. Not a young woman and never a beauty. Still, she is decades younger and far preferable to the white-haired Mr. Barrymore who is turtle-ish in his movements, laboured in his breath.

"Dinner will take some doing," Mrs. Barrymore says without a hint of apology, and so Eugene tends to Ariadne, cleaning her scratches and feeding her tender shoots of grass found thriving 'round a stagnant pond. She presses her muzzle to his chest. Eugene wraps his arms 'round her neck and they stay in that attitude, propping each other up until the mosquitoes become bothersome and a chill breeze cuts through.

Mr. Barrymore is at the table poking at a collection of feathers when Eugene returns. Eugene sits opposite him. Mrs. Barrymore stands rigid over the stove and throws bacon hissing into the pan. On the wall is a large portrait of the Queen in her mourning cap and widow's weeds. On the table, floor, shelves and window ledges are heaps of well-handled books. Framed in the kitchen window are two small and well-tended graves.

"Good you shot it," Mrs. Barrymore says. "They're evil, those beasts."

"Not evil, my dove, an animal cannot be evil," Mr. Barrymore says without looking up.

"They're worse than evil. They're always biting their handlers and terrifying the horses and the mules because of their evil smells and evil ways."

"One should blame Mr. Laumeister, my darling, not the camels themselves. He is the one who brought them here."

Mrs. Barrymore hands Eugene a plate with crumbling biscuits, burnt bacon, a round of fraying meat.

"It's all we have. I hope you're not particular."

"On the contrary, madam. It makes me feel quite at home."

"That German, Lomister. He was the one who brought them here."

"Mr. Laumeister, my dear, and he is an American."

"That Lomister said they were stronger than mules or horses and they don't need water, just air."

"No animal subsists upon air, my sweet, not forever."

"On air, and people's shirts. They rip them right off your back."

"Ah, so they are not wild?" Eugene asks.

"No, but Lomister's letting them full loose soon enough."

"Laumiester!" Mr. Barrymore shouts. He hurls a feather, watches with dismay as it drifts leisurely to the floor.

Mrs. Barrymore smiles faintly at Eugene. "Don't trouble yourself, sir. We won't say a thing if Lomister comes asking around. Evil beasts. Evil god-forsaken country."

She pours Eugene a coffee. Eugene looks hopefully to the door. The light is gone. A howling begins somewhere in the hills.

"Aha, *Canis latrans*, the coyote," Mr. Barrymore says, looking greatly cheered.

A second howler joins then both cease abruptly as if embarrassed at beginning before moonrise. Mr. Barrymore's enthusiasm vanishes. He stares at his feathers. His harsh breathing fills the room.

"Madam, may I ask if you have any stronger refreshment? Claret? Brandy?"

"All I have is whiskey, if you're not too particular."

Whiskey. Again. After Yale he had sworn to avoid it at all costs. But he needs bulwarking if he is to survive in this cesspit of despair.

Mrs. Barrymore fills his glass and sets the bottle before him. Eugene reiterates how the camels came charging at him like a herd of maddened bulls. "But I stood my ground, friends, and took down the leader with one shot between his eyes."

Mrs. Barrymore pours a small measure in her own cup, mentioning that it helps with sleeplessness and ague, then says: "I wish you'd shot the evil lot of them."

"I was fortunate that my mule was unharmed except for scratches from being entangled in the brambles. Still it took me several hours to coax her down from her hillside sanctuary. If she had been harmed I would have had to seek out this Lar, Lor, that German-American fellow and demand compensation. Yes."

At this Mrs. Barrymore bursts into sobs and rushes out. The door creaks shut behind her. Eugene sits wide-eyed and certain that he is far too tired for any dramatics besides his own. "I offer my apologies, Mr. Barrymore, and my . . . my condolences for whatever is the cause of her distress. I hope I did not speak wrongly. I do at times. Indeed, I do."

"They are from Bactria," Mr. Barrymore says. "It is a country in the high reaches of Asia, and hence they are called *Camelus bactrianus ferus*. Of course, they do not subsist on air any more than we do, but they can manage for a year at a time without water. I have told Amelia this, but she forgets."

"Quite so."

"To our eye they appear ugly, but in the place where they belong, in their home. There, I suspect they are something quite remarkable to behold."

"Indeed, I . . ."

"It did seem a good idea. Mr. Laumeister hoped to make a fortune, but their feet are too soft for the roads here, and the damp in some regions is enough to drive them to madness. But then one is often plagued with bad luck. The road is not built where one expects. The cattle do not arrive. The land does not thrive without great effort and much water brought by hand. One does what one can."

Eugene murmurs his sympathy. Suggests the hour is getting late.

Mr. Barrymore lights a lamp. "May I show you my collection? Please, we so seldom have guests."

"Your collection? Ah, the feathers. Lovely. A fine array."

"No, the collection in the shed. Come, please."

"Ah, perhaps I should look to my mule again. And I am exhausted. The adventure of the day, and . . ."

"It will only take a moment. It is a fine collection." He grips the lamp and walks to the door. He is smaller even than Eugene had thought. Is slightly hunched, certainly forlorn.

Eugene fills his glass. Soon enough wishes he had taken up the entire bottle. Odour of half-cured hide, of something like vinegar, of something fetid, musty. The feeble light shows jars in which float snakes, fish, a chick, its great eyes closed and blue-veined, its claws at the glass.

Mr. Barrymore beckons Eugene along a narrow passage. The creatures could be out of a medieval bestiary; they are that crudely, that grotesquely stuffed. Their eyes are made of bits of bottle glass. Their hides bulge here and there as if possessed of cancerous growths, great boils.

"I realize they are not the finest examples of the art. I have been experimenting with a sort of plaster and with a frame of wood, to create the greater illusion of life, you see."

Eugene swallows the last of the whiskey. "Splendid, now . . ."

Mr. Barrymore holds Eugene's arm. His grip is surprisingly tight. He leads Eugene to a squat creature the size of a large dog. Brown fur. Yellowish stripes from shoulder to tail. Lips pegged back with small nails. Great teeth. A heavy jaw. "*Gulo gulo*," Mr. Barrymore says. "Or skunk bear. They are solitary animals that scavenge and hunt. They birth hanging upside down, like bats."

"Are they numerous?" Eugene asks, affecting curiosity, affecting something other than a desire to run.

"I do not know. I am sorry. I have written many learned men on that question and others, but none have replied. It is difficult living here. Now this." He stands beside a catlike beast. From the seams in its belly stuffing spills like guts long atrophied. Eugene peers closer. "Puma?"

Mr. Barrymore smiles. "Yes, you are absolutely right. A puma.

Felis concolor. It is also called Indian Devil, Catamount, and Deer Tiger. It is the most fearsome of the cats about. Its young are born in winter storms and its scream is like a banshee. It is heard only in the night, however, and always at the time between waking and sleep, though why I do not know."

"Quite so, and now, I . . ."

"And this . . ." and so it goes. *Felis lynx*, its paws as great as its head, its ears tufted so it may hear its mate's cry at a distance of three hundred leagues. *Erethizum dorstum*, the porcupine, and naturally the most difficult to stuff. *Marmota caligata*, the easiest, being no more than a walking ball. Mr. Barrymore imitates its piercing whistle. Eugene gives an idiot's smile. The spread-winged bird is *Falco peregrinus*, a bird that can live for weeks afloat in an updraft. A handful of red fur is *Tamiasciurus hudsonicus*, or a pine squirrel. A great skull is *Ursus arctos*, the largest and most vicious of bears.

Mr. Barrymore casts the light on a mess of brown feathers, smiles modestly. "I cannot identify this one, not at all. I am hoping that it will be named for me, its discoverer. It is not much, I know, but it would create a legacy of a kind."

"Quite so. Did I not see the beaver? There, near the door."

"Ah, yes, good eye, the mainstay of the Company of Gentleman Adventurers. Is it still called that?"

Eugene assures him it is.

"We value only its fur, but look at its tail, how remarkable. It is used for trowelling the plaster over its home, which can have as many rooms as ours."

The moulting antler is *Rangifer tarandus*, the caribou. "The creature is most numerous where you are travelling; this is why the territory is named so. It breeds in the untold millions. The young are born near full grown and need no tending but bound off the very day they are born."

"Would that children did as well," Eugene says, attempting to lighten the mood.

Mr. Barrymore's hands stop in mid-gesture.

Eugene thinks of the graves in the yard, the black dress of Mrs. Barrymore. Inwardly curses. He might well have stepped into a Russian novel, what with these multiple, complicated names, the sense of certain tragedy.

Mr. Barrymore clears his throat. "And this is *Procyon lotor*, raccoon, or little bandit. Cleaner than most men, and wiser."

Eugene stresses he must respond to the call of nature. Mr. Barrymore relents. They pass the graves. The moonlight shows them clearly enough, the whitewashed crosses, the white stone borders, the white flowers in earthen jars. Eugene quickens his step.

The door is ajar. A candle drips wax on the table. Mrs. Barrymore sits by the red mouth of the stove. The sight of her perplexes Eugene until he realizes she is engaged in nothing. No needlework, no knitting, no mending, no preparation of food. She is not even reading. Perhaps the woman is mad. Then Eugene smells the whiskey, notes that the bottle he left behind is empty. Not mad. Worse. The mad can entertain delusions, false hopes.

"Good night, my love," Mr. Barrymore says.

She begins a tuneless humming.

"And good night, Mr. Hume. I hope you will be comfortable on the side bench there. Merely set aside the books, carefully, if you please. You will find a quilt in the trunk."

"Thank you. And for the lecture as well. It was most informative. Indeed, I believe I will never forget it."

Mr. Barrymore nods. "We have few visitors. So very few. Good night now."

"Yes, good night, but, your wife. Is she? Does she?"

"Ah, she will come in time." He shifts aside a curtain, disappears from sight.

Eugene spies another bottle. Helps himself and sits opposite Mrs. Barrymore. He notices she is wearing a large mourning brooch made of dark hair. It is poorly made, resembles a hairy spider more than an adornment. He looks to the portrait of the Queen, the wildflowers in a jar before it.

"She has the loveliest voice. Sweet, gentle, like a summer breeze."

Mrs. Barrymore ceases humming. Stares at him. "Who do you mean? Who?"

"Our Queen. I met her once. I had an elder cousin who was an earl. He took me along for an audience once when I was a boy. She was younger then, and oh, so very pretty. She wore a splendid green dress and green gloves and she had a golden circlet on her brow."

Mrs. Barrymore leans forward. Her hands are clutched together. Her eyes are large, dark, even lovely in this uncertain light. "You spoke to her?"

"Ah, a Queen is never spoken to. She spoke to me. I recall the words as if even now they are being whispered in my ear."

"What did she say? Tell me. You must."

"She said . . . she said that I must be good, that I must struggle against adversity. That I and all her subjects must make for themselves the best of what they have. To not forever long for what was and for what cannot be. I suspect she ascertained that I was distressed. I had recently lost my mother, you see, and . . ."

"She has nine children."

"Yes."

"What more? Tell me."

Palace halls hung with damask and panels of carved ivory. Marble fountains. Shoes embroidered with golden thread. Topiary trimmed into the shape of griffins. He did see the Queen once. The royal carriage was being pulled along the Mall and Eugene, barely eight, saw her gloved hand flutter from the window and the shadowy outline of her face before the crowd drowned him. Yet he does not dissemble too greatly. His father as a knight did have the right of audience, though thank God he never exercised it. He would have been brought drunk and farting before her majesty, then fondled the handmaidens, sneered at the courtiers. They would have been banished then, to languish on some rocky isle à la Napoleon.

He pours whiskey into Mrs. Barrymore's outstretched glass. She asks for the story again, and then again. And so again and again Eugene tells it, adding details until the palace is fit to bursting with luxuries and the Queen is as garrulous as a fishwife, until Mrs. Barrymore has fallen asleep in her chair, her face nearly peaceful. Eugene covers her with the quilt from the trunk. Stokes the fire then clears the bench of books and settles in his bedroll. Mrs. Barrymore faintly snores. From behind the curtain Mr. Barrymore breathes as if each breath was his last. The Puma has a banshee wail. Tonight is not the night he would want to hear it. He does not sleep. He scratches and shifts. Bad enough that he has seen Injun Hank, now he has partaken of the food and drink in this necropolis. He knows of Persephone and the grapes, or was it plums?

How she ate of them and so was condemned to live on in Hades. There are warnings in these old tales.

Ah, Dora, Dora, Dora. Not for her these morbid rituals, these ghoulish half-lit rooms. Damned if he doesn't miss her, like an ache, like he's been stripped to the bone.

FIFTEEN

"Ma'am, you the Mrs. Jacobsen?"

"I am. Yes? What is it I may do for you? Are you wanting a room? Victuals? Come into the light and shut the door behind you. Drafts, sir."

She looks Boston over with suspicion even though his hair is now short to his ears, his beard trimmed. She stares pointedly at his hat. He takes it off reluctantly and holds it tight in his hands as if it has a will of its own and has to be kept down.

"Asking about your painting."

"My painting? Are you indeed? Which one? For what purpose? I do not understand. Not at all."

Boston motions to the parlour off the entrance. "The one over the sideboard there. What you take for it?"

"For the Picnickers? You are asking to buy it? That I part with it?"

"Yes, ma'am."

"Have you been drinking? Have you been taking opium? Because I do not tolerate such indulgences in my establishment. Not at all."

"Haven't been doing that. It's just . . ."

"Just? Yes? I am listening."

"Need a gift, that's all, to even it out."

"Have you stayed here, sir? You are familiar. Have we been introduced? What is your name?"

"Name's Jim. Boston Jim some call me. Not staying here. No. But . . ."

"Well, that painting, Mr. Jim, is a cherished heirloom. Have you heard of the French Revolution? The rule of the unwashed mob? That is my family, as it once was. They had their heads removed. Guillotined.

Unjustly so. And so you see, I would rather sell my soul to the devil than sell that painting."

Boston is considering whether to argue the worth of such a trade when pots crashing in the kitchen take up Mrs. Jacobsen's attention and she leaves him abruptly. Boston peers into the parlour. It is much like the Dora woman described it, is a jumble of tassels and drapes and furnishings, is awash with ambers and clarets and purples of all hues. There on the mantel is the golden clock and there the stereoscope. There on a table the Wardian case, ornate as the cage for some foreign bird, its ferns and odd pale flowers pressing at the misty glass. The Dora woman spoke of it: "It's a strange and lovely thing, it is. When you peer into it you'd half expect to see a naked jungle savage peering back at you. I'd never know how to care for such a thing."

She did not speak, however, of the many doilies and antimacassars. She should have, for they festoon the backs and arms of every chair and every surface and bring to mind the skeletal remains of some delicate sea creature.

That is not all that is amiss. The windows are large, but not large enough, as she had proclaimed, to drive a carriage through. The piano is not the size of a Cathedral organ, and there is a sweetish odour she forgot to mention entirely.

A wan light struggles into the room. It is a damp afternoon at the beginning of July. Two men sit near a low-burning fire, periodicals propped before them. They are well-dressed, big-bellied men about whom pipe smoke lingers as if in some kind of homage. Neither look at Boston and he has that feeling, as he has from time to time, that he is not quite real.

He steps into the parlour to get a closer look at the painting. He holds his hat close to his chest so as not to send crashing the many gimcracks. "It's an astonishing picture," the Dora woman said. "It's like they're inviting you in. Like they're saying come and laugh with us now, and eat grapes with us. I could look at it all day, I could, and did, too, when I should have been dusting."

But the picnickers are not laughing. Grimacing perhaps. And their eyes suggest a warning rather than an invitation. As for the grapes, there are none in evidence, only the remains of some on the blanket. Flies hover near. A crow tears out the eyes of a half-eaten fish, and the juice of a hacked-apart orange stains the hem of a silver skirt. It troubles him that so many things are different from her descriptions. Mrs. Jacobsen, for example, though not slim, is not as wide as a wagon wheel. Her hair, though bright, he supposes, for a woman her age, is not the red of a peony. And he has yet to see her be swept up by gusts of rage, has yet to see her behave like a music-hall singer who has lost her stage and voice but not her grand entrances and exits.

Mrs. Jacobsen returns with a rattling of keys. "Now who is this gift for? Who is asking for my painting?"

"She isn't asking . . ."

"She? Who? What are you talking about?"

"Mrs. Hume," Boston says, though he had not meant to. He had meant to buy the painting and then leave. It was to be simple. But never has Boston encountered such an effective fusillade of questions.

Mrs. Jacobsen presses her hand to her chest. "Mrs. Hume? Do you mean Miss Dora Timmons? Is that who you mean? Is it?"

"Don't know about Timmons. Dora, though, that's her given name." He has not said the name "Dora" aloud before. To do so now seems strange, as if he were giving up some secret.

"I am astonished. I am astounded. Understand that while she may use the name Mrs. Hume, society does not, the holy church does not."

"What the church says don't matter. She worked here. Heard that."

"Indeed. We had a contract and yet she left me. I was told. I was warned. Mr. Jacobsen said she'd be off with a fellow in no time. But what are you to her? Are you a friend? A relation?" She puts a hand to her chest. "Have you taken up with her? Is that it? And Mr. Hume gone barely eight weeks. Why am I surprised? Why did I not expect this?"

"Not like that. No. Just owe her, see. She liked the painting. Said so."

"Did she? Did she indeed? Well, be assured, sir, the painting is not for sale. Not for any price, and certainly not for Miss Timmons. No, certainly not. Now, Mr. Jim was it? I must bid you good day."

Boston clamps his hat on, but makes no move to leave.

Mrs. Jacobsen twists the keys at her waist. "Should I call for Mr. Vincent? Should I send for the constabulary?"

The bronze at the head of the stairway is of a woman twisting away from some pursuer. Her lower limbs are turning into a tree trunk, her fingers into leafy branches. The Dora woman described it briefly, but added that she had not liked it much. Fortunate. It would be heavy and difficult to pry from its place. Boston says: "The stereoscope then. What you take for it?"

"The stereoscope? It is for my guests. No, no indeed, this is not a shop. This is not a marketplace. There is nothing available here for Dora Timmons. Nothing."

Boston tries once more. He describes the Dora woman as best he can, the bonnet slipping sideways off her straw-yellow hair, the blue dress, the pink cheeks, the blue rounds of her eyes.

"I am well aware of the woman's appearance. I had the pleasure of her face and company for the greater part of a month. Throw your love away on someone else. That is my advice. In any case, she has taken up with Mr. Eugene Hume, has she not? They are suited. Both have the most troublesome characters. What will he say, indeed, when I tell him anon that a disreputable man is trying to buy a gift for his woman, that is to say his mistress, his whore? Now good day. I am a busy woman. I have many people to attend to."

She rustles off, calling to her servants, throwing an irritated glance back at Boston who is staring at his boots as if they have just appeared there.

Boston breathes in sharply. Love. The landlady spoke the word so casually. Was this love, then? This confusion? This sense of obligation? He considers hate. That is love's opposite and something he understands. Is what he feels for the Dora woman the exact opposite of what he feels for the man whose face is in shadow, always in shadow? This face that, with all his vast memory, he cannot recall. At first it was only an insistent pressure, a warmth even, then agony. What Boston knows, and knew then in that inarticulate, gut-certain way of children, was that the man was dying and did not want to be forgotten, that it was not enough to carve his own name and that of his city on some tree or rock. He wanted a living, walking testament to his time upon the earth. And so he carved his name on Boston and muttered some incoherent incantation and in doing so he worked a curse. Did he know he was working magic? Magic was often stumbled upon. One had to be careful. But that did not matter. What mattered was that only after the man had at him with his knife did memories begin imprinting themselves upon him, as indelible as the words on his skin. It is for this burden of memory that Boston hates him. When Boston is dead, the man's name will rot away with his flesh and so be forgotten as if he had never existed. Boston hates his scars and he hates the man, and the hate is like nourishment. But this love, if that is what it is, does not nourish him. He is weakened by it.

He makes his way slowly to the restaurant at the front of the Avalon. He sits at a table in the corner and orders a whiskey from the waiter, and then a steak with eggs and bacon for he has not eaten once this day. Next to Boston a boy is being applauded for the arrival of his seventh year. What happens on your birthday? Do the years turn like a great wheel inside of you? Is wisdom parcelled out? At Fort Connelly, Christ's birthday was celebrated with fresh-killed game and free-flowing rum. The men danced together until near to morning when they sprawled out where they had fallen. Lavolier told him that all were marked on God's calendar, that the Lord had decided in advance the day of one's birth, and that of one's death. Boston believed him. He had no reason not to then. But now it makes no sense that this Christ could trade his life for the salvation of all the living and all the dead and for all those yet to be born. For a hundred people perhaps, for a thousand even. But all exchanges must have a limit, even those with the divine. And certainly Boston can't believe that any greater power notices when another being slips into the world, or slips out, or visits for a fraction of time, as do newborns who open their eyes and then die as if they have seen all they wish to and have realized it is not as they were promised. Boston knows it is unlikely that he is accounted for. There is no record of his entrance into the world. No people who will mourn his death, pass on his name, pray for him to interfere in their worldly matters. There is only the Dora woman saying: "For your birthday, then." There is only the Dora woman giving him a day in late spring, giving him back the one hundred and twenty-six pounds and ten shillings as if to remind him of the purpose for it. There is only the Dora woman telling him her stories so that he may step into them when he chooses the way one steps into a clear, warm lake.

When he finds the appropriate gift he will return to her cabin.

They will talk again as she promised, sitting inside the cabin this time. Bread will be rising fatly by the stove. No one will come and go. She will ask for his life and he will give it to her. He will tell her of the scars, of Fort Connelly, and perhaps of its demise. He will tell her of Lavolier and of Illdare. He will tell of the village near the fort and of Kloo-yah, how she cooked his meals and warmed his bed in exchange for protection from her people. He will tell her how he spends his seasons hunting and trapping and how occasionally when he skins an animal and leaves its bloody carcass in the snow he shivers briefly, as one does when a door opens onto a warm room and lets in a fragment of brutal cold.

He will tell her, also, of how he once awoke and found himself floating near the blackened roof of his cabin, was able to see his own form sleeping on a bed of furs, the half-chewed bones on the table, the tangle of his traps hung on the walls and roof. He spent that day cleaning the floor planks and the table and the windows even, which were of true glass. His cabin was not like the lair of some animal at all.

Of what else can he tell her? Of the summer last, the summer of the pox. It had swept through before, but never like this. He headed for the coast. The Indians were not allowed to trade in Victoria unless they had the mark of the pox on them already, so it made sense that he would find good trading as a middleman.

Once he came near the salt smell of the sea he decided to head further north, curious of a sudden to see again the village near Fort Connelly. On his eighth day of walking along deer paths and trading paths, along the shore, he began to recognize the trees and rock formations. Saw an overhang with the carving of a square masted ship. It was a carving that Illdare had told him of, though Boston had never seen it. The moss thickened and deadened noise, the mushrooms pushed up through the earth like pale thumbs. Everything, even the light, seemed soft and slightly rotted.

He came upon the remains of the fort first. The moss and ferns had long taken over the charred logs, though the black still showed through the green. He studied a pail that was so rusted it seemed made of lace and then the lichen-encrusted skulls that were heaped where the gates once were. One of the skulls might well have been Illdare's, but it was impossible to tell.

Near the village the trees began filling with carved boxes. About them were hung blankets and trinkets, pots and axes. Nearer the village the corpses were no longer housed in carved boxes, but were cradled in the branches as if they had fallen from the sky. He stood at the shore of the curved bay, near where canoes were drawn up. The pinnacle rocks called the three sisters had not changed. They stood out in the waves at the edge of the bay as they had always done. But the village was not as it had been, was smaller, bore evidence of less prosperity and evidence of rampant death and recent abandonment.

He covered his face with his neckerchief. Walked on. The corpses lay between the houses and in the houses themselves. There was the sound of the wind and surf and that of dogs and carrion birds quarrelling and feasting. And there was an odd, absolute stillness that did not mark the absence of the living, nor even the presence of the dead. Boston wasted no time, took four seal skins and a beaver skin and two sea otter pelts that he found at the bottom of a great wooden chest. He took also a carved wooden ladle and a carved wooden bowl. He took nothing more. The sea otter pelts alone were worth the trip, so rare were they by then that they commanded twenty times the worth of other pelts. In exchange he left the goods he had brought—chisels and pots and a bolt of plaid cloth—in the house of the headman and his wives and clan. Left them beside a corpse that wore the otter and cedar bark cloak of a headman. He did not recognize the man, however, and would not have, even if it were the same headman as when Boston left, he who had offered to let Boston stay with them and be one of them, since Boston helped them so. The pox had so melted his countenance into a mass of pus and lesions that even Boston could recognize nothing of what he had been.

He camped a good distance off that night. Decided that, in all, he had received just value for his goods. True they had not been of the finest quality, but then he had walked for two weeks and the rain had dogged him, and there had been the stench to contend with, and all this added to their worth.

He traded the furs in Victoria that summer for a new stove, nickel-plated and steel-bound. He paid for its passage to the Cowichan and from there spent a week hauling it to his cabin with the help of a hired Comiaken who alone of all his family had been lanced against the pox.

Why had he bothered trading with the dead? Do they take a reckoning? No, the dead have no use for possessions. He could have taken as much as he could carry, could have left nothing in return. Ghosts could haunt him all they wanted. They did, in fact, and a few more leering on the periphery would not trouble him. No, it was that strange stillness in the village that prompted him to leave the goods. It was the stillness of a cycle broken, of nothing owed and nothing offered. He'd left the goods behind not out of fairness, but out of a sense that if he did not that strange stillness would hound him until he, and all the world as well, might cease to be.

His food arrives, steaming and brimming over the plate. He eats morosely. Pushes the plate aside, then takes out his latest purchase: good unlined paper and a portable inkwell. He writes the letter carefully to better mimic the angular manner of Kines' handwriting, seen briefly on a bill of sale during the occasion of Boston's false accusation. He is nearly finished when he looks up and sees the satin wall of the landlady.

"You are writing letters to Miss Timmons? Is that it?"

"Not to her, no. Going now."

"It is not that I mind if a woman, married or otherwise, has admirers. It is not that I mind if she makes conquests here or there. Only that it all remain honourable, above reproach, only that her reputation be kept spotless. And so if you must persist then I suggest flowers. They are the simplest way to show regard. Yellow roses would suffice. They imply friendship. Either that or marigolds. They mean health. If you wish to express gratitude as well, arrange them with a spray of sage. Place them on her doorstep and then quickly leave. For it is best the admirer remain unknown so that she may imagine at her leisure."

She speaks loudly enough so that all the men about can hear. They glance over; some smile; some nod.

The flowers must be boxed, she tells him. The stems must be wrapped in sodden paper. Boston says nothing. After a few days the stems will be rotting, the petals brown. In any case, the Dora woman could grow flowers. They are the free bounty of the earth. It would be a worse gift than the paltry marten pelt he had offered in the first place.

Boston thanks her gruffly and concentrates on folding the letter. She eyes him, then turns to the next table. She says good afternoon to a man there, all abruptness gone from her manner. The man wipes his nose, then grasps her hand and kisses it.

Boston puts the letter in his pocket, pays his bill, and then man-oeuvres past Mrs. Jacobsen. He is not looking at her, but of a sudden she cries: "I recognize you now! Yes, I knew I had seen you before. I have a good eye. I have a fine memory. The chain gang. They worked on the street outside my door on several occasions." She directs her voice to the diners. "I finally had to send Mr. Vincent out to tell the guard to move them on, to tell him it was bad for business. That I do not want thieves and criminals eyeing up my establishment. No indeed. I have guests to think of. I have my honour to think of."

"Leaving now," he says, and surveys the seated men. None seem about to challenge him.

"Oh, the lot of you are useless," Mrs. Jacobsen sighs.

Boston makes his way to Poodle Alley. Waits for the diminishment of light. Obed Kines will be coming this way as he does every day on the way home from his shop. For now Boston has time to think and think some more on what gift would satisfy the Dora woman. Round and round the thoughts go, clattering relentlessly like iron wheels over stone.

SIXTEEN

Eugene wakes to the crowing of the roosters, a view of table legs, a floor that is a landscape unto itself—swamps of ale, rivulets of tobacco, ridges and valleys of crumpled tablecloths, a leaf-scattering of playing cards.

He crawls out from under the table, hauls himself upright, neither sways nor stumbles. Hah. Not every man would manage so well after a night of such liberality, of such, such . . . the word fails him, as, in truth, does the remembrance of the night itself. He surveys the common room: two long tables pushed beneath gingham-curtained windows. A long bar with a locked spirit cabinet. A spinet with a sampler and crucifix above it. Plates roughly stacked and food-streaked. An army of glasses and bottles, mostly fallen or smashed.

The room shifts abruptly, like the backdrop in a pantomime. Perhaps he should retire again beneath the table. Let the morning sort itself out. Let him hear all about the heroics over breakfast. Remembers now the room spinning in a reel-de-deux, a galop, a cotillion. No wonder he has blisters blossoming on his heels. Remembers some cordial, bright as new-pricked blood, strong enough to fell an ox. No wonder he has a mighty desire to piss. Just before he reaches the door he glances at the bar mirror. His hair is in disarray; his moustaches and beard bristle like a scullery brush and his half-buttoned shirt shows the pale flag of his underclothes. In this state he would terrify small children. Are there small children about? He has some vague image of two boys running through a forest of booted men. He pats his hair. Where the devil has his hat gone? Halts in mid-motion. The coffin is half-propped against the far side of the bar. The lid is askew beside it. It is lined with a sheet and contains the carcass of a chicken.

Eugene would dearly love to turn away. And yet the enigma of the night insists. Cautiously he approaches the bar; cautiously he leans over it. The corpse is seated on the floor, his back against the far wall, his filmy eyes fixed on the ceiling. In the stiff spray of his fingers is a bottle, in his lap a few stained playing cards. He is a small man. His hair is thick and grey and dishevelled, his belly rotund. At his temple is a bloodless gash.

Eugene stumbles over an upturned chair. "Christ and damnation!" he shouts, and then composes himself. The previous day, at least, has now returned. He left Lac La Hache house—owned by a rule-spewing former steamboat Captain—near the crack of morning. Delightful country. Delightful day. Golden plains dotted with cattle and wood groves and, the long glittering waters of Lac La Hache itself. A breeze sprung up 'round the noontime and dispersed the mosquito haze. He and Ariadne made reasonable time. The air must have agreed with her, the succulent grasses.

Late in the afternoon he came upon the Mactavish roadhouse. It was a fine establishment—two stories of well-chinked logs, three gables, and a freshly painted fence about a thriving garden. There was a large barn, and several tidy outbuildings, and at least twenty people bustling to and fro. He had not planned to stop so early. He was making admirable time. But how could he ignore the certainty that a splendid party was at hand, one that could not be missed?

He was correct. The Mactavishes were preparing for the lyke wake of the brother of Mr. Mactavish, one Tricky Ole Amos who laid his head on the table while playing at poker. The other players carried on, thinking this was merely a bluff. Only when he repeatedly refused to take up his hand did they become alarmed.

Eugene hobbles into the grey light, curses the blisters on his heels, the constant itching of mosquito bites. He pisses by a pig trough. A thought chills him. Perhaps the man in the front room is not the only one dead. Perhaps all the others are dead as well. Poisoned by Mrs. Mactavish's meat pasties. But then he, too, would be cooling his heels in purgatory, as he had eaten six early in the evening, and in record time, and for this won a silver dollar from a Spaniard who had breath to make a dragon cower.

Something else about the night. A Norseman squeezes an accordion.

A crab-limbed Frenchman saws at a fiddle. A string snaps and he continues gamely on. The floor shudders with the stomping of boots. Eugene is leading them in song. He is leading Mrs. Mactavish in a reel. She is apple-cheeked and lively-eyed, her dark hair all scattered out from its pins. She is here, now, in the common room, picking up glasses. The coffin is flat on the floor, the lid in place.

"Good morning to you, ma'am."

She glares at him tight-lipped and continues in her task. A door bangs open. Mr. Mactavish the Live stands with suspenders in loops against his thighs. He resembles his brother to a disturbing degree and is glaring at Eugene, though for what reason Eugene certainly could not say.

"Here's the dancer, then."

"Ah, yes. Good morning to you."

"Think so, do ye?"

"I think it is good enough. Good enough. Pray, tell me, where might I find my rucksack and hat?"

"Pray? There's something ye might wanna be doing."

"Upstairs, the second room," Mrs. Mactavish says sharply. "I'll be donging the bell soon as this mess is cleared."

"My thanks, madam. Sir."

Eugene mounts the stairs. Walks as upright as possible, as if to deflect the eyes boring into his spine.

"Ye know, Violet, I'm thinking to get a trap door like the Pole's at Horsefly. That way when the roustabouts get half-screwed I can spring it, and wham, they're cooling their heels in the cellar."

Eugene can hardly blame the man for this outburst. He, too, would be in a foul temper if another man had danced so enthusiastically with his woman, if his woman—if Dora—had looked at a man the way Mrs. Mactavish looked at him the night before.

Nothing like the smell of a room crowded with at least thirty sleeping men, all of whom are in need of a bath, all of whom have been partaking in the joys of Dionysus. A few are belching and scratching their way to consciousness. Others are sprawled fully clothed on the floor as if dropped there from a great height. His rucksack is beside a bottom bunk where two men sleep head to toe. He picks his way over. Grabs his rucksack. His hat. His belongings are intact. Splendid. Excellent.

One of the men pushes the socked foot of his companion away from his cheek. He looks bleary-eyed at Eugene. He is a mere stripling, barely old enough to shave.

"Larky, you're Mr. Hume. Morning," he says, his accent that of a Londoner.

"Ah, Good morning, good morning." Eugene cannot place him, but that is not what troubles him. What troubles him is the smirking and pointing in his direction that is going on as the men rise.

Eugene whispers: "Young sir, in your opinion, is an apology required?"

"An apology? Larky, it'll hardly matter to the man."

"Which man?"

"Which? Why the dead man. Amos was it? The brother of Mr. Mactavish."

"Ah, quite so."

"But to the Mactavishes, an apology there might be swell."

"For anything in particular?"

"Anything in particular? For the dancing you were doing. You don't recall? Larky, I'll be."

"I have been praised for my dancing. I cannot imagine it was so offensive."

"You don't remember?"

"It seems not. Humour an old man, will you?" But even as he says this memory's door creaks open. Eugene stands on the threshold. The common room is crowded with men. The windows are white with steam. The men are dancing with each other, which is nothing unusual, except for the boisterous vigour with which they are conducting themselves, a vigour that only free liquor engenders. They are stomping about in the parody of a quadrille. A keg of ale on the bar dribbles out its last into the glass of the Spaniard who peers at the spout with a look of betrayal. From somewhere in the house a clock strikes three slow dongs. Mrs. Mactavish, the only woman there, looks distraught and defeated, does not even notice her two young sons drinking from abandoned glasses. Eugene rearranges his memory. He takes her elbow, bellows at the rabble to disperse, to give the lady some peace, to respect the dead. But, no, edit as he might, such is not the scene. She is on her own. As for Mr. Mactavish the Live, he is in a chair, his head in his hands. He seems incapable of movement, much less controlling the situation. Mr. Mactavish the Dead surveys the proceedings from his propped-up coffin. His hands are clasped on his belly. A glass is in one breast pocket, a pack of playing cards in the other. He is comfortable, no need to disturb him, his dancing days are done. So why, why does Eugene berate him for being so quiet? For looking so deathly tired? None doing, sir! He cannot but feel contemptuous of the man, as if dying were an expression of weakness, of lack of will.

The smell is of something ripening. The man's new-shaven cheeks are pressed against Eugene's. His rotund belly has a womanly softness. His limbs have a peculiar heaviness, as though filled with clay.

Mr. Mactavish the Live shouts and struggles to rise from his chair. But he cannot move forward. The vomit pooling all about his boots seems to have ensnared him. He sits back down heavily and is not heard from again.

Eugene hauls Mr. Mactavish the Dead about the room, knocks over chairs, bangs against a table. Bottles smash to the floor. The other men are cheering, huzzahing, calling: "Amos, Amos, Amos. Back to life with you!" What splendid affairs, these popish wakes and lyke wakes, these attempts to roust the dead, to ensure they are not merely sleeping deeply, playing a trick. How much better than all the weeping and vast expenditures of his experience, the hired mutes and mourners, the women so decked in black mourning apparel they seem like macabre Christmas trees.

Eugene drops the man and trips over him, hauls him upright. He has never felt so alive, so certain of his own strength. It wouldn't surprise him in the least if those feet started tapping on the floor, if those filmy eyes sparked with life. Injun Hank and his evil eye be damned. The ghoulish Barrymores be damned. There was enough life and hope emanating from Eugene Augustus Hume to animate the dead man's limbs long enough for one last dance.

Eugene now sniffs his lapel and detects a rotting, sweetish odour. Finds a grey hair and then another. His gut churns. He'll throw the coat out. Or have it washed in lye. And, oh, for a tub of steaming water, a scrub from sympathetic arms.

Mrs. Mactavish is in the kitchen plating flapjacks, looking older in the hard light of full morning. Two Chinamen stand guard over the stove. The younger one takes a step back as Eugene comes closer. The older one makes an intricate motion with his hands and mutters what might be a protecting spell, as if before him stood not a proper Englishman, but some foreign devil.

Eugene places his hand on his heart, begins his apology. Without a word, Mrs. Mactavish brushes past him to the common room. Eugene follows close behind. No vestige of last night's festivities remains. The men at the long table look up in expectation, though whether for the food or for the spectacle of Eugene with his hat in his hand is not clear. The Spaniard is picking his teeth. The French fiddler is holding onto his mug with both hands, the way an orphan might.

Mrs. Mactavish slaps down the platter of pancakes.

"Madam, I meant no disrespect."

Still she says nothing.

Eugene joins the others at the table and does his best with the fried eggs and meat pasties and coffee, all of it settling poorly in his belly. Afterwards he makes his way to the anteroom to settle his bill with Mr. Mactavish. He waits patiently in line, barely hearing the talk all about him. These Catholics should be more forgiving. It is not that unusual to dance with a corpse. He has heard of worse, lyke wakes where the corpse is taken out for a spree, or sprung-wrapped so as to leap out of the coffin, or used as a table for cards. No, he has not lost face, perhaps, hah, merely a nose, or an eyelid. He was not alone in his carousing, after all. Still, what was he about? He is not a grave robber, not one of those physics who hack open the dead for experiments and grotesque proddings. He is not one of those men who are spoken of in hushed voices in the lower taverns of London, men who love only the passivity and carnal coolness of a corpse, male or female, it matters not.

Mr. Mactavish hands Eugene a lengthy bill in an illegible hand. "Ten pounds or fifty dollars. What ye prefer?"

"Ten? Fifty? There is a mistake, I . . ."

"Ye smashed twenty-two glasses and fifteen plates. The coffin's wrecked. Ye ripped my brother's suit and gashed him plenty. Need to get him plastered up so he looks fit to bury. And here, two kegs o' ale and ten bottles o' whiskey. 'Put it on my bill. I'll pay in the morn, ye said.'"

"On my bill? You there, Larky-boy, is he correct? Two kegs? Ten bottles?"

"Name is Evans, but Larky is what they call me, true enough, and that's right, meant to thank you, sir."

The Spaniard, the Frenchman, the assorted Yanks and Canadians, the Norwegians, the Balkan, all voice thanks. Some slap Eugene on his back. His head is pounding. His underarms are sticky with sweat. He must smell as wretched as these others. He must look as wretched as well.

"I must protest the bill. It is outrageous."

The men are now hurrying off with barely a sympathetic glance. Mules are being loaded. A whip cracks in the yard. Mr. Mactavish calls out the window and several farmhands promptly enter. They smell of manure and hay and are standing about with an air of cheerful menace.

"'T'ain't outrageous. It's what you owe, damnit."

The farmhands move in closer. Mrs. Mactavish comes in from the common room. "It's the mess I kinna abide," she says to no one in particular. "I like a place spic and span."

"I apologize for the mess, madam. If I may assist in any way."

"You kin pay, that's what," Mr. Mactavish says.

"'Tis better now. 'Tis clean and fit for anyone to see," Mrs. Mactavish says.

"Ten pounds. You're lucky I dinna charge ye more . . . well?"

"Mr. Mactavish. May I ask? Do you intend to expand? Provide separate rooms at some future date?"

"What in damnation business is it of yours?"

"I am only asking because I am writing a guidebook."

"A what?"

"A guidebook. Surely you have heard that coaches will be in use as soon as the road is fully complete. Soon there will be many more travellers and, if I may say, of a higher quality and with thicker purses than the ones to which you are accustomed."

"I heard that, Pete, 'tis true," Mrs. Mactavish says.

"And in this guidebook I could most certainly include your establishment. Your meals, madam, are the finest I have yet had. Finer than

Madame Hautier's, if I may say. My God, I can still taste those meat pasties! Those sausages!"

"Oh, 'tis nothing. But you're not the first to compliment them. No, sir."

"And your raspberry cordial. It is ambrosial. Nothing less."

"My grandmother's. I make blackberry as well."

"And your preserves! They are as sweet as sunshine."

"Losh! I make five kinds. I only had three on the table this morning. The mess, ye see. Usually we have five, nothing less." She pats her hair and gives a dimpled smile. "Pete, get yourself into the common room for a minute."

While the Mactavishes confer, Eugene congratulates himself. A guidebook, indeed, why had he not thought of it before? Good then that he so often stops to refresh himself and rest Ariadne. He will warn of dissembling blacksmiths and vicious camels. He will clarify the confusing mileage. He will write of the Cornwall brothers and their hunts that make use of Indians got up in red coats and a coyote instead of a fox. He will write well of 47 Mile House in the Cut-off valley, for it had pulu mattresses free of vermin and a fine bar where any manner of spirits could be purchased. He will write well of Pollards, just north of 47 Mile House. He will reserve his highest recommendations for Saul, the kindly proprietor of 59 Mile House at the Painted Chasm. Such a vista. The chasm, blued into the distance, was layered with rustic colours like some tertiary pie. Once he has finished his guidebook he will write of this Painted Chasm to some geological society or other. By then he will have the money to take up a hobby or two. Why not geology? Rocks have the advantage of being sedentary, of not taking one on a merry chase as might beetles or birds. No more merry chases for Eugene Augustus after this. No indeed.

The Mactavishes have returned. Mrs. Mactavish's hand is on her husband's elbow. He looks well and truly defeated. Already he is folding the bill and putting it away.

"What ye ginna call this book, then?" he asks grudgingly.

"Ah, quite so, sir. It will be called *A Gentleman's Guide to the Goldfields of the Cariboo Including Recommendations and Advice on Supplies, Most Favourable Routes, Modes of Travel, Hunting, Dangers, and a Full Description of Creatures and Natural Wonders as well as*

Colourful and Informative Descriptions of Way Houses and Settlements, and in Which of These the Discerning Traveller May Find the Finest Meals, the Cleanest Beds and the Trustiest Proprietors."

"'Tis a mighty long title."

"Well, my good sir, 'tis a mighty long road."

SEVENTEEN

The shacks on the inner harbour are braced partially on stilts and stand one apart from the other. They have verandas of driftwood, chimneys of tin. Two fly the union jack. A seal heaves itself onto a rock then flops back into the waves as Boston comes near.

The shack he stops before is mere detritus arranged into a semblance of a dwelling. Boards protrude at odd angles. Tin siding faintly glints. No windows, not even one of greased paper. The doorway is torn burlap arrayed with mud and mould. Boston brushes it aside. The warmish light of the afternoon vanishes. A whale oil lamp gutters in the dimness. Inside, smells of spilled whiskey and spoiled milk, of damp, unwashed wool and rotting, un-dried fish. A place, in all, of Whitemen.

"Ah, Mr. Jim? Yes? The terror of shopkeeps. I did not much recognize you. You look a gentleman. Trimmed so, and cleaned. Compared to you we must appear as vagabonds or cannibals, yes? No matter. I am glad you have found us. Not difficult I trust. Sit with us. A drink, yes? Whiskey? A glass. Where's a fucking glass?"

Petrovich stands up from the lopsided table where two other men sit sprawl-legged. One is Tom McBride from the chain gang. The other is a thick-armed Kanaka with wisps of black moustaches and an inscrutable gaze. All three are armed. On the table is a bottle of murky green glass, a rind of bread, a mess of cards, and a chicken carcass without a platter.

"Like cannibals. Hah, good one, Petrovich," McBride says, chuckling.

"You recall Mr. McBride, yes? Tommy, we call him. And this is Lano from the Sandwich Islands. He was telling us of a black bird that can speak like a man, and a lizard that can walk in the air. Remarkable. Yes?"

"Forty-five dollars. Here for that. That's all."

"Ah, a man of few words, so it is not just the sorry victuals and melancholy decor of our Majesty's hotel that makes you so . . . so . . .. taciturn. That is the word, yes? Compared to you we must be as chattering monkeys."

"Chattering monkeys, that's right, hah," McBride says. Lano thumps his glass on the table and McBride falls quiet.

"Took a thrashing for you, that was the deal. You paid fifteen. Agreed on sixty. Makes forty-five more."

"Mr. Jim, you have been free for only a day or so, yes? And so, please, take a drink. Our finest."

"Don't drink fucking tanglewood."

Petrovich sighs mightily. "Would we serve such a thing to a guest? For the Indians, it is elixir, for us we keep the Scottish whiskey."

"Not here for drinking or talking, for dealing neither. Forty-five more. That's what we agreed on."

Petrovich chews the stem of his pipe. McBride nervously runs a finger across his teeth. Lano yanks out a chair and gestures to it. Boston considers, then sits, keeping his knees free from the edges of the table.

Petrovich says: "We have a fine business here. Yes, boys?"

"That's right, Ivan, that's right," McBride says. "Just like you said, if it weren't for the son of a bitch bluejackets we'd be so rich we'd be wiping our asses with money."

Lano rocks back in his chair. Boston gauges him as a man who plots and patiently waits, who gives no warning before an action, as indeed, the most dangerous of the three.

Petrovich is nodding sagely. "You intrigue me, Mr. Jim. And thus I have inquired about you. And I was told many things. You understand the languages of the Indians, yes? And you have many dealings with them. And they have some trust in you. What else have I heard? You are a likely half-breed of some kind, though one who lends himself to neither side. And you are a man who would uphold a bargain to the death, but who must not be crossed. And I said, Petrovich, such a man may be interested in a business proposal, yes?"

"Who you hearing this from?"

"Different sources. You have some minor fame. A reputation. Yes?"

Boston has observed how others speak endlessly of this man's actions, that woman's proclivities. He understands it as their attempt to fix in their minds what has occurred as they are unable to conjure the past with any ease, and rarely with any accuracy at that. Yet he has never thought that when he leaves another's presence they dwell on what he has said or done. Whisper of it. He does not like the thought of this at all. Has the Dora woman spoken of him to the people of the bay? To the Smithertons, Mrs. Hickson, Mrs. Bell, and to others who come visiting to see how she is getting on? Has she called out his name through that bull's horn? "It booms over the bay, Mr. Jim. The ducks are scattering when they hear it. And then you hear an answer back on theirs. Without seeing the person, mind, because them are too far off. It's like you're winds calling to each other, or clouds, or spirits. It's queer, and marvellous, too. But it keeps the loneliness from eating at you, it surely does."

"Not interested in your damned fool bootlegging, only the money you owe."

Petrovich stares at the wall, says: "I heard of Mr. Obed Kines' misfortune."

McBride snickers. "Misfortune. Hah, me too."

"Shut your trap. I was speaking to Mr. Jim."

"Forty-five dollars," Boston says.

"Ah, then perhaps you have not heard. Perhaps I should tell you. He was found terribly beaten, in Poodle Alley, yes? A sacking was thrown over his head and so unfortunately he did not see his assailant. On his coat was tacked a paper and it read that he was a traitor to the Queen. A letter was in his pocket. And what was in the letter, Mr. Jim? . . . Ah, such silence. The details of a plot, yes, a plot led by him and his clerk to explode the Governor's mansion, to arrange a revolt by the Americans and so take our blessed isle for the American cause."

"The money."

"And so he and his poor clerk are to stand trial for conspiracy and such, yes? Alas, though the circumstances are suspicious, he will have few to vouch for him; his hatred of our lovely Queen and all monarchies is too well known. Indeed, I hear he has many enemies among the British, yes? And so, fortunately, the finger of justice will not point straight to you."

McBride looks uneasily from Boston to Petrovich. Lano pours himself a measure of whiskey, swirls it in his glass.

"Forty-five dollars," Boston says.

Petrovich is about to answer when the burlap sways open and a wind funnels along the planks. The girl has a pole slung over her shoulders. One bucket swings from either end. She is dressed in a torn calico shift and in black stockings that at second glance become a layer of fresh mud. She is perhaps ten years of age, certainly no more than twelve. Her skin is the shade of a coal lamplight turned low. Her hair is cut raggedly to her ears. Lice move along the strands. Still, she is pretty, remarkably so. Her nose is exactly like that of a girl Boston saw once in the village near Fort Connelly. That girl played with an English doll and wore a skirt of bark. A raven clucked nearby her. A small cloud crossed over the sun.

The girl sinks to the floor and ducks out from under the pole. Catches her breath. Petrovich jerks his head and the girl squats between him and Lano. Petrovich gently squeezes the back of her neck. Lano hands her the chicken carcass. She glances up warily at the surround of men, then retreats to a space beside the stove and chews determinedly on gristle and bone.

"You are interested in our young charge, yes? We keep her safe from the Indians who would have her as a slave. We keep her safe from the nuns who'd lock her in their orphanage, and teach her all the popish hokum. Isn't that the truth, boys?"

"Sure is, Petrovich. Sure is," McBride says.

Petrovich taps the table. His fingers are long-nailed, seamed with grime. He smiles in the manner of someone going along with a joke. "But what of my business proposal? At least hear me out, yes?"

"You can bugger your offer, yourself while you're at it."

Petrovich looks at a point over Boston's head. "You see, we are having difficulties in our dealings these days. The authorities are always making new laws about the trade of spirits with the Indians, and some of their muck a mucks do not like our trade either. You could help us, yes? I speak that bastard Chinook, of course, but some of the Indians do not. Or pretend they do not. You could speak to them in their own tongue. You could make clear we are only businessmen. We will pay you, what say? Ten percent of any profit of which you are part? Yes?"

Boston curses silently. Petrovich might well not have the money the way he is going on, or else will not give it up without violence done.

Boston's hand is already close to his gun, has been since he arrived. He could certainly kill Petrovich, most likely the other two as well, though Lano may give him trouble. Three bastard lives for his own, for he would be shortly hung if he left the shack blood-splattered and body-heaped. A poor exchange, certainly, but unavoidable perhaps.

He notices the girl out of the corner of his eye. She has cast aside the chicken carcass and is crouched over her knees as if to make herself as small as possible.

Boston says: "Take the girl instead of the money."

McBride chuckles nervously. The girl looks up, her expression unreadable.

Petrovich's hand rests on his belly just above the butt of a revolver. He stares unblinking at Boston. Lano puts his glass down slowly. McBride's eyes shift from Petrovich to Boston and back. His swallow is audible in the silence.

There is a clear space in Boston's head, something akin to joy. He makes no movement

Petrovich whispers: "I am very fond of her. She came to me one night. She came from out of the dark woods. She was naked, caked in filth. I cleaned her, yes? I fed her. And now in return she brings water. Cooks for us. Her worth spans time."

That fixed stare. Boston has seen it on others. Madmen. He has no time for the breed. They find ways to complicate the simplest of transactions.

"It good trade," Lano says calmly. "Injun girls her age only twenty dollars. Thirty most. We buy another."

"That's right, that's right. And she's a biter. Nearly took my finger off the other day," McBride says.

Petrovich looks at the girl. She ceases chewing.

"She not worth trouble," Lano says.

Petrovich speaks as if to himself: "Why does she watch us? I have told her not to watch us."

"Give her Mr. Boston and she not watch us. We buy you better girl," Lano says.

"She is only alive because of me. Her life is mine, yes?" Petrovich says.

"Sure is," McBride puts in. "Sure is."

"Won't hurt her. Throw that promise into the deal," Boston says.

Petrovich pulls off his glasses, wipes his eyes, is suddenly cheerful. "Oh, I'm sure you'll take fine care of her. What do you think, boys? Mr. Jim drives a hard bargain, yes?"

McBride reaches for the bottle. His relief is nearly palpable. "A hard bargain. Sure, that's right."

Lano says: "She free, anyway. You get best deal." He takes the bottle from McBride. How long before Lano cuts Petrovich's throat and takes the business for his own? Not long, Boston supposes, and reaches for the girl.

She begins shivering once they have climbed the bank. Boston wraps his coat about her shoulders, not wanting her ill. He looks over the bay to the Songhees village. The smoke from the long houses tunnels into the dimming sky. Three figures move along the shore. He hesitates, then turns and walks toward the town. The girl follows along beside.

"Speak English, do you?"

"Little."

"Good. Taking you to a lady. Do what she says. She had a girl near same age as you. She died. You'll be her new girl. Help her out. Be good company. She'll look after you, then. Understand? English all she speaks except for bits of Chinook. So speak it, hear. For practice."

The girl says nothing. Her shoulders curve in further. The wind lifts her hair.

"Won't hurt you. Don't fear that. Not like them, understand?"

"Yes. Far?"

"Two days. Maybe more. Your people, who are they?"

"People. No."

"Your name then."

"Girl."

"Half-breed?"

"Girl."

"Talk in your first lingo."

"No."

Boston is quiet for the space of four steps, then says. "Call you Girl, then. Don't know what the lady will call you."

"Friend?"

"She'll be your friend, yes, if that's what you want to call it," Boston says, then lets a silence fall. He is weary of speaking, weary of dealing with madmen and children. Friend? What difference does that make in matters of owing?

They walk back through Humbolt Street. An old woman in a company blanket grimaces at them. A constable passes and Boston draws Girl back into the shadows. Likely the constable would not even notice them, but if he did? It might be difficult to explain what he is doing with a barely dressed Indian girl.

A man on a ladder is lighting a street lamp. They are a new addition to the town, these few gas lamps with their piss-yellow lights. And in their light Boston sees anew her tangled hair, her dirt-streaked face, the sacking that barely covers her bony shoulders, the filth of her legs. She is nothing like the well-groomed half-breed and Indian children he saw through the jail yard gates. What will the Dora woman make of this dredged-up offering? The Dora woman's petticoats flapped bold and clean on the line. Her blue dress shimmered faintly, as if shot with light. There was the smell of lye about and her teeth were white as polished shells. She might well refuse Girl as no fit substitute for Isabel Lund. Such is her right. She might well shut the door on them both.

Laughter swells out from some distance, then fades. It is never as he plans; it is as if some force is out to thwart him. He would not be surprised to see the great form of Raven alight on the high buildings of the Whites. Plotting and chortling.

He grips Girl's shoulders and turns her to face him. All is not lost. She merely needs a washing. At a bathhouse. No. There will be questions. At a lake or stream then. And she needs clothing. Shoes. Stockings. A dress of some kind. The kind the white children wear. Her hair. He will purchase a comb. Yes. But that will have to be on the morrow. The locking of shop doors can be heard all around them. The town crier bawls out *seven o'clock*.

Girl mewls faintly.

He releases her and she rubs her shoulders. They walk down Broad Street, keeping to the alleys when they can. In Poodle Alley there is still blood where Obed Kines fell. Even if Kines does not go to jail, he and Boston are even enough. Kines' right hand will not point at Boston again, for it was broken at the wrist. Nor will Kines' mouth be accusing him again, for it is missing several teeth.

Near Chinatown is an unused lot with high brush and a mess of stumps. They settle hidden in the middle of this lot. Boston takes bread and hard cheese out of his rucksack and they eat by the smudged glow of a candle. A time later a man stumbles through, mumbling a song. He stops for a long piss not two steps away, but doesn't notice them, so exquisite is his relief, so quiet are they.

Girl sniffles. Is she crying? He thinks of the Dora woman telling stories to Isabel, how she said it calmed the child.

"Want a story? That keep you quiet?"

"Story, yes, story."

He tells the story in English, though he heard it first in the Nu-chah-nulth tongue, from the old woman who cooked at Fort Connelly. Equata was her name, and she knew of spells and medicine, and was often called upon to intervene between the living and the dead. And she knew all the stories that ever were, or so the People of the village said.

A great headman had three daughters from his favourite wife. Each one was more beautiful than the last, and the chief was very proud of them. "Have you ever seen such beautiful women?" he asked Crow and Bear and Black Whale, because this was a long time ago, when the People could talk to the Animal People as easily as I talk to you. And Crow and Bear and Black Whale said no, they had never seen such beautiful women, and they asked to marry the daughters, but the headman laughed and said his daughters would never marry. They would stay with him all their lives for no one could love them as well as he could.

Now the headman and the nobles of this village were very rich and owned rights to many hundreds of harvesting grounds, for shellfish, oolichan, salmon and deer, for berries and camas and ferns. And all these grounds gave such abundance that the People never feared the starvation times and had so many goods to store that their longhouses took three days to walk from end to end. And they could have had more, but they were careful to give much to the Animal People, and to give them songs and rituals also, because this is pleasing to the Animal People and is why they return to feed us all.

Now it happened that the headman's favourite wife died. The headman tore at his hair and wailed for ten days and now he loved his daughters more than ever as they reminded him of his dead wife. And he ordered his People to now give all the food they would have given the Animal People to his three daughters and to give to them also all the songs and rituals.

"But what will they give us in return?" A nobleman asked.

The headman grew so furious at this question that he ordered the nobleman impaled on a stake. This terrified the People altogether and they began to give all their food and all their rituals to the three sisters, just as the chief commanded. And so now the three sisters sat about all day and ate and ate and listened to the songs and took all the presents they were given and hoarded them. And because of all the food they grew and grew and grew until they were taller than the highest trees and fatter than the fattest whale, and still they grew. And now there was not enough to feed them, for they were always hungry and demanded more and more. They had never been without, you see, or had to share or be moderate. And they weren't beautiful anymore, but hideous, with greasy chins and bulging eyes and hair tangled with animal bones and skin stained with berry juice. And the headman himself was wondering if this was all entirely a good thing. His People, you see, were thin and starving because they gave every-thing to his daughters and the great longhouses were nearly empty and to make it worse the Animal People weren't interested in returning in their seasons to the rivers and forests and bays, but went to grounds where other people gave them rituals and songs and food in return for their flesh.

"This has to stop, my daughters, no more can we give you all this food and all these gifts. The People are all starving. Look, even I am starving." And he showed them his arm that was thin as a stick.

"We're hungry," cried the three sisters. "What do we care of your arm! What do we care of the People. We're hungry and we want gifts."

"No, my darlings."

And then the three sisters flew into a rage. Never had they been denied. Never had they gone hungry. The eldest grabbed her father 'round the waist. The second eldest grabbed his arms. And then the youngest bit off his head and swallowed it in one gulp.

"It's delicious," she said. "Oh, it is the finest thing I've ever eaten!"

After the three sisters ate their father they strode out in the village capturing all the People and eating them raw and eating all the dogs as well. In fact, they ate everything they could find—insects and birds and fishes and berries and oolichan oil and the houses and the canoes— everything that is, except Mouse Woman, who was very old and wise and hid as soon as trouble started. This was easy enough because she was very small and could hide in the crack of a plank. And she listened with her mouse ears as the three sisters munched and belched and fought amongst each other for the choicest portion of human flesh.

Now all this disturbed Mouse Woman mightily, as you might suppose, for she loved a balance to all things and hated what the foolish Chief had done and though she tried to warn him many times he always thought she was just chattering and so chased her off.

Raven, he can help, Mouse Woman decided. But she knew it might not be easy to persuade him because he was selfish himself, and vain and a glutton, too, and often up to no-good tricks. Still, he was the most power- ful being about and so she went off in search of him. After many days she found him high in a cedar. He was grooming his feathers and looking proudly all about him.

"Raven, have you heard of the three terrible sisters? They are walking all over the land and draining the streams dry and using whole forests for firewood and eating whole villages of humans and animals both, and they say they are going to eat you, too, because you are said to taste better than anything."

"Who says I taste so good? Who says? No one has ever eaten me before!" Raven cried.

"Oh, but they can just imagine! And why wouldn't you taste good? Look how handsome you are and shiny and large."

"That's true, I probably taste delicious, but they'll never know, will they?" And off he flew in search of the three sisters. He searched and searched until finally he saw them roaming around a valley, picking their teeth with trees and scratching their asses with boulders and nearby were shit-heaps the size of mountains and all was quiet because they'd eaten all the birds and anything else that made a sound including the wind.

"Hey, you three! Hey, you three," he called and they looked up and saw the largest, choicest bird they'd ever seen. The eldest one reached up to catch him. Raven flew just out of her grasp. Now the second eldest

leaped up. Now the youngest. They missed him every time and so in this way he led them back to their home village, them jumping and jumping and him bobbing just out of their reach. In fact, they jumped so much that they threw up all the People that they had eaten and all the animals and then all the water from the rivers they had drunk. And they became skinnier and smaller so that by the time they reached the bay of their home village they were only half the size they had been, which was a fair size still. And then Raven turned them to stone. Even now you can see the three sisters, standing in a row out in the waves on the edge of the bay. They must act as guardians of the village for all eternity now, and no thanks do they get for it. That is the price for their greed and gluttony. And every time the People see them they remember to give to the Animal People and to make sure that all is kept in balance. But even so the People were never as rich as they once had been, because that was the price for their foolishness.

Boston falls quiet. His throat is dry from talking. Never has he talked so much at once. But it has worked. Girl has fallen asleep, is wrapped in Boston's coat and huddled in the grass.

Boston does not sleep. He sits with his back against a stump, his revolver on his knees. He positions himself so he can espy people passing in the street. It was near here that Boston saw the Jesuit, Father Gaspar, give Christian names to three Samish in the Spring of '52—John, Joseph, Jeremiah. Father Gaspar was missing the middle finger of his left hand and the sun gleamed through the gap as he blessed them. Would that things had not changed. It was simple enough once, Fort Victoria abuzz with trade, the rules of the company clear, Douglas ruling it all. One thing was given for another. Everyone's function was discernible—the blacksmith's, the cook's, even the priest's trading reverence for salvation. But now? What to make, say, of these loud revellers sauntering down Government Street, illuminating their way with no less than four lamps, the three women in bright swishes of dresses, two of the men in regimentals, the third in a top hat and black jacket that forks like a swallow's tail. They are off to a night of dancing, on one of the Navy ships, perhaps, or at one of the houses of the wealthy. The two men in uniform are Navy men, certainly, but of the women and the other man, who can say?

The men begin singing. Boston knows the song. It is "The Yellow Rose of Texas." He heard it eight years and ninety-five days ago. Another trapper, distant from him, sang it as he skinned a beaver. And so Boston could sing it, certainly, if he were one for singing.

The song crescendoes, then transforms into laughter. Singing was the first sound he heard when he awoke at Fort Connelly. The memory comes unsought. Boston scowls. Others complain of memories springing up unawares, but this has not happened to Boston since he was beardless and had not yet learned how to keep the myriad images and words trussed until called upon.

He lies on furs on a narrow trestle in a narrow room. Through a doorway he sees an old woman tending a pot. He wonders if he is dead. It seems heaven enough to be warm, to have the smell of food nearby. The woman's song is a chanting refrain. He did not understand the meaning of the words then, but he recalled the sounds of them, as he was to recall everything he heard and saw from that moment forth.

He is naked but for the binding on his chest. The pain starts from his collarbone, radiates to his shoulder and down to his pelvis. In the old woman's fire are flames of blue and yellow. On the beams above hang ropes and traps and dried salmon. Stacked against the walls are furs, barrels and sacks. The room is white-washed, though streaked with soot, and it smells of smoke and fish and half-cured hide and of other things he has no name for yet.

The old woman sees his open eyes. She wears a labret and her lower lip juts out like a small shelf. He has never seen such a thing. He reaches out as if to touch her. "Equata," she says, before she shuffles off, chuckling.

"Can you speak English?" The man has a lean face and a sparse beard and a thick, incongruous nose. His hair is a thin net over his pale scalp. "I am Mr. Hiram Illdare, the Chief Trader. The leader here. Do you understand? Good. What do you recall? It is important you tell us. The Indians who brought you here spoke of a ship."

"Yes."

"Speak, lad, louder."

He explains as best he can, with what words he knows as the

fragments tumble one on top of the other. A great cracking. A rush of water. Immense cold. A battering of waves. A pebbled beach. A canvas overhead. A shadow figure of a man, cursing and weeping.

"A wreck then, not an assault by the Indians?"

"Wreck. Yes."

"Do you recall any landmark or positioning? Anything that would help lead us to it."

"No. no."

"More survivors. Can you at least recall that? We could hunt for them. It is our duty to do so."

He clenches his fist to his cheek.

"You believe yourself the only one?"

He nods and fire courses down his chest.

"Is James Milroy your name? Are you from Boston? Is the ship?"

"Forget."

"Is Milroy your father, then, a relation?"

"No, no father."

"Well, well. We have two Jameses here already. That's two enough, eh? We'll call you Jim, then. Jim of Boston. What of that?"

"Good. Yes."

Illdare studies him with an odd expression, then abruptly reaches down and strokes the hair from his eyes.

"*Mort?*" A pockmarked face. Lashings of dark hair. Pale eyes. A coat worn over his shoulders like a cape.

Illdare straightens. His countenance changes, becomes stern as the others crowd in. Their faces are pale and dark. Curious and impassive. Scarred and smooth. They shift aside and the boy sees two women with white blankets around their shoulders, beads in their dark hair. One has a nose ring that glints in the guttering light.

"'Ere, now, sir, did he say where the wreck was? Did ya, boy?" The man has yellow hair, a face raked with lines. The boy cringes before the rankness of his breath, looks to Illdare.

"The Indians would have scavenged the cargo by now. Leave him, all of you. Now."

The one with the pockmarks and pale eyes says: "Last rite, if die. It duty."

"You are not a priest, Lavolier. You seem to have forgotten that."

"He go purgatory."

"And where do you think he is now, you popish ghoul?"

The night is half gone. Boston watches Girl sleep. She is curled up in the grass, his coat covering her completely. She makes no sound. He crouches beside her and draws the coat back from her face. Her head is pillowed in her arms. Now he can hear her breathing faintly. Briefly he places his hand on her forehead, on her damp hair.

EIGHTEEN

ADDENDUM TO THE GENTLEMAN'S GUIDE
Should the Gentleman find that he is short of monetary accoutrements or, indeed, that he has been robbed most ignominiously while he peaceably slept at the way house known as Mrs. Jones House at the mark of 145 miles from the town of Lilloet of the Harrison route—a way house this author most strongly recommends avoiding like a house with the mark of the plague—then he may find that it is not unnecessary (unless he be one who can subsist upon berries and squirrels) to labour to thus have the means with which to eat & with which to later stake his claim in the goldfields which are so close they beckon like spirits in the mist.

The foreman bawls out *eight o'clock* and the road-clearing crew ceases their hacking of trees and brush. Eugene dumps his wheelbarrow for the last time, wipes his brow clean of the grime engendered by the burning slash. A horse is unhitched from a go-devil and stands exhausted in the waning light. Some distance behind, the road-building crew takes up their mattocks and pickaxes and hammers. All the men carry their own belongings, even the crew that builds the bridges and culverts and that is paid more than any, and certainly the crew of Chinamen and Indians that is paid the least and works apart from all the others entirely.

"No storm tonight," the foreman announces with the certainty of a prophet.

Eugene rubs bacon fat on his mosquito welts until he feels fit for the frying pan. From his flask he dribbles water onto his hands that are admirably begrimed and calloused after only ten days of labouring like a convict. A week more by most calculations. Then the road will be built entirely to the steamer dock at Soda Creek. Then Eugene will have fulfilled his contract and will have his pay, though the $1.50 a day will hardly make up for the £50 the thieves took from his pocket while he slept. Thankfully it was not the entirety of his money. The piddling rest was lining his boots. Fortunate he often sleeps with them on these days. Only in the last few days has he been able to think of his misfortune and not grow near apoplectic with rage.

From the back of a chuckwagon a stout Chinaman serves up stew, pigeon pie, beans, pemmican, bread, blueberry cobbler, coffee. Eugene is ravenous. Looks about for his tent mates—Young George Bowson and Langstrom the Swede. Spies Langstrom far up in the line, sidles next to him, tin plate used as a shield. Men mutter, too tired to protest outright.

"Are we ready for this evening, Langstrom? Ready?"

Langstrom vigorously nods, his ever-present pipe dangling from his lips like an elongated tooth. He has a perpetual squint, a heads-down walk, a beard that lies flattened against his chest. Seems in all as if he were raised in the brunt of a fierce wind. How he arrived this far and this alone is a mystery to Eugene, for Langstrom has barely any English and relies on energetic pantomime and gestures that might be taken for those of a madman. When Eugene asked after his family by indicating the shape of a woman, the low height of children, Langstrom gathered perhaps thirty sticks. Sticks ran away, lay with forbidden sticks. Sticks were born. Sticks were orphaned. Or abandoned. It was difficult to tell. Sticks fought. "Bad," said Langstrom and snapped a stick in half and cast it into the fire.

"Quite so," said Eugene, as if he understood completely, and perhaps he did. One story or misery and failed hope was, after all, becoming much like another.

They sit on rocks, their plates balanced on their knees. Young George joins them. Greets Eugene as he always does, as if he has not seen him for days. Mosquitoes settle on his thick shoulders like a mantle, on his flaxen hair that is already thin enough to show the vulnerability of his scalp. Poor bastard, thinks Eugene, not for the first time. It must be the young man's taut ruddy skin that attracts the damned bloodsuckers like beggars to a banquet. Unfortunately for Eugene and Langstrom,

Bowson believes that unwashed skin and fervent prayer will keep the mosquitoes at bay.

"Have you said grace yet, sirs?"

Eugene, his mouth stuffed full, mumbles they have not.

George presses his palms together. "May I? Is it all right with you, Doc? You, Mr. Langstrom?"

The Swede shrugs. Eugene nods. He likes that George and some others call him Doc out of respect for his learning and gentleman-like ways. Professor would be preferable, mind, but when was Eugene Augustus Hume one to quibble?

George squeezes shut his eyes. Eugene and Langstrom put down their forks. "And God bless my mother and sisters, and my father who's in heaven and the cows and make it rain enough for them so as there's hay in Ontario and please, Lord, find cousin Adair a good husband. Oh, and God bless Mr. Hume for all his kindness and good advice, and keep Mrs. Hume safe for when he returns. And God bless Mr. Langstrom too. . . . Wait, sirs, there's more."

Eugene puts down his fork again, says as jovially as he can: "I am sure there is, George, vast multitudes to bless. The food, however, is growing cold."

"And God bless the Queen and all her children and help her in her sorrow for her husband, amen," George says in a rush and then smiles.

"Amen," Eugene says.

"Amen," Langstrom echoes and touches the rough green stone about his neck.

"Are you prepared for this evening, Young George? I sense luck once again in the air, good clean luck."

"Gosh, Doc, I dunno if it's a good idea is all."

"The Lieutenant is away, not to worry."

"It isn't that so much. It's the gambling. I promised mother I wouldn't is all. She says that gambling is a terrible sin."

"A sin? Come now. You need not gamble yourself. Merely ring the bell. We can win money this evening as we did last week. Money we will need for our claim. Do it for us, lad."

"All right, then, all right," he says and smiles bravely. Eugene claps him on the shoulder, feels an avuncular affection for the young man, a comrade-in-arms friendship for Langstrom. They are all partners now. Have sworn on George's Bible to pool their capital and buy a paying claim. Eugene has great confidence in their success. Langstrom appears to have some expertise in mining, certainly he keeps gesturing knowledgeably at the ground. George has a strong back and is a good hand at the carpentry. Eugene has the best suggestions for a name. The Golden Bough or the Dora Dear is what he favours now. Ah, dear George, good Langstrom. If not for them, Eugene would have tossed aside his axe and barrow the same day he began. The money is hardly worth the while. Only the promise of a partnership has kept him here, the information that good claims can still be found for men willing to seek them.

Full dark and insects halo the lamps hung from cross poles. Perhaps fifteen men jostle for position in their tent. Their shadows, thrown up against the canvas, meld into one writhing form. A bottle of whiskey is being passed round. Eugene takes a drink. And then another. Whiskey is not as despicable as once he thought. In any case, he is not one to put on airs, to refuse the offers of honest men.

A droplet falls on Eugene's neck, and then another. He does not look up for a spitter, for someone sweating more profusely than most in the fuggy air, the challenge before him is too important. The four contestants—Langstrom, Eugene, a bandy-legged Philadelphian, a thin-faced Mexican—crouch at the ready. Before each is a tin plate bisected with chalk lines. It is their fifth round of the evening. Langstrom's Gustavus has won once, Eugene's Lilith twice.

"Lilith! Lilith! Lightning Lilith," Eugene sings out. "Win this race and you'll win my heart. I'll write you an ode. I'll sing your praises to the Gods."

An enormous Irishman holds aloft a kettle that is stuffed with bills, ajangle with coins. "Place your bet, lads, place 'em, place 'em!"

The shouting comes from all corners.

"Three on Doc Hume's Lilith!"

"She's got nothing on the Swede's what-ya-call-it. Three dollars says the Swede wins."

"Six shillings on the Señor's Migro."

"Milagro!" the Mexican shouts.

"Don't matter the name, it won't live fucking long enough to be remembered!"

"Over here, Paddy, we're betting two dollars on Mr. Washington."

"He damn well deserves more than that!" the Philadelphian shouts.

"Doc, how you know she female!"

"Because my darling, beautiful Lilith does as she's told!" This draws a gust of laughter from the men, a doubtful glance from George. Ah, so at least two of them understand the jest. For Lilith, the first wife of Adam, was transformed into a succubus when she abandoned her husband. Lilith was a fitting name for a louse then, though not, of course, for an obedient woman.

"Smith! What you betting? Place 'em! Place 'em!" the Irishman shouts.

"Saving my bloody bets for a bloody craps table in Camerontown! Lice racing, hah. You're desperate, the bloody lot of ya!"

"Count on the English to be miserly! Last call! Last call!"

Money shifts hands. The Irishman dashes out chits. George rings the bell. Langstrom's louse Gustavus immediately crawls over the lip of the plate. Langstrom slaps his forehead in a parody of despair. Grinds his louse into the dirt with the heel of his hand. Roars with laughter.

Howls. Shouts of disappointment. Men elbow each other for a view. The Mexican seems to be praying as his louse Milagro steadies on. The Philadelphian's Mr. Washington is nearly to the dividing line. Stops, turns. The Philadelphian pounds his fists on either side of the plate, yells: "Get a move on! Stay the course, damn you. No turning and running like a yellow coward!"

Mr. Washington stops completely. The Philadelphian tips the plate.

"You! Out! Illegal that is!" shouts the Irishman.

The Philadelphian throws up his hands.

Here is a scene that would give even a Londoner pause. What are rat pits and cockfights compared to this? What a colourful interlude for Eugene's guidebook! What a.... "Lilith! Lilith, my love."

She trundles over the dividing line of the plate, a louse breadth before the Mexican's. Men huzzah, wave bottles over their heads and punch the air. Even George is grinning now.

Eugene gives a champion's salute, takes a champion's drink from the proffered bottle.

The Irishman is doling out the winnings. Arguments erupt, subside. Eugene knows there will be no fights, no grudges. The mood is too jocular, the losses too minor, and the event too ludicrous. It was his most excellent idea to set the maximum bet at three dollars each, to make it merely a lark, merely a way to pass the time. Still, he has made near two weeks' wages in one fell swoop. Let Lilith return to where he found her, nestled snug in his beard with all her sisters. Let her feast to her heart's content. Christ and all his saints! Is he now so uncouth? Ah, well. When in Rome. When in Rome.

"Mr. Hume!"

The tent falls silent. Men shuffle behind each other. Look about as if they have lost something. Their senses perhaps.

"Lieutenant. Lieutenant. Quite so. You have returned. You are here. Ah. Well."

Lieutenant Olsen speaks through gritted teeth, through thick moustaches. "Yes, I am here. Most certainly here. You there, pick up those plates. And you, Mr. Hume, step outside with me, sir." He turns smoothly on his heel, back ramrod straight, as if he is nailed to a door.

The men mutter in sympathy as Eugene slowly follows. The tents are clustered in a swale near a small lake. Fires flag out thick smoke from green wood to keep the mosquitoes at bay.

The Lieutenant waits by a skid some twenty paces off. He seems a tin soldier in the moonlight, his regimentals drained of their scarlet and gold. The sight heartens Eugene. He strides forward, gathering his thoughts, putting his limbs into some kind of harmony with each other. He has imbibed too liberally. It happens at times. No matter, he must merely consider himself alike to an automaton with ingenious hinges and wooden limbs that must be lifted just so for effect.

"How was the expe . . . expedition, Lieutenant? Is the trail well-blazed? I met one of your number at the great canyon several weeks ago. Did I mention this? Ah, but we had a splendid chat. A fine job you gentlemen do, a fine job. I was in the Crimea you know. Sevastopol. And I can tell you, most certainly, that her Majesty . . . Majesty . . . would be . . ."

"Proud? I think not. Not with such as you reeling drunk and inciting gambling in the camp when I clearly stated that such things were forbidden."

"Sir, I would scarcely call it gambling. There were no cards, no . . . no roulette wheels, no dice. It was small wagers only. It was mere entertainment after a hard day's toil." He throws a sweeping gesture toward his tent, to the men outside of it, their stances those of eaves-droppers. "Have pity on the men. Punish me if you must. But have pity . . ."

"Oh, for God's sake, man, shut it. It is hardly as if I can send you swinging from the gallows, much as that would appeal."

"Ah, quite so."

Lieutenant Olson sighs in exasperation.

Poor man! Such an amorphous authority. Not that it was a foil, what Eugene just implied about sacrifice. For he would. Yes. He would, in a heartbeat, sacrifice himself for these admirable men of all nations and creeds, and they for him. They would protest mightily if he were sent packing, the Lieutenant must realize this. They would refuse to work until he was reinstated. His name would become a rallying cry. And surely the Lieutenant will consider that he is as strong as two men, or at least a man and a half. And educated enough to give advice on the positioning of the blazes, the possible trajectory for the road. Will consider that there are barely enough men, Chinamen and Indians in-cluded, to finish the road in the required time. The Lieutenant cannot afford to lose even one man; thus, he must walk a tightrope between appeasement and command, and must do so while retaining his honour. Well, by God, Eugene Augustus Hume will not force him into a corner.

"I believe we are cut of the same cloth, sir. My great third cousin is an earl, you see, and my father a knight and they . . ."

"Your father may well be the King of Spain for all it matters here."

"Ah, but."

"And we are not cut of the same cloth. My father was a barber, so do not attempt to ingratiate yourself with me, sir."

"Ah, quite so, the man has no gentility."

"Speak louder if you have something to say. You sound like a tinker in his cups."

"I was saying . . . saying . . . that you are at least a man of sensibility. I have seen you in the evenings, silhouetted on a promontory, paying homage on bended knee to the vista below you, the great swath of stars above you."

"Paying homage!" the Lieutenant shouts. "I am gauging our latitude and longitude by the stars so I may make a map that will stand for generations to come. I am not composing pointless odes like some consumptive poet!"

"Quite so, but . . ."

"Gambling and drinking! Merrily in hand they go. And then what happens to the calibre of the work for which I am responsible? It becomes shoddy. And what happens to the men? They become fools. They leave blasting powder too close to the fire. They blast Old John sky high. Do you follow, Mr. Hume?"

"Old John?"

"And now I am without a foreman for the Chinese crew. Fools and shoddy work. Merrily in hand they go."

"Sir, you have my word of honour that it will not happen again, but to explain. It is just that I won. It is just that I cannot stop winning."

The Lieutenant sighs, says quietly now: "Everyone stops winning sooner or later, I assure you."

"Quite so, quite so, but fortune is smiling at me. Her lovely arms open. Never mind that I have been fleeced by innkeepers, by ferrymen that could be kin to Charon, that I have been robbed by bandits, have fought against ferocious beasts, have toiled on this road like an Antipodean felon. I, Eugene Augustus Hume, am a lucky man."

"I assure you, there is no such thing as luck. You won. The others lost. As such one man's *luck* is always another man's despair. Where was Mr. Sang's luck?"

"Whose?"

"My Chinese foreman, Old John. Have you not been listening?"

"Perhaps their luck is not useful here?"

"Don't be ridiculous. It is a false equation to think that luck can be owed or used as money is, or favours for that matter. Luck is not stored. It is not parcelled out. Luck is a random ordering. A matter of ratios. Never have I encountered so many gamblers as here, men who believe in ridiculous amulets, who believe in a destiny they need only step into as if it were a pair of boots. Toil and restraint, such are the key to one's success. Not luck. Not at all."

"Listen, I beg you. I, too, am a man of reason. I, too, have more than a passing acquaintance with rational thought. But the evidence is accumulating that I am . . . well? What should it be called? I am lucky. Yes. There is no other name for it."

Eugene speaks of the aura some have seen about him, like a bluish halo. Of his certainty that a grand destiny is in store for him. It is why the others consider him a kind of a talisman, why they wish to gamble when he is about. Eugene's voice rises as he speaks, becomes insistent. Even he can hear it in a sort of whine. Even he has trouble believing himself.

"My friend Judge Begbie claimed he had never met a man whose destiny was so evident. He said . . ."

"Enough of this. You are rambling like a madman. This is your second infraction. You will be deducted three days' pay. See my clerk in the morning about the rest and then be gone."

"My second infraction? What . . ."

"The strike. You were the instigator there as well."

"I . . . I did not suggest it. I am being wrongly accused. It was the Americans. The Dutchman. Some others. I forget."

"We cannot afford strikes. The road must be built."

"But we relented after only one day."

"Why should the Chinese and the Indians receive less than you? What matter is it of yours? They work harder than the lot of you and without all the drinking and gambling and carrying on and complaining. If I had my druthers they'd be out-waging you."

"I did not say their wages should be lowered. I merely voted, along with the others, the many others, that we, the white crews, should receive more. And in hindsight, in hindsight, I agree with you entirely. Allow me to quote my great friend, the High Judge Begbie: "The yellow man and the red are all the same under British law and . . .""

"You admit it then. You were involved."

"No, I merely went along. Please, consider that if you send me packing you must send us all."

"You rate yourself too highly. Not a man will protest your departure. You will stand as an example. Good evening, Mr. Hume."

Eugene watches the Lieutenant stride off. Calls out: "Fine, good, splendid. I hardly care. Hardly. Do not expect charity from me, however, once I have struck the lead, as they say. Once I am rich, indeed."

The Lieutenant gives no sign that he has heard him. Eugene stands alone. The other men have lost interest in the spectacle and have drifted back to their tents, many no doubt thinking of the proximity of the dawn when the taste of road dust will overlay that of stale whiskey and bad dreams. Eugene should be angry, furious. A scapegoat, that is what he is, nothing more. But instead he feels an even greater certainty of his coming fortune. It is as if it is all going to plan.

It is a night full of shadows and quicksilver light, a night that can trick the mind and the eyes. Still, something, someone, shifts in the thickets.

"Who's there?" He parts the brambles. A small, furred creature rushes past his legs. Night hare? Fox? Goblin? Eugene yelps and falls onto his back. The earth shifts like a raft on a gentle sea. A warm wind is scattering the mosquitoes. The swath of the Milky Way arches over him. So this Olsen sees no poetry in the firmament, only latitudes and longitudes, only angles and degrees. A pity for him. Likely he also does not notice the crickets that sound like the mutter snores of night itself, nor that haunting fluty call of some nocturnal bird. Likely he never bore affection for woman or beast. Ah, faithful Ariadne, waiting hobbled in the fields. Everyday he slathers her with mud as protection against the insect hordes. When it dries she seems to be in the process of hatching. At least the grass is good, as least she is growing plumper by the day. Dear girl!

A mosquito has burrowed under his collar. He lets it suck its fill. Where is Lilith? He has forgotten Lilith. Ah, but not Dora. Not Dora.

"Doc. There you are. Gosh, you all right?"

"What? Dora?"

"It's George."

"Wife? Hah. He think wife."

"Who are you? What?"

"It's your friends, is all. I'm George. Here's Langstrom."

They haul Eugene to his feet.

"Ah, the Good Swede, the Saintly Young George. I have failed. I must be on my way come the morrow. You will join me? Will you?"

George clears his throat. "We would, 'course. I would, anyway. But our contracts. We won't get our pay, is all. None of it. And Mr. Langstrom and me, well, we've been working near a month."

"Of course, of course. Do not fear, I will find us a claim. We will be rich. I can sense it as surely as I sensed that Lilith would win. Did I not say Lilith would win?"

"You did," George says.

"Ya, win," Langstrom says.

"Say a prayer for me, will you, Young George? There's a fine chap. I need a prayer."

"Easy now, Doc. Easy. Let's get you on to bed for some shut-eye."

The black powder explodes and Old John hurtles upward and stays balanced in the crux of a gigantic tree. On a nearby branch brocaded ladies dangle their jewelled shoes over the abyss and clap as if witnessing a feat of acrobatics. Old John has wispy grey moustaches and wrinkles about his panicked eyes. He waves his bloodless stumps and voicelessly screams. Eugene can see clear down his throat, clear to the green sea churning in his gut and a square-sailed ship careening there, can see clear to the man's childhood in a misty village adorned with pagodas and white flags. The Lieutenant is there, dressed in silken robes. He is berating Eugene. "Your fault. You fool. Shoddy work and fools. Merrily they go. Merrily down the lane." Dora stands beside Olsen. She is coyly smiling and holds her breasts in her hands the way a baker might hold out two round loaves of bread. "Do you want them, or not, Eggy? There are others waiting. Make up your mind." Eugene cannot breath. Cannot move. Why is so much asked of him? He is only a man, only a man.

NINETEEN

Boston prods Girl awake at first light. They eat the last of his food. Girl eats her share ravenously, gulps water from his flask, then picks up the crumbs that have fallen in the grass.

"Getting a dress for you. The Lady wants you looking nice. Stay here. Lie low. Like a mouse in the grass. Don't be talking to anyone. Send you back to Petrovich if you do." He repeats this in Chinook. She grabs his hand with her own. It is cold and surprisingly rough. It does not feel like a child's hand, more like some small sea creature, a starfish perhaps, or something with a similarly slow and stubborn life.

At the Hudson's Bay Store Mr. Gifford looks nervously at Boston. "Excellent to see you again, sir. You are here to collect your goods I take it. Not to worry. I have kept them safe for you. Ah, your receipt, thank you." He heaves Boston's goods onto the table, checks off the receipt, then hands it back to Boston. "I heard of your misfortune, Mr. Jim. That I did. I was speaking of it to Farlane and Bennet, who are just here, just in the store room, sure to be back in a trice. I doubt Mr. Kines . . ."

Boston is holding up his clasp knife.

"Farlane! Bennet!"

Boston places the knife on the counter. "What'll you give for it."

"Give for it? Ah. I see. I see." Gifford dabs his forehead with his sleeve. Boston waits without moving while Gifford settles himself.

"May I?" he asks finally and reaches for the knife. Gingerly he tests the blade with his thumb. The handle is of ebony and is inlaid with mother-of-pearl. "I can give ye one pound."

"One pound is it."

"Or one pound, ten shillings."

"You can take the coal oil back, then. And won't take less than two pounds for the knife. Cost more than that. It's got good silver."

"I kin see that. It is just that we have an abundance of knives at the moment."

Boston frowns. His hand drifts over his bowie knife. It is a fine piece, easily finer than his clasp knife. The double-sided blade is ten inches long, the quillon is of silver, and the engraving on the handle is of a creature half-horse, half-alligator, and is wrought so well the creature looks as if it might spring to life. He got this knife off an American two years and seven days ago and has used it near every day since, for the bowie is designed for the ordinary tasks of skinning and gutting as well as for the killing of men.

Gifford is swallowing nervously. "But as you are an excellent customer, or so I have heard, then the clasp knife. . . . Let me look again."

A time later and Boston is walking through Bastion Square, a package under his arm. Soon he will be telling the Dora woman that Girl belongs to her now, and the Dora woman will exclaim. "Ah, well and so! It is just what I was wanting! Why she even looks a bit like Isabel."

Two children brush by him calling: "My turn, my turn now." A man with a brace of bottles calls out the price for a gross of jalap, a pound of opium, a bottle of Turlington's balm.

Boston buys potatoes and camas roots from two Indian women. The younger one pulls them steaming from a coal-laden pot. Wraps them in leaves.

"*Mahsie*," he says.

"*Mahsie, Kahpho*," she replies.

Older brother? Why not? Once an exchange is made it creates a bond, however tenuous. All about, exchanges are being made and contemplated and weighed. All about him, the world is being held in balance.

Girl leaps out of the grass. "Dress? Dress?"

"Not for you. For the Lady. It's for her you're being made pretty."

She prods the package. "Want see."

"No. Have to clean you up. Then put it on you."

She pats his arm, as if in some kind of thanks. Why is she crying?

Will she cry when she is with the Dora woman? Will she be of any use to her? But then Isabel Lund was weepy and she apparently inspired in the Dora woman a type of courage. Girl might well do the same. Boston puts his hand on Girl's head. His smile is a brief upward movement of his beard.

They stick again to the alleys, walk around shattered bottle glass, a pool of black sludge. A woman pounds a ragged carpet with a stick. A man squatting at his morning stool grimaces as they pass. Soon enough they are through Chinatown and then onto the path through the marshlands. The day is fine and hot. The salal quivers with small birds. Frogs croak from the reeds.

Girl trots to keep up with his strides. Soon she is breathing hard and limping. He crouches and peers at the thin lines of blood. It will take more than the usual two days to reach the Cowichan, that much is obvious. He pulls the thistle from the hard sole of her foot, then tears a strip from her sack dress and tightly binds her foot. She does not whimper. "Good," he says.

By late afternoon they reach the base of an inlet. A stream fans out from the immensity of the trees. Sunlight through the poplars and cedars casts fragmented shadows on the rocky shore. Boston finds a long, thick branch and sharpens it with his bowie knife. He wishes briefly for the clasp knife that is now in Gifford's keeping, for the bowie knife, no matter what its many uses, does not have that knife's finesse.

He waits at the stream, spears three salmon in succession. He turns to show Girl but she is gone. He calls her and she appears after a few moments, holding something in the hem of her dress. Shows him the fiddleheads, mushrooms, fern roots.

They stuff the gutted salmon with her findings, then roast them over a fire, rocks acting as a brace. The meal tastes finer than any Boston has had in a long while. It is the clean smell of the breeze and the clean sound of birds that makes it seem so. The prison was rank. The shit bucket overflowed. A roach crawled sideways along the floor. Coom shouted out that they were damned.

Boston sucks a salmon head. There it is again, that sense of elongated time, that sense of fullness. He felt it at the Dora woman's place, once he had resigned himself to staying. He felt it years ago, with

Kloo-yah. A word appears to him, an English word: contentment. He supposes it might suit best.

"Wash now," he says.

Girl grins and a gap shows where a tooth has gone missing. She pulls the sacking over her head and runs into the water up to her waist. She shivers and hugs herself.

"Under. Get your hair," Boston calls. She dips under and rises spluttering. Boston throws her the store-bought soap and makes the motion of washing. She does so, eyes shut tight. Her hip bones and ribs prod through her skin. Her nipples are as small, puckered scars on the flatness of her chest. Boston turns his back to keep a sudden anger at bay. She need not be so oblivious to her own vulnerability. She looks as if she would crumple in a minor wind. She looks as fodder for a puma, or for those colossal birds of prey seen on rare occasions catching the high winds. She looks, certainly, with that hairless, unguarded sex, as prey for men. Boston sees her again in the shack, Petrovich's hand on her neck, her wary gaze.

He squints into the lowering sun and aims his revolver. Girl yelps at the shot and a green-winged duck flaps its last.

"You need more food."

She crouches naked by the fire while Boston cuts the duck and spears its parts for the embers. "I clean. Dress. Dress now," she says.

"No. Tomorrow, when we're close. Don't want it getting dirty. Put that on again." He points to the calico shift. She shakes her head furiously. Not until they have finished the duck and she has washed her face and hands again does Boston relent.

She unwraps the package with great care. The simple dress is the blue of an autumn sky at dusk, darker than the shore-water blue Dora wears, but of the same company: sky and water, one reflecting the other. Girl touches it with reverence, strokes the black stockings, the shoes, the comb. "We know what looks pretty on a girl," the old woman at the haberdashery said. "We knew you'd come back and let us help you, that we did."

Girl awkwardly pulls on the stockings, then the dress. It is slightly large for her, but this does not signify. "They grow," the old woman assured him.

"You," Girl says, pointing at the many buttons of the black shoes.

Boston does them up for her, but slowly as the buttons are needlessly numerous and small. Girl walks unsteadily along the rocky shore, her limp made worse. She laughs, returns to the fire. Now sweeps a rock clean and sits and forces the comb through her hair. The snarls are too great and she holds it out to Boston with a sigh of exasperation. She winces when he pulls too hard, once swats gently at his hands. He crushes the lice in his nails. In all, it is a task that takes until the sun is gone.

Boston adds more wood to the fire. He sits with his back against a log. Girl sits beside him.

"Lady. Pretty?"

"She's good. She'll be good to you. Lives in a nice cabin. Her and her husband. You be like a daughter to them."

"Yes. I good help. Get food. There. There." She points to the forest, the water.

"Not with your dress on."

"No. Dress clean. Good."

"Yes."

She points to Boston. "Visit? Visit me?"

"Suppose. Yes," Boston says, though he had meant to say no.

Girl smiles. "Story now."

Boston pokes at the fire. "Just one."

"Yes."

And so Boston tells her a story that Kloo-yah told him. How in the beginning of the world the moon was always fat and full and satisfied and was bright as his brother the sun. And Raven became jealous because even he, with all his power, never knew if each day was going to be better or worse than the last. And so how could he be happy? How could he be satisfied? Why should the sun and the moon never know melancholy? The sun was too bright and strong for the Raven to steal and so he stole the moon and locked him up, and the moon mourned for the sky. Soon the moon was only half himself and then a silver splinter, but before moon could disappear Raven let him out. And then he was like the rest of the world—satisfied and glad and full for a time, and then lean and aching and nearly lost.

"Story. More."

She is insatiable for stories. She should sleep. He should sleep.

They must leave early in the morning. Yet now he does not want the next morning to arrive, nor the moment when he stands before the Dora woman again. Strange that he should dread it and yet desire it.

He tells her of Gulliver and his strange travels. These tales were some of Illdare's favourites. They spent long evenings with Boston reading aloud, and then Illdare. Boston now abridges the stories as best he can, for it would be days before he recited all of Gulliver's adventures. He tells of Lilliput and its tiny inhabitants, of Brobdingnag and its giants. He tells of the flying island of Laputa, and then of the island of the wise and virtuous talking horses, and how among them lived creatures called the Yahoos, who were a form of degraded people. Boston dwells on the last part, for this was Illdare's favourite. How Gulliver came home to England and could not bear to be about people, not even his wife and children, for they reminded him of the Yahoos and filled him with loathing and disgust.

"So this Gulliver spent at least four hours a day with his horses because even though these ones couldn't talk, he liked them better than people. And after a while he'd sit with his wife, but the smell of Yahoos was too much for him and he had to stop up his nose with rue and lavender and tobacco leaves. That's it. The story."

Girl yawned, stretched out closer to the fire. Held up one finger.

Boston settled down beside her. "One more. That's it, Girl."

She nodded.

"The lady told me this one. You should be hearing it, since she likes it so much. It's about a poet fellow. He drowned. Had seen it coming . . ."

He looks down. Girl is sleeping. He covers her with his coat, stokes the fire. Now gets into his bedroll. The waves lap noisily at the shore.

"Oh, but he were famous, Mr. Jim. Eggy told me of him. Percy Shelley his name was. He drowned after he saw the ghost of his little girl. Poor mite. He saw his own double, too. There's a German word for that; I think it's German. Eggy would know it. You can ask him someday. Well and so, this double person warned Mr. Shelley about his coming death. It were a premonition, like. That's the word. He was on a boat. His own boat, I'm guessing, and it sank in a terrible storm. I know about terrible storms now and I can't but think how wretched it would be to die like that. His friends found him washed up on the shore. In Spain, it was, or maybe Italy. They sounded like strange folk to me, this Shelley and his friends and their wives, but my Eggy admired them because they weren't afraid of flouting society and all its rules and that. Eggy said takes more courage than fighting battles and the like. They didn't bury the poor man, see. They burned him on the beach, right there where he washed up. Just like they do in India and such. And when it was nearly done his friend, I don't remember the name, but he saw that Shelley's heart didn't burn up—it must have been such a strong heart, don't you think?—and so he snatched it out of the fire and put it in a nice box and gave it to Shelley's widow. They found it with her things when she died, oh, years and years later. That story always sets me going, it does. It's so sad and beautiful, and at the same time, like. I envied Mrs. Shelley when Eggy told me that story. I said I'd never heard anything so romantic. It's like she had some part of his love forever, right there on her mantel."

Boston stokes the fire for the last time. He turns onto his side, his revolver near to hand. Girl stirs and curls into his back. She is a pocket of warmth and not unwelcome, no.

Girl is gone when he wakes to a grey sky. He did not hear her leave. Odd. Usually he sleeps lightly enough to be aware of any movement. He rubs his beard, spits, then nudges the fire. The embers are faintly alive. She must be at her morning stool, must be in the bushes near. His coat is there. The dress as well. It is laid out neatly on a log, the stockings and shoes on the rocks below. It is as if she has melted from within her garments. He calls her name once, twice. He shouts louder and a flock of ducks rises flapping out of the rushes. She must be seeking breakfast—berries or camas, yes, and did not want to dirty her dress. He had warned her not to, after all.

The nearby bush shows no evidence of her passage. He searches in an ever wider circle about their camp. Strips and wades into the water. Searches for a wave of hair, a shadow of thin limbs. There is a faint ringing in his ears, a hollowness in his gut. He curses her, curses the sky, pounds at the water. Back on shore he hauls on his clothes. Again he searches the brush, the nearby forest. Again he calls her name. In the afternoon he spears another fish and eats it raw and with an intense concentration, as if the eating were a test in which the reward was his own life.

The day is windless and hot. He pulls out a few strands of her dark hair from the comb and winds them tight around his thumb. Grips the comb. The teeth bite into his palms. He saw her vulnerability. He should have told her not to stray. He should not have wasted his breath on stories about Raven and Gulliver and that idiotic poet, Shelley. He should have told her of the horrid creatures who lurk at the border of the forest and shore, at the borders between men and beasts and who were worse than any Yahoo. He should have warned her of the Boqs who are hairy and stooped and have penises so long they have to be carried rolled up in their arms, of Matlose—black-bristled, with great claws and a voice so terrible that it alone could kill—of Skookums in all their varieties. Then she would not have strayed off. Would not have dared.

He searches and waits. Searches and waits. Calls until his voice is hoarse. Clouds filter over the sun. The day is drawing to its end. He is searching further and further into the forest. All is shadows and green. All is oddly quiet. A faint crack. He whirls. "Girl!" he shouts.

The bear shuffles toward him, then settles on its haunches. It is a small bear, barely old enough to be on its own. Boston holds his revolver ready. It should run. It should not be looking at him unafraid. Looking at him as if it wants to speak. He knows then, and the knowledge is a hard thrumming in his chest. She did not know her people. Or would not say. She came naked to Petrovich from the forest. She left Boston in the same manner. It is what they did sometimes, the bear people. Traded off their skins and tried on those of a human for a time. It is evident enough that of all the animals the bear is the best at adopting human form. Anyone can see how they favour human company, how they favour human food. Anyone can see how a skinned bear has a human shape.

"You shoulda told me. Wouldn't of taken you then. Bear people aren't what the lady needs."

He thrusts his revolver back through his belt. She became caught in the human world. It happens to those who are too young. At least she is fine, after a fashion, at least she did not wander off in search of food, become lost, meet some bitter end. No.

"Go on back to your people, then. Go on then. GO!"

She dashes off. For a while he hears her crashing through the bush.

And then the forest is still. No breeze and no sound excepting his own harsh breathing.

He stays that night by the shore and does not sleep. It is as if he is mired there, unable to move forward, unable to move back. He feeds the fire but he does not eat. He has failed, yet again, and so again he relives the day he met the Dora woman. He sees the Dora woman returning the tobacco pouch. Hears the words "for your birthday, like," as clearly as if she were whispering them in his ear.

A second night comes on. Still he has not eaten, nor slept. Her stories of London parade before him until he finally steps firmly onto the cobbled street. He doesn't move, cannot move. He is not one for astonishment, and yet. . . .The crowd presses into him. He stumbles forward. "Get outta the way, ye bloody idjit!" someone yells. There are the Hindu tract sellers she spoke of, the piemen, the muffin men, the match girls, the bird sellers. There are the blind beggars, the crippled beggars, the drink-sodden beggars. There are the women who dance on stilts, there the street orchestras. He walks on haltingly past the gin shops and shoe sellers, the rag and bone shops, past shadow men who lounge against the dank walls and watch him intently, without curiosity. The smells are of shit and smoke, of rotting things, of sweat, of ash. He knows such smells, but here all are intensified, as if it were here that such odours were born. Of other smells he has no reference. And the noise! All around costermongers are crying out their wares amid the clopping and rumbling of innumerable carriages and carts, amid the pipes and organs of the musicians. A boy passes him at a half run. He is holding up a tract, throwing out promises of seduction, murder, betrayal.

He turns 'round in bewilderment and it is a night in early winter. Newcut market now battles with the light the Dora woman so adores: tallow candles, grease lamps, tin lamps cut with stars and angels, the stoves of the chestnut men glowing red. Glowing globes of blue and green dangle from the roofs of coffee vendors where men in top hats and long coats converse with women whose skirts are hiked to their ankles.

He knows, somehow, where he must go. Finds the narrow street where the roofs of the opposing buildings lean together, nearly touching. Finds the drapery store. The door is thrown open. The interior is smaller than the Dora woman suggested. Her mother is folding a length of white cloth behind the high counter, a paraffin lamp beside her. She is wrapped in several shawls. She is comely, according to the white men's standards. Her skin is white, against the dark shine of her hair. Her throat is long. Her eyes wide. Does she look, as Dora insisted, as might a queen? Boston cannot compare, having never seen a queen in the flesh before. There. Coming along the street. Dora's father. So it is before her father's misfortune. A large man turning to fat, he holds his own in the street. Others part around him, return his hearty greetings. Boston draws back into the shadows. Dora walks beside her father. She is half-grown; her hair hangs down her back in a pale mat. She is chatting and showing her white teeth. She holds her father's hand. He is grinning also, nodding. He is also proud. Of her, of himself, of the world he inhabits. Dora's mother is now at the doorway. Dora's father throws an arm about her, kisses her cheek. "My dove, my wife." And then to Dora, "Ah, my favourite girl. Promise me you'll have a marriage as blessed as ours then, eh?"

"I will, I promise," Dora says fervently. And then these three lock arms about each other so that they block the doorway, are as one dark form.

The Dora woman never spoke of such a scene. Boston grips the wooden post beside him. A splinter drives into his thumb. The pain is sharp and true. He is truly here, then. He is about to step forward and ask this Dora what she wants of him when the ground shifts and he is back again at the shore where he lost Girl.

Never has he fallen into memories. His own or others'. Never has he heard of it happening before. Equata said that in her dreams she travelled to the lands of King George's Men. There she saw spires piercing the clouds, saw men of bronze, and houses large enough for ten thousand families, saw children pleading before wheeled boxes made of gold and led by four-legged beasts that were larger than bears. But it was the present Equata saw; never had she claimed to fall into the past, nor into another's memories.

He studies his thumb by the light of the fire. Yanks the splinter from it.

All through that night he tries to fall into her memories again. But he cannot. Dawn is now a red smudge over the trees. He is in this time, in this world. And yet a message must lie in the scene he witnessed between the Dora woman and her parents. What of the endearments? The embrace? Her promise to have a blessed marriage?

"He's all alone on that road, Mr. Jim, with no one to watch out for him. Riches are nothing if you're dead. Mr. Hume home with me, that's all I'm wanting. I'd be so perfectly happy then." Five times she mentioned her husband, always with sighs and sad smiles. She returned what was precious to him. He must return what is precious to her. An action for an action. Boston was a fool not to have realized this before, to have wasted his time on gimcracks, on Girl even. It will put all back in balance. He stands. It is good to know such absolute resolve.

TWENTY

A country stroll from Quesnel to Barkerville? What cretin told him this? Damn his eyes. Damn him and his bloody damned relations to the tenth generation.

"Arie, please, I beg you. Do not fail me now. I'll fête you with the finest oats, with a warm stable, mash. Golden bloody horseshoes, muleshoes." Eugene is speaking urgently, softly, swallowing his panic. He must for her sake.

His boots are braced in a labyrinthine fall of logs that is slick with moss and smashed slugs. He yanks on her bridle with one hand; his other has hold of a stunted, twisted tree. All about him are plants with oily leaves and sickly yellow flowers. Carrion eaters? He has heard of such diabolical plants. Likely they entice the unwary with some intoxicating vapour. Only this could explain how they stumbled off the main path and came to this. Eugene had faithfully followed the wavering needle of his compass. He had not led them astray.

It is no use. The bog has her. She is up to her belly now. She is exhausted from her thrashing and rimmed with sweat and her eyes roll in panic.

They are not alone in their predicament. Dotted about them are dead horses, mules, cattle, even a moose. Many are mired upright so that it seems they might totter on forward at any moment, decayed and fly infested and reeking like some hellish visitation.

"Goddamnit! Bloody hell. Fuck!" Eugene grapples with the supplies on Ariadne's back, nearly tumbles into the bog himself, so far does he have to lean. He unlashes the trunks and sacks. Struggles under their cumbersome weight, finally thrusts them clanking and thudding into the bush. The bandana falls from his face and he inhales innumerable flies. Gags from this and from the stench of rot. Would vomit if he had anything left in his belly.

He looks upward and apologizes profusely for his lack of observance to Sundays, his poor attendance at church, his belief in luck over prayer. Grey clouds stretch apart in a high wind. He shuts his eyes. Hears Ariadne's laboured breathing and his own, hears the quarrelling of the birds, the hellish symphony of the mosquitoes and black flies, feels the bite of those miniscule demons that tear hunks out of a man's flesh, that could no doubt flay him slowly alive.

He left the road crew three mornings ago. Bid farewell to George Bowson and Langstrom and arranged to meet up with them in two weeks' time in Camerontown. Promised to stake out a fine claim. Good that he was going early, they all agreed. It was already the second week of July. The season had already begun.

He disembarked from the steamer at Quesnel, a town so full of celestials he might have disembarked at Canton. He walked with a party of Cornishmen for the first day. The trail was a thin slash through murky forests, over logs and stumps. At times the mud was knee-deep. Other trails led off from this so-called main trail. Did prospectors make these? he wondered. Or did the beasts in these parts? Didn't Mr. Barrymore mention a bear? Yes. Ursus something or other. They are big as bulls, vicious as lions. Are man-eaters. Likely they prefer English flesh to all others.

"Keep going east," the Cornishmen advised just after they told him he was slowing them down, just before they tromped off without him. The youngest, a boy no more than fourteen, gave him bannock and a fill of water from his own flask and then that frank look of pity that children sometimes bestow upon the cursed.

He spent that night under the protection of some fallen trees. He huddled in his bedroll, wondered where his splendid luck had gone, where the way houses had gone for that matter. They existed on the route. He had heard that. What he would have given for a bed, even one infested with vermin. Ah, but he was too slow, always too slow. And now it was not all Arie's fault. His feet were as heavy as if his boots were filled with lead shot. His head ached as if held in a steel clamp.

She is up to her chest now. Her breathing is harsh. She has not brayed for some time.

ADDENDUM
If the Gentleman should find himself trapped in the Quagmire of Despair he is advised not to thrash as thrashing will only encase his limbs in the putrid mud & if he does thrash, he should then be advised to say his prayers & if it is only his pack animal that has succumbed to the embrace of the bog, then he should be advised to carry on regardless. For what is a pack animal? Or let us be specific, what is a mule? It is, good sirs, a creature without a soul, a beast of burden created by God for our use & thus I recommend that you leave it where it lies with no thought of rescue, for any rescue may needlessly endanger yourself.

Eugene is sobbing only because he is exhausted. Lost. Only because his splendid luck has deserted him entirely.

The light itself seems muddy, difficult to move in. He fumbles at his revolver. Clenches his hands to stop them from shaking. Ariadne stares at him. Her eyes are filled with flies.

At the shot the birds wheel upward like ash from a fire. There is a roaring in his ears, a pounding in his skull. There is a sense that he must escape at all costs.

TWENTY-ONE

The steamer plies the water to the mainland. On the wharf a crowd waves *goodbye,* white handkerchiefs flitting in their raised hands. Now it is only grey sky above, grey water below. Off the starboard rail the monstrous blackfish leap from the waves and show the white of their great bellies before crashing back. The People near Fort Connelly hunted the blackfish in the month of the ripe salmonberry. The women slice at the corpse that is drawn onto the shore. The headman takes first share and then the shaman takes his and then the nobles and then commoners and then the slaves. There are rivers of blood. Strips of flesh as long and thick as trees.

The blackfish plume and vanish into the deep. A man vomits over the rail. Boston hunches in his coat and pushes down his own nausea. He does not go below. He does not like to be sealed up within a boat. Does not like boats at all, not even canoes, though he uses them when he needs to. Feels uneasy in the territories of the salmon people, the whale people, the seal people, and all those creatures of the between worlds in which he half-believes. Not only that. Boston presses his knuckles to his forehead. The remembering comes unbidden once again. He is crouching behind barrels, backing away from an arm that gropes for him. The hold rocks; a barrel tips. The arm grasps his long and matted hair and hauls him out. The arm is thick-muscled. Sinewy. Blue tattoos of a turtle, a bird, of whorls, a cross. What else? It is beyond. In the time before. He struggles and bites. Laughter. Is held up. A lantern blazes into his eyes.

"And when did you sneak on board, you damned little wharf rat, eh? When'd you start thinking you could be eating up old Milroy's stores, making him look the fool, eh? Well, now. You owe me, boy. You owe."

TWENTY-TWO

"Hold his head. We must not let him gag."
"Poor bastard."
"Where?"
"Be easy now. Lie back."
"You're Negroes? What?"
"Shit, and here's I thought we was lily white. Sure is a revelation."
"Yes, it certainly is, Lorn. Sleep now, Mr. Hume. Sleep is the finest of remedies."

The red eye of a stove glows red then clanks shut. Warmth of furs against him. Dora? Is he home then? Has he dreamt? But why two beds and not one? Ah, yes. The goldfields. The road. The Negroes. Placidly he watches them. They are eating at a rough table. A candle is between them. On a shelf above them is a line of bottles, a mortar and pestle, two chipped mugs and four neatly stacked books. Drying plants hang from the rafters. Though the cabin is scrupulously clean and well-appointed it does not look a place that one would call home for long. No woman's touch, that is the trouble.

One of the men stands and becomes so thinly tall his head nearly scrapes the roof.

"Good, you are awakened. How are you feeling? Any palpitations?"

Eugene croaks out a *no*. The tall man hands him a mug of water from which Eugene gratefully drinks.

"Visions of any kind?"

Eugene manages a smile. "Visions, no. You, indeed, seem real enough. Though it would help if I knew what I may call you."

"I am Napoleon Beauville." He gestures to the man still sitting at the table. "And this is Lorn Hallwood."

The second man sneers mightily. "I had a fever once and I thought the angels themselves were sitting around, gossiping and playing tiddly-winks and whatnot."

"Do you know your name, sir?" Napoleon asks.

"Yes, of course. It is . . . is . . . Eugene Augustus Hume."

"Excellent. I believe you are recovering." He hands Eugene a cup of syrup. Eugene nearly gags. It smells of mould and vinegar and of something putrefying.

"I cannot. I apologize."

"It will help."

"He knows his remedies," Lorn says. "He fixed up a family dying of the fever and whatnot. I saw it myself. And he fixed me up right, didn't you, Nap?" Eugene now notices that Lorn is not sneering. He only seems to be sneering because of a scar that has pulled up the corner of his top lip and exposed his teeth and gums.

"I did my best," Napoleon says modestly.

"You are a physician. I see, quite so. I am most lucky then."

"I suppose you could look at it thataways," Lorn says. The scar has slurred his speech, has made him sound as if he has been drinking. Curiously, spirits are not something that appeals to Eugene at the moment. Not even brandy, that fine cure-all.

"Drink the syrup slowly. And you must take more water with it." Napoleon's hair is grey at the temple. His face grave. He certainly seems the sort who knows of what he speaks.

Eugene sips as docilely as a patient should. "I feel its benefits even now. My thanks. Pray tell me, how long have I been here?"

"Three days," Napoleon says.

"Three days?"

"Yes. And for several more you must not exert yourself. I believe you have mountain fever. It has killed many men in these parts."

"Good Christ! Will I . . .? That is . . ."

"Settle yourself, Mr. Hume. The worst has past. You will not die of this occurrence."

"What of contagion? Do you not fear . . . ?"

"I have observed that the mountain fever thrives only where there is filth and vermin. Cleanliness is what keeps it at bay."

Eugene now notices the cleanliness of his own hands, that he no longer smells ripe. These good men must have cleaned him while he lay senseless. "My thanks again, my thousand thanks." He swings his legs over the edge of the bed. Winces as he puts weight on his blistered, swollen feet. He is wearing a clean night shift of coarse linen. It is not his own. A panic grips him. "My boots? Damnation if . . ."

"Here by the fire," Napoleon says. "Do not trouble yourself. Your money is safe."

"Ah, quite so, of course, I did not doubt . . . and my apparel?"

"Washed and drying outside," Lorn says as he jams a log into the stove.

"Sirs, I have to, I must immediately."

Napoleon hands him a bucket. Turns his back.

Lorn glances over. Difficult to believe that he is not sneering at Eugene's incompetence, his stupidity, his struggle to piss.

When he is done Napoleon gazes into the bucket. "The colour is too deep. You need well-boiled water. Two quarts a day at the least."

"Should I be bled?"

"I have never seen it help a man or woman. It only serves to weaken them. Your guts are dry. Simple water well-boiled, more restorative syrup, as well as tea with a suffusion of willow bark and balsam fir. Bitterroot would not be amiss, but none is to be had, unfortunately."

"As you have cured me thus far, Mr. Beauville, I will comply. I must, however, I must search for my supplies. I . . ."

Lorn gestures to a dim corner. Eugene's two trunks and assorted sacks are there. Filthy, but there.

"Again, my thanks. How the devil did you find them, or me for that matter?"

"I heard someone shouting in the bush." Lorn says. "Found you crawling 'long a deer path. You were so filthy you looked as black as us, and some awful, too, all splattered with blood and whatnot. We figured from what you were raving on about that you'd got yourself caught up in Iverson's Bog. It's not so far from here. We thought this Ariadne was your woman, so Nap hauled you here and I headed straight off. Didn't find no woman, just a fresh dead mule, and your stuff half-ripped up by birds and whatnot."

"My mule served me well. I must apologize. I hope my delirium was not too disturbing."

"Do not trouble yourself for it. I am certain that you would do the same for us," Napoleon says.

Eugene assures them he would. He is not one to judge a man for his colour. What matters is his bearing, his deeds.

Napoleon folds himself into a chair and studies the roof. Lorn looks at him with that false, mocking sneer. Eugene's voice winds down. He is miring himself, thrashing about for some appropriate phrase, and they are content to let him do so. He falls quiet. A log sizzles and snaps. A night bird trills out. Lorn chuckles. Napoleon smiles gravely. Eugene laughs, feels as if he has not laughed in a century. An age.

Later Napoleon gives him broth and mashed beans and then his remedy of bark tea. The strength pours into him, and with it a sincere gratitude. Indeed, he would save them as they saved him. Ah, better. When he has his fortune he will buy them something fine. Clothes. White shirts to set off the walnut dark of their skin. Embroidered waistcoats. He had seen a footman of their hue wearing one. How remarkable he looked.

"I am writing a gentleman's guide to the goldfields, gentlemen. I will make mention, no, write reams of your generosity."

"A gentleman's guide," Lorn says. "Good idea. Lots of gentlemen around here could use some directions and whatnot. Need more than a title, mind."

"I have more than a title."

"Not from what we saw," Lorn says.

"Saw? Where? My journal? You read it?"

"Not me. Napoleon, he's got the knack for it."

"My apologies, Mr. Hume. I needed to discern your name and any information that would give a clue to your affliction." Napoleon pauses. "You made a note of lice racing. Mountain fever might well be associated with such vermin. As such it was perhaps not the wisest form of entertainment."

"Quite so," Eugene says.

"Yup, need more than a title for that guide book of yours." Lorn says. "Title won't get you far, even one as long as yours."

"I have been making notes in my head. When I have a spare moment

I will write them down. For now, they are safely here." Eugene taps his skull. Winces. Sinks back against the furs, now recalls the gory mass of Ariadne's head, the blood on his hands and face, recalls the brush tearing at him like witches' hands, and how the world shifted between black and grey as he floundered. Poor Ariadne. She had not lived up to her name. She had not lead him through the labyrinth at all, but had fallen victim to it herself.

He sleeps in one bed; they in another, head to toe, Napoleon's long legs dangling over the side. The next day Eugene feels much stronger and so asks to be outside. Napoleon takes his pulse, looks into his eyes. "Yes. But you must remain bundled and you must not move." And so Eugene, swathed in blankets, watches from a bench as they work with a dedication that he can only admire. Their cabin is in a stand of poplars near a puny creek, which, though it gurgles with charm, does not seem big enough to hold a motherlode. It seems unlikely, indeed, that they have found much gold at all, otherwise they would not trust a stranger to be on their claim, in their cabin.

Lorn swirls a pan, then prods at the remaining sand with tweezers. Napoleon works the rocker. His expression is distant. No doubt he is dreaming up some fantastic panacea. A squirrel dashes over a man-high pile of tailings. Sunlight spatters through the poplars. It is almost hot this day, almost tranquil. The hellish bog might have existed only in Eugene's fecund imagination if not for the scratches on his hands and face, for the lack of Ariadne.

On the night before he is to leave, Eugene tells them of Dora, his Intended, his beloved. He asks if they have wives, children, family of some kind. They glance at each other, tell him little, except that they intend to bring what is left of their families to the colony of British Columbia whether the Rebs win or lose, whether Lincoln keeps his promise to free the southern slaves or not. There are ways, Eugene learns to his surprise. There are people, white and coloured, who risk their lives to help escaping slaves. But what it comes down to, truly, is money, gold. For that can buy near anything.

It is a Saturday when he leaves. He takes only his rucksack and what supplies he can fit into it, as well as his revolver and rifle. The rest of his supplies he leaves with them until he can return. He thanks them and praises them so profusely that Napoleon shifts his ever-grave expression to one of embarrassment and Lorn says Mr. Hume might consider being a preacher instead of a writer of guidebooks.

Now on what passes for the main trail he holds his rifle at the ready, for Lorn has warned of bears and of men less charitable than themselves. He stops and listens closely. Hears nothing but birdsong, water song, and then the poplar leaves softly clapping in the breeze, as if in gentle mockery at his endeavours.

TWENTY-THREE

For over forty miles the road runs straight as a needle through the high plateau. Offers no corners to hide attackers, human or otherwise. No precarious bridges. No falling rock. Is monotonous in all. And yet Boston walks more rapidly than ever before, keeps his rifle ready, keeps a watchful eye. It is the peculiar density of the place that makes him wary—the clouds of mosquitoes so thick they seem one presence, the warm heaviness of the air, the fetid odours of swamps and rotting things, the wall of stunted trees on either side of the road, the sodden sky that presses down, and the way the daylight dies so quickly, as if night grows from such a place. He was caught yesterday in utter blackness. Not so tonight. He stops at mid-afternoon, finds a decent sized clearing in the woods not far from a roadhouse. Makes a fire of green boughs to ward off the mosquitoes. Shoots a duck in a nearby marsh, roasts and eats it. Now walks to the edge of the road-house yard. Lanterns burn in the windows. Smoke curls thickly from the chimney. The door swings open and shut as men piss outside, as they smoke and spit and hold up mosquito-haloed lanterns to latecomers. Laughter. A harmonica. A man stumbles outside. Exclaims "Capital View! Bloody marvellous!" The chasm is perhaps a mile deep and many more miles long, is layered with shades of ochre, brown, and dun. The lowering sun fires it red and gold. Why is it that the Whitemen choose such foolish places to build their dwellings? A hard rain could easily tear both the rim and the roadhouse away; easily the drunken man could tumble into its depths, his cry echoing those of the birds wheeling there.

The man steps back from the edge of the chasm. Calls to his companions to come see, but they laugh and beckon him inside. He

199

throws up his hands and strolls back to the roadhouse, as certain of his welcome as if it were his home entirely.

Boston walks back to his camp. Builds up the fire, and as he does Fort Connelly builds itself—stone by stone, plank by plank. Like the nearby roadhouse the fort is likewise foolishly situated. Has been built on a shoreline promontory, as if safety could be found in proximity to the sea from whence the builders came. During the highest tides the waves lap at the fort's western wall. During high winds they bang like a giant demanding entry. When the tide recedes it leaves slime and amber jellyfish and great nests of sea kelp. A weak tide also leaves, or fails to carry away, refuse from the village, those who built the fort not having realized that this is near to where the People come to shit, and to dump animal remains and rotten oil. Except for this unfortunate positioning and its small size Fort Connelly is a trading fort much like any other, has four bastions and an eighteen-foot high palisade, has a great gate inset with a postern, has an armed night watchman to toll the bell and call out the hour and announce that all is well.

Nootkans, the fort men call the People of the nearby village, as they call all those who live on the northerly west coast of the Island. The People, however, is what they call themselves. Their village begins some five hundred yards off, is built higher up on the sandy shore of a long bay. At the far end of this shore three pillars of rock rise from the crash of waves and act as a barrier against the northern winds and as nesting grounds for seabirds. These are the three sisters—the guardians of the village.

The village was smaller when the fort was first built. Now, because of the trade, it has grown to several hundred strong, more in the winter months, less in the summer months when the People go to their harvesting grounds. Others come to trade as well—the Kwagu'l, the Haidas, the Tsimshians—but all must pay the People to do so.

The Indians are allowed only in the trade room, and then only in groups of no more than three. They trade furs of seal and sea otter, of beaver, mink, bear, cougar, deer and racoon, as well as venison and dried salmon and oolichan grease. In exchange they receive molasses and iron tools, mirrors and beads, sheets of copper, lengths of rope, red baize and buttons, and blankets, most of all.

"This is the fort's purpose," Illdare tells Boston. "Good trade. Fair.

The company is fair. We bargain hard but our goods are of quality. Unfair trade brings only an upsetting of the balance, and oftentimes, disaster. Remember that, lad."

Boston is healed enough now to partake in the rituals of the fort, to do his part in return for sustenance and shelter. The morning bell tolls at six. The engagés eat from their individual rations, then each begin their tasks—pressing furs, gathering seaweed to fertilize the small gardens, whitewashing the buildings, sawing lumber. And most of all, repairing and rebuilding, for the drizzle, the fog, the vegetation itself, eats constantly and moistly away at wood and steel alike.

In the evening the postern is locked and the keys given to Illdare who then eats alone in his chambers, the old woman Equata cooking for him. The engagés cook their own dinners. They help Boston at first, show him how to measure the cornmeal, how to keep bread safe from the wet. He learns quickly, without whining, and soon enough they leave him to his own devices. On Saturdays the engagés have the afternoons free to mend their clothes, to relax and drink their rations of rum, or to bathe if they are of the inclination. Sundays are a day of rest, a day when Illdare is to read aloud to the assembled men from the book of common prayer. It is a regulation of the company, and one that Illdare completes as quickly as he can.

Twice a year the supply ship comes. The outer gate, twenty feet high and twenty broad, is opened only at this time. The engagés row out to the ship, return with the barrels and sacks, visitors, news, letters. All day the loading and unloading goes on. In the evening Illdare allows a regale while he entertains the ship's officers or dines on board the ship itself. For at least a week before the expected arrival of the supply ship, Illdare is in a foul mood and the engagés avoid him as best they can.

Of the sixteen engagés at Fort Connelly eight are Kanakas from the Sandwich Islands. They were taken aboard en route by the supply ships and, though lured by promises of fortune, they know nothing of the fur trade and so have became the common labourers and are paid in half portions to the others. Of the other eight engagés, five are mixed-bloods from the east—Abenaki, Iroquois, and Snake—and two are Upper Canadians, one of English background, one of German. The Orkneyman, James McNeal, he of the yellow hair and rank breath, acts as the clerk. There are three Indian wives who live within the fort and five children. And there is Illdare, raised on the borderlands of Scotland and England, and the sole officer of the place.

Boston listens and learns from them all.

The carpenter Kanaquasse Fleury tells him of Fort Edmonton. "Fifty men in all. And a great house for the gentlemen and another for the Factor, and a Bachelor's hall and a married man's hall. Here. Hah." He waves his hand about the compound, complains of each in turn—the single hall for the married men and bachelors both, the damp storerooms, the damp trade room, the decrepit smokehouse and reeking outhouses, the paltry saw pit, the creaking fur press, the single forge under its shed, and most of all, the lack of dances and good Métis women.

"Only us dregs are sent here. It's alike to being sent to Botany Bay," says James McNeal and adds that Fort Connelly is more an outpost than a fort and that Illdare for all his strutting, for all his glove-wearing like some Montreal gentleman, is more a postmaster than a Chief Trader, as he fancies calling himself. "He insulted Governor Simpson, I heard. Simpson! Hah! Illdare wouldn't take his gloves off to shake the Governor's hand. That's why he was banished here. I'd watch out for him. He's naught but bad luck, that man."

"Rain," the Kanaka Peopeoh says mournfully, and the other Sandwich Islanders nod. They speak little English or French, but "rain" is one word with which they have become distressingly familiar. For the rain turns the compound into a quagmire, beats on the roofs, leaves the stores mouldy, the blankets damp no matter how they are protected. The Kanakas trade their own provisions for the conical hats the People wear, and which the other engagés scorn, though these hats are so tightly woven of cedar bark the rain slides off them as if they were made of pure gum.

Anawiskum Tulane shows Boston the workings of the bow and arrow, of the musket and rifle, teaches him how to throw a knife and an axe. In return Boston beats the dust and dirt out of the furs and grinds the clamshells for whitewash. Both are duties that Tulane loathes.

He would rather be hunting, or making more children with his wife. Not something Illdare would understand, he says, and calls Illdare a half-man, a dried corn-husk man.

"Why are we not allowed out at night, as if we are children or criminals?" ponders James Thomson, a blacksmith from Upper Canada. He hammers at a spike that glows red. Boston heaves more coal into the forge. The question does not need an answer. Thomson knows as well as anyone. Even Boston knows. The women. Wives are allowed; they bind the village to the fort, are an alliance the People recognize, but whoring and carousing, as Illdare calls it, are another matter entirely. At no fort are such things allowed. They lead only to disaster. "But then he's not one for women, is he? I'll agree with Tulane on that," Thomson says. "Fact you never see him touch a living creature."

Lavolier teaches Boston the rituals of the Eucharist. Has Boston act as altar boy as he raises the cup of wine over a rough altar. He teaches Boston French, as well as phrases from the Latin mass, from the catechism, the Gloria. Lavolier himself does not understand all the words. No matter, they have the power of the holy spirit. "*Repetéz,*" he commands. When Boston does so without faltering Lavolier eyes him with suspicion and says it is remarkable how he can remember so, that God must have graced him, or perhaps the devil.

Ettoine Moreau grips Boston's chin. Presses his thumb into his cheek. Later, reeking of rum, he fumbles at Boston in the dark. Boston makes no move, no sound. Ettoine groans and hauls himself off and pats Boston's hair before he leaves. The next night an infernal screaming and the engagés crowd 'round the pallet where Boston sleeps. Candles are held up. Moreau dances and yowls. A small trap dangles from his bloodied hand.

"The rats have indeed been a problem," Illdare later says. "They came with the supply ships. They are able creatures that can live anywhere, eat anything. Much like men, eh, Jim?

Boston stares at the ground. He will be beaten, but that is of no matter, what matters is the displeasure in Illdare's voice.

Illdare sighs. "You should have come to me. For now Moreau cannot work, can he? His hand is crushed and likely maimed for the rest of his miserable life. He'll be sent off on the next supply ship, three months hence. As for you . . . you will stay. I can make much of you yet."

They are in Illdare's sitting room. A kettle hangs over a fire and puffs out steam. On the floor is a rug of black bearskin. Boston sits at the table. His feet dangle just above the padlock of the strongroom below. On top of the table is a writing set and pipe rack and behind this table are three shelves stacked with books and journals and rolls of Protan charts. On the wall is the company crest and a rough map of New Caledonia with the name of Fort Connelly written, in Illdare's exact hand, high up on the island of Vancouver. "So I will not forget where I am," Illdare explains and then chuckles dryly, as he often does at his own remarks. Boston smiles though he does not understand the jest. Still, more and more is becoming clear to him, the markings on the page, the habits of numbers and calendars, of cooking pots and rifles. Languages are becoming more clear as well—the language of the People, the trade jargon, the French and Kanaka and Gaelic of the engagés themselves, even the Latin of Lavolier. It is English, however, that springs most easily to his tongue. "You're an American, it seems, a Yankee," Illdare tells him. "That cannot be helped. Be warned, however, that the Indians use the term *Boston men* for all the Americans, just as *King George man* is used for all the English. This is because most of their wretched ships are from Boston ports—as was yours, we presume. Best then that you introduce yourself to them as Jim, no matter what the others call you. The Indians do not like the Americans, the Boston men, you see. And why is that? You recall, do you not?"

"Bad traders. Bad goods. Not company men," Boston says.

"Exactly, they are a lawless rabble who ply these shores like pirates. They take. They deceive. Sooner or later they pay the price. The Indians attack their ships, slaughter them all. You were lucky to escape."

"Good here," Boston says.

"Good? Hah! Well, let us see if you have earned your keep. Have you been my eyes and ears as I asked you?"

Boston nods. Recites what he has heard, how McNeal said he, Illdare, is a miser of the first order, that he measures out the grog rations to the drop, that he secretly trades with the Indians for rare goods, keeps hundreds of pounds stashed in the strongroom along with the rations and rum. For whether he can spend it or no, a miser without money to fondle will be as miserable as a baby without a teat to suck.

"McNeal, that Gaelic goat, he said that, did he? And Lavolier, what does he say?"

"That you give nothing to the Church and keep your soul for the devil. That is why you hate to read the Sunday sermons."

"Hah, indeed. He is correct there, perhaps. Steer clear of him. He fancies himself a Jesuit though they would never have him. And Anawiskum, that black hearted half-breed, what does he say?"

"That you have nothing between your legs, that's why you won't take a woman. That you are a half-man."

"Remarkable. You, I mean. You do not coat what you have heard with honey as most would. It is why I can trust only you. Why I invite you here. Only you. As for the others. Don't trust what they say. They tell lies so much they cannot distinguish them from truth. Ah, but it'll be one of Lavolier's blasted miracles if we don't all kill each other before the New Year's contracts are signed."

Illdare falls into silence as he often does before sending Boston off. But Boston does not want to leave. Not while the fire still burns. Not while Illdare might stroke Boston's forehead with his gloved hand as he did once before, not while he might say again that it is only Boston he trusts.

"What are dregs?"

"Dregs? They are the bottom of the barrel. The sweepings from the floor."

Boston scowls at the table. "How can a person be a dreg?"

"It is a manner of speaking. A metaphor."

"You not a dreg."

"And how would you know? What have you to compare it to, eh?"

TWENTY-FOUR

Eugene rushes to the window of Tang Lee's store. It was he. Eugene knows that coat, that manner of strolling as if he were on a leafy Paris Boulevard and not in some slapped-together town in a valley of ravaged hills and heavy clouds.

"I shall return directly, Mr. Lee." He pushes the sack of beans back over the counter and elbows past several men who threaten him absently in broken English. The Judge must have been coming from Richfield a mile or so on. The courthouse is there. And the Judge's abode. Twice now Eugene has attempted to call on him, but that ungrateful scrivener Arthur Bushby seems to have forgotten how Eugene saved him from a thrashing in Yale. Certainly this Bushby was quick to tell him that the Judge was busy indeed with disputes of all kinds.

Eugene runs past a Tong house, past a Chinaman carrying a vast back-load of vegetables. Spies the Judge towering over all others in the narrow gauntlet of Barkerville's main street.

"Sir! Wait!"

The figure does not turn. Eugene bounds up the steps to the board-walk, narrowly misses toppling a stack of barrels, clips his head on the low-hanging sign of a livery, and then, cursing, blunders into a gang of men who are singing drunkenly and off-key. It is not, it seems, a boardwalk for pursuing old friends. It is not a true boardwalk at all, but a series of rough porches of varying widths and heights protruding from structures built on stilts in defence of the spring floods, the tailings that slide into town from the nearby mines, though to a green hand's eye the purpose of such building techniques might be to avoid the refuse, the offal and manure, the all-prevalent mud. And what would a green hand make of the flumes crossing over the town, sometimes at a height of fifty feet? They bring fresh water from the hillside springs, though some (not Eugene) famously believed they were filled with liquid gold, as were all the streams about.

The sidewalk ends abruptly before a grog shop set back from the main street. The door is accessible only by a propped-up plank. Eugene crosses the street and heaves himself up onto the other side. Dammit to hell. He has lost sight of the Judge. He cannot have turned a corner, nor gone down a side street or alley. There are no such things. There is so little flat land in this narrow valley that the peak roofed buildings are squeezed against each other tight as the keys of an accordion, and the sparks from the tin chimneys swarm together like fiery flies.

No sign of the Judge in Wake-up Jake's. Nothing there but the smacking of jaws, the clink of cutlery, the guffaws of satiated men. Nothing but odours at which Eugene's mouth waters and his belly seethes. He lingers by the stove. It is in the centre of the room, as all stoves are in the gold towns. It is as large as a hog, has ornate carvings on the door and plates, and has a boot rail gripped with tiny nickel-plated hands. A canister for hot water fits over the drum, a tap on one side. Here in this distant, frigid place such a fine stove is a measure of wealth, carted as it is over hundreds, even thousands of miles, each mile compounding its worth.

"Pleasance!"

A well-girthed woman nods at him. In one hand is a pitcher, in the other a platter with a steaming roast. She drops the platter at a table of four men who cheer her as if she has performed some feat of magic. Points toward the one free table.

"Not today, later perhaps," Eugene says, than asks if she has seen the Judge. She has not. He lingers. Perhaps she will say: "Come, Mr. Hume, it will be on the house." Perhaps his hat will turn into a beef-steak, perfectly fried.

No sign of the Judge in the butcher shop. Nor the tin shop. Then, in the crowded murk of the Denby Saloon, Eugene smells the heartening waft of an expensive cigar. An imposing figure by the roulette wheel lifts a hand in greeting. Eugene steps closer, arms outstretched: "My friend, so excellent to . . . to . . ."

"What's the matter, Hume? You look fit to sob. I'll give you some comfort. Fair price for it, too." Miss Anna wears the tight breeches of a man as if born to them. She wears a bowie knife and a revolver. Her blouse is opened to show the moon-risings of her breasts. She is no beauty, true, is tall and raw-boned, has a paucity of teeth and manners, but her charms, Eugene has been assured, defy description.

"Ah, Miss Anna. Indeed. Quite so. I am looking for the Judge. Have you seen him? He is a friend, you see."

"The Judge. A friend of yours? I'll see him. I'll see the both of you at the same time. Fair price for it, too, seeing as I only gotta peel down once."

"So you have not seen his face hereabouts."

"Truth is, I ain't one for faces."

Eugene stands outside, not yet disheartened; it takes more than a small setback to dishearten a Hume. The door of Sin Hap's laundry opens and the man himself emerges from the steam. A herd of cattle low through the streets, horns knocking on the high boardwalks. Great turds steam under their feet to be nosed at by the dogs and pigs. Indian packers walk by with their mules. Ah, Ariadne.

He presses his hand to his brow to ease the thudding there. Napoleon's willow bark tea, that is what he requires. It hardly helps that it is as noisy as only Sundays in the gold towns can be—is an orchestration of blacksmiths' hammers and clanging bells, of emptying refuse buckets, and clunking billiards, of concertinas, fiddles, calls for patrons, drunken arguments, and in the distance the ever-present thump of the water wheels. What he does not hear—though this is one of the reasons he came to town—is the preaching of a Methodist who has offered twenty cents for every man who comes to service in the shack behind the Platonic Saloon, and fifty cents for every woman.

A runner for the White Dove Lottery edges past him. Eugene catches his sleeve. "Mr. Tien!"

"What bet, Mister?"

"No bet today. I am looking for the Judge."

"No bet. No Judge."

"What? You devil."

Mr. Tien smiles.

Eugene scowls and fishes in his pocket for coins. He has sworn not to bet on the lottery again, but it seems he has little choice. In any case, he might win this time. He has not given up all hope.

"What number?"

"1847." It is the number he always uses. It is the year he first bedded a woman and is enshrined in memory as one of the finest years of his life.

Mr. Tien hands him a paper marked with writings in English and Chinese then points to the pole wrapped in red flannel. Of course! A man such as the Judge would have himself barbered often. And where else but at Wellington Moses's? The man is so deft with a razor it is said he could shave the whiskers off a mouse without the creature knowing it.

The shop is small and neat. On a counter are rolls of ribbons and ladies' gloves—an optimistic display, given that the manly population of the gold towns runs from 6,000 to 10,000, the vast majority of whom are destitute and struggling. It comforts Eugene not a little, this knowledge that he is hardly alone in misfortune. Of the women, he has heard estimates of 150, and this includes the Klootchmen who have married Whitemen, and the 'dressmakers' and 'Judys' such as Miss Anna, and the grass widows about whom rumours swirl like flies but never settle, for they could be divorcees, or women who have borne a child without wedlock, or women who have abandoned husbands and sought better, richer ones here. Would Dora bear the title of grass widow if he should perish? Would that he had married her properly. Would that she could properly mourn him.

Eugene's eyes water and smart. He curses Wellington's Hair Invigorator. Bottles of it line the shelf behind the counter and a batch of it brews on the stove. Odour of lye and lavender and something else. Tar?

"Good day, sir," Wellington places his book on a lace-covered shelf and stands up from his barber chair and motions Eugene toward it. He wears a striped vest over a white shirt that gleams against skin that is darker than Napoleon's, darker than Lorn's. His accent is not as theirs, however, but hovers somewhere between England and warmer climes.

"Shall it be a full shave today, sir? Followed by a vigorous washing of the strands? I provide a discount for before-noon patrons."

Eugene glances at Wellington's looking glass. His hair laps at his collar. His beard is a tangled mat, is seeming to grow more rapidly than usual, as if in defence against the damp chill that wraps Barkerville most days, though it is still August. He has lost so much weight that his clothes seem the worn-out ones of a larger man handed to him on charity. His blanket coat is frayed at the cuffs, the soles of his boots are near worn through, and his blue serge shirt is stained and stiff with use. None of his apparel has been properly boiled since he left Victoria. Instead he washes his clothes in the cold waters of Lickety creek, his hands aching as an old woman's might. Yes. He would love to stretch out there in Wellington's chair with a steaming towel draped over his face, blotting out all his disappointment, would love to hear the blade sharpening on the strop and then the clean edge of it against his throat.

"No, I thank you. Another time. The Judge, have you seen him?"

"Indeed, I often have the pleasure of his patronage."

"When?"

Wellington heaves out an enormous journal. He flips through muttering "no, not it." Eugene shuffles from foot to foot. The wall clock ticks over to nine o'clock. He looks over to Wellington's book, there on the lace covered shelf. *Bleak House*. At one time he would have found such a novel fascinating, but these days he has troubles of his own aplenty without needing to read about the maudlin denizens of Mr. Dickens' imagination.

"Ah, here, the 10th of August. The Judge came in at 2:30 sharp. He said 'Hello Mr. Moses, the weather is peculiar today, is it not?' I said: 'Indeed it is, sir, more peculiar than usual. I saw a rainbow over the white-dressed mountains in the North though it was that the rain still drove.' He said he wished he had seen such a splendid sight then asked to have a trim of his moustaches. I said . . ."

"Quite so, but have you seen him today, just recently."

"Today? Well now, no, I could not say that I have."

"My thanks, my thanks. If you see him again tell him his friend Mr. Eugene Augustus Hume is seeking him. Tell him I can be found at the Dora Dear, formerly the Praise to God, formerly the Highstakes. It is out on Lickety creek. Tell him . . . well, that is sufficient."

"The Highstakes? Did not the Greek and Holy Dunmore own that one?"

"Yes, quite so."

"And it is now in your possession?"

"Not *just* in my possession. I have shares in the claim. I have partners."

"Well now, sir, well. I wish you luck."

"Thank you. I have been hearing I shall need it. Now if you will excuse me," Eugene says, for he feels an abrupt need for air.

He leans against the wall of a tin shop over which the flag of Prussia flies. Indeed, the flags of all nations crack high on poles over the bakeries, liveries, blacksmith shops, supply stores, and stables. The flags are the only bright colours in his view besides that of the blood of freshly slaughtered pigs. Valley of the Flags, some romantic soul has dubbed it. Valley of the Fools more like.

Again the disappointment. Like a knocking in his gut. It was not that Eugene expected much. Not that he had believed the oft-repeated line that Barkerville was the greatest city north of San Francisco. A mere glance at a continental map would disabuse one of that notion. What of Seattle? Of Victoria, in fact? Indeed, *crap-heap* was the only description that came to Eugene's mind when he first saw Richfield, then Barkerville, then Maryville, then Camerontown. Do the others notice? They seem not to. They are too busy peering into the gaping holes left in the earth for that one golden vein, that one spark of beauty. It is up to Eugene to notice. To point out that the environs look as if they have been pillaged by a marauding tribe, or ravaged by a volcano's fiery blast. The once merry Williams Creek beside which the towns are strung is now dissected and butchered, made filthy with refuse and tailings and drained to a trickle by flumes and ditches and troughs and shafts and by those great clunking water wheels of which the Cornishmen are so proud. And in the surrounding hills not a tree is left standing, nothing to offer respite from the rain, nor from the occasional ragged blasts of sun. It is a landscape of jagged stumps and smouldering slash piles and stagnant cesspools; it is a breeding ground for the massive horsefly, the cunning mosquito. It is avarice given a home.

Enough of this. Enough. Eugene presses his brow. If he were the Judge where would he be off to on such a morning? The Occidental Hotel? It has true glass windows, a grand piano that was hauled famously from San Francisco. There are further attempts at gentility— velvet embossed wallpaper, a chandelier, a carved billiard table, a gilt mirror behind a lustrous bar. There is an elaborate gilt scale as well. It is the largest in all of Barkerville and is said to be able to weigh, not just the largest nugget a man can offer, but the value of a man's word.

The Judge is not in the Occidental's saloon. Nor is he in the reading room just beside it. A fire burns lonesome in the grate. An unironed copy of the Colonist is open on the card table. It is over six weeks old. A headline proclaims the victory of the Union Army over the Confederates at Gettysburg. War. Battles. Is there nothing else to discuss?

Back in the saloon he leans heavily on the bar. "Whiskey."

"No jawbone here, Hume."

He spills a few coins onto the bar. "What is that? Tailings. Lumps of coal?"

The barkeep counts them with maddening slowness, then pours out a shot of the cheapest whiskey. Eugene gulps it down. Astonishing the flow of reason it engenders. With most people it is the reverse. For now he suspects that it was not the Judge. For he would have turned if he had known it was Eugene. Besides, Eugene's senses have not been the most trustworthy of late—had he not smelled roast pork when it was only his boots being singed by the fire? Not felt, just before the unwelcome dawn, Dora's minty kisses? Certainly the darkness of the mine has done nothing to invigorate the senses. It has a texture, almost, like damp wool, and an absoluteness that the merlin candles can barely challenge. If he is not on his guard he will become like that Finnish miner who started tearing off his clothes and raving in his own queer tongue. Disappeared to God knows where. Poor sod. Here's to him.

The saloon is becoming crowded, tobacco fogged. A man in his shirt sleeves searches through the song sheets atop the piano, settles at the stool.

> *Then sleep, let her sleep in the grave we have made;*
> *From the cares of this World she is free;*
> *Then weep, let us weep, while the tall willows wave*
> *O'er the grave of our own Carrie Lee.*

Carrie Lee? Again? Why not Cariboo Cameron? Now there is a tragedy worthy of a song. Eugene has written Dora of the cautionary tale in case she is still wishing she had joined him. Women did not belong in the goldfields, as well he warned Dora, as someone should have warned Cameron. Instead he brought his wife Sophia and their little daughter who died before the goldfields were even reached. And then came a winter so cold that metal snapped like twigs. The Camerons stayed and worked the claim with partners. Sophia huddled in their tiny cabin. The fever was raging on the creeks that winter and it was not long before the lovely Sophia fell ill. How would the song go?

> He struck the lead, two months after she was dead
> Poor Cameron! Poor Cameron!
> A town with his name, but no wife in his bed
> Her last sweet request, to be buried in Ontario
> To be buried in Ontario, oh, ho.
> And so thro' ice and snow, thro' bitter winds and mountains high
> Twenty-two men did to Victoria her coffin take nigh
> To be buried in Ontario oh, ho.

Yes. John Angus Cameron. A high price for his riches. He now has three shafts and near a hundred men working for him and the gold is coming out by the bucket. The diminutive Billy Barker can be seen strutting about as well. He is a Naval deserter, a Cornishman. No price has he paid for his fortune.

More men enter with much stomping of boots and much calling for coffee and grog. Eugene hunkers over the bar. Tips his hat over his brow.

"Mr. Hume? Is you?"

Eugene grudgingly admits it is his very self indeed. Manages a smile and a handshake for Herr Boots who wears a fur-lined overcoat and a voluminous green scarf, who no longer looks the shabby merchant, no indeed. Manages a nod and mumbled good day for Oswald who wears a towering top hat, a scarlet waistcoat, and an ill-fitting coat adorned with fat brass buttons, who looks, in all, like a well-dressed troll. Fortunate for Oswald that he arrived in the goldfields a good two weeks before Eugene, and thus before the opportunities were taken up. Fortunate that Herr Boots sold his gumboots for a staggering sixty dollars a piece and with that purchased shares in Oswald's mine, The Jessica Bell. Fortunate that The Jessica Bell chanced to yield while all the claims around them yielded nothing. Expertise had some hand in their success. Eugene can admit that. But it was luck as well that led them to the pay dirt. The Jessica Bell now employs over twenty men who work 'round the clock and who thus leave the main shareholders—Oswald and Herr Boots, or Herr Schultheiss as he is better known—with leisure time aplenty to strut their wealth.

"You are liking this Sunday?" Schultheiss asks. He rubs his nose with a vast handkerchief and calls for the door to be shut against the dangerous drafts, mentions an ache in his neck that will not cease.

"Yeah, how's your Sunday, Hume?"

"Swell, gentlemen."

"And what about that played-out hole you and them others bought, how's that?"

"It is not played out."

"I heard it's emptier than an old whore's heart."

"It is not."

"Find the god-blamed gold did you?"

"Not as yet. There is gold. I saw it. It is only a matter of time."

"Christ's turds. Never heard of spiking, Hume?"

Eugene is silent.

"Wouldn't catch me crapping in that hole, never mind going down it. Mouse fart got more chance of holding up in a storm."

"Go it easy, Os. He has hard time," says Schultheiss.

"It was vouched for," Eugene says, louder than he intends. "It was vouched for by two others, no less. They had no interest in the mine."

"You can pay a man to vouch for fucknit anything, can't you? Shoulda asked me."

Eugene snorts. Asked Oswald? Cussy Os as he is being called? This troll?

He excuses himself, dashes down the whiskey, then slams the glass on the bar to show that he is not to be trifled with. The short bark of Oswald's laughter follows him out the door.

"Good day, Mr. Hume!" Schultheiss calls out, sincerely enough.

Damn Oswald. He is right, of course, the Dora Dear is a miserable mine. She is plagued by quicksand and flooding and weak-timbered shafts that groan and weep as though the earth itself were in torment.

But it is not as if Eugene threw himself into it with no consideration. Indeed, he had been about to tell the Greek and Holy Dunmore that he was no longer interested in their claim. Then he overheard two men, hardened miners by the look of them, discussing the claim in a saloon and saying how they wished they could buy the majority of shares in the Praise to God. The mine was yielding some now, and would soon enough be showing pay dirt. Lucky for someone the Greek's wife died and he had to return to his ten motherless children. Lucky for someone that Holy Dunmore is a holy fool for selling the mine so cheaply. This was in late July. Eugene had met up with George Bowson and Langstrom and the three of them were working a surface claim far from the major, known-yield streams as these were unfortunately already staked out. On their claim they found only enough flecks of gold to keep them from starving. He told Langstrom and George what he overheard and they agreed in due course that the Praise to God seemed their only chance. The Greek and Holy Dunmore were asking eight hundred dollars for the paying claim, the cabin included. Between the three of them they had only five hundred and ten dollars, provided they could sell their claim, which they did, though for less than they had hoped.

Lorn and Napoleon were less easy to convince. Even after they saw the gleam in the sand dug from the shaft. Even after the Greek and Holy Dunmore showed Napoleon the books and swore on the Bible that the claim was honest.

"Surface mining is not the way to riches, men," Eugene told them. "We have learned that. Let us now band together."

Napoleon and Lorn looked at him doubtfully. In the end he promised that if the mine did not yield enough to cover their outlay before the season was out he would repay them in full. When they questioned how he was to do this, moneyless as he was, the lie came to him unbidden. His rich widowed aunt—the very one who gave him five hundred dollars to journey to the colonies—was sending a draft note for one hundred pounds to the bank in Richfield. It would be the equivalent of another five hundred. He was expecting it by September. And so it was decided. Lorn and Napoleon would sell their claim and buy into the Praise to God. "You wouldn't fool the men who saved your skin and whatnot?" Lorn asked. No, Eugene assured him, he would rather die, then wondered if he truly should write a beseeching letter to Aunt Georgina, that harridan. He soon shook off the notion. She had given him the money to travel to the goldfields only if he promised never to darken her door again. She had then made a promise herself, which was to feed any letters from him to her hounds.

They agreed to rename the mine the Dora Dear. Eugene, after all, was the one who had convinced them all to buy it. Eugene was the "lucky one," as Langstrom said so often that Lucky Hume nearly became his nickname. In retrospect he should have chosen a less sentimental name, as so many others seem to. Now he understands why. The Cowshit Claim. The Sheep's Balls Claim. The Whore's Hole. Such names suit an endeavour likely to bring only curses.

He makes his way back to Tang Lee's. *Only a few weeks' more credit, sir,* he practices silently. *My word as a gentleman.* He is nearly there when his path is blocked.

"You have been asking for me, sir?" The Judge is looking at him strangely. He takes Eugene's proffered hand. His dirty paw.

"Your Honour! Matthew! I am pleased. So pleased."

"Have we met?"

"Yes, yes. At Yale. In June. I helped your clerk."

"Ah, of course, Mr. Toom was it?"

"Hume. Eugene Augustus Hume. It is understandable you don't recognize me. My appearance has altered. It seems I am accommodating myself to this place rather too well."

"Do not apologize for the evidence of honest labour."

"I saw you. I shouted."

"There is much shouting in this town."

"Quite so. It is good, excellent, in fact, to see you. May I stand treat for a coffee? Or perhaps a refreshing draft of some kind." Is the Judge one for spirits? Three pounds and some odd shillings is all Eugene has left in his pocket, is all he has left in the world.

"You have a legal matter to discuss?"

Legal matter? Another understandable mistake. Eugene is twisting his hat in his hand like a supplicant. And the Judge is a busy man, a man immersed in legal minutiae. Let them first talk of legalities then, if that is the way things must be done, for Eugene does, in fact, have a grievance. "My claim. I believe it was spiked. I believe they altered the books. I, we, bought it in good faith."

"And when did you put your good money down?"

"The mid of July."

"Did you report your suspicions immediately to the gold commissioner's office?"

"No, I would not say immediately. It took some time to realize that, well, that . . ."

"That a mistake had been made?"

"Quite so, exactly so," Eugene mops his brow with his sleeve, grateful for the Judge's tact, that he need not admit that he, they, have been made fools of, have thrown their money down a bottomless pit and that never has an analogy been more apt.

"They are surely long gone," the Judge says. "*Caveat emptor* and such."

"I was told by others, you see. It was in their opinion."

"A man should not be easily swayed by the opinions of others."

"Quite so. I agree entirely."

As they speak, men jostle past Eugene but part around the Judge like water around a stone. They tip their hats, say *good morning* to him in German, French, Spanish, Gaelic. The Judge replies in kind. It is not surprising he barely recalls Eugene. He must encounter a hundred men a day. Must hear constantly of their dilemmas.

"Mr. Hume?"

Eugene's knees buckle. "I am . . . it is just, just that . . ."

The Judge grips his elbow and steers him toward the New England Bakery and Saloon. The waiter calls out his pleased salutations, shoos away a table of dawdlers, helps ease Eugene into a chair. Such solicitousness. Such vicarious respect.

"Two plates of your flapjacks, Mr. Wilkins. Ham and potatoes, coffee, and some of your ambrosial pie to finish. I take it, Mr. Hume, that you could use a meal? Do not worry, *I* am standing treat."

"Thank you, yes," Eugene whispers. "I will repay the favour. On my honour." He pats his breast as if searching for something.

"Do not trouble yourself. You were of help to my clerk when he was in his cups. I have not forgotten. Such things have a way of coming full circle, much as justice does." He folds one of his long legs over the other and stuffs his pipe. Appears quite at home, even in the cramped space of the New England.

The waiter sets down the steaming plates. Eugene dredges up his manners. How quickly they have fallen by the wayside. He must not stuff his mouth full, though he would like to, though it seems he has never tasted a finer repast.

"You will find it difficult to believe the misfortunes I have had," Eugene says after a time.

"There is little I find difficult to believe," the Judge says and instructs the waiter to bring them more coffee, more pie.

Such a relief to have such a sympathetic ear. Eugene tells of his encounter with the camels, of being robbed, of having to labour on the road gang, of Ariadne's gruesome death. His fever. The kindness of Lorn and Napoleon. He tells how after a day in the mine he feels as one who has been locked in the stocks and pelted with apples. He mentions his guidebook. How it had once seemed a grand plan that would bring him some notice, some respectable earnings. Now it seems all folly. The Judge is nodding. It is as if he has experienced similar deprivations, or at least has heard of them. He seems different from the man Eugene met in Yale. He was more aloof then, more keen to show his learning and not his heart. Amazing how the frontier can change a man. But then Eugene himself has changed. The peevish tone in his voice is something new entirely. He who was never one to complain. *Who could liven a graveyard*, as Dora once said.

"And then this mine. This pit. This, ah. But you see, I had been lucky. At one point I could see my fortunes turning sure as the tide. Lily, that is . . ."

"Lily is your wife?"

Eugene notices again the immaculate state of the Judge's attire, the cleanliness of his person. The man must bathe at least once a week. "No, my wife's name is given Dora. Lily, well, it is of no importance."

"Dora, that is it. I recall now. I recommend caution, Mr. Hume. There are certain women who are best avoided in this town."

"Yes, of course. It would not occur to me, not at all. Lily was not a woman, but a . . . a lucky charm of sorts, not that I hold with such superstitions."

"Of course not, and thus, your dear wife, how is she faring?"

"She was well the last I heard from her, though I am planning this afternoon to wait once again in that purgatory of a post line. It troubles me not a little, I must confess." Eugene sighs. Fortunate that he is fortified with food or he might well begin to weep.

"The line troubles you?"

It is difficult to tell if the Judge is jesting. Eugene smiles obligingly, just in case. "No, that I have not heard from her lately. She is alone, you see, in the Cowichan. Not all alone, of course. She has paid Indian help and neighbours close at hand."

"The post is not the swiftest as yet. However, I am certain you will be rewarded for your efforts and that you will hear from your charming wife. And so, Mr. Hume, I will not keep you any longer from your duties. I wish you the best of luck and God's Grace. As for myself, I have a great number of matters to attend to."

The Judge stands. Eugene stands. The waiter rushes over, takes payment from the Judge only after much prompting. Eugene elects to stay where he is. His chair near the stove is pleasantly warm, the odour of fresh baked bread and brewing ale most comforting. He stares into his coffee cup. He has heard of women who can read one's destiny in the dregs, though to him it looks like all the same black sludge.

Good that he did not ask the Judge for a loan, even the smallest of ones. The mention of money would have tarnished their friendship, though what, after all, are friendships for if not mutual assistance?

Addendum
If the Gentleman should find that he has miscalculated his opportunities and finds that he is missing his beloved wife, that he is longing for a helping hand, a charitable ear, then he should be well advised not to despair but to recall Errare human.

Or *Errare humanum?* Yes, that is it.

TWENTY-FIVE

Beyond Fort Connelly is the village and the forest and the sea. It is two months after Boston's arrival before he ventures outside the gates. With him are Lavolier, James Thomson, and Peopeoh. They have been sent out hunting, the People having brought no meat to trade for some time.

Peopeoh grips his musket and look sadly upward. "Sky," he says.

Boston looks up also, at the vast mossy branches of the cedars and firs. The bit of sky is a mere platter for these towering trees with their trunks as wide as five, six men abreast. And the moss. It covers all. It mutes their voices and their steps, has made soft forms of rocks and fallen trees. Great fringes of it hang from the branches, become entangled in their hair as they walk along a faint path to what might be called a clearing, though it seems more like a green cave, so dense and over-arching are the trees about, so muffled are all sounds, and so odd is the light, denser somehow and green of itself. The glimmer of the sea is gone entirely. James Thomson points to a group of knobbly forms that are thickly covered with moss. "Don't it look as if some family sat down to rest and then waited too long and were done for?"

Boston stares.

"Don't see them?" Thomson asks, half-smiling. "It's what happens if you sit too long. The moss creeps over you and chokes you. It's true."

Boston still does not see the family, sees only a totality of green, a place where they do not belong.

"*Taisez-vous,*" Lavolier whispers. He points to a shadow. A movement of ferns. Raises his rifle; the shot resounds. They clamber to where the deer is thrashing, its blood seeping into the green. Lavolier thanks Christ and Mother Mary, then cuts the deer's throat.

"Bloody hell," James Thomson says when they come into sight of Fort Connelly. Lavolier half raises his rifle, then eases it down. Just outside the fort gates is Anawiskum Tulane. He is tied to a post, his bare torso striped with blood. A whimper escapes from his gritted teeth. A number of the People look on, as do all of the engagés. Illdare holds a whip in his gloved hand. His breath trails in the chilly air.

"It is not to be tolerated," Illdare tells Boston that night. "He can say what he wishes of me, but he cannot steal from me nor from the company. Not even rum. Everything must be accounted for. Everything must be balanced. Every action countered. Every item paid for. And the punishment for infractions must be witnessed by all. Does that make sense to you, Jim?"

Boston is sitting at his customary chair at the table. He nods.

"And what happens if these rules are ignored?"

"The world falls apart."

"Yes, our world cracks into great unequal pieces. You remember. Excellent. Now tell me what you have heard."

Boston tells him what Lavolier has told him, of Solomon and his wisdom, of Jezebel and how she fell and how nothing was left after the dogs had at her but the soles of her feet and the palms of her hands. He repeats the Latin Lavolier taught him: *Quia tu es, Deus, fortitudo mea; quare me repulisti, et quare tristis incedo, dum affligiti me inimicus.*

"He goes about in sadness does he?" Illdare says. "While the enemy harasses him. Hah! Here, lad, this is all the Latin you need." Illdare taps the motto under the company crest. "*Pro pelle cutem.* For skins we risk our skins. Don't forget it. Well . . . look upon it."

Boston does so, then glances curiously at Illdare. For why should he look at the crest and motto, since he has seen it before?

"What else? What has McNeal said, or Thomson?"

"Don't speak of you now."

"Ah, they suspect that you inform me. Well. What are we to do with these evenings then?" He looks hard at Boston.

"Sit here while you write, sleep. Won't be a trouble."

"No, I shouldn't think you would. But would it not be better to learn something of use besides Lavolier's Latin and foolish Bible tales? Would you like that?"

"Would like that. Yes."

"I would as well. It is good to have someone to speak with of an evening."

It is three months later. Illdare taps the map of New Caledonia. "And here is our island. Named for Captain Vancouver. It is near the exact latitude and longitude that Swift placed his Brobdingnag, which was?"

"Land of the giant people."

Illdare paces the sitting room. It is late in the evening. The fire burns low. Illdare's bottle of brandy is empty, as it always is by the end of their lessons. The pipe rack, the writing set, the books, all are in the same arrangement as they are every Thursday and Tuesday evening. It gives Boston comfort, this sameness.

"Exactly, the land of Swift's allegorical giants. It is why I was drawn to take the command here. Not, hah, that I believed I would discover giants, but that I might see something of Swift's mind. He knew Man and of what he was made. It is why he lived alone. Why I do as well. Why I do not like others about me. You know, I am often plagued by a dream of a young man. It is not me. Perhaps it is the man you will be. Hah, don't look so Jim, I am jesting. This young man is on a narrow, treacherous path that is cut into a cliff. Behind him are icy mountains, and though I never see what is below, I know the abyss is endless. His journey is of utmost importance, but he cannot find the way forward, nor back, not that it matters, for he is the only soul left in the world. What do you make of this?"

"Don't know. Don't dream."

"Truly? Well, you are a singular creature then. Truly, Jim, I do not know how you came into this world, though oftentimes I doubt you were born of woman. Perhaps you were shaped by this James Milroy out of sand and sea water, given then to me as both a gift and a curse."

"Not a curse."

"No, I am rambling." He lifts the empty brandy bottle and sets it back on the table, precisely in the same spot. "How disappointed I was when I first arrived here. No respite for my melancholic mind. Not here. People pressing all around. Tighter than if I lived in Edinburgh or in London. But I have found some comfort in the thought that I might write a book of the island. It would suit my temperament, to be a writer, to sit alone in an empty room with only a candle and a page. Many have been here, did you know that, Jim? We Englishmen believe nowhere exists before we set our boots upon it, spear our flag in its soil, and claim it for the monarch. But we were not the first. The Indians, of course, they have been here since before time. But there is evidence of others who have washed up, as did you, on these treacherous shores."

Illdare sits on the chair opposite Boston, leans forward, lowers his voice. "I know of a rock carving of a square-masted ship such as the celestials use. I know of jade beads and of an Oriental idol. I know of Spanish swords and Spanish armour. And I know of the most remarkable thing—coins from the time of the Virgin Queen, evidence that Sir Francis Drake himself discovered this island on a secret voyage, more than two hundred years before Vancouver ever clapped eyes on it."

"What of the company?"

"What of it?"

"The others say it was here before Christ."

Illdare laughs. It is a choking, guttural sound, one that Boston has never heard before. "Here Before Christ. Hah! The Hudson's Bay Company. They have reworked the meaning of the lettering. Not they as in the men here, not these half-wits. Others. They are alluding to the power and longevity of the company. It is a compliment in its way, not wholly a joke."

Boston scowls at the table. "The company is not so old, then."

"Exactly. Oh, lad, you understand so much so quickly, and yet so little withal."

Another evening. Illdare places a slim book on the table. "We feast on Voltaire again."

Boston handles the book carefully, as Illdare has taught him. Illdare pours out a precise measure of brandy and settles in his chair by the fire.

"Recite now?" Boston asks.

"What? Yes. Good. But do you not want the lantern closer? Your eyes, young man, they will fail you if not given light. Better, but careful now, not too close. You do not want to spark the pages. For where would we find another copy here, eh?"

"Now?"

"Yes, now. Any page you please."

The University of Coimbra had pronounced that the sight of a few people ceremoniously burned alive before a slow fire was an infallible prescription for preventing earthquakes; so when the earthquake had subsided after destroying three quarters of Lisbon, the authorities of that country could find no surer means of avoiding total ruin than by giving the people a magnificent auto-da-fé.

They therefore seized a Basque, convicted of marrying his godmother, and two Portuguese Jews who had refused to eat bacon with their chicken; and after dinner Dr. Pangloss and his pupil, Candide, were arrested as well, one for speaking and the other for listening with an air of approval. Pangloss and Candide were led off separately and closeted in an exceedingly cool room, where they suffered no inconvenience from the sun, and were brought out a week later to be dressed in sacrificial cassocks and paper mitres. The decorations on Candide's mitre and cassock were penitential in character, inverted flames and devils without claws or tails; but Pangloss's devils had tails and claws, and his flames were upright. They were then marched in procession, clothed in these robes, to hear a moving sermon followed by beautiful music in counterpoint. Candide was flogged in time with the anthem; the Basque and the two men who refused to eat bacon were burnt; and Pangloss was hanged, though that was not the usual practice on those occasions. The same day another earthquake occurred and caused tremendous havoc.

The terrified Candide stood weltering in blood and trembling with fear and confusion. "If this is the best of all possible worlds," he said to himself, "what can the rest be like?"

Illdare looks up from the fire. "Astonishing. How quickly you learn your letters. Read on."

Boston does so, looking now at Illdare, his hand on the page already recited. He speaks clearly, loudly. Illdare might say astonishing again. He might let him sit with him before the fire and share a measure of his brandy. He might unfurl the map of Great Britain as he did once and ask him to point out the village where he, Illdare, was born. When Boston does so without hesitation he will nod and smile and say again what an excellent pupil Boston is, how diligent, how attentive. He might even tell Boston of his dreams.

"Cease."

Boston falls silent.

"You are not reading. You have not even turned the page. Why are you not reading?"

Boston looks to the lines before him. He can make out most letters, but many words elude him as yet.

"Reading hard. Easier this way."

Illdare approaches the table. "What way?"

Boston has done wrong. He is not certain how, but he has. He must *atone,* that is what Lavolier calls it. "Heard it from you. You read it out by the fire."

"I did? Yes, perhaps. But weeks ago. Nay, a month ago. How is it you recall it?"

"Heard it."

"And so you recall it after hearing it once? Can repeat it just so."

"Can. Yes."

Illdare tilts the book so that Boston cannot see the page. "Recite again. I shall read along."

Boston does so through to the end of the chapter and then half-way through the next. An old woman consoles Candide. She salves his wounds and later brings Candide his lady love. Candide is astonished. He heard that his lady love had been disembowelled. People do not always die of such things, his lady love assures him.

Illdare's lips move as he reads along. His eyes grow wide with astonishment. "Stop now. Enough. It is exactly so. Word for word. What more do you remember?"

"What more?"

"Take, say . . .say, something I might have said to Anawiskum."

"When?"

"A month ago, a week ago. Anything you recall."

"You said those bear hides will combust if you pack them that way, you half-breed mooncalf. Were in the storeroom then. Was a Tuesday by the calendar. The fifth of October."

Illdare hauls a company journal down from the shelf. He folds back the great pages. "Describe the weather of twelve days past."

"Morning mist. Then it rained. Sun. Rain again."

"And how many Indians came to trade? What did they trade?"

Boston says: "Was helping press the furs that day. Weren't in the trade room."

"Then on a day you were."

"Was there the day it stormed."

"When was that?"

"Twenty-third of the September."

"What occurred?"

"Two of the Kwagu'l came in first. A man and a woman. They had an otter skin. They spoke a form of the jargon. Asked to see you. Said they had more to trade. Certain thing you'd want. They'd heard that. McNeal told them he was the only one trading. They insisted and he went and got you."

"That I remember, yes. Go on now, spare no detail."

And so it goes. Boston tells what the man and woman wore, their gestures, the way the woman bargained more forcefully than the man, the way she berated him in their tongue for relenting so quickly to such a low price.

"Astonishing. Astonishing. You will make a remarkable clerk. Would you like that?"

"Yes. Would like that."

"Keep this as our secret, Jim. Do not allow others to know, ever, of your ability. Not the engagés, not the Indians, not anyone you should meet in your life. Few others have any reason and will see in your talent the devil's hand. Do you understand?"

"Won't say, no."

"The shipwreck. But what of that, then?"

Boston shakes his head. Usually a scene fills itself in until all details are there, in the order that they were. Immutable. Exact. The time before is different. Full of shouts and crashing and the pounding of feet and shouting and water hurling down. The images are in a chaos. Are missing great gaps.

"Don't remember. Not details. Parts. Faded half-bits."

"Strange."

Boston places his hands on his chest. The wounds have healed but still they ache at times.

"Ah. It is the magic of this James Milroy of Boston. Is that what you are believing?"

"Don't know."

"Hear me, Jim, it is coincidence only. The belief in witchcraft is best left to Yorkshire villagers and savages." He shakes his head. "You recall everything. Everything. Without change. An odd expression travels over Illdare's face as he adds: "You poor bastard." Boston has seen this expression on Illdare's face only once before. That was when, nearly thirteen months past now, he stroked Boston's forehead as he lay battered and aching, in confusion as to where he was.

TWENTY-SIX

The hills are dense with water wheels, flumes, and windlasses that clank and creak like medieval siege engines. Eugene makes his way over the ragged trail, over low flumes and logs, over planks and ditches, past a broken cart wheel, a growling dog, past men labouring, ever labouring. He walks with exaggerated caution. Last week a Dutchman broke his leg at just this time of day, when the grey light smudges the borders between this thing and that.

The miners have constructed crude cabins, earthen pits roofed with split logs, tents, even brush shelters, the sort better fit for hermits bent on suffering and sainthood. At least his cabin is chinked with moss and has a solid bark roof that leaks only in hard rains. He should thank the Lord for His small mercies and not grumble that goat pens are as large, nor that the beds are as narrow and hard as trestle tables. "Matters could be worse," as Young George is wont to say. True, they could be eight men to such a cabin. They could be sleeping in shifts, in the stew of each other's dirt and sweat. They could be dead. That would be worse, Eugene supposes.

The stench of an abandoned mine shaft near drops him to his knees. He soundly curses. He himself championed an end to using such shafts as receptacles for shit and piss and refuse of all kinds, or at least *hear-heared* the idea in a saloon at some point. He will mention the problem to the Judge when he sees him again. Perhaps there is a legal angle to it all. Filth should be criminal, leading as it does to pestilence.

Lanterns begin speckling the hills. Eugene strikes a lucifer that hisses uselessly. It will be dark as pitch by the time he returns to the cabin. Without a lamp he will be lost. He will wander into the woods and die of hunger and exhaustion and cold as others have done.

Only his bones will be found. Only his bones and his last desperate attempts to scratch out his name and fate. Or perhaps they will find no sign of him. Bears and pumas will consume him whole. He will. . . . The second lucifer strikes. Flares. Eugene sighs. Holds the lamp high. Who is that singing? What language? It is syllabic and off-key and seems to be forming itself from the gloaming. Eugene pulls his blanket coat closed. Peers this way, now that. Lost, are you, Eugene Augustus? Yet again? No. There is the Dewlap claim and to the right of it is the trail that leads eventually into the forest and then to Lickety creek. He whistles in false cheer, wishes mightily that his flask were full of good brandy. Recalls those morbid old tales of children lost and witches found, recalls a childhood belief in a vast skeletal hand that crept from an abandoned manor to claim the wayward, and now, least welcome, recalls a leafless tree that at first seemed full of rounded, sleeping birds, which on closer inspection proved to be the heads of Russian soldiers.

A good hour passes before he hears the rush of the creek and spies, with great relief, the black form of the cabin and then the mine some fifty yards past it.

He is greeted with *good evenings* and with the sight of the cabin's tin stove that faintly rattles as if something were hopelessly trying to escape. Smoke hovers near the roof and steam rises from a line festooned with socks and underclothes. The odours of wet wool and boots reign perpetual, Napoleon having insisted that boots be pried off at the end of each day. It is the only protection against the gumboot gout, he claims, an affliction that marries the boot to a man's foot, creating a green and putrid hybrid.

Langstrom stirs a black pot. Napoleon is at the small table reading his book of remedies. Lorn is hacking wood outside. Bowson is lying on his lower bunk, staring upward, possibly thinking.

"You have caught us some dinner, Langstrom, splendid," Eugene says, his mouth watering though his belly is still half-full from his afternoon meal.

Langstrom nibbles at his fingers, puffs out his cheeks.

"Rabbit?" Eugene asks hopefully.

"Actually, it is squirrel," Napoleon says.

Langstrom is the best shot of them all and as well the best cook. For these reasons they recently agreed that he should spend a half-portion of his time hunting instead of mining. Any gold would be shared equally with him, of course, just as if he were digging himself. It took some time to convey this plan to Langstrom who from their gesturing thought perhaps that they were threatening to shoot and eat him. But it has paid off. Though they are never full, they have not starved, and now and then there is enough gold scratched from the claim to buy some beans, flour, sugar even.

Eugene sits across from Napoleon who barely glances up from his reading. Calls a *good evening* up to George.

"And good evening to you, Doc. How was your afternoon?"

"Excellent. Splendid. I was strolling through that shelving known as a boardwalk when I was hailed by the Judge and . . ."

"The Judge! Gosh!"

"Yes, we struck up a friendship in Victoria, you see."

"That's right. You told us that," George says.

"Plenty of times," Lorn says, coming through the doorway, thudding down a load of wood.

"It's just that the Judge, well, he's something."

Eugene agrees with George that the Judge is something indeed. Tells how the Judge treated him to a coffee. "We talked of a great many things. We have much in common."

"Did you tell him 'bout the mine and whatnot?" Lorn asks. There is no accusation in his voice. Still it is hard not to take umbrage when confronted with a face frozen into a sneer. It is such that Eugene can barely look at Lorn, otherwise everything Lorn says seems riddled with contempt. "Pass the biscuits". "Good night." "No gold again."

"I did, yes. He said it is not unusual for mines to not yield for a time. Patience is required."

"I'm patient."

"Yes, you are, Young George. You are indeed."

"Food? Lee?" Langstrom asks.

"The Chinaman's generosity has been exaggerated. As has his judgment of good character."

"Gosh. Is it no credit then?" asks George.

"For the moment, no."

"There's a surprise," Lorn says.

"Gentlemen, all was not in vain." Eugene takes the packet from his breast pocket. Holds it high.

George leaps from the bunk. Lorn surges forward. Langstrom stares into the cooking pot as if seeing something hidden from lesser cooks. There is no letter for him. There never is.

George carefully slits open his gummed envelope, is immediately puddly-eyed over his mother's handwriting. The woman must have a scribe's heart for George receives just such a fat letter nearly every week.

Lorn sits on the edge of his bed and hunkers over a slim letter that is stained and battered. Eugene does not offer to read it to him, nor does George. They were told clearly enough the last time that Lorn trusted only Napoleon to read his missives.

"I waited for over an hour, gentlemen," Eugene says.

George nods. His lips do not cease silently moving. Lorn makes no sign that he has heard Eugene at all. Napoleon politely echoes "an hour." Langstrom tastes the stew and grimaces.

"It rained. A Frenchman and an American fought with knives near the steps. They were separated before blood was shed. I was fortunate not to be drawn in."

"Gosh, I'll go next time," George says. "I don't mind the waiting."

"I did not mean that I minded the waiting."

"Did you receive any letters?" Napoleon asks.

"No, I unfortunately did not."

"Nothing from your wife?" George asks.

"No, nothing on this occasion, though I waited for near two hours in the hail."

"Thought you said it rained," Lorn says.

"It rained and then it hailed."

"I'm sure she's doing swell. I'll pray for her anyway."

"Thank you, Young George. Thank you, indeed."

Eugene thinks of the mere three letters Dora has written so far, or rather that Mrs. Smitherton, that epistolary chaperone, has written him in her spidery hand. Young Mr. Hartworth fell asleep in the butter church and slid to the floor. Mrs. Bell delivered Mrs. Hickson's second child. The Sisters of St. Anne have come to see if the Cowichan would make a good home for Indian and half-blood waifs, orphans, and strays. They stepped out of the boat looking like giant crows. Later Jeremiah asked if they had bodies or were merely faces floating in cloth. He was jesting. Or so Dora thought.

Why has Dora not written him twice a week as she promised, as he promised he would write her? At least he has proper excuses. He has been plagued with hindrances, the like of which she cannot imagine. Certainly if Dora were aware of the letter that sits heavy in his breast pocket she would go running for Mrs. Smitherton and her pen. He is avoiding thinking of this letter with all that he can muster. For Mr. Jacobsen has died. Mrs. Jacobsen found him in the pantry among jars of smashed preserves. Shocking, yes. And how difficult it is for her on her own. How lonely. Eugene steps outside with a candle. Sits on the low bench along the wall and smoothes Mrs. Jacobsen's letter over his knee, having crumpled it impulsively upon first reading.

And thus, Mr. Hume, I shall be selling the Hotel Avalon & returning to Toronto. There I intend to use the capital from the sale & the capital which I have saved over the years to open a new & even grander establishment. In this I would like your assistance. I will be plain. I will be frank. Such is my nature. You have not yet married Miss Timmons. You are, in effect, a free man, a bachelor. You may take opportunities should they present themselves.

And so on. Eugene is flattered by the offer. Indeed, he can almost see himself as the guardian of a rosewood bar. He would stock it with spirits from far-flung ports of the empire. There would be ten varieties each of champagne and brandy. He might even stock vodka. Why not? The war with the Russians is barely remembered here. The gentry of Toronto would be his clientele. There would be evenings of uproarious laughter and quieter, more contemplative evenings with adventures related and philosophy discussed. He will wear grey suits for summer. Black for winter. A monocle might not be amiss.

George calls out that supper is ready. Back in the cabin Langstrom carefully ladles the exact small portion of stew onto each plate. Hands a plate to Eugene along with a hard biscuit. Eugene ponders mentioning how he already ate once this day. But why should he, truly? Would his partners mention if they had been treated to a large meal? Would they say: and so please, divide mine among you? Certainly not.

He hunches over his plate and afterwards wipes it clean with his fingers and gives his compliments to Langstrom. He does enjoy Mrs. Jacobsen's company well enough. In certain lights she hardly looks her age. In any case, he is feeling older by the moment. And she might not demand too much in the way of husbandly duties. Stranger unions have been made. It is possible. And he might not have to give Dora up entirely.

Ah, Dora, Dora. One word from her would be enough to torch these idle thoughts. He would not even bridle at the ridiculous sobriquet "Eggy." Perhaps his latest letter, penned three weeks ago, is only just arriving. She is at the pier, bathed in the glow of the setting sun. She is waving at the sloop. She is inquiring breathlessly. Now Mrs. Smitherton is reading:

The mine is going well & yielding a steady outflow & I have no doubt that if we dig deeper we will find a rich strain though I must constantly assure our young Bowson that we will not fall into the pits of hell & see the damned there cooling their heels. He is also fearful that we will stumble upon the remains of the creatures and sinners swept away by Noah's flood, at which I could not resist suggesting that, according to that fellow Darwin, we are more likely to find the bones of our monkey ancestors, who were replaced slowly & surely by the wily specimens of men who rule the earth in these modern times. Poor boy! I believe he would rather encounter a demon than such evidence of our paltry, animal origins.

Or some such. In any case, she is smiling and saying how witty is her Eggy, how hopeful, how brave. One distant day he might well agree.

TWENTY-SEVEN

Eleven years, three months and nine days have passed since Boston first awoke to Equata's singing. Though he has only a youth's sparse beard, he is never called Young Jim anymore, not even by Illdare. "It's like you were born old," more than one of the engagés have said, and they offer no complaint when he is placed in charge of the trade room after McNeal's death from apoplexy. Boston is, after all, the best at bartering, and he speaks the language of the People as fluently as if he had been born among them. He speaks the jargon as well and all its variations and all the languages of the engagés, though some with a roughness he has never cared to improve upon, wanting as he does, less and less over the years, to hear pointless talk. Of the men who were there when he arrived only Illdare and Kanaquasse Fleury are of the originals. Some engagés Illdare sent off for thievery or insolence. Others, such as the Sandwich Islanders, died of gangrenous fever or by accident or suicide. As for Lavolier, he left Fort Connelly on April 17th four years previous. He walked into the forest dressed in a black robe that he had sewn himself. It was of no great surprise, for Lavolier had taken to claiming he was Saint Ignatius of Loyla himself, to lying prone with arms outstretched in the mud, to saying repeatedly that he must save ten thousand heathen Indian souls before his life was done. Without the ten thousand he would never be received into heaven. Such was the Lord's price in return for eternal bliss.

The new engagés complain even more bitterly of Illdare and his ways. True, he has grown harsher in his punishments over the years, is more likely to flog a man, or make him run the gauntlet, or clap him in irons, though he has told the engagés that he is more just than most company officers, and for this they should be grateful. He does not, after all, inflict these punishments in a drunken fit, nor to satisfy some prejudice or private grudge, nor for simple blood lust. He inflicts them for distinct causes, and only if the evidence against the miscreant is clear, and even then without any sign of enjoyment, rather a revulsion that it must be done at all. Often he reassures the miscreant that he should not blame himself, for all men are debased, some are merely better at suppressing their bestial nature. Boston he never touches with a whip or a fist, but then Boston does his tasks well and does not join in the combinations that happen from time to time, when the engagés refuse to do work other than that of their craft, or demand better wages or better food. And he does not steal, nor raise his voice against Illdare, nor drink more than he is allotted. No longer, however, does Illdare invite Boston to his sitting room to read from the books of Voltaire and Swift. No longer does he invite him to sit by the fire in silence. The last occasion he did so was when Boston's voice was beginning to change. Illdare did not drink brandy on this occasion, nor did he ramble. But then not once had he done so since he learned that Boston could not forget. "I have taught you what I can. There is no need for us to meet here again. You are too much the man now." Then Illdare added that an officer should not befriend an engagé.

"Not an engagé," Boston said. He had never signed a document binding him to the company. Illdare and he had agreed that it was enough that he had his life, his food, the roof over his head and the clothes on his back. And he is allowed a small share of the profits, taken from Illdare's own, and a small share of the trade goods to trade again or to do with as he pleased.

"No, you are not formally an engagé, I will grant you that. But you are an underling and a grown man now and I am an officer and should not show favouritism."

And he hasn't, not since that day, but greets Boston in the same clipped tones as he greets the other engagés. He asks him mostly of the details of the trade and often reminds him, as if Boston might forget, that he be informed if the Indians have brought any items out of the ordinary to trade. Now and then he commends Boston on always making his quota, and now and then he mentions that he trusts Boston more than any other man at the fort. Boston takes pride in this trust of Illdare's, and in the trust, also, that the People show him. For lately he has been invited, though none of the other fort men have, to the potlatching where the guests witness the taking of names and songs and privileges, and receive goods in return, each according to his rank. He attends, as well, the potlatching for the dead and the newly born. At these ceremonies long speeches are given and tales retold. These tales have been passed down through the generations, are as old as the mythic times. They give evidence of hereditary rights and are not the free-form stories told for entertainment. It may take half a day to recite the history of the headman, or a family, or the collective history of the People, and a type of sacredness is in each immutable word. Boston knows the People's remembering, though greater than that of any Whiteman, is not the same as his. It is practised and learned. They do not recall the mundane details of each and every day. Still, this vague sense of commonality is enough to draw him back to the potlatching, as does the latticework of reciprocity that is so formally acknowledged, that maintains a balance that is almost palpable and satisfies him in a way that the religion of the Christ never has.

"Tell us what they are planning," Illdare said when Boston first began attending the village ceremonials. "If you do not, you cannot go."

Boston agreed to gather what information he could. But the People tell him nothing of much use, and instead ask him questions about the Ghost People. Why do they rely on books? How many guns at the fort? How strong are the gates? Boston brushes off the questions and goes to the ceremonies less and less. For it is not an alliance between Fort Connelly and the village, but an uneasy truce with advantages for both sides, and Illdare knows, as Boston does, that many in the village would like to see the fort burned and plundered and the heads of the men arranged in neat piles.

TWENTY-EIGHT

The single shaft is some twenty feet deep. The drift runs west under Lickety Creek, following the downward flow. Today Langstrom is responsible for cranking on the windlass and emptying the bucket into rockers manned by Lorn and Napoleon. Eugene and George are to go down into the mine itself. It is their turn. Nothing can be done about it.

"Today the day, sir?" George calls. He is full of his usual appalling good cheer though it is barely light.

"Assuredly, yes. Pay dirt as they say," Eugene says, with no conviction whatsoever. Except for dustings and a few slivers here and there the mine still refuses to show up. The first week they took out only three ounces. Barely enough to maintain the mine and themselves, though enough to keep their hopes up. Now they are working at a loss.

They sling their shovels on their backs. Eugene hooks the lantern into his belt and looks wistfully at the clear field of the sky. It has been raining steadily since he saw the Judge last week, the sort of persistent drumming rain that seems to mock a man.

Now the descent. It is what Eugene hates most. The air becomes cool and thick as he passes the fraying rope and rusted bucket of the windlass, and then the canvas that flaps against his face like torn sails. The support timbers creak and weep, as might those of a sinking ship. And all smells of wet wood and ancient earth. Of things best left where they are.

Their gumboots are treacherous on the ladder that is slick with slime. "Careful now!" he calls when George nearly slips, nearly drops on Eugene's head.

"Gosh darn it all. Sorry about that."

What would it take for George to soundly curse? Surely he has it in him. Eugene tried to bet Langstrom that George would curse before the season was out. The Swede refused the bet, saying, as far as Eugene could surmise from his gesticulating and paltry stash of English words, that if George did swear it would bode ill indeed.

Eugene drops the last few feet to the bottom of the shaft. The water splashes up to his booted calves. George drops behind him. The darkness is lit only by Eugene's lantern. Eugene, a good head taller than George, is bent nearly double in the shaft. Already his neck and back dully throb. What he would give for a bath, a true bath, not this sponging of his visible parts with water heated on the stove. Not this washing in the creek as Langstrom is wont to do, and which Eugene and the others can only watch with amazement. For Langstrom settles into the cold waters of the creek as happily as if he were in a Turkish bath, leisurely rubs himself with sand and then returns to stand naked before the stove, his broad body white and scarred and steaming, his pipe soon enough clamped again between his teeth.

They trundle on. Eugene's throat constricts. If only the possibility of being buried alive did not present itself with every trickle of slum through the timbers. No, it is not his element. He is no Welshman. No Cornishman. It is not in his blood, this toiling in the dark like a mole.

They come to the end of the tunnel where the barrow was left the previous day.

Eugene stops. George bumps up against him.

"Here then?"

"Yes, yes. Where else?" Eugene regrets his tone. But why is it that George looks to him for even the most minor of decisions? Eugene is not the young man's father, nor has Eugene shown any great wisdom in mining. Indeed, by now it should be obvious that he is a charlatan, a fool.

They pound their sticking toms into rock and timber, and then into their sticking toms they shove their merlin oil candles. Six hours it takes for one to burn. A shift half-gone. A life melting to a puddle of ooze.

They shovel dirt, water, and gravel into the barrow. They are down at the bedrock, where the stream ran eons ago. The gold should be on this bedrock. It was where Barker found it, and Cameron, and Oswald, though to be certain, to be thorough, they have gone at the rock walls with both mattocks and tweezers, looking for a vein as well, for a colour, a glory hole.

Eugene pushes the loaded barrow to the opening of the shaft. He fills the bucket, then calls "haul up," to Langstrom. Would they had a long tom with a flume to feed it, or at least extra hands to load it with water. Oswald and his partners have three long toms that are fed by flumes that are higher than the trees of which they were made. He has four shafts. Says, smugly, that he is doing "not so damned bad." But then who admits to high yields? Tax agents and thieves is all that would lure.

The hours drip on. Eugene strains at the shovel. There is a burn of pain in his back. A burn of cold in his feet and hands. These discomforts occupy the whole of his thoughts. It is not as he had thought it would be. He had thought that while his body was labouring his mind would be free to devise philosophical theories, or design the house in which he and Dora would one day live, or decide upon the manner of his lecturing (for a lecture circuit would no doubt follow the publication of his guidebook). And for a time he did ponder such things, as well as old mistakes, past injustices, the whereabouts of a spinning top he lost when he was a child (the gardener took it, he decided), any number of plays that he has seen, ditties he has heard, the names of the daughters of Zeus, the way Dora sheds each layer of clothing as if it were a hindrance, then him gazing at the rounded sheen of her limbs. Then, one afternoon, doing his time at the rocker, he realized that his mind was perfectly vacant. This is a great deal different from one's mind being perfectly clear or at peace. Eugene had known the approximate of such feelings on those afternoons when he and Dora lay together after love. No this is a mindlessness; it is a realm where nothing moves and nothing comes to light. It is a dark vat, the black waters of his soul. He can only imagine his expression when he is mired there—dull, fixed, like that of a gravedigger, or of a beggar who sits all day in the shadow of a church.

Lunch is a respite of a half an hour or so. The clearness of the morning is gone. The air is green and aqueous. The clouds thick on the horizon. It is as if they have stepped into an entirely different day from the one of this morning. It is as if time follows a different stream below.

Langstrom hands them biscuits, then holds up his rifle and motions to the trees. Would that Eugene could go with him. He'd rather face a bear, a charging stag, a poisonous snake than a return to the shaft. But the more they work on the mine the better are their chances of finding the motherlode. He was the one who said this just yesterday, during a fit of hopefulness.

Eugene rubs his neck. Does Napoleon suffer as he does? He is the only one taller than Eugene and when he is in the shaft he walks in a crouch with his hands pressed on his knees. He must suffer, and yet he never complains. A stoic man. A good man. A weary affection for them all suffuses Eugene. For Langstrom trudging toward the hills, humming a tune from the cold regions of his youth. For Lorn who is spitting into a ditch. For Napoleon who is inspecting a plant and no doubt dreaming up concoctions that will cure the ague, the palsy, the black dog of melancholy. And most of all for Young George Bowson. He is snoring softly on some canvas sacking. He can sleep anywhere, at any time. Only the young are so blessed. Only those who owe nothing to anyone.

"Come, up with you, lad. It is time we all became wealthy men. It will happen soon. I can feel it in my very bones."

Eugene and George again descend into the shaft as grey clouds roll over the sun. When their candles are a quarter burned Lorn calls out that it has begun to rain. When their candles are half burned they hear the muffled boom of thunder. Then, a few seconds later, they see the rain, now pouring down the shaft and transformed into an illuminated pillar, thick and glorious enough to hold up the sky.

"Lightning!" Eugene shouts.

"What do we do? What!" George's face is stricken, his mouth agape.

"Calm yourself. We can't stay below. That is for certain. The lightning may well fire the timbers."

"But no, no. We can't go above! My brother, he was killed by lightning when he was ten, walking in a field. Why him? We prayed for answers. By God, we did." George backs further down the shaft, out of the round of lamplight.

Someone shouts down to them. Another muffled boom. Another illumination of the pillar of rain. The water roils under their boots. Eugene hefts his lantern, points wide-eyed at the slum oozing thickly between the timbers.

"Jesus H. Christ!" George shouts.

"Run! Get above! The timbers won't hold!"

George whimpers and makes no move. Eugene grips him by his shirt. He stumbles along with Eugene. The shaft opening. Was it so damned far? Eugene catches a glimpse of a figure coming toward them. "Lorn!" he shouts.

Lorn raises his hands, shouts back. And then a great cracking as the timbers give way. A torrent of dirt and mud and shattering wood. Eugene is flung back into George, into the tumult of water. He is scrambling on his hands and knees, gulping at air. The lantern has shattered. Such darkness. He spits out dirt, struggles to his feet. Scraped and bruised. Nothing more. Nothing more.

"George! Young George! Are you alive?"

Silence and then a faint: "I think so."

"Where?!"

"Here."

Eugene gropes about until he finds George's arm. Can feel it shaking, as his own must be. "The lantern!" Eugene says. "Smashed. Dammit. The lucifers. Where are they?"

"I have them. I have them."

"Dry?"

"Think so. Hope so. They're wrapped. Oh, God."

"A candle. Here I have it. Strike the lucifer. Let there be light, eh, lad?"

"Right, Doc, Right. Here. Damn you, match. Strike! Strike! There."

George lights the candle that Eugene clenches in both hands. Their harsh breathing slows. Eugene turns at George's look of horror. Rubble blocks near the entire tunnel.

"We're bloody doomed!" George shouts. "We're dead. Buried!"

"Easy, easy. Lorn's the one who's buried. He was coming this way when the mine caved. Come. Dig. Let us do our part to save him. Ourselves as well, eh?"

George dashes tears from his eyes and nods.

Where has Eugene found the courage? Though how can it be courage while he is shaking, while he is battling bile and tears? Ah, but he can act the part. Has always acted a part.

They jam the candle into a crevice and begin to claw at the rubble.

Eugene is oblivious to the splinters driving into his hands, the pounding in his head. He hauls aside a beam, marvelling at his own strength. George runs back for the shovels and mattocks. They hack away until they hear faint shouting from the other side of the rubble. Eugene ceases his labours. Holds his ragged breath. The shouting grows louder.

"Hello! Hello!" Eugene calls. "We're alive, boys! But Lorn's buried. So dig! Dig! The tunnel may cave again!"

"Please, Mr. Hume! Quiet. We're trying to listen for him."

"That you, Napoleon?"

"Yes. Quiet, please!"

"Quiet," Eugene orders George.

A timber shifts. Dirt and mud flow over their boots. It is a disaster of Eugene's making. He is as certain of it as if he called up the storm like some warlock. He led them here, the lot of them. It was his enthusiasm. His blindness in the face of the obvious. And now Lorn. Poor Lorn! Lorn who saved him from the demon bog, who nurtured him like a child. This is his thanks.

"Here, damnit, here!" The voice comes faintly from the right. George presses his hands together in prayer.

"Be easy. Careful. We do not know his condition," Napoleon calls.

"Yes, be careful now, George," Eugene says and has a vision of Lorn stabbed with a shovel, crushed by an ill-moved timber. They work as methodically as possible, speaking little except to call to Lorn from time to time. Lorn answers with curses, with demands to hurry up. A current of air. Eugene spots a hand reaching over the top of the rubble. Langstrom?

"We're nearly there!" Eugene shouts. Now sees Napoleon backed by a font of lantern light. He is breathing heavily and there is a tightness along his jaw. Aside from that his face is, as usual, surprisingly calm.

Lorn is face-down. They uncover his thighs, his shoulders, his head over which his hands are clasped. His cheeks are grooved with scratches. But he breathes. He breathes in Napoleon's arms, is standing with the help of steadying hands. "I'll be Goddamned. I ain't dead."

"The timbers formed a bridge over you," Eugene says.

"Thank the good Lord," George says.

"Amen," Lorn says, as does Napoleon, then Langstrom. No one is thanking Eugene.

"Storm! Finish!" Langstrom yells as he looks up the shaft. He and Napoleon help Lorn to the ladder. Lorn limps and pauses, limps and pauses. Eugene and George follow close behind. The enormity of the close call is only now becoming apparent to Eugene. They all could have been buried alive. Yes, of course, they must give thanks as George is insisting. They will all praise the Lord for delivering them. It is enough to make a faithful churchgoer of him, though if the Lord truly had his interests in mind, a little gold might help. He looks back to the pile of rubble. It must be cleared. The walls must be reinforced. More futile work. This whole operation is pure foolishness. He will leave in the night and return to Dora. In time he will send the money to Lorn and Napoleon for their shares. He will sell all he has to do so. It will be as he promised. For the claim will not prove up. Cannot.

"Maybe we could go 'round it, Doc," George says, following Eugene's despairing gaze.

"What?"

"Go 'round. Make a bend. What did I say? It wasn't a joke."

They clamber out of the shaft. The storm has passed as quickly as it came. Patches of sun through the cloud. Glistening leaves. An earthen smell. Eugene strides into the centre of the stream. He is filthy, soaked, cold to his very bones, and yet. Yet! That knoll 'round which the stream bends. Why had he not noticed it before?

The others stand at the bank. Look at each other, then to Eugene. Lorn eases himself onto a rock and Napoleon attends to his foot. George sways with hands clasped. Langstrom lights his pipe. Takes a great inhale.

"Picture it, gentlemen," Eugene says. "A thousand years ago. Two. Three."

"Before the Flood?" George asks.

"That I could not say. And this mountain which shadows us, it did not bear the concave shape it does now."

"A what shape?" Lorn asks.

"Concave. Inward. Dished out," Napoleon says dubiously.

"Exactly. You see, once this mountain was as whole and round as the rest about. And then, a great torrent. Days of relentless rain such as we have had. Though worse, assuredly worse."

"During the Flood, then?"

"No, George, no. It was a great torrent, not as severe as Noah's Flood, but severe enough to cause the side of the mountain to slide as does an ill-cooked pudding."

"A pudding would be grand. I wouldn't care if it were cooked," George says.

"Pudding? Eat?" Langstrom asks.

"It is merely an analogy, gentlemen. Think of a moulded pudding, one that stands upright like so and if it does not set properly it slides and . . . and the comparison matters not. What matters is that *this* knoll was once a part of *that* mountain until it slid into the depression below, burying the path of the stream that once ran straight. The stream then angled itself past it."

The others stare at the mountain, the knoll, Eugene.

"Do you mean that the old stream bed would have travelled beneath the knoll, and not where we've been digging?" This from Napoleon.

"Yes!" Eugene shouts. "I can see it as clearly as if the earth were an open book. The debris slid into the hollow. That is where the gold is, gentlemen. The motherlode. It has collected there over the hundreds of centuries, the thousands. It is there, awaiting us like Briar Rose awaited her prince."

"Who?" George asks.

"It's an old story. Old as the hills."

"I cursed, Doc. I took the Lord's name in vain."

"Indeed. Let's take it as a good luck sign, shall we?"

TWENTY-NINE

"Do you have a wife, Mr. Jim?" the Dora woman asked.
"No."

"Have you ever had a wife, then?"

"No," he said and she looked as astonished as if he'd said he'd never eaten, never breathed.

When he returns he might tell the Dora woman of Kloo-yah. But then she might well ask if he loved her. Women are free enough with that word. No, he will not speak of Kloo-yah to Dora. Speaking of her will only bring on a surround of memory. But even as he decides this, Kloo-yah is wrought whole in his mind. Boston curses. She looks precisely as she did one morning in the time when the salmon were returning to the river.

She sits on the floor of the trade room and quietly weeps. She wears a finely woven dress of cedar bark and a cape made from no less than a four-point trade blanket. Her forehead is flattened and trade beads are woven into her hair, though even without these enhancements she would have been fine enough to look upon. Boston has seen her before, several times, though the first image that comes to his mind is that of her holding tight to a giddee dog pup, its skin pink and scabrous.

She has nothing for trade. Still, he gives her water and some hard tack. She eats in delicate bites though it is obvious from her shaking that she is wracked with hunger. While she eats, Boston notices that her nails are rimmed with blood and her hands scratched and swollen and raw.

"I will stay here now," she says in her language.

Boston keeps about his business as if he has not heard her. After she has finished the water and hard tack he locks the trade room and leads her back to the village. She says nothing, nor does she take her eyes from the ground as they walk past the canoes drawn up on the shore, past the welcome figures, the racks of drying salmon, the great square houses with their flags of smoke and tall carved figures before the rounded doors. She glances only at the three sisters, the three great pillars that stand out in the waves at the end of the bay.

The People stare as they pass. An old woman slaps a child's pointing hand. Two slaves, their hair cut short, fall silent and draw back.

The house where the headman lives is larger than any other. Boston ducks through the doorway; Kloo-yah follows. Women are cooking at the numerous hearths or weaving mats and clothing. The cross poles above are hung with dried herring, fern roots, fishing hooks, and packs of roe and berries. Black and red painted boxes line the walls and baskets are scattered here and there. The place is thick with the smell of cedar smoke and fish, with the sound of rocks hissing into pots and of children crying and calling out, and with the slow beating of a drum.

The headman's hair is grey and he wears a cloak of otter fur, a rare thing now, for it is otter fur the Whitemen covet most of all. He gestures to the raised bench beside his hearth. Boston sits and Kloo-yah stands behind him, still as a house post, silent as a shadow. A wife hands Boston a platter of whale blubber and small fish heads and a bowl of berries soaked in oolichan oil. He eats these delicacies and afterwards the wife hands him cedar strips and a bowl of water with which to wash his hands. The wife offers nothing to Kloo-yah. Does not look to her, nor speak to her.

The headman hands him a pipe and some good trade tobacco. They talk of the abundance this year of the black clam, of the impending ceremonies to thank the salmon for returning to the rivers. Boston asks after the headman's family and the headman tells him that he is still grieving for his niece. She was to be married to a man from a neighbouring village when she was wracked by a strange fever. She ranted in a voice that was not her own, in a language they had never heard. Equata came and made her best chants and best tonics but all to no avail. Ah, but Kloo-yah had always been strange, one whose spirit wandered, Equata said, and often inhabited the trees and waves. Did she not prefer to gather food alone in the forest though this was dangerous?

Was she not always more fond of the sea than was normal for a girl? And she had never liked the winter entertainments, but preferred ever to be on her own, staring at something they could not see. She was of another realm and so it was no surprise when she was called away. They gave her full ceremony and dressed her in fine garments and folded her into a box and covered it with a white blanket and left it high in a tree. Nearby they hung trinkets and calicos and torn trade blankets. All was done according to tradition. The women had lamented, the songs had been sung. Thus it was to the horror of all when banging and screaming was heard from the box. Equata said her chants but the One-who-had-been-Kloo-yah broke free. She lingered in the village for several days, one of those who are too stubborn to accept that they have died, and so must be convinced of it. They ignored her until she faded. The headman himself had seen her fade. Does Boston see her now? Is she visible to him?

Boston says that he does see her now. That she is standing behind him.

The headman is quiet, then says "She will fade for you in time also. Merely assure yourself over and again that she is a ghost."

Sweat trickles down Kloo-yah's cheek. Her wrists show red marking where her bangles have rubbed. Her arms and hands are scratched. She smells as all the People do, of salmon and cedar, and of the grease they use in their hair. She does not seem about to fade, not at all.

Boson gives his formal farewells. Gestures to Kloo-yah. They are nearly out the door when the headman calls to Boston.

"Can she hear you when you speak?"

"Can. Yes."

"Then tell her I will see her soon. Tell her that I am old and that soon I, too, will make the journey. Tell her I will bring her that which she loves—a young dog and the ladle carved by her brother, and berry cakes and vermilion paint."

Once within the fort walls Kloo-yah shows him the pulse of veins at her wrist. "I am not dead."

"No."

"I will stay here. I will cook for you and lie with you."

"Don't like pointless talking. Should know that."

"Nor do I," she says and places her hand on his arm.

247

Later Illdare says: "You know how I feel about consorting with the women of the Village. It leads only to trouble."

"Kloo-yah not like others."

Illdare snorted at this. "No. But neither is she your wife. No formal exchanges have been made."

"Can't. The People don't see her."

"Yes, the circumstances are unusual. Damned superstitions. Look, Jim, I will allow this as a favour to you, but only if you and your concubine live outside the fort walls. Is that clear?"

It is as if the world were holding its breath, not only him. He lies very still at first because it is possible that she *is* one of the dead as the People claim. To embrace her would be to embrace death. He has heard the stories; he knows as much. She will lull him to sleep and feast on the marrow of his bones.

She smoothes her hand over his chest, as if to wipe it clean of the scars. What does it matter if she is something not entirely human? There is some comfort in knowing she is different from all others, as he himself is, that she, too, by some turn of fate, has been exiled from the human realm. In the nights that follow he studies the seams of her hands and feet, the arc of her brows and the shape of her ears. He studies them closely because, unlike most things, he wants them etched firmly in his memory.

THIRTY

"Mary. A whiskey. For me. I friendly."

"*Kah* Madame Blanc?"

"*Pus iktah?*"

Boston tells her why. The woman flounces out her dress of crimson and black. She once was a woman of status; the tattoos on her hands tell of it. She was once possessed of beauty; the pox marks on her cheeks cannot wholly destroy it.

"*Klootchmen kimta kloshe, wikna?*" she says loudly, as if daring any man to refute her saying that Indian women are better than white.

"*Kunje yahka chahko,* Madame Blanc?"

"*Nekhwa* buy me whiskey, then tell you."

Boston buys her a whiskey and she tells him that Madame Blanc will come when she pleases, then laughs and moves off to more welcoming customers. A large woman in breeches slaps a hand of cards on a table. The men haul back as if faced with a venomous snake. She is Indian as well, or partly so. Of the Tlingits, Boston guesses, as her broad gestures, her straight stares, are common to their women.

Faces turn upward. Madame Blanc descends from the stairs behind the bar. She is corpulent and coarse-featured. Her dress is of gauzy yellows, purple lace, and silky greens. Her hair is a golden construction of loops and waves, is a beacon in the overall drabness of Barkerville's Denby saloon. She sits laboriously at a table in the corner from which the shifting clutch of men can be best surveyed. She notices Boston's stare, does not shift her eyes from his, nor blink. Does not, unlike most, seem uncomfortable under his full gaze. She smiles knowingly, lifts two beringed fingers.

Boston approaches, takes off his hat. "Ma'am."

"Please, dear boy, sit yourself here." She has small red-painted lips. Her voice has the cadence of the Southern States.

He sits with his hands on his knees. Madame Blanc glances at his fingers. They are stained with ink. "You are interested in Mary? I must tell you she is not the most tractable. I do have also a Mabel and a Mavis. Clean girls, none of them cannibals." She smiles sweetly.

Boston lifts his chin to indicate Madame Blanc herself.

She breaks out a fan patterned with Chinese palaces and trees in pink bloom. "Madame Blanc is retired, respectable if you please. If it is a white woman you require, Miss Anna, our splendid card player could pass well enough."

Boston looks again at Madame Blanc. Unfortunate that her eyes are not in the same realm of blue as the Dora woman's. Hers are the blue of a summer sky. The eyes of Madame Blanc are the grey of wet slate, of winter clouds.

"And Mariette. She is occupied at the moment. She is the finest I can offer. She learned her skills as the mistress of a Montreal merchant. Her father was a Jesuit sent to convert her people to the book. Is not that an enticing lineage? Is not it enticing to imagine a conversion taking place between a savage and a man of the holy cloth? Though not the one the holy man intended. Not at all."

"You."

Madame Blanc strokes a stiff curl. She leans close to Boston, whispers in a tone that carries to his ear alone: "You flatter me. Prefer a woman of some substance do you? Or something motherly? Or perhaps something of a darker bent? Tell me, whisper it in your dear Malva's ear. Perhaps something can be arranged. Nothing will surprise Malva Blanc, I promise you that. And not to worry, dear boy, keeping secrets is my own personal commandment."

A man bumps against their table. Apologizes in Dutch, stumbles on. Boston whispers in her ear though his eyes remain fixed on the wooden table, the lines in the grain indicating the uncountable passing of years. She smells strongly of violets.

"My dear boy, I am truly intrigued." She cites a hefty price.

Boston counters. Madame Blanc mentions that in New Orleans in her days of fame she could ask five times such a fee and still be able to pick and choose. Boston holds. Madame Blanc offers a price slightly lower. Boston counters again, but she will no longer bargain. She looks over his head at the bull-necked man who has been awaiting her signal. Boston agrees to her price, knowing he has little choice, for she has seen a need in him as clear as if he has been branded.

The room is plainly furnished and criss-crossed with drafts. A lamp has been lit though it is not yet dark. "Shall I sit here? Would such a position please you?"

Boston nods. Madame Blanc draws the curtains and settles in the chair by the window. She sets the lamp on the table near to it. Her hooped skirts are so voluminous that they hide the chair entirely, make it seem as if Madame Blanc is sitting on an uphold of air.

Boston hands her the pages and sits on the edge of the bed, there being no other place. She strokes the pages in her lap. "And these are your writings?"

"Thank you to read it quick," he says and curls his fingers to hide the ink stains upon them.

"We have time."

"Ain't that, it's the way she talked, see."

"Yes, of course." She takes spectacles from a beaded purse and perches them on her nose, tells him that she wears them only to see the small matters of the world.

Boston shuts his eyes.

Madame Blanc reads: "We had a flat above the shop. Did I tell you that, Mr. Jim? Oh, it were small, two rooms only, but lovely. We had oval pictures of my Mother's family and a chair with clawed feet and a sideboard with grapes all carved in it. Had a rug, too, that came from the Indies or somewheres and that Mother brought when she left her house to marry Father. And we had a real chimney piece. It was of the famous murderer, Jack Delane. He's the one who murdered his wife and made her into a stew . . ."

"Your accent. Thank you to make it a London one."

"But I am not a Londoner."

"Know that. But you can do any kinda accent, can't you?"

Madame Blanc looks sharply at Boston over the rim of her spectacles. "Ah, dear boy, no need to disrobe. We see through each other quite clearly, don't we now? Where was I? Ah. On an evening we'd sit 'round the fire. It were always warm in the times before Father was hurt so. He'd point into the coals and tell us what was there—rubies and Turkish delight, villages with glowing windows and doors and step-ways, dragons, and trees with magic birds. I could see it all straight away. My sister and my brothers couldn't so well. My sister even said it was a silly game, but I think she was jealous because, though he never said it, I know father loved me best of all his children. . . ."

Boston shuts his eyes again and Madame Blanc begins anew. Her accent is not quite like Dora's, but is passable. "It's my favourite story, it is. It's of how my father met my mother. He and his mates were putting on a play called *The Widow's Return*. For charity, it was. In the cellar of a church. Father was the widow because he was the tallest and the most manly and so the most hilarious. They decked him out with crepe streamers and ornaments and covered him up with a thick veil. Oh, I don't know how he could see a thing. You should have heard him wail! You should have seen the way he'd swoon into the men's arms, and how the men would be falling over because of the weight. He, or she I should be saying, was right upset about his small inheritance, and he was upset, too, because this husband had the bad manners to die in bed "while they were in the midst of making an heir." That's what the line was. Oh, how the crowd laughed. After the play his mates dared him to go out in his widow's weeds, and he did, too, because he couldn't resist a lark, my father. They went into a right fine haberdashery near Regent Street and straight 'way he saw my mother Ethel sorting through buttons. He looked at her through his veil and it were like he was seeing her through a fairy mist. His mate said that this poor widow here has lost a button in a paroxysm of weeping and that she needed another like it, and then they pointed to his bodice that was stuffed up gigantic with a pillow. But my father, he lost the taste for the game. How could he be tricking this angel? He couldn't lift his veil, she'd scream for sure. Or she'd think him mad, or worse, this big man out dressed as a woman.

Oh, how my mother searched for the perfect match. Finally she found one. And, you know, she didn't charge him a farthing. She couldn't, see, because she felt so sorry for this big, blundering widow. She just held out the button. Her fingers were like lily stems, my father said. Their fingers barely touched. Oh, but it were enough. He was her slave for ever after. That's what he always said."

Madame Blanc turns the paper over. "My mother didn't find out till her wedding night that father was the widow who needed the button. Ah, well and so, she thought it was terrible funny. Oh, she was always telling us how father made her laugh and . . . are you awake, dear boy, shall I continue? The tale is not bad, though certain details could be added, yes indeed. Shall I embellish for you?"

Boston opens his eyes. Madame Blanc looks at him coyly.

It is not working. Perhaps if he turns the lamp lower. Perhaps if Madame Blanc were not Madame Blanc. He has not fallen into the Dora woman's memories again. Has not stepped from the alley where he watched Dora and her mother and father embracing, has not gone further still and followed them up the stairs to their flat above the shop and sat quiet and unnoticed while her father told his tales and her mother looked on adoringly and Dora and her siblings grouped 'round, their cheeks reddened by the coal fire.

"Would you care to dress in women's garments?" Madame Blanc asks when the silence lengthens. "Is that it? Most men will take any opportunity to do so. The fee will change, of course."

"No, ma'am." He takes the letters from her.

She begins talking of New Orleans. How she ran away from the orphanage and lived on her wits until she discovered "the way." How she would charge ten dollars to wear a habit and pretend to be seduced. For many men like to believe their charms are that great.

It is all amiss. The portents are part of it. Normally he takes no note of them. Finds it idiotic, in fact, that others imagine them in spiderwebs, entrails, teacups, in the weather, the stars, that they believe they are singled out from the multitude by that nameless power that moves the world. And thus he has ignored up till now the obvious signs that the balance is threatened. That so much depends upon his actions.

He thinks of the three-legged dog he saw just yesterday, of a tree splintered by lightning and still smouldering though there had been no storms for days. Of a one-eyed, white-Indian who stared at him from a hillock near Yale. And of Girl, certainly. She crossed between the worlds to show him that much depended upon his actions. A curious ache when he thinks of Girl, of pulling the lice from her hair, the pattern of blood on her foot. It is as if he should have somehow stopped her from returning to her realm. What of these damned females? Kloo-yah. The Dora woman. Girl. It is as if they hold him up on one of those children's see-saws, each after their own fashion. It is as if they weigh more than he does, and thus he is high in the air, boots kicking futility in search of the ground.

He crumples the paper in his fist. He prefers the life he had before. Part of the landscape, part of the air, passing his time before the grave. He is strange. He knows that. But never had he imagined that this strangeness might have some purpose.

"Are you feeling badly?" Madame Blanc asks, without much interest.

Boston shakes his head.

"Then, dear boy, if you no longer want the pleasure of Madame Blanc's reading voice . . ."

He pays the agreed price. Madame Blanc counts it out discreetly then assures him that on another occasion she would be happy to accommodate him in any way he pleases.

THIRTY-ONE

It shall be called Humeville. The square shall be named for Dora, the streets for their children. Likely there will be a statue in time. Nothing ostentatious, no horse or grand uniform, merely him standing top-hatted, gazing benevolently down. Travellers arriving by coach and train will exclaim: "Here I am in Humeville, at long last! Do you know that it is famed across the continent for its sumptuous hotels, its race-tracks, its fine spirits? It is said that fortune flows over the gabled roofs, the canals and cathedrals, over the stone bridges, the splendid shops. It is said that at dawn the light is such that the entire town seems wrought from the very gold that begat it."

Lorn and Napoleon opt to stay and guard the claim.

"Do not be disappointed, friends," Eugene says. "There will be many nights such as this. We shall return with champagne!"

"And cakes!" George says.

"Women!" Langstrom says.

"Just bring yourselves back in one piece and whatnot," Lorn says. "And don't let on what happened, you hear?" His leg is still splintered. He will not be working below for the duration of the season, though he is quite capable of working the rocker. Was, indeed, the first to see the shimmer, the first to raise a shout. Good that the new drift proved up so quickly. Building it had taken the last of their pooled resources as well as the last of Eugene's unsold supplies: his pocket watch, his good suit, and the flask inscribed with his name, all of which was now the property of the local pawn shop. If the new drift had not proved, they might even now be stumbling back to Victoria, skedaddling on their debts, eating grass, begging charity. Eugene shudders at these thoughts, real as any nightmare. Heaves in a great breath. "Are we prepared then?"

Napoleon hands Eugene a scrap of paper. "Give this to Mr. Lee. It is for some herbs the Chinamen use."

"That is all? Not a new waistcoat, a bottle of claret, porter?"

"How about cake, sirs?" George asks again.

"Yes, Young George, let them eat cake," Eugene says.

"Pardon?"

"Ah, never mind. A jest."

"The herbs will suffice for now."

Eugene looks to George, Langstrom, and Lorn. "Quite so, it has yet to sink in, I would say. For Mr. Beauville can buy whatever remedy he chooses—balms and purgatives, even a magneto-electric machine. I am sure one could be ordered."

"Oh, it has 'sunk in' Mr. Hume," Napoleon says and looks at him with an expression that Eugene would have called anxious on another man.

They walk through Camerontown and then into Barkerville. They are not hollering out. They are not even whistling. They are as nonchalant as you please and still heads turn. It is as if they have the odour of fortune, the aura, as if the others can see clear through their pockets to the sachets that are the size of a chicken's egg, though a great deal more weighty. The gold inside was a mere afternoon's work.

First to Wake Up Jake's where they order steaks with potatoes, eggs and beans, and with George in mind, apple cake and molasses cake, where they plan for their spree with the thoroughness of explorers in search of the pole. When Pleasance brings the champagne Eugene presses into her palm a nugget the size of an infant's nail. "A new dress, dear lady. A garland for your hair."

Her cheeks flush; her eyes sparkle. In her gratitude she is almost pretty. The men at the other tables stare as Pleasance half-curtsies.

"A toast, gentlemen!" Eugene calls.

"I promised mother I wouldn't touch the spirits," George says uncertainly.

"Ah, but champagne is not truly a spirit. It a celebratory tonic. A child's draft. A glass of stars."

"Star! Lucky!" roars Langstrom. He downs his glass in one gulp.

Eugene pours for George with a liberal hand. "Just one. None of us will inform your dear Mother. In any case, she is far, far from here."

George considers this. "Gosh, all right then. Just one."

Here's to luck. Here's to the Dora Dear. Here's to Cussy Oswald, that goblin. Here's to Herr Boots. Here's to those good men, Napoleon and Lorn. Here's to Lieutenant Olsen from their road building days, he who needs not a toast, but a humping from a good, experienced whore.

George, cheeks ablaze, stares at the empty bottles with something akin to awe.

Langstrom gives a gap-toothed grin. "Lucky Hume!" he shouts.

"To Lucky Hume," Eugene says. What a splendid evening this will be! He has not a doubt of it. Senses it more clearly than he has ever sensed the course of an evening before.

At the tobacconist George mutters about the devil's temptations, inspects a snuff box.

Eugene asks the proprietor, an Italian, if he has Turkish smokes. "They are the latest invention. They are the most convenient little cylinders."

The Italian confesses he does not. Directs Eugene's attention to the cigars. "Good for celebrating. For handing out," he says, smiling at them, as everyone seems to be.

"I didn't know you smoked, Doc."

"I do not. But it does one good to try everything once or twice. For how can one devise a method of critical analysis based on hearsay and assumption?"

"Gosh, I never thought of that. It makes sense though, don't it?" George is speaking slowly, carefully. Sweat trickles into his reddened eyes.

Eugene decides upon a box of good Cuban cigars and a new matchsafe made of silveroin from which a penknife and cigar clipper ingeniously spring. Langstrom buys three folds of Virginia tobacco and a meerschaum pipe large as his fist and carved with a pirate's head. Once outside he hurls his old pipe into the street where a man in a ragged coat scoops it up from the mud. George holds his purchase cupped in his hand. The snuff box shows an enamelled scene of three women languishing under a green bower. Their rosy-tipped breasts are clearly visible under their dresses of diaphanous white. One looks in mild concern at the man spying at them from the bushes.

Eugene claps George on the back. "That's it, take life by the horns! I'm proud of you, that I am."

George grins. "Now where?"

Mr. Lee works for a long while at his abacus.

Langstrom indicates Eugene's pocket. "Napoleon."

"Ah, yes," Eugene hands the paper to Mr. Lee who studies it, glances curiously at Eugene, then orders the clerk about in his peculiar chiming tongue. The clerk brings out a jar. Mr. Lee fills a cone with greyish powder, then cites the amount, plus the amount of credit owed. Though it is more than Eugene expected, he does not hesitate to add an extra shard to Mr. Lee's scale. "In thanks for your generosity, sir, your trust." It astonishes Eugene that such fragments have any value at all. Astonishes him that the gold is there for the taking, should one only know where to look. One need do nothing to deserve it. Look at Oswald. Look at himself for that matter.

At Itlebod's Pawn and Supply, Eugene retrieves his pocket watch, his folding candlestick, and his flask. Tells Itlebod to keep the suit for now, he will buy another, then looks about, as giddy as a schoolboy in a sweet shop. Buys an ornate brass scale the size of his hand and with it a neat case with velvet lining. He also buys a sheaf of the finest paper, envelopes, sealing wax, good steel nibs, ink of indigo blue. Dora will know immediately when his letter arrives, the news in the weight and worth of the paper itself.

George cannot decide between a brooch of entwined flowers for his mother, or a silver money clip for himself. Buys them both at Eugene's encouragement. Langstrom decides on a handsome colt revolver. He aims it at the pots hanging in the window. Something in his look of anticipation gives Eugene pause. How much does he know of Langstrom? Or of Young George? Or of Lorn and Napoleon, for that matter? He trusts them all, but why? All they have done is swear on the Bible to be honest with each other. Langstrom might be some Laplander who worships trees and water sprites, George a stupendous con man, Lorn and Napoleon anarchists or poisoners. They might all begin tucking gold away in their pockets and boots, might even now be getting the dead wood on him, as the yokels here about say.

Bowson hiccups. Langstrom grins and tucks his new revolver into its holster. Both are looking to him the way men look to a respected leader. Eugene's fear passes. He'd trust these good men with his life. And they would trust him with theirs. Certainly.

"Gentlemen, our attire must now be attended to."

The tailor shop of Overlander Pearl is small and overheated by the stove. Cloth is piled high in neat bolts.

"Your finest shirts, sir!" Eugene says. "And good collars!"

"Gosh, but I'd give a cracking lot for a pair of my mother's socks."

"Good," Langstrom says and indicates his flannel shirt that is so faded and mended it threatens to drop from his frame.

"You must have new apparel, Langstrom," Eugene says. "What of trousers? A cravat? Mr. Pearl has ready-made. Or so I have heard."

Mr. Pearl agrees that he does have ready-made. Mr. Pearl would agree that he has cashmere and silk-stuff, just allow several weeks for delivery, gentlemen. He is a lanky Upper Canadian with bristling orange hair and a tape measure strung over his neck. He need only clamp pins between his teeth to become the very caricature of a tailor. Apparently he and his party of two hundred and fifty thought the British Columbian gold fields only a five-week journey from the Red River settlement of Manitoba. Four months later those who were left limped into the gold-fields, their great carts long since abandoned. Some straight away took a ship 'round the Horn back home. As for Nathaniel Pearl, henceforth Overlander Pearl, he went back to the work that he had thrown in for better. Poor bastard, Eugene thinks. But then it cannot be the same for everyone. It takes fortitude to achieve riches. It takes tenacity.

"We shall need good wool coats for our eventual journey home. Can you supply us, good man? One should not be caught unprepared in the winter storms, is that not correct?" He winks at Overlander Pearl to show that he sympathizes with the man's past travails. Pearl stares at Eugene, then cites an exorbitant price. Eugene does not even blink. He has already sworn to spend this entire first sachet of gold on this one night. It is an offering of sorts, in thanks for their fortune. Do not the Indians of Mexico lay their first harvest at their snake temples or what have you? Do not the Indians hereabouts do something of the same?

They stand on stools before Overlander Pearl as he darts about them, tucking and sewing. At last they are fitted. Overlander Pearl weighs their gold, then wraps their old trousers and shirts in brown paper. Langstrom tugs at his new collar and grimaces. It was not easy to convey to him with single words and broad gestures the abstract ideals of fashion, not easy to convince him that they should appear in sartorial harmony, one with the other.

At the bathhouse the attendant leads them to a room divided up by curtains. A vat rests on an enormous stove. An old Indian woman stands at the ready with a bristle brush. A Chinaman brings in the steaming buckets.

"We will be as the phoenix from the ashes," Eugene promises. "We will emerge as new men entirely."

George yelps as he settles in. Langstrom thrashes about as if just thrown in the drink. Eugene eases expertly down in the tin tub, his legs vanishing in the steam. It is as close to heaven as mortal man can come. Eugene will have a grand tub in his house in Victoria. It will be large enough that Dora may lie with him, here in the calm drifts of heat.

Wellington Moses says: "Come in, come in. I have been expecting you. Ah, how well appointed are you all. I recognize Mr. Pearl's merchandise. Sit yourself here, Mr. Hume. The Praise to God. My apologies, the Dora Dear. I would not have bet on it. No, indeed."

"How'd you know it proved up?" George asks, then claps his hand over his mouth.

"I am a barber, sir, there is little that I do not know before the rest."

"Quite so, the secret is out then," Eugene says. "Do not forget to write this moment down in your great journal, Mr. Moses."

Mr. Moses assures them he will not forget, asks Eugene what barbering he would like.

"Off with it all. Leave only the moustaches."

"May I recommend burnsides as well. They are all the rage in New York."

"Work your art as you see fit. I am in your most capable hands."

Languorous strokes of the blade. Thick applications of Macassar oil. Liberal drippings of wax on his moustaches. He is transformed. They are all transformed. The years drop from George Bowson with each scrape until he seems barely old enough to be wearing long pants. Langstrom, clean-shaven and trimmed, is nearly handsome. And Eugene? He studies the looking glass. Gauntness lends him an ascetic dignity. Surely the Judge will now agree that he would suit the position of a Victoria magistrate. He is well-dressed enough. Barbered enough. Wealthy enough.

Oswald and Herr Schultheiss find them at the New England Bakery and Brewery.

"I tell Cussy. It true, the Dora Dear. Wonderful! Fabelhaft!"

"Ah, so you have heard," Eugene says. "Please join us for tarts and ale. And you also, Oswald. We are standing treat, of course."

Oswald scowls. His mine, The Jessica Bell, is not proving as rich as reported, or so Eugene heard from an Irishman who Oswald had recently fired. Certainly Oswald has lost a brass button or two. He has lost his swagger.

Herr Schultheiss sits at the table, his fur collar hiking 'round his cheeks. He coughs heartily, says his cough is a mystery to all the physicians he has met.

How will he manage in the howling autumn winds? But then Eugene's grandmother was likewise full of ailments and chills, a preoccupation that kept her alive into her eighty-fifth year. Likely she was disappointed when death came with such quickness and stealth, and in the night, without a herald. Eugene, however, can think of nothing better than departing the living great-aged and unaware. Certainly such a fine death is possible now that he is rich. Anything is possible now.

"I may have interest in shares," Schultheiss says. "You are selling shares?"

"Not as yet, but you shall be the first to know of it when we do," Eugene says.

Oswald is still standing. "I'm leaving, Otto," he says, then turns abruptly and bangs into Schultheiss's chair. He grimaces, mutters a curse or two in what might be a humbled tone. Eugene thinks of Oswald's fiancée, the Miss Jessica Bell. She must see something good in the man.

"Oswald. May I ask your advice?"

"What the damned hell you talking about now?"

"Advice. We are wondering if a long tom would be a reasonable investment. The rockers are hardly adequate now."

"Mary's tits. You mocking me?"

George stares horrified at Oswald. Schultheiss coughs into his handkerchief. Langstrom stares dreamily at the tin-plated ceiling.

"I am not mocking you. No, indeed. It is just that my knowledge of mining is somewhat wanting, as you yourself once pointed out. And yet I must make the best of this opportunity so that I may shower my Intended with riches."

"Your fiancée?"

"Quite so."

George stares at Eugene. "You're not married to her? But you said . . ."

"We are married in our hearts, as poets are, but not by the church, not as yet."

George looks doubtful. Takes a good drink of ale.

"What's her name, then?" Oswald demands.

"Her name is Miss Dora Timmons. I confess that I am not good enough for her, though some would have it the opposite. For you see, she is of common stock. Her people sold patches of cloth in the market. She drops her h's so often the ground before her is strewn with them. And yet she waits, waits with the patience of the regal Penelope for me to return so that I may keep my promise of marriage, so that I may give her a life far removed from the trials of her youth."

Eugene's words catch in his throat. What else might he confess? How he stole from the collection plate when he was a boy? How he lit a cow's tail afire?

Oswald looks at him suspiciously, though Eugene no longer takes offence. It is how Oswald looks at all things, animate or otherwise. "Who's this Penelope, then?"

"Ah, it is a reference to an old story, to a woman who waited years for her beloved to return from his adventures, who was assailed by suitors and yet still she waited, even though she did not know if he was dead or alive."

"You're full of them fucknit made-up stories, ain't you, Hume?"

Eugene has to agree that he is.

Oswald sits down, allows Eugene to buy him an ale. "Need a steady supply of water for a long tom," he says and then regales them for the better part of an hour with the minutiae of mining. Eugene, feeling hugely proud, hugely at right, nods occasionally, as if he truly is hanging onto every word. Later Oswald shows him a locket with a painted miniature of the famous Jessica Bell. She is buck-toothed, as plain as a boot.

"Lovely woman," Eugene says.

"No she god-blamed ain't. I knows that. I got eyes. But I ain't fancy to look on neither. And she's good. Never met a woman so good. She gives to the poor, see, and teaches the black uns to read. Her Pa don't approve of me, the fucknit, but she said she'd wait no matter what."

"Ah, such loyalty."

"That's right, we swore to marry whether I got gold or not. Without his word a man ain't worth pig shit. Don't you forget that. Don't be forgetting your promise to your fiancée."

How good is Oswald's advice. How true are his thoughts! He is a peasant philosopher, one of Rousseau's children of nature.

"I will not forget my Dora, I swear it as a gentleman," Eugene presses his hand to his heart, the drama of the moment as apparent to him as if he were lit with limelight on a stage.

By the time they reach the Saloon of the Occidental Hotel, the news has gathered force and a crowd has gathered inside and out.

"How much deep?" someone yells.

"How did you know where to look?"

"Come look at our claim, boys, we need advice."

"Lend me a hundred quid. I beg you. It's all I need."

A cacophony of requests, questions, demands. George is grinning foolishly and stumbling. Oswald and Herr Schultheiss have begged off, citing an early rising, of all things. Langstrom is oblivious to all but the ever bold Miss Anna. No doubt she hopes to lure him to the Denby saloon nearby. No doubt she is about to succeed.

It is up to Eugene. But then, is it not always? He holds up his hands. The crowd settles. "All I can state is this: look to the lay of the land, gentlemen, study the expressions of nature as if they were those of a beloved woman. Ask yourself. What truly lies there? What has been hidden from you? If you are correct you will be rewarded beyond your wildest dreams." The laughter is suitably ribald, suitably loud. And when Eugene clangs the bell that hangs over the bar and declares that he is standing treat for each and every man, the laughter turns into a great cheer, thunderous applause.

He calls to the barkeep: "Mountain Howitzers, good man. Chain Lightning. Scorpion Juice." It is the same barkeep who ribbed him about jawbone not two weeks ago. Quite so, Eugene need ask no man for credit ever again.

The barkeep, well-tipped and obliging, brings out bottle after bottle. The men clamber over each other to reach the glasses. They cheer in a multitude of tongues. Never has there been such an admirable collection of toilers and adventurers! At this moment Eugene cannot believe that he is on the crumbling edges of civilization, for this seems the cynosure, the heart of the world.

A man in a drunken stupor sits on a Cariboo tipster chair. Such a mischievous invention, these chairs, found in most every bar and store. Eugene asks for bets on how long before the man is sent sprawling. The man's head nods toward his breast, now he is being dumped, is cursing in some foreign tongue. Twenty seconds. Eugene wins and with his winnings he buys drinks for the tumbled man and for all the others about.

The candles and lamps are now ablaze. Eugene throws back a brandy. Gasps like a man coming up for air. George is vomiting into a spittoon. Langstrom is nowhere in sight.

The saloon is as raucous as only a room full of drunken men can be. Voices stack one upon the other. Laughter erupts. The roulette spinner calls out bets. The piano pounds. Waves of song crash over the crowd that reeks of tobacco smoke, onions, liquor, the long-unwashed. The floor shudders under pounding feet as men start to dance. Eugene would not be surprised if the floor caved in and miners tunnelling below stared up in wonderment. Hadn't just such a thing happened at a livery? Certainly the barkeep is looking troubled as he pours still more drinks at Eugene's behest.

Langstrom has returned. Is imbued with a fire. Ah, the charms of Miss Anna! Like water to a man dying of thirst. Not that Eugene will indulge. No, indeed. Though surely sheep's gut overcoats could be found. If he could avoid infection. If he were careful. Ah, no.

Langstrom clambers onto the bar amid shouts of encouragement. He hollers in Swedish and does some kind of a jig. He waves a bottle of champagne. The men roar, and when Langstrom upends the bottle over their heads, they reach to touch him as if he were a saint.

"Off the bar!" yells the barkeep. He shoves at Langstrom's legs and Langstrom leaps into the crowd and disappears amidst a tangle of limbs.

"Young George!" Eugene yells. "George Bowson!"

"'Misser 'ume!" The throng jovially pushes George from side to side as if he were a straw man in one of those queer village festivals.

"Easy there. Moderation is the key, I should have mentioned that. Here, wipe your face." Eugene gives George his handkerchief and props him up against the bar, looks over the crowd for the Judge. Surely he has heard of Eugene's fortune and is even now making his way to the Occidental. Ah, no Judge, only a slew of half-familiar faces seen in the towns or encountered on the journey. Many, in any case, seem to remember him. "Show us the dead man's waltz!" someone shouts.

The dead man's waltz? Ah, yes. Tricky Ole Amos Mactavish at the Mactavish roadhouse. "Not unless you are prepared to meet your maker this night," Eugene shouts back, pleased that his fame has preceded him, pleased that no matter what he says he is greeted by a gust of laughter. Is this how a king feels? A prince?

From the edges of the crowd a man is scowling at Eugene. He is of average height, has a reddish brown beard, a vicious countenance.

"You there!" Eugene calls to the man just as he vanishes into the throng. Eugene searches over the celebration, but already he has forgotten what the man looked like; he can only think how his own face must look: stunned and red-eyed, over-indulged, with a fool's manic grin.

George sags. Eugene props him up on one side. Langstrom, unharmed from his leap, props him up on the other. Eugene fights back uneasiness. The evening will not turn, no, not as long as he is standing.

"A song to revive my young friend, gentlemen! A song!" Eugene shouts and launches into "My Darling Clementine." The crowd joins in a booming chorus. Even the foreigners seem to know it. And thus the celebration, with Eugene at the helm, sails on into legend.

THIRTY-TWO

"The trade is down, Jim," Illdare says. "How many times must I say this?"

Boston shrugs: "Animals hunted too much. Otters near gone. New headman."

Illdare eyes Kloo-yah weaving there in the corner. It has been seven months since she came and the cool foggy damp of winter has turned to the warm foggy damp of summer. Since she came they have lived in a rough cabin beside the fort. Boston does not mind this in the least. Though he had his own partitioned area of the sleeping hall, he hated the proximity of the other men, their snoring and mutterings and laughter at evenings when they played at cards or bones. The cabin suits him far better. There is a rough stockade and a plot of potatoes and a wood basin for boiling clothes. There is Kloo-yah, quietly at her tasks, looking intently at him from time to time, warming his bed at night, just as she said she would.

"Indians claim the fort is haunted," Illdare says. "Skookums and such nonsense. And the engagés can't but notice how she stares. They say she has the power of the evil eye. They say that is why Merrymont has fallen sick."

"He were sick before."

"And Fleury. They say she has afflicted him also."

"He's old. Near dead anyway."

"I agree, though the half-breed prick has been surprisingly tough until now. I am merely setting it out as the others see it, fools that they are."

"Yes," Boston says. It has been four years, three months and a day since Illdare spoke to him like this—as if he and Boston shared the same mind, the same space, separate from the rest.

"Come to my chambers at eight o'clock tonight, Jim. We have further matters to discuss."

The map of New Caledonia is now yellowed at the edges, the bearskin rug worn in patches. Boston counts four more books on the shelf, notes a new pipe in the rack. The pen set, however, is the exact same, and is in the same position as years ago. Neither has the table been moved, nor Illdare's chair before the hearth.

But Illdare has changed. His hair is completely grey and no longer does he have enough of it to comb over his scalp. Nor does he have as many teeth as he did. In all, he is smaller, more hunched, and though he wears gloves still, these are not the fine moleskin they once were, but cloth gloves tattered at the fingers and stained at the cuffs.

"Sit here." Illdare gestures to the chair at the table, the one Boston sat at when he was a boy and Illdare taught him to cipher and to read. He sits and is half-surprised that his feet are solidly on the floor, near touching the padlock of the strongroom beneath.

Illdare pours himself a measure of brandy, then offers a glass to Boston. Boston takes it and drinks slowly while Illdare makes himself comfortable by the fire. For a few moments they say nothing. It is the same sort of silence that Boston recalls from their lessons. Peaceful, perhaps that is the word.

"We will not meet our quota for this quarter."

"No?"

"No."

"Quota's always been met. Always."

"Yes, I was as surprised as you."

"Must be a mistake."

"Not on your part, I should think. Your books are impeccable, not surprisingly."

"Trade changes. Value of things."

"I agree, but that can be worked around. New trade goods have been introduced, have they not? No, the truth, and you know it, Jim, is that the presence of your woman has hampered the trade."

Boston brings the glass to his lips, but he cannot swallow.

"*Pro pelle cutem*," Illdare says and taps the company crest. Speaks of the quota in the same tones that Lavolier once used for his God. The quota must be attained. The quota is all. This is something Illdare has impressed upon Boston again and again, ever since he first arrived at Fort Connelly. What will happen if it is not reached? The world shatters. Boston can near see the shards of it at his feet.

Illdare clears his throat. "The Kwagu'l have asked of her again. She is lovely by their standards and young and strong. The noble who would have her will treat her well. He will take her to wife. He has promised me. He has upped his price considerably."

"No."

"The People will come back to trade if she were gone. You know it is not just because of the season, not just because the furs are scarce. And the price offered will be enough to nearly make the quota. I will make up the rest from my own pocket. You can leave it to me. She will be much better off. She will have status again. As will you. Ah, such a face. Come now. Turning off is the custom. Even Simpson has done it on several occasions."

Boston stands without finishing his glass, without asking for permission to leave.

Illdare stands also and places his gloved hand on Boston's shoulder. "My mother bore sixteen children and nearly all lived. We slept five to a bed. There is no quietude once women are involved. Leave such a life to others. We are not as they are, the damned fools. . . . Agreed?"

Illdare offers his hand. Boston has never seen him offer his hand to any man. He raises his own, and shakes Illdare's gloved hand, once, twice.

A week later Boston returns from hunting and finds her gone. Illdare gives him one otter skin; the other has gone to meet the quota. In this year, the otters are so rare they are worth fifty four-point blankets each. It is a hefty price, nearly unheard of for a woman, especially one said to be of the spirit world. Boston sets the fur aside, crouches in the cabin by a cold hearth. A pain is in his chest and a coldness is in his limbs. No matter the otter skin. It was a bad trade. It should not have been done. Kloo-yah's worth lay in her actions, and actions do not calculate like molasses or furs. She cooked for him, gathered clams and quamash bulbs and fern roots and sea kelp. She combed the lice from his hair. She mended his clothes. In return, he gave her a hearth and protection and pleasure also, for often at night her sighs and groans mingled with his. Was this what was meant by love? This pact?

He ponders again the idea of forgetting. If he were capable of it, one day he would no longer know what she looked like and her every gesture would be impossible to conjure. One day he would no longer see twin flames reflected in the darkness of her eyes. He would like that. He crosses his arms over his chest, for the scars ache near as much as when they were newly made.

"Need the wages."

Illdare glares at him. "What do you mean, wages?"

"Been here twelve years, three months. Take off three years for an apprenticeship. Owed for nine then. Figure thirty-five pounds a year for the clerking and translating and trading. That's less than you'd have to pay any other. You know it. Makes three hundred and fifteen pounds. Take nothing less."

Illdare stands. His voice is low, his fists clenched. Boston has seen him angered, but never has Illdare's anger been directed at him. "How dare you come into my chambers unasked? How dare you beg for money? You have received food, a roof. You have been allowed to conduct your own trade. I have given you monies from my own profits. You ungrateful bastard. You came to me like a bloodied cur and I saved you."

"Need the wages."

"You are not on the books. As such you do not exist. You are more like a noxious odour that has vanished. Are you aware of that quandary?"

"The wages. Worked for them. Don't matter if not on the books."

"You might have left with her, you stunted idiot. Did you consider that?"

Boston says nothing.

"Hah, you see, that is your trouble. Your head is so stuffed with the pointless details of life it leaves no room for imagination. Well, then. Here is the deal, Jim, my boy. Either take your belongings and leave now, or cease your begging and stay. Think on it. Now get out! Out!"

Boston stares at him. Illdare drops his gaze. "Out, Jim," he says almost gently now.

Boston leaves without another word. Illdare would only deny the assertions of Fleury and of the five Kwagu'l that Boston questioned. Kloo-yah was not traded to a noble for otter skins. These came from Illdare's private hoard. Boston was a fool to believe otherwise. He knows that now. For what noble would take to wife a woman said to be of the spirit world, no matter what rank she had formerly? "He trade her for a sword, rusted one, not fit to chop wood," Fleury told him. "Bad deal. Woman like yours be sold to the Indians at new fort down south. Sixty pounds, that is the going rate. The Whitemen, they use them for whores."

The new headman listens carefully to what Boston proposes. He is young, this headman, and known for his prowess as a warrior. Lately he has been insisting that the fort men owe the People for the wood they have taken and the water drawn and for the birds shot from the sky, which is their sky and ever has been. The old headman gave away his privileges for nothing, not even for status. And in return the Whitemen—King George men and Boston men both—have brought the pox and the coughing sickness and have infected their women, and for this the new headman wants that the fort men should be gone from his lands entirely.

"Want the old pallet back," Boston says to Illdare.

"Ah, so you've given up on your ridiculous demands."

"Yes."

"Jim, I was perhaps harsh. Perhaps . . ." Illdare is about to say something more, then shakes his head, as if to ward off the thought.

Later Boston stretches out on his old pallet behind a partition of canvas. Listens as the engagés settle in for the night. A new engagé, a young Irishman, cries in his sleep, a victim of that sickness for home that afflicts many of the newly arrived. Boston waits until the crying subsides, until snores are constant throughout the room. Now he crouches and lights a shielded candle and picks up a hand mirror and applies the black grease and then puts the red painted clamshell 'round his neck, all as the headman instructed him. Next he wraps his boots in cloth and takes a mallet and three lengths of coiled rope from out of his trunk. Walks past the sleeping engagés to the compound. It is a half-clouded night, the moon waning. The tide is high and is lapping at the western wall of the fort. Smells as always of sea brine, of rotting things.

He climbs the ladder to the northwestern bastion. The watchman is already half-insensible from the rum Boston left for him and drops without a sound when Boston swings his mallet. Boston gags him and then binds him with cording. Next he secures the three ropes to the spikes of the palisades. The ropes thud against the fort walls as he hurls them downward. He takes a long breath, then gives a soft whooping call to the men ranged in the darkness beyond.

They tear the goods from the trade room shelves. A sack of flour spills open, covering all in a pall of white. Once or twice a warrior nearly falls upon Boston but halts when he sees the red clamshell, the black grease on Boston's face and remembers that he is the one they have been told not to harm. Boston waits until the shouts and screams subside and then returns to the compound. It is lit with oolichan torches now. The body of the watchman lies hacked to pieces. The bodies of many engagés are in bloodied heaps. The wives of the fort men have been herded to one side, are rending their hair, holding fast to their wailing children, are cursing their own people for what they have done.

Shots and shouts. Whoops of triumph. Someone cries out to God and all that is holy. Another curses God in French. Another gives a strangled scream that ends abruptly.

It takes several rammings for Illdare's door to splinter open, so well is it locked. The headman and his brother drag Illdare from his chambers. He is not screaming or shouting, only grunting as he struggles against them. He wears a night shift, a nightcap, and stockings. His legs and forearms are thin, show a fish-belly white where they are not covered with purple-red stains. The men point, rip his shift from him. Laugh. The stains continue up his groin and chest. It is as if has been splashed with wine.

Illdare tries vainly to cover himself. His hands are grotesquely gnarled and darkly splotched. The nails are oddly white.

Illdare does not recognize Boston until Boston steps past him with axe in hand. He reaches out, mouthing some words that Boston cannot hear above the din. Boston hesitates. No. It is too late to explain that allowing the People to attack the fort was the only way to get inside Illdare's well-locked chamber, into the strongroom. The only way Boston could think to get what is rightfully his.

The headman is true to his word: Boston is allowed in alone. He thrusts aside the table and hacks at the trap door that leads to the strongroom. No time to search for keys. The door gives way. In the cool depths of the strongroom he finds only barrels of rum, bales of furs, the rations for the next quarter. He clambers out. Rights the table. Puts the pipe rack back in its place. Picks up the pieces of the writing set that have fallen—the closed box of sand, the blotters—then sits at the table. Illdare says. "Well done, Jim, you have read all of Candide." Read, yes, and now kept whole in his memories. He has only to imagine the leather binding and the pages fold out before him. But he cannot say he always understood what he read. Likewise he does not understand why he so wanted to please Illdare, would have done anything for him, and without desiring anything in return

Enough of this. He has not much time. He opens a company journal to the entry of several weeks past. Illdare's hand is upright, heavy-inked. In places the page is punctured by the pressure of the nib.

September 14, 1847. Drizzle in the morning. Thick Fog in the evening. Traded 20 made beaver skins for 3 two-point blankets. A bolt of red baize for twenty salmon. Boserviet again ill with Venereale.

There is no mention of Kloo-yah. No mention of Boston.

He flips backwards, reads of Jackinaw who stole tobacco and so had to be clapped in irons. Of the combination that lasted until Illdare agreed to one half-hour less of work a week, though not to the full hour the men demanded. Of the water supply again cut off by the Indians, of the lumber stolen from the stockade, of the broken fur press and the amount of furs traded. Never a mention of Boston, though it was he who knew the diplomacy to stop the People from stripping the stockade to nothing, and he who saw to the repairing of the fur press, and he who acquired so many of the furs and other goods that were needed to maintain the fort and reach this quota that had once seemed of such terrible importance.

He flips through the journal of 1835, the year he was brought to Fort Connelly. No mention of him here either. Only that the fort is nearly finished, only the mundane details of the weather and trade. Only observations on the Indians and on the conduct of the engagés.

He has never been in Illdare's bed chamber. The bed is made of iron and is covered with a rumpled patchwork quilt. A trunk. A lamp. A basin with a water jug. Except for the continuing noise outside it would seem as if nothing were amiss. He finds Illdare's personal journal in his trunk. *All men, red or white or black are vessels of folly and despair. Some calamity will wipe the earth clean of us.* And so on. Ideas of his own, of others. There is no mention of Boston. Illdare was telling the truth, then. It is as if Boston does not exist and never has. Good, then no one will ask him what he knows of the pillage of Fort Connelly. No one will ask him what he knows of Illdare.

The headman will not wait much longer. Boston upends the trunks, slashes the mattress, the quilt, the pillows. Feathers float through the air, settle on his hair. He smashes the glassed picture of an English field. Nothing behind it. He grabs a poker and pries up the floorboards. Still nothing. He stands perfectly still, his breathing harsh. Recalls Illdare at the map of New Caledonia, recalls him reverently touching its shorelines and parchment seas.

Boston rips the map aside. Finds a seam in the woodwork. Pries at it with the flat of his axe until the large cavity is exposed. Finds what he seeks—the treasures of Malcolm Illdare. Before him is an ivory statue, a basin of jade beads, rusted armour, a single worn coin that bears the face of a queen, and there, a sword that still shows evidence of exquisite craftsmanship though barnacles are encrusted on the hilt, though the blade, as Fluery said, is rusted. A burning wetness fills Boston's eyes. He presses the heels of his hands to them, then searches further, finds a fold of pound notes and some coins in a tasselled smoke pouch, an image of Raven embroidered upon it with beads. He counts the money quickly—one hundred and twenty-six pounds, ten shillings. Not enough to cover his wages, but more than enough to buy her back. He will not even bargain. It is at this instant he realizes that Kloo-yah is not a memory like others; her absence is nearly tangible, and has a constant presence, a dragging weight.

He travels to the lands of Kwagu'l. Learns, as he feared, that she has already been taken South along with other women captured in raids or cheaply bought.

At this new fort called Fort Victoria he hears that Fort Connelly has been attacked and overwhelmed and all the men butchered though they fought bravely, surely.

The man who tells Boston this is young and English. His eyes are wide-spaced and pale grey, as if sucked dry of colour. "A gunboat was forthwith sent, a mighty ship with splendid guns, and flags . . ."

"The People. How many dead?"

"The People? Ah, you mean the damned savages. Several hundred I should say. The guns have a fine range." ·

It is all Boston can do not to spit on his hair and buttons and boots and cutlass, all of which gleam in the sun. This gleaming, as far as Boston can tell, is what makes these Englishmen believe they are of greater worth than any other creature that walks on two legs.

"Only sixteen at the fort."

"They were Englishmen and others. They were butchered."

"Hundreds for sixteen. No reckoning there. Any damned idiot can see that."

The man rests his hand on his cutlass. Glares at Boston as if he has just recognized an enemy from long ago. "Which tribe is yours then?"

"What are you on about?"

"Which tribe? I assume you are something of an Indian yourself. A half-breed perhaps?"

"The Chief Trader. What of him?" Boston asks, though he knows the answer well enough.

The Englishman looks at him askance. "Dead like the others. He was tortured it seems, and for a good long while."

Later Boston looks again about Fort Victoria. It is larger than Fort Connelly. The buildings are numerous and well-built. A flag snaps crisply on a pole. Perhaps he has overlooked her. Perhaps she is tilling potatoes in the field. The one hundred and twenty-six pounds, ten shillings is safe in the tasselled smoke pouch in a sewn-over pocket of his shirt. The small weight of it is like a talisman. It is for Kloo-yah and only Kloo-yah that the money is meant. Once he finds her and buys her back it will not matter that he caused the death of the fort men, that Illdare was tortured. Nor will the quota of the company matter, nor the demands of the Christian God, nor the demands of the spirits and gods of the People. All will be balanced again.

She is not to be found. None have heard of her. "If this is the best of all possible worlds. What are the rest like?" These words of Candide come unsought, leave him with the sensation that he is tilting in a gale.

THIRTY-THREE

On the day of the hiring Boston waits in a queue for the better part of an hour. Now stands before The Hume who sits at a makeshift desk near his cabin. It is the first time Boston has seen the man up close. His eyes are amber flecked with green, and are fairly bloodshot. His moustaches and beard are short-cropped, as smooth and shiny as mink pelts. Below his hat brim are wisps of brown hair. "Handsome, he is," the Dora woman said. "Handsome as the saints, the devil even." Boston studies the straight nose, the fine teeth, and supposes this is true.

The Hume asks questions in quick succession, barely waiting for the answers: "Do you have experience? Do you speak English? Do you have any ailments?"

"Some," Boston replies. "Yes." "No."

The Hume scribbles at his papers.

"Work cheaper than the others. Work harder."

"I do not doubt it. I'll keep that in mind. Yes. Thank you for coming." He looks past Boston to the man behind him. Boston stands before the Hume a moment longer. The Hume's hands are patterned with freckles; his forehead has three distinct lines. In all, an older face than the one from the tintype the Dora woman showed him.

"Good day then," the Hume says and motions Boston aside.

Boston follows the path back to the towns. He curses himself for not having dropped his gaze, for it unsettled the Hume, that was obvious. He might have hired Boston otherwise. And then Boston could have kept a proper eye on him, could have made certain he came home safe, just as the Dora woman so wanted him to do.

He looks about, then veers off into the trees and crosses the stream. On a slope he finds a vantage point behind some boulders and bramble. Takes out a telescope. He bought it with the last of his money, not with the one hundred and twenty-six pounds ten shillings still in the smoke pouch, still in the sewn over pocket of his overshirt. That is not truly money anymore, is more a portion of Kloo-yah's spirit that presses against his chest like a small fist. He finds the mine and then the Hume's partners busy at this task or that, and then the Hume himself, talking now to a Chinaman. Boston holds the Hume steady in the round of glass.

Dusk, and the long queue of men has gone. They have hired two Chinamen and a Canadian. The Hume sets off to town with the blond young man and the Swede. Boston follows at a good distance, keeping the figures the size of his hand. He cannot let the Hume out of his sight, that much he knows.

In the next two weeks the Hume goes to the towns six times—twice with the black men, Napoleon and Lorn, four times with the Swede and the one called George Bowson. On three of these occasions the Hume visits the Denby saloon. But he does not indulge in Madame Blanc and her women, as do Langstrom and George Bowson. Out in the street the Hume roars that he would rather be boiled in oil, rather be drawn and quartered and his entrails left for buzzards than betray his love. This comforts Boston some. "He's faithful to me, he is," the Dora woman said. And if the Hume is not faithful? Does Boston's task extend to keeping him safe from other women? He hopes he will not have to decide. He is being kept busy enough following the Hume and his partners about, keeping a discreet distance, shifting himself behind the crowd that gathers 'round the Hume wherever he goes. For the Hume is known to give a hundred dollars' worth of gold to down-and-out miners. He has used champagne bottles for bowling pins, has wrapped a ten pound note 'round a cigar and smoked it. Boston overheard Lorn Hallwood, the scarred black man, reprimand the Hume, and Napoleon Beauville, the tall one, nod in agreement, saw George Bowson stare in astonishment at the Hume's spending. The Hume's antics, however, do not surprise Boston. It is the sort of generosity expected of those with wealth, particularly those who find it in the earth, or win it, or gain it suddenly, for no apparent reason. The Hume's giving is providing him with status, a name, with admirers who vow, for the time being, to follow him. It is ever so in the world. The headman Wa'xwid smashed the copper *Quail Before* to show his power and to defeat a rival. The copper was worth twenty lynx blankets and twenty slaves and thirty wide planks and forty boxes of grease. He burned three canoes that day, and he gave away four machines that stitched clothing, eighteen rifles, and a hundred three-point blankets, each person receiving according to his station. Boston has heard the missionaries call the potlatching wasteful and knows they are keen to stop it. But it is no different from what the Whitemen practice when they receive bounty, unexpected or otherwise, any idiot can see that.

No, what worries Boston is that the Hume is drinking without restraint and does not seem to notice the ones who glare at him with envy instead of hope. On the last occasion the Hume went on a spree to the towns he stumbled back to the cabin alone, singing drunkenly. Langstrom the Swede and George Bowson were still at the Denby. The night was full of wind and odd rustlings. The Hume, drunk as he was, did not notice the two men following behind him, closer than Boston ever dared. They carried no lanterns and walked with the stealth of thieves.

The two men stopped when Eugene stopped. Boston stopped also. For a moment all four were stock-still, as if waiting for some cue, and then Eugene swung his lantern this way and that, searching for the path, as if he'd never been that way before.

The two men were whispering together when Boston came upon them. He hit the large man on the back of the head with the butt of his revolver. The large man thudded to the ground and as he did Boston clamped his hand over the other man's mouth, pressed his revolver to his head.

"Who's there?" the Hume called.

"Don't make a fucking sound," Boston whispered. "Kill you if you do. And stop squirming."

The Hume called out again and then blundered off. Boston waited until his singing faded, then released his hand from the man's mouth and searched him for weapons. Threw an old pistol and a knife into the ditch.

"Damn. I think you killed Jevowski."

"Shut your mouth."

"You a constable? Christ, how's a man supposed to get by around here?"

"Leave the Hume alone, hear?"

"Whaddya care about our business?

"Nod or I'll blow your head off."

"I'm nodding. Ouch! Fuck Christ. Easy now. Hume owes me, the fucking idiot. Interfered with me when I was trying to make a living. Harmless game it was. And here he comes along and calls me a sharper, a cheat. I never cheat at Find the Lady. He set the Judge on me and poor Jevowski here. Damnation, now you."

"Get going. Kill you if you bother him again."

"Oh, fucking hell, fine, fine. I'm going. I've had it for tonight. What about Jevowski?"

"He'll live. Get going, that way."

"Christ, I don't get it. Like they say, Hume must shit out horse-shoes."

Another week passes and now the days are rimmed with frost, spiced with cold. On the tenth of September Boston wakes to snow, to an unasked-for remembrance of Kloo-yah lifting her face to a thick snowfall. The snow dissolved on the wet ground, showed white against the dark gloss of her hair. A raven on the roof of their cabin dislodged a piece of bark the size of a plate. The bark plunked on the woodpile and the raven flew into the sixth branch of a spruce. Boston had seen snow eighteen times before in his life. And yet it did not seem familiar, not with Kloo-yah standing in its fall.

Boston crawls from his bower. From his chosen vantage he peers through the telescope. The Hume and his partners come into view. The Hume is safely above ground. He is gesturing at the snow and scuffing at it with his boot. He looks surprised, as if just aware that winter is coming on. The Hume, to Boston's relief, has not been to the towns since the night he was nearly set upon.

It is now just past nine. The Hume and Napoleon Beauville have been working a sluice together for four hours. Two whiskey jacks flit from branch to branch. One alights on Boston's boot and pecks at the straw and mud caked upon it. Boston pays it no attention. The second bird careens down to the mine workings. Its partner soon joins it. The Hume smiles at the birds, as if they were a rarity, as if they were anything but a nuisance.

THIRTY-FOUR

ADDENDUM TO THE SECOND EDITION
While working assiduously at pulling riches from the earth the Gentleman will no doubt often be assailed by the cheeky whiskey jack who is always to be seen with its mate twirling about in skyward dance & who is bold enough to snatch food from one's very hand & who is ever together with its mate, ever plotting thievery, ever playing the coquette. One assumes the bolder of the birds is the male though in truth which is male & which female is impossible to tell for any but the most enthusiastic naturalist. Consider, Gentleman, how would the world figure if women and men were indistinguishable? Would one be wracked with indecision if one female were exactly like another in form or in temperament or in speech? Would life be simpler or merely dull?

"How are you feeling, Mr. Hume?" Napoleon asks.

"Salubrious. Fit as a fiddle. Merely pondering some philosophical ideas. Is it not warm today?"

Napoleon looks at him curiously and says he finds it quite brisk. Eugene nods and comments on the paucity of gold this day. Napoleon says "patience." Simple enough for him to say. He is the most patient man ever born, never raises his voice, never looks to his pocket watch. He unnerves Eugene at times, but then so does Langstrom heaving on the windlass. By the warmth of their new stove he is often polishing his new revolver with the same look of expectation he gives to his cooking. At the moment he is singing tunelessly in Swedish, a habit Eugene does not find as soothing as he once did. As for Lorn, he has made Eugene uneasy since the day they met. It is that perpetual false sneer, his slurred speech, as if his mouth were filled with bile. It is his comments that could be taken this way or that. At the moment he is below, overseeing the hired men, a task to which he has taken with considerable relish. Who can blame him? The world is inverted here. Eugene must emphasize this in his guidebook, or at least direct his secretary to do so. As for Young George, he is bringing over endless buckets from the shaft. Bringing them their fortune. Dear George. He heaves a bucket into Eugene's sluice, bellows: "Number 103!"

Yes, dear George. He has hummocks of dark flesh under his eyes. A manic cheer that has manifested itself in the last week or so. What has happened to the wide-eyed young man, diligently rereading his mother's letters? Diligently praying by his bunk? He has been transformed by wealth. They all have, certainly, but none more than George Bowson. In truth, it is somewhat disquieting. For George has developed a taste for unwatered whiskey, for chewing tobacco, and smoking cigars, for dancing the hornpipe until all hours, for shouting and singing himself hoarse, and for the ladies of the Denby saloon, Mariette in particular, said to be the daughter of an Indian woman and a Jesuit priest, said to be able to turn any man heathen. If these were his only pastimes, Eugene might console himself that George is merely a young man testing the waters of life. George, however, has recently acquired a taste for the Chinamen's opium. It was not just Eugene who suggested sampling it. Langstrom by his gesturing seemed to have some expertise in the matter. It was a mere lark in any case. He, Langstrom, George, and Miss Anna. The three of them in a small room that smelled foreign and acrid. On a square table were numerous gaming tablets inscribed with the Chinamen's fanciful writings. On the floor were straw mats. They stretched themselves out. Tang Lee's assistant took a pin and poked the sugar-brown chunks into the long pipe, then lit the pipe with a practiced hand. The opium bubbled in the small bowls. Ah, so this was what blue tasted like. The room melted, expanded. A flow of colours, a sense of half-dreaming. Joy, then, was not some philosopher's concept that Eugene secretly doubted. It inhabited his body. His bones. It had form and shape. It was lavender and white as well as blue. An age passed. And then, the following day, a sore throat, a headache which has plagued him since, a weakness in his limbs, and worst of all a melancholy and loss of appetite that had no place in the breast of a wealthy man. George, however, was barely afflicted.

In fact, he was agog, and became distressingly poetic as he described how he had communed with angels. Now he smokes a portion each night and each morning drinks whiskey to combat the ensuing lethargy. Eugene's insistence that opium is an invention of the devil, his tales of sordid opium dens, white slaves, rotting skulls, have not deterred young George in the least.

Eugene straightens laboriously. His head pounds and there is a swath of pain in his lower spine, a swath of sweat on his brow. The droplets reach his eyes and the gold particles for which he is so keenly searching disappear in the swim of brown water. Absurd, this thought that it is all an illusion, a spell, this idea that the gold does not exist at all. It is only that the day is surprisingly warm, no matter what Napoleon says, only that he is surprisingly tired. Come now, Eugene Augustus, you are no longer young, that is all. True, true. Time was he could sleep for two or three hours and wake refreshed by the noontime chimes and the shouts of friends at his door. Time was he could drink prodigiously and awake with only a gentle throbbing in his temple, as if some disapproving teetotaller was tapping him with her fan. Now when he imbibes it seems a drummer has taken her place. And his throat. So parched come the unwelcome mornings, such a longing for simple water. It is as if he has dragged himself through the Sahara instead of the saloons and gambling dens of the town. Come now, has it not been worth it? Of course. Most certainly. Already one of his exploits has been put to song—the footrace between Miss Anna and a boasting Oregonian. He, Langstrom and Young George bet on Miss Anna, out of loyalty, out of show, and were astonished as any when she won by two strides. Later she accompanied them to the Occidental in a dress patterned with dots, a cigar still firmly between her teeth. Miss Anna tromping about in a dress! What magic had they worked, or rather what magic had Langstrom worked, for it is his side she never leaves as they make their way through the towns, betting on the roulette, the black-jack, the dog fights, the bare-knuckle fights. They come away, roaring with laughter, marked with droplets of blood. Win or lose, it hardly signifies. Lucky Hume he is being called, and not just by Langstrom now. He could sell the buttons on his coat, clippings of his hair, certainly his advice. Even the Judge hinted he would like to question Eugene on one or two matters, a roulette game, for example, in which the wheel kept responding to his number. The Judge approached Eugene as he was scraping up his winnings. Arthur Bushby, nearby as usual, was humming some annoying tune. The Judge complimented Eugene on his good fortune, then posed his questions with impressive tact. He nodded at Eugene's explanation of astounding luck at work, gave his good day and turned to leave.

"Ah, I nearly forgot. I must warn you, Mr. Hume, that Kinnear and Jevowski are about."

"Kinnear? Jevowski?"

"The sharpers from whom you rescued my clerk. In Yale?"

"Ah, yes, quite so. Surely they cannot still hold a grudge. I shall buy them some champagne, yes. And you as well. Come, your honour, Matthew. I owe you. I have not forgotten your generosity."

"I would take up your offer, Mr. Hume, but I am occupied at the moment. And do not worry about repayment. The lunch was my pleasure."

Eugene watched him leave with something like exasperation. Felt much as a child might when given a bemused glance, a pat on the head.

When the noontime arrives Eugene sets aside his portion of cold beef and settles against a stump. "I might take a nap, gentlemen, if that is acceptable."

"Rest all you want, Doc!" George shouts.

Lorn scowls. Or is he deep in thought?

"Is there something vexing you, Lorn?"

"Not at all. Just seems that lately you're doing a lot of napping and whatnot."

Eugene reminds him that it was he who realized where the gold could be found, he who encouraged them all to invest in the Dora Dear.

"That's true enough. Just worried you might be getting that sickness again."

"I am feeling fine, thank you. I apologize. I thought. . . . Well, shit."

Eugene closes his eyes, wishes away the thumps and slooshes. Only several weeks more if the weather holds. And then the mud and water will begin to freeze and he will return to her. Napoleon, Lorn, and Langstrom have agreed to stay on through the winter to watch the claim even though Eugene has reminded them that it is well-known that he is a friend of the Judge, that terror of claim jumpers.

Ah, let them stay and shiver here then, if that is what they desire. Let them watch the mercury freeze. He will take Barnard's new coach from Quesnel to Victoria. It seems years ago now that Eugene posted a letter to Dora by the confluence of the Fraser and Thompson Rivers while Barnard himself waited and offered unasked-for advice. Astonishing how quickly a letter carrier can become a man of substance. Astonishing how a journey that took five weeks now takes only a week or so. Yes, he must be frugal now. He must not go to the towns. He must be certain he saves enough for a pillared house, for silken dresses, for the wedding. He is a man of his word, a man of honour. He will buy Dora status. She will have lessons in managing servants, in dressing, in speech. Dora. Ariadne. His father. The Judge. They clatter through his imagination like bone puppets on a stage.

"Mr. Hume, can you hear me?" Napoleon is studying him with the same quiet intensity that he studies his drying herbs, his bottles and concoctions.

"I am resting a little longer. I hope that it is not objectionable."

Napoleon's voice booms in his ear. "The fever has returned."

"Nonsense, man."

"How is your throat?"

"Sore, yes, sore, but only because my humours are balancing themselves out. I have not drank spirits for several days, you see." He struggles to his feet, but it is as if Napoleon's utterance of the word "fever" has brought it on in full. "Damn you," he says. Lurches onward. Napoleon shouts to the others. The whiskey jacks hurl upward past the knoll. Eugene watches them. Imagines taking wing. A shadow on a rocky outcrop forms into the vague shape of a man. "You there!" Eugene shouts, desperate to ask the man a question, though what this question is he cannot recall, not for the life of him.

The figure melts even as Eugene stumbles forward, even as the others catch him and lower him to the ground.

THIRTY-FIVE

The Hume has been ill four days now. He is kept in the cabin. Napoleon Beauville collects roots and buys powders from Tang Lee's store. The others take turns at the sickbed. Boston sleeps only in fits. Eats next to nothing. Does nothing because there is nothing he can do and yet he is more clear in his understanding than he has ever been. He understands now why Kloo-yah returns to him unbidden each night. He understands why his ears have been ringing with the cries of Illdare and the fort men as the People overwhelm them. And he recalls, finally, the words of the man whose face is in shadow, always in shadow: "You owe me, boy. You owe James Milroy. I saved your worthless flesh, and now I'll mark it like it's mine. You're the bad luck that wrecked us on this godforsaken shore, knowed it. Should have killed you when I found you stowed away in my hold, thieving my stores. Now you owe. You owe." It worked some magic. For the sense has been growing all of Boston's life, a great unease, as if the world itself is growing more and more unbalanced. The woman, this Dora, she is not of the spirit world herself. Spirits cannot manage the faint throb of a blue vein at the temple, the sweet stale odour of womanly sweat. But they are directing her, of that there can be no doubt. They sent him into her memories so that he might realize the importance, not only of her return of his money, but also of her stories, of her request that her husband be returned to her. The spirits sent the changeling Girl as well so that he might be set back on the proper path. They did all this so that he might know that all his fine exchanges cannot balance his poor ones. So that he would know that this is his reckoning.

THIRTY-SIX

Eugene's eyes are as dry and raspy as balls of twine. His joints ache as if they have been nailed together. Night. The stove gives off a hellish heat. He is lying in a stew of his own sweat that is rank with sickness. The blankets are leaden slabs spiked with wire. His name floats just beyond his grasp. He hardly cares. What matters is this raging thirst. The heat. The wretched air. It is cutting off his breath. Is it the cholera he has? Ah, God. Has he returned to Sevastopol? In the harbour the corpses are as thick as schools of fish, but they are not turning as fish do, all at one mysterious cue, but bobbing senselessly this way and that, each in its own lonesome death.

He twists his neck. A man sits at a table, sleeping with his head on his arms. He is young, blond-bearded, a long thin pipe near his hand. The place is empty otherwise. Eugene wishes to beg the young man's forgiveness, but why? And why, for that matter, is he here? He should be with his wife. Her name? He has forgotten. Ah, his father is here. His hair is in frightful disarray, and he glares, how he glares. "Failed, have you, Eugene Augustus? Failed is it?"

Eugene gasps out an explanation. He had not wanted to be a soldier. It was just that the uniforms were so splendid, and the crowds cheering the departure were so jubilant and so certain of victory, so proud of them all. So proud of Eugene Augustus Hume.

What does Eugene want? Truly want? He has forgotten. It was so clear once. No matter, all he wants at this moment is water. Coolness. He shoves the blankets aside. He is naked but for a night shift that hikes up and shows islands of curious rashes on his belly and thighs. Dora, that is the name of his wife. She is gay, robust. Her golden hair twists to her hips. She is standing at the fence of a stone house that is covered with flowering vines. Now only a silver light, a wind that fills his lungs. His feet are bare on the stones, on the layer of snow that is not enough to cool his tongue. Not near. He could drink a river dry. Some distance off lanterns hang in the black. A muffled thumping. Ah, but for silence, cool silence. The creek. Below. A mine. Companions. Wealth. The earth drops under him like a wave. He stumbles. Doesn't fall. The embankment is impossibly long. He can hear the rush of water. Can see the stars spattered in the firmament. He falls before the creek. The stones burrow into his knees. His hands are shaking as he cups the water to his face. On the other side is a figure formed of shadows. A crashing of brush. Dora? She has come. She said she would not leave him, not ever. He is wading toward her, swimming. Small stones scrape his chest. Her face, silver and round in the waters of the creek, shimmers just beyond his grasp.

THIRTY-SEVEN

They have him in a small room. He is tied to a chair, for he has given them considerable trouble.

"Shall we start again?"

Boston stares at the floor planks. Chief Constable Chandler sighs in disappointment, says he can wait all day. He is a clean-shaven, jowled man whose flesh hangs heavily on his bones. He is standing to one side of Boston. Constable Bearn, hare-lipped and stocky, stands on the other. A clerk is seated at a small table with an inkwell and paper before him. Boston has seen him in town, following the Judge about. The clerk is nervously stroking his beard, which is very dark, and so long that it flows under the edge of the table.

The silence stretches. Bearn looks at Chandler with raised brows, a balled fist. Chandler shakes his head, then, true to his nickname, Whistling Pete, begins to whistle a tune that is slow and melancholy. Boston has never heard it before and suspects it is of the man's own devising. He seems the sort. "Beware the inventive man," Illdare told Boston and held up an ingenious tong made by the new blacksmith. It was January of 1842, a Tuesday, and ice marbled the pathway to the trade room; a mottled rat scuttled over the counter.

Chandler pauses in his whistling. "Come now, you must have a name."

The Dora woman asked if he was truly from Boston, or if he was just an ordinary American. "In the Chinook lingo all the Americans are called Boston men, aren't they now?" He shrugged and said that some still used the term. He could have said more. Could have said he had no true name, just as he had no true birthday. He could have told her of

289

Milroy, the blade in the firelight, the muttered incantation. She might have had some answer to it all.

Chandler comes to the end of the tune. Gestures to Bearn who gives Boston an expert wallop that resounds in the small room. Arthur starts. The ink trembles in its jar.

She will remember the name of Boston Jim because she had found it odd. And an oddness is the only thing that enables others to recall a person they have met only once. And so she'll remember him, remember his name, and she'll not understand that he was protecting the Hume—her husband, lover, what he was called mattered not. She'll not understand that, although he failed to bring the Hume back alive, he'd tried to return at least some portion of him to her. She was the one who told him of this custom after all. She was the one who told him of the poet Shelley and how he drowned and how, on his funeral pyre, his heart had not burned and so his friend had snatched it from the flames.

Boston spits out blood, a tooth. The men take form again. He says the name slowly, under his breath. Surprising that the name has no substance. He has always assumed it would, that it might choke him by its mere utterance.

"Speak up," Chandler says.

"James Milroy."

"Lovely. Well, where are you from Mr. Milroy?"

"Boston."

"You have some proof of this? Someone to vouch for you?"

"Got proof."

"Well?" says Chandler.

Boston tells them to unbutton his shirt. Bearn snickers.

"It's there," Boston says. "Your fucking proof."

Bearn takes out his knife. He slices through Boston's shirt and undershirt, the blade scraping from his belly to his neck. Boston's chest is very pale compared to the rest of him, so rarely has it been bared.

"I'll be fried," Bearn says.

"Well, Mr. Milroy," Chandler says. "Worried you would forget who you were?"

Boston says nothing.

"Such a quiet man for an American. But we have British law here.

We have a determination to discover truth. Perhaps, then, you shall be so kind as to tell it to us."

"Told you."

"We don't believe you."

"That's your damn problem."

"I rather think it's more yours, seeing as you are the one who will be tried for murder."

"Didn't kill him, the Hume."

"No?"

"No."

"Tell us the story again. I am slightly confused."

"Me too," Bearn says.

"Shut up, Constable."

"Yes, sir."

"Drowned."

"He drowned, did he?" Chandler asks and smiles.

A cart rumbles past outside. The clerk scratches furiously at the papers, recording it all, and the sound of the scratching is that of a blue jay scratching at the window of Boston's cabin. It was trying desperately to get out, though how it had gotten in he couldn't say. He killed and ate it and then swept the blue feathers from the hearth.

"Hauled him back to shore, but he was already dead. He's a fool. Never seen such a fool."

"Ah, so it was a rescue you were attempting. Intriguing."

The clerk pauses in his writing and mops at his brow with a handkerchief. The Dora woman spoke of handkerchiefs. "We had the loveliest ones in our family shop. Ones with pictures from the Duke of Wellington's funeral and from the Crystal Palace. They weren't for using; they were so people wouldn't be forgetting things. So as they could tell their children about what they'd seen and done, like."

Perhaps a simple handkerchief would have sufficed. Perhaps that was what the Dora woman meant.

"Mr. Milroy," Chandler says.

"Rescue. That was it."

"Ah, well, you see, though you say it was a rescue attempt it certainly didn't look like that to Mr. Hume's partners. Indeed, to them it looked like something far more foul."

"Was it for some rite or other?" Bearn asks. "I've heard of the Indians in Canada carrying on like that."

Chandler turns to Bearn. "Damn you, I'll ask the questions. . . . Well, was it some rite or other?"

"Not an Indian. Wasn't no rite. Was to even things out."

"Ah, revenge. That's not particularly original. I put it to you, Mr. Milroy, that you were waiting to rob Mr. Hume. Indeed, that perhaps you justified doing so because he did you some injury in the past. He was an annoying man, after all, the sort who is always putting his foot in it, or so I have heard from Mr. Bushby here, and others."

Boston stares at Chandler's boots which have been so polished that Boston can see a rough blotch that must be his own image.

Chandler continues: "I put it to you that you thrust Mr. Hume, a sick and weakened man, under the water to force him to confess where his gold was hidden. And then you committed the second foul deed while he still breathed, hoping, perhaps, that some innocent Redman would hang in your stead."

"Seems a damned fool way to rob a man."

"Not for a damned fool."

Boston spits. It is a poor spit as his mouth is so dry. Still, it lands close enough to Chandler's polished boots to warrant another wallop from Bearn.

"Easy. We don't want him so thick tongued he cannot talk."

"Fuck the lot of you."

At Chandler's nod Bearn punches Boston in the stomach. Boston slumps groaning in the chair. Arthur Bushby hunches miserably over his papers. Chandler whistles the tune of "Greensleeves." This tune Boston has heard before. In the Victoria jail the idiot Toolie sang it seven times over in his high, cracking voice before the jailer stuffed his mouth with straw.

Chandler taps the clerk's papers. "Mr. Bushby?"

"Yes?"

"Is it all transcribed there?"

"Yes, I think. Yes. Should we not help him?"

Chandler gestures to Bearn who unties Boston and then manacles his hands and pulls him to his feet.

Bushby watches white-faced, anxious-eyed. "I'm a musician, you know, I'm not really cut out for this law business."

"One does get used to it." Chandler says.

"He didn't deserve this," Bushby says.

"Mr. Hume? I quite agree."

"I meant Mr. Milroy. It hasn't been proven. He hasn't been tried."

Chandler claps Bushby on the shoulder and steers him toward the door. "Let's get together for some music making sometime, shall we? I have a modest talent for the notes myself."

Bushby twists in Chandler's grip and looks back at Boston. With what? Curiosity? Revulsion? Years past, Illdare gave him such a look when he passed his gloved hand over Boston's forehead, and then again when he learned that Boston could not forget. Kloo-yah, too, gave him such a look when she traced the scars on his chest, as did the Dora woman when first she saw him, there at the shore.

THIRTY-EIGHT

The Judge has left the makeshift jail. Boston settles back against the iron forge to which he is manacled.

"It's odd, Mr. Jim, but it feels like I've known you for ever such a long time."

The Dora woman was quiet then, as if she was holding her breath. It seemed there'd never been such a quiet in the world. Boston stood and stomped his foot, for it had fallen asleep.

"You're leaving? Well and so. I've kept you here so long, haven't I? All my stories. Oh, I talk, yes I do. But you'll be coming again, won't you? When Mr. Hume returns? We'll have scones with butter. I'm sure to know how to make butter proper by then."

He muttered that yes, he might. And when he did his throat constricted, as if he had eaten juniper berries, as he did once at Fort Connelly, when he was still a child.

He recalls this part of the conversation, recalls her restless movements, the Quamichans working in the garden, the clucking of the chickens, the spider making its web in the join of her cabin door. Now recalls all she said from when he first saw her on the shore, and how she looked when she spoke of the Hume, of her family, of London. There is still time. He might fall into her memories again. He might find himself again in the alleyway watching the young Dora with her mother and father. This time he will come from out of the shadows. "Join us," they will say, and the jail will cease to be, as will the dull pain in his ribs and eyes, the fierce pain along his jaw, as will the knock-knocking of the scaffold being built outside the doors.

The next morning Bearn ties Boston's hands behind his back and hobbles his legs

"You are a sight," Chandler says as he takes Boston's hat.

"Give it," Boston mumbles, his lips being swollen and split.

Chandler says he cannot wear his hat in the presence of the Judge, which is like being in the presence of the Queen, which is like being in the presence of God.

"Bugger them all."

Bearn dutifully punches him in the ribs. Boston drops to his knees.

"Mr. Milroy has drawn a sizable crowd," Chandler says. "You are lucky to witness it, Mr. Bushby."

"Lucky?" asks Arthur Bushby, standing in the doorway.

The shorn hills are the first thing Boston sees, then the morning sun fractured by clouds, then the crowd murmuring and shifting. One eye is suppurating and nearly shut, but the other recognizes most in the crowd as clearly as if he has known them all his life. Others might find this comforting when approaching a scaffold, seeing such familiar faces. Boston does not. He would much prefer to die in his cabin alone.

Madame Blanc, carrying a green parasol, is talking with several men, her face averted. Boston thought she would be at the trial, that she would tell of what he wrote, of what she read aloud. But Madame Blanc did not appear. Keeping secrets was her own personal commandment, that was what she had said to him at the Denby saloon. Good that she was true to her word. Otherwise the jury would have construed he murdered the Hume because he coveted his wife, not his gold. Not that it mattered. The outcome would have been the same. Still, he was relieved when the Dora woman was not mentioned. For he did not covet her. To do so would be a betrayal of Kloo-yah, and he had betrayed her enough. No other word suffices. He can admit that now.

The Swede lunges at him. Bearn shoves him back into the arms of Miss Anna. She is wearing a plaid dress this day and a bonnet. The one called Mariette stands in a plain brown dress, her hands folded before her. She will be busy when the hanging is done. All the whores will be.

Boston's lawyer, one Jedidiah Smithe, falls in beside him and mutters his regrets. He is a clerk at the assizes office, though lawyering, he said, was always his ambition. He has a high voice, a nervous habit of knuckling his cheek. Boston didn't give a horse's ass about a lawyer and told the Judge so. "You must do your part as well," the Judge said.

A short man in a high top hat shakes his fist and hurls a litany of curses. His companion wraps his scarf more tightly around his neck, as if it were he who needed protection from the noose. The two black men from the Hume's claim are at the edges of the crowd. The tall one is walking away. The scarred one hesitates and then follows. The jury men jostle for position and place their bets, likely on how long his dying will take.

Now Boston passes this George Bowson. He is sniffling and mouthing, fish-like, to the sky, his hands pressed in an attitude of prayer. He was the first one called to the stand, swore fervently on the Bible, then said: "I fell asleep. It was my turn to watch him, your honour, and I fell asleep. I can't never forgive myself for it. I've been praying night and day every since but I don't think I can ever be forgiven for it. . . ."

He wiped his face with his sleeve. Chandler, acting as prosecutor, asked George Bowson what transpired on the night of September 14th. "Be specific. We must not shirk the specifics."

"Mr. Hallwood there and Mr. Langstrom, they woke me up when their shift was finished. They said: where's Eugene? And I said I didn't know. We went looking outside and then one of us, I don't remember which, but one of us said that we should check the creek. When . . . when . . . we got there it was bright from the moon and it was cold. Terrible cold. And there was the sight the like of which I'll never forget. Not if I should live to be a hundred by God's grace. . . ."

"Take your time," Chandler said.

"Thank you, sir. Mr. Hume, he was . . . was stretched out on the bank and that man there he . . . he was crouched over him. He had a great huge knife. There was an awful lot of blood. It was horrible, horrible."

And so on.

Jedidiah Smithe asked Bowson if it weren't possible that the Hume had drowned first, like the defendant had claimed. Smithe's voice cracked as he spoke. He ruffled through his papers and sheaves of them fell to the floor. Chandler stood with his thumbs hooked in his vest, at ease with the world. Above them both sat Judge Begbie, black-robed and be-wigged, his hammer near to hand.

"But I saw Mr. Hume move, sir. I heard some terrible moaning, too," said Bowson.

"Ah, but you'd just woken up," said Smithe.

"That's true I suppose."

"And had you indulged in spirits, or opium, or well, anything of the like?"

Bowson admitted to the opium. "But it wasn't much. And I'll never touch it again. I swear it on my father's grave."

"Your honour," Chandler interjected, "If a man's testimony was to be discounted because of some indulgence then justice would never be done, not in this town, certainly, where hard-working honest men need some respite."

The jury nodded at this. Smithe stammered some objection. Why did he bother? Boston thought. It was all show, all sham.

Through an interpreter whose English was not much better than his own, Langstrom told much the same story as Bowson had, added how he had seized Boston and likely would have killed him but for Mr. Beauville, who came running when he heard the ruckus and demanded he be held for the constable.

"And why did you not want him killed on the spot, Mr. Beauville?" The Judge asked Napoleon when he took the stand.

Napoleon looked at the Judge curiously. "I have seen justice taken into the hands of the mob, your honour. I have seen innocents murdered. Restraint is the only cure for such madness."

Lorn nodded at this. Chandler frowned.

"You would make a fine lawyer, Mr. Beauville," the Judge said.

The details were wrong. The Hume had not moved, had not groaned. Boston had tried to revive him first, had turned him over and thudded his back to get the water out. But the Hume was already stone dead. And Boston had not been howling in some foreign tongue as George Bowson said, as the others agreed, even this Napoleon Beauville. He had not been covered in blood. He had not fought with the strength of ten men. His limbs had been numbed from the cold stream. His fingers seemed frozen to the handle of the bowie knife. In any case, the desire to struggle fell from him as soon as Bowson and then the others were upon him. No, it did not occur the way they said. But then that is always the way with others. It is as if they inhabit a thousand possibilities. It is as if the past shifts for them to suit the present. They cannot be trusted, not ever, only the Dora woman. Only Kloo-yah who is gone from him.

Chandler passed Boston's bowie knife to the jury. Told them to note the blood still on the blade. Then he passed them a small wooden box. "Final evidence. Look well." One of the jury men retched as he opened it. Not long after, the Judge reached for his black cap.

The crowd falls nearly silent. Chandler and Bearn lead Boston to the four steps at the base of the scaffold. A priest of the Anglicans waits with his head uncovered. To the left of the scaffold is the Judge. Smoke curls from the pipe in his fist. Arthur Bushby is beside him, scuffing at the dirt.

Boston spits. He had told them he wanted no priests, had told them he was making no deals with their conniving God.

The priest says a prayer, then asks Boston for his last words. Boston's mouth is too dry to spit again and so he ignores the priest and steps up on the scaffold. Bearn follows, holding Boston's arm.

Chandler pulls the hood over Boston's head. Boston hears his own breathing and then the creaking of the boards as Chandler reaches for the noose. A weight is around his body, a slide of cloth that is rustling and smooth. His body is of a sudden larger, softer. It smells chalky and sweet. His heart quickens, his blood. Something scratches at his neck, a tendril of hair, such a bother at times, so unruly. Need more pins. Such a warm day. Ah, well and so, must talk to keep this worry within its banks. Poor man. I've never seen anyone so dirty and tired, it's as if he's been walking for centuries, like. And such misery in his face. Like that of a tragic actor. How could I have been frightened of him at first? He is as lonely as I am, worse I'll guess, for he lives off in those mountains with only dead animals about him. And he's listened so well. I chatter. How I chatter. Good that I gave him back that old pouch and the money. How astonished he looked! Good that I said it was for his birthday, poor sod. But who wouldn't give him back his own? Who wouldn't pity him enough for that?

THIRTY-NINE

The crowd disperses slowly, as if there might be a second act, another show.

The Judge congratulates Chandler on a job well done, then tells him to see to it that the body is buried in the Chinese graveyard.

"I could make up a cross," Arthur Bushby says.

"I do not think so. Such men are best forgotten."

The Judge's pipe has gone cold. He relights it. The odour of the smoke is reminiscent of the Guernsey shores over which he roamed as a boy. Good that the hanging was done in the morning and not at sunset as is the custom in some parts. Best one have a long, busy day stretching before them. He is thankful once more that he chose the law over the army. He has never killed a man, doubts, indeed, if he has the stomach for it.

The Judge reaches to his pocket. The money this Milroy gave him last night is there. Perhaps he should not have visited the man, but Milroy had made no other requests. It did not seem unreasonable. The Judge came in alone. Bearn waited outside. Milroy was manacled hand and foot to an iron forge that it had taken six men to haul inside, the building itself being too flimsy to keep anyone for long. A proper jail would have to be built soon.

The Judge studied Milroy by the light of a coal lantern. The beatings had made him into a grotesque. He made a note to remind Bearn to keep his enthusiasm in check.

"Got money for the Hume's woman," Milroy said. "She lives in the Cowichan. Her name's Dora Timmons."

The Judge hid his surprise. Milroy did not seem the sort who would trouble himself about recompense. "I will see that she receives it," he said.

"Good then."

The money was in a well-stitched-over pocket on the inside of Milroy's torn shirt. The Judge cut the pocket open with his penknife, took out a tasselled smoke pouch. Milroy stared impassively past the Judge's shoulder. Indeed, the Judge had never seen a man so impassive to his fate.

"Here. One hundred and twenty-six pounds, ten shillings. Take the money. Not the pouch. Thank you to give her new money for that," Milroy said.

The Judge emptied the pouch. It was English money of many decades past, the notes worn soft as fabric. Likely it was no longer even negotiable. He put the money in his breast pocket, then left the pouch at Milroy's feet.

"Crisp new notes. You have my word."

Milroy nodded, then looked at the Judge. Even through the swollen eyes the gaze was unsettling. "Where is it?"

"The heart of poor Mr. Hume, you mean?"

Milroy nods.

"We buried it with him, as is civilized."

"The Dora woman. Thought she might want it, as a gift, see."

All the Judge could see was that Milroy was most certainly mad. "It is not the most appropriate of gifts."

"Now it's not right. Still not right."

"Things have a way of righting themselves, Mr. Milroy. Now I suggest you make peace with your maker, whoever, whatever that was."

The crowd is gone. The body has been cut down from the gallows; the morning is promising to be fine. Poor Miss Timmons, the Judge thinks. But then Hume was a fool. More than that. He was a drunkard, an opportunist, an exaggerator, a sycophant, a poseur. He was the sort who stayed about once a conversation had reached its natural conclusion, like a porter waiting for a large, unnecessary tip. And he was a gambler no matter what justification he gave. Not a bad man for all that, however. No, the Judge would not say that; but neither would he say he was surprised that Mr. Hume's end was very bad indeed.

"Milroy's last words," Arthur Bushby says. "They were strange, weren't they, your honour?"

"No stranger than many."

"Chandler was the only one who heard what Milroy said. Maybe he invented them."

"Chandler is not one for imaginative tellings."

"Then whose birthday do you think Milroy meant? Someone in the crowd? Was he working some kind of curse?"

"Perhaps, perhaps, though likely it was simply a morbid jest."

EPILOGUE

My life, dear? Ah, well and so. It has been full, rounded. It smells of Cantonese silk newly unwound from the bolt, of the talc I sprinkled so liberally on my children, of the apples ripening in the yard. And of roses, certainly. Blooming in my garden. Plucked by children who giggle like wind chimes and think I do not know. Even the dear old Judge Begbie praises my roses. Such a compliment coming from him, the champion at the Rose Festival three years running. I must invite him to tea. Ah, no. Dead. Dead these twenty-odd years. No longer does he sweep down Yates Street with his cape and cane and little dogs. No longer does he send out elaborate invitations to his parties. Pity he never married. All the women said so. And the dear Governor with his sashes and medals. He and Amelia are dead also, aren't they? And my first husband Eugene, my darling Eggy. And my beloved Jacob. At times I forget that even he is dead. Sometimes I am certain he is in the room with me. After being with a man for fifty years you are allowed such mistakes. Indeed, I must admit that lately I have begun to see my lost loved ones clear as day. Not so the blessed living. My eyes have always failed me and now those I love are mere dim, glimmery shapes, until they hove suddenly into sight, as if a door has been flung open in the air. Ah, yes, my spectacles would help. I have them hereabouts. But I have some vanity left. And so you must come closer. There. Ah, you remind me of my daughter now. She is so much like Jacob, mild and firm, and looks of him, too, not lovely, poor lass, but pleasant-faced, and gentle in her ways. And isn't she a wonder at the business? The Empire of Lace and Petticoats as you called it in your newspaper. Was that last week? Last month? Odd that you are here again. Never mind. I must tell you that "Empire" is a rather grand way of describing five shops scattered about the West, though certainly the shops are more successful than I would have ever dared dream. I do have a talent for knowing what looks best on men and women both—what style, what fit, what fabric, what colours are needed to bring out the eyes and make the complexion glow. It is why my patrons are so loyal. That and my habit of chatting with them, for remembering their birthdays and the names of their children and my habit of giving out small gifts: perfume, lace, collars, handkerchiefs, small notebooks. I learned all such things from my father. He died by fire and I miss him even still.

My Eggy had a talent. His was for knowing exactly when a party was at hand, as well for the way it would play out. He could nearly smell the charge of it, he said. It did not seem a useful talent, but then neither did mine, and look what I have done with it. You must make use of what you are given. Eggy told me that. Or was it my father? Or was it Jacob?

Is that grey you are wearing, dear? I don't understand the fashions these days, though my granddaughters adore them. They say they are "emancipating" and go on about how the women of my time were jailed in their corsets and great hoop skirts. Perhaps, but at least in my day a woman made an entrance. At least you knew when she was in the room, being that she took up such a great deal of it. But nowadays! Not a flare, not a ruffle, no waistline at all, and all to make a poor woman seem as flat-chested as a boy and thin as a wood panel. And, oh, the hair! It is as if the women are fevered, as if there is some wretched epidemic and their hair has been shorn to give them strength. And then, then, they jam those little hats so far over their heads I fear they will disappear into them, as in a magician's trick. Ah, now my hair was glorious. Golden and thick and long it was. Ah, well and so, I was not "emancipated." I loved those hoops. It was as if I were a splendid ship and men mere rowboats bobbing about. I loved what came later, too, the intricate hats, the bustles, the mutton sleeves, the hair arranged plump as a Christmas goose on one's head.

You are quiet now, so quiet. Did I mention that I am forever astonished that I live in this grand house, that I could have petit fours at any hour of the day if I should so please, though I do not indulge often, for otherwise I would be a globe and you would be searching out the Hebrides or the Indies on my person. Ah, I am talking on so. You do

303

not mind? You know, I feel quite at ease with you, quite at peace. I have always talked a great deal. I know that. Of course. I have always noticed how eyes would dart to windows and doors and rooftops. It were as if people thought they were tethered and a fire were advancing. And yet they could have just excused themselves, just moved on. I would not have minded. Well and so, I do not talk as much as I once did, I can assure you. My voice is too frail for that and too full of old-lady warbling. Ah, but my thoughts, they splash against each other and the past bumps against the present like paper boats in a pond. My daughter says that lately I have been talking to myself and I admit sometimes I do, but only when I remember something that I should have mentioned years ago, to Jacob, or to the dear Judge, or to my darling Eggy, and I must say it, to get it off my chest, you see. Ah, well and so, at least the worry no longer courses through me, like a dreaded wind that has no source or cause.

Have I thanked you for writing that I am Victoria's Greatest Philanthropist? Yes? Did you know that time was I wouldn't have known such a word as philanthropist? Indeed, I recall thinking it was some kind of insult. My Jacob changed all that. Such patience he had in teaching me my letters. He was not interested in teaching me how to speak properly, however. You see, even though my mother tried to iron it out of us, you could still hear the London market in my voice. Jacob said he liked the way I spoke. But Eggy had told me there was no point in wearing fine clothes if one were not wearing fine speech. And so after his death I moved to Victoria and took lessons in elocution and diction. All to remake myself, as so many people here have done.

I apologize. I drift from one thing to the next. Indulge me, dear. And now, you were asking of the pioneer days. Everyone is so intrigued by those times. Exciting, they say, to be forging a new land and all. The paintings? By Miss Carr? Yes, I have seen them. So strange they are. No, they do not look like the great forests did before they were cut down. The great forests didn't flow together like dyes from a vat. And yet her paintings feel the way the forests did, as if they might fold you in. Ah, but in all, pioneering was so very dull. Imagine being alone in a cabin, the nearest neighbour a good mile off, animal sounds all about, and endless toil to fill your days. Perhaps I was simply not cut out for it. I was never one for churning butter and tilling the soil and pounding the washing. I was born of London and its throngs, its cobbles, and great churches. Bustle is what I like and shops aplenty, and the sense that the world is pulsing all about you. I can mend a shirt or two well enough, but that is all the domestic arts of which I can boast, and that only because I did my time as a seamstress. Did I tell you of this? And did I tell you of the *Tynemouth*? Everyone wants to know of the *Tynemouth*. A brideship. *How archaic*, people say. You would think we were white slaves the way they go on. But we had our pick of men and I picked a fine man, but he died. Yes, he died, and it was the greatest sorrow of my life. I understand the Indian women now, the ones who carry the bones of their dead husbands on their backs to show the weight of their grief. We called them the Carriers because of it, though I don't know what they call themselves, nor if they follow that custom still.

Do you know the tale of the Princess and the Pea? Such a delicate, useless princess, I always thought, to feel a pea through a hundred feather mattresses. Yet I understand her now. I understand how things can press through all your luxuries and comforts and trouble you in your sleep. For, you see, sometimes I am certain my father is alone in my attic rooms and has been for these sixty-odd years and the loneliness has driven him mad beyond remedy. Sometimes I think that the younger Mr. Haberdale is weeping for me still, or Isabel from the *Tynemouth* is crying out that she is not a thief, not a thief. Sometimes I weep with regret that I was so guileless and trusting then and so did not insist upon travelling with my Eugene to the Cariboo and so keep him safe. And sometimes I weep when I think how angry I was when he left, and how I did not write to him each week as I promised. You see, I wanted him to fret and worry same as I did. I wanted him to yearn for me, as I yearned for him.

I can't ever forget the black day the letter came. I can't forget, either, when I met the Judge for the first time and he told me that Eugene was a worthy attribute to his class and that he, the Judge, had considered him a friend and a rare gentleman. He gave me some money then, over a hundred pounds it was, and some shillings, and he told me a collection had been taken up for me in the goldfields. I always suspected, however, that the money was his very own. And now do you understand? My fortune was all built on one man's Christian charity, for it was with that money I started my first drapery.

Eugene's partners? They all came to see me at one time or another. Mr. Hallwood and Mr. Beauville came first. Though they were near broke they still tried to give me a bit of money. The mine only had one good seam, they said, and it had been exhausted soon enough. I told them to keep the money, I had enough from the good Judge. They were surprised by that. They hadn't realized the Judge and my Eggy were such close friends. Well and so, Mr. Napoleon went into business with a Prussian fellow, Mr. Shillmice I think. They made a fortune on restoratives and balms and cigarettes. Mr. Hallwood, now he became something of an agitator, trying to right the wrongs done to his people. They both lived in Philadelphia with their wives and children. We corresponded for a time but fell off as people do.

As for Mr. Langstrom, he and his wife Anna moved to Hastings Mill, the place they call Vancouver now, and later went to the Yukon. I never heard of them again. They loved each other so very much. How you could tell! And Mr. Langstrom said that all the bad luck went to Eugene and that he'll never forget him, at least it seemed that's what he said in his poor English.

One Mr. Oswald came to see me also. I was living in Victoria by then. He was a curious fellow, fidgety and full of cusses, but kindly withal, and he said that he and Eugene were more different than oil and water, but that Eugene loved me as fierce as he loved his Jessica and that was enough to bind them. From time to time, I received a letter from him as well. He did splendidly. Went into making steel and though he and his wife had no children they gave plenty, as I always have, to the good causes of this world.

Mr. Bowson? He became a tent preacher, one of those in America who move from town to town and preach eternal salvation and eternal damnation and breathe fire in general and all come from afar to listen and be amazed. Hard to believe, it is, for when I met him he was wretched with guilt. He blamed himself for my Eggy's death, you see. He fell asleep when he should have been watching, lulled, he said, by the opium, the devil's smoke. He added quickly that Eugene did not suffer much and I felt, as I had felt with the others, that there was more to tell, but then isn't there always? He begged my forgiveness and I gave it quick enough. I didn't blame him. Eggy's death was the fault only of this James Milroy. That was his name. Even now it catches in my throat. That bastard. That black-hearted soul. Excuse my words, dear, but how else can he be called? How else can he be remembered?

Ah, they are all dead, all dead. That is what is unfortunate about living so long. I am the grand old dame of the town, as your paper said. Was it your paper? Ah, and I have forgotten your name. No matter. At least I will not outlive my daughter. I will not outlive my granddaughters. For that I am grateful.

Do you see them, dear? They fill the room. Why, the dead, of course. There is dear Mrs. Smitherton. She never left the Cowichan, even after Mr. Smitherton died and that not five years after Eugene did. Often I went to visit her and bring her food and coal and any new-fangled invention for the easing of a woman's work. She was such a solace to me when I was alone in the Cowichan. I would have died for want of her advice and friendship and nourishing food. There stand Mary and Jeremiah. Oh, I would have died without them, too. It was they who taught me the jargon of the Chinook and in time some of the words of their own language. These words had the weight of gifts, so gravely did they give them. And Mrs. Jacobsen of the Avalon Hotel. She is standing behind your chair, her hands on her hips. I worked at the Avalon for a time, that was where Eugene courted me, that was where we fell in love. She moved to Toronto after her husband died, murdered it was whispered, by her very hand. I did not believe it. She was a hard mistress, but she meant well and I never held a grudge against her. She loved my Eugene, you see, as so many people did, men and women both. And how can you dislike someone who loves what you do?

Ah, there is Eugene taking up an entire doorway, bellowing for his beloved Dora. And there sits Jacob, his head against the antimacassars that must still bear the imprint of his hair. Ah, Jacob, he was a fine man between the sheets, but I never feared I would lose myself in him, not as I feared, gloriously feared, that I would lose myself in Eugene.

My dear, you are such a fine listener. And so I will tell you some-thing that I have never told anyone. After my Eggy died I fell into the blackest despair. I did not want to live, for I could not imagine living without him. And so one morning I walked into the bay. Further and further. My skirts swirled about me like some great sea creature. How cold, it was, how terribly cold. The salt waves broke over my shoulders and neck. I did not know how to swim. I still do not. One more step.

And I might have committed such a sin, oh, I might have, but for the sense that came upon me, certain as the icy cold, that happiness would be returned to me. It was as if I had been given a glimpse of my lovely shop and my devoted Jacob and my daughter's kindness, and of all my wonderful friends and even of you, dear, listening so patiently to an old woman's talk. And so it was that I floundered back to shore.

AFTERWORD

Although Eugene, Dora and Boston Jim are fictional, many of the people they encounter are historical, including Governor Douglas, Judge Begbie and his clerk Arthur Bushby, Isaac Oppenheimer the provisionist in Yale, Francis Barnard the postman cum stagecoach operator, Cataline the packer, Wellington Moses the barber in Barkerville, Miss Burdett-Coutts and Edmund Hope Verney of the Ladies Immigration Committee, and of course, Karl Marx. The brideship *Tynemouth* is also historical. The events I describe on-board, however, are fictional. The camels Eugene encounters were brought over as pack animals in 1862. They proved ill-tempered and ill-suited to the terrain and were soon let loose to puzzle travellers until 1905 when the last of them died. Eugene's waltz with a dead man was inspired by the historical account of a wake at 150 Mile House.

Work on the Cariboo Wagon Road began in 1861. Only two years later the majority of the work was done. Eighteen feet wide and four hundred miles long, the road cut through canyons, cliffs, and mountains and was indeed an engineering marvel. Much of today's Highway 97 follows the route of the original wagon road and towns such as 100 Mile House are named for the roadhouses that once stood there. Barkerville is now a national park with over one hundred and twenty-five restored buildings and is well worth a visit.

Although I used many books in researching this novel, I am particularly indebted to Branwen Patenaude's *Trails to Gold: Roadhouses of the Cariboo, Volumes I and II*; *Barkerville* by Richard Thomas Wright, and *Wagon Road North* by Art Downs. I am also indebted to the classic anthropological work *The Gift: the Form and Reason for*

Exchange in Archaic Societies by Marcel Mauss, as this provided that first spark of inspiration. Lastly, I am indebted to my husband Benno for all his patience and support.

CLAIRE MULLIGAN was raised in Kelowna, British Columbia, but calls Vancouver home. Before completing her studies in English and Anthropology at the University of British Columbia, Claire backpacked through Europe, Southeast Asia and Central America. To fund her writing habit, Claire has worked in ski resorts and fishing lodges and has been a waiter, chambermaid, freelance editor and ESL tutor. Her short stories have garnered awards and appeared in many literary publications. She now lives in Pennsylvania with her husband and three children. *The Reckoning of Boston Jim* is her first novel.